INTUITION

Other Books by Anna Durand

INTUITION

Psychic Crossroads, Book Two

ANNA DURAND

JACOBSVILLE BOOKS · MARIETTA, OHIO

INTUITION

ISBN: 978-1-934631-71-3 (paperback)
ISBN: 978-1-934631-74-4 (ebook)
ISBN: 978-1-949406-86-3 (audiobook)

Manufactured in the United States.

Jacobsville Books
www.JacobsvilleBooks.com

Publisher's Cataloging-in-Publication Data
provided by Five Rainbows Cataloging Services

Names: Durand, Anna.
Title: Intuition / Anna Durand.
Description: Marietta, OH : Jacobsville Books, 2015. | Series: Psychic crossraods, bk. 2.
Identifiers: ISBN 978-1-934631-71-3 paperback) | ISBN 978-1-934631-74-4 (ebook) | ISBN 978-1-949406-86-3 (audiobook)
Subjects: LCSH: Man-woman relationships--Fiction. | Amnesia--Fiction. | Psychic ability--Fiction. | Family secrets--Fiction. | Romance fiction. | BISAC: FICTION / Romance / Paranormal / General. | FICTION / Romance / Suspense. | GSAFD: Love stories. | Occult fiction. | Romantic suspense fiction.
Classification: LCC PS3604.U724 I58 2015 (print) | LCC PS3604.U724 (ebook) | DDC 813/.6--dc23.

Chapter One

GRACE POWELL SLAMMED THE FRONT DOOR, AND THE COOL AIR IN-side the house expunged the sultry October heat that clung to her skin. She stalked across the living room, down the hall, and into the bedroom. As she fumbled for the light switch, her fingers slipped off the plastic. *Dammit.* No one but David Ransom detonated her temper like this. At last, she flicked the switch, and light flooded the room. The bed stood empty, the sheets crumpled at the foot.

They'd fled the house in a near panic, racing from their home to the Cincinnati airport with tires screeching, all because of a thirty-second phone call David had received at one a.m. Another tip from a questionable source. Another threadbare clue in his quest for vengeance. Another search that yanked him away from Grace, away from their home, their life.

The emptiness of the bed tore at her heart like tiny claws, sharp and hot. Fresh tears pricked her eyes, and she gnawed her lip to stave off the downpour. *No crying.*

She fingered her engagement ring. A tear sneaked out of her eye to roll down her cheek, painting a hot trail on her skin. *No crying, dammit.*

Grace resisted the impulse to tap into their telepathic bond and check on her fiancé. It was an invasion, one she understood all too well, but how else could she know David was all right? She had to trust their latent connection, however faint, to warn her. If he stumbled into trouble, though, what could she do from here, over a thousand miles away?

Her heart clenched. Losing her parents had ripped her world asunder. She could not lose David too. Her head told her she wouldn't, yet the fear chilled her down to the essence of her being.

She trudged into the bedroom, kicking off her shoes. The lonely tear crept into her mouth, infecting her tongue with a salty tang. She tugged the cell phone out of her jeans pocket and tossed it onto the bedside table. Her muscles, stiff and sore, begged for a rest, so she collapsed onto the mattress on her back. Her gaze hit the ceiling where little acoustic balls clung to the paint, stuck there against their will. *I know the feeling.*

When they'd reached the security checkpoint at the airport, she'd longed to plead with David to stay. Instead, she cranked her lips into a smile, pecked a kiss on his cheek, and all but shoved him through the gate. Her stomach wrenched into knots as she recalled that moment when he strolled into the main terminal. When he paused to glance back, she prayed he would change his mind. But he simply waved, then strode out of sight.

Grace rolled onto her side. Her nose bumped into David's pillow. She drew in a long breath and let the spiciness of his aftershave flood her senses, along with another scent—a subtle, masculine smell unique to David. It was indescribable and delicious. Warmth suffused her, seeping into her heart and mind, smoldering in parts of her that ached for him. She inhaled another draft of his scent, her body responding as if he were there, caressing her. He might drive her nuts at times, but...

Oh, the way he kissed. Her lips tingled from the memory of it.

A chill whispered over her skin. Every hair on her body stiffened. Her sixth sense burst out of its slumber, clanging alarm bells in her psyche. *Someone is here.*

She bolted upright and whipped her head left and right. Nobody there. She swung her legs off the bed and pushed up onto her feet, nabbing her .357 Magnum revolver from the bedside table. A chill trickled down her spine. Eyes watched. Invisible, ethereal, but real. She turned toward the doorway. Nothing lurked there.

Why couldn't she pin down the source of the sensation? Her paranormal radar was blanked out as if overwhelmed by input.

Psychic energy crackled through her. *Behind you.* She whirled around, thrusting the gun up, clamping it in both hands, and confronted—

The lamp.

Hell. She'd let her unease blossom into paranoia. Nobody hunted her anymore. Probably. Tesler wouldn't find her here.

Her cell phone buzzed. A text message had arrived.

David. She snatched up the phone, tapping the screen until the message popped up. As she scanned the words, a shiver rattled through her.

"Come to me," it said, "I can help you. 1325 Meroz Road."

She didn't recognize the phone number the message came from, and no name was given. Oh sure, she'd rush right out to the address texted to her by an anonymous whackjob.

The phone buzzed again. Another text message: "Your lip is bleeding."

Her lip? She dabbed a finger on her mouth. It came away wet. Blood stained her skin. How did the texter know she'd bitten her lip? Without moving, she searched the shadows for a figure, a camera, something to explain this, though she knew she'd find nothing. A thick curtain shielded the window. The person sending the messages could either see through solid objects or had another means of viewing her. Extrasensory means.

The phone tumbled from her hand, clattering on the floor.

No, she was jumping to conclusions. An intruder must've stolen into the house. With the revolver in hand, she sprinted out of the bedroom, down the hallway, through the kitchen, and into the living room. Vacant. All vacant. She rushed back to the bedroom and dug through the closet, scoured the dresser, even dropped onto her belly to investigate the space under the bed. No cameras. No stealthy intruders. Not a damn thing. Which left her with one unthinkable possibility.

Maybe she should call the police.

What for? They couldn't help her with this kind of problem.

"You belong with me."

She jumped. Her head smacked into the bed frame. She clutched the gun tighter. Where had the voice come from?

No, no, no, not again. Nausea swelled in her stomach, bile rising high in her throat. The voice did not originate in this room, or from outside. The source was much, much closer. Someone had rammed the words into her mind.

A psychic intruder had just hacked her brain.

Grace crawled out from under the bed. She pushed up onto her knees, set the revolver on the carpet beside her knee, and grabbed her phone off the floor. Her heart implored her to call David, but her head warned against it. What if the psychic intruder had bugged the phones? She shuddered. An invisible stalker needed no bugs or cameras to track her every movement. He might spy on her anytime, anywhere.

Grabbing the edge of the mattress, she heaved herself up and onto the bed. Her eyes stung. Her lip throbbed from chewing it. She yearned to lie down and drift to sleep. As if she could sleep now.

Her phone buzzed.

She lifted her hand. On the screen, a message appeared. "Come to me when you're ready. No pressure. Last message, promise. Good night."

Grace gulped. The rock in her throat stayed put.

Good night? Sure, she'd sleep. Like a freaking baby—if the baby had guzzled a pint of tequila. Unfortunately, she didn't drink, never had. Thanks to her new "friend," however, she craved a big, tall glass of anything alcoholic, to soak her fears in the vaunted bliss of drunkenness. Maybe then she could pretend nothing happened.

David needs to know. Given her past, he'd want to hear about an intruder hacking into her mind. She punched the button to call up his cell number, but then froze. He was in the air right now, on his way to Utah. Did the airlines let passengers use cell phones in flight? Better stick to the one means she knew would work.

Ohhh, David wouldn't like this.

Screw it. He ought to know.

Grace slapped the phone down on the table. She slumped onto the bed on her back, folded her hands over her belly, and shut her eyes. Tension tugged her muscles taut. Thoughts swirled in her brain. If she couldn't block out the anxiety, she'd never tap into her powers. Drawing in a deep breath, she let it out bit by bit. *Relax. Picture the target.*

David. His face glimmered in her mind as if lit by heaven's own glow.

Her mind snapped free from her body. She floated in nothingness for a second, and then whoosh. She rocketed up through a dark tunnel into a field of blackness dotted with stars. Her mind drew lines between the lights, sketching out the connections between places and events and psyches in the crossroads, the ethereal source of all psychic power. A white line stretched out toward a pinpoint far away. The star pulsed. David. She'd found him.

Grace hurtled toward him through the darkness into the light, smashing through it into another tunnel. Psychic gravity hauled her downward, closer and closer to her destination. To David's mind. His presence cascaded over her, through her, penetrating deeper with each second, overwhelming her with warmth and love and belonging.

She tumbled out into the world. Shapes blurred into each other. Up, down, her senses struggled to separate the two. Precious seconds ticked by until her mind acclimated to the change. It shouldn't have hit her so hard. Something was different this time, but she couldn't deduce what.

Solid earth supported her feet. Though she lacked a physical form, her mind conjured an image of her body that behaved like the real thing. She turned in a circle, inspecting her surroundings. Trees loomed overhead. Green moss squished under her feet. The sun blazed behind the treetops, its rays puncturing the shadows below. This made no sense. She'd watched David walk into the terminal. He should've been in the air, not down here in the woods. Down where? She'd figure that out later. First, she must find David.

She stopped. Her heart thudded. A dozen feet away, David crouched in front of a thick pine tree. Facing away. Hands bound behind his back. Ankles bound too. Head tipped up. Grace zeroed in on the object of David's attention. A man, engulfed in shadows. His face obscured.

She tiptoed closer. Still couldn't see.

The stranger swung his arm up. His hand. He clutched something. A shiny metal object. He hoisted it higher. *Shit.* A knife.

"David!"

Her cry ricocheted off the trees. He didn't react. She charged forward.

And whacked into an invisible wall. Pain exploded through her, and she staggered backward. What the hell?

The stranger drove the knife downward, plunging the blade into David's chest. He gurgled. The stranger tore the knife out and raised it high. Blood drenched the blade, but he jammed it downward again. David convulsed and crumpled to the ground.

Grace screamed.

She flung her arms out to David, but the barrier hurled them back. She toppled over, scrambled to her feet. The stranger ripped the knife out and braced for another blow. Grace flailed for the knife. Her fingers smacked into the barrier, and pain racked her joints as she attacked the barrier with every ounce of psychic energy in her, pounding on it with both hands. It shattered with a whoosh of air that bowled her over backward. She scrambled to her feet, rushing toward David, and grappled for the knife. Her hand sailed right through it.

No body, dammit. No hands. No hope.

Like hell.

The stranger stabbed David again. A red stain erupted on his shirt. The blows wrenched Grace's astral body as if the knife shredded her own flesh. The slickness of his blood oozed over her skin, and his life spewed out of her as if it were her own.

No, no, no. I won't lose him too.

The assailant tossed his knife aside.

Manifest now, dammit. Construct a body. Nothing happened. She staggered forward, gasping, tears cascading down her cheeks. They stung like the real thing, and her chest ached from the pain of her hammering heart. She must manifest a physical form *right now.*

But she couldn't.

She pumped every ounce of psychic energy she had into the task, draining her metaphysical power lower than ever before. Her head throbbed. Everything twirled around her. The tether between her and David unraveled.

"No."

The word whispered out of her. Faint. Distant. Every bit of energy inside her vaporized.

The stranger waltzed into the light.

Grace peeled her gaze away from David and stared at the assailant. The sunlight glistened on the bald spot atop his head. A breeze ruffled his gray hair, and his freckled face warped into a smirk. Recognition jolted through her. She knew this man.

Karl Tesler.

He was the scientist David had hunted for six months. The man who captured and tortured psychics. The object of David's obsession, and the reason he fled to Utah.

Tesler surveyed the area. A cold draft whispered over her in the wake of his gaze. Goosebumps prickled her skin. He couldn't see her. Could he?

The scientist sneered down at David, his dark eyes narrowed and burning with amber fire. He fingered the blood stain on David's shirt, then lifted his hand to his face to sniff the blood—and grinned.

Grace clenched her fists, gritting her teeth. "Tesler, you bastard. You'll pay for this, I swear it. You'll pay."

Anger boiled inside her. Scorching. Swelling. Obliterating reason. Propelling her to do something. Anything.

She could do *nothing*.

He would pay for this. Somehow, some way, she would summon the strength to rip his heart out.

The tether snapped.

Her mind crashed back into her body, ramming into it with a force that punched the breath out of her. A vice bore down on her head, the pain so intense she nearly vomited. She jerked upright, still on the bed. A salty flavor drenched her mouth. *Tick, tick, tick.* Dampness pasted her clammy shirt to her chest. *Tick, tick.* Sobs twisted her gut as tears dripped off her chin to plop onto her shirt, ticking like a countdown timer. One thought consumed her.

David was dead.

CHAPTER TWO

The sun had long since breached the horizon by the time David smacked the car door shut and leaped up the front steps of their home, two at a time. The morning light glared in his eyes as he grabbed for the knob. It slipped in his damp palm.

What would he find inside the house? Was he too late?

He wiped his hand on his jeans and seized the knob.

The front door swung open, releasing a blast of cool air from inside the house that chilled the sweat on his face. Grace hunched in the doorway, her bleary gaze aimed at him.

He staggered backward half a step, the air trapped in his lungs. She was *okay*. Freaked out, but alive. He hauled in a breath, shoving aside his own anxiety, and moved toward her.

Grace's hazel eyes widened. Her face blanched. "You're alive."

"Obviously." He tilted his head, baffled by the way she stared at him like he'd hopped off a unicorn's back. "Are you all right? I sensed… something."

More than something. A tidal wave of fear and anger had battered him with such power that he'd nearly tumbled off the hard, plastic chair in the Denver International Airport, where he'd been waiting for a connecting flight. He recognized in a heartbeat the source of the icy burst of sensations. Grace. He'd sprinted to the ticket desk, his pulse racing, seized by a wild panic that hammered one thought into his brain over and over.

Grace is dying.

Yet she wasn't. No blood, no bruises—unless her clothes masked them. Other than her bloodshot eyes, nothing betrayed the terror that had coursed down their connection and skewered his heart. He touched his fingertips to her cheek. Warm. Smooth. Undamaged. The electrical charge of adrenaline that had buttressed him on the flight home flooded out of him. The world seemed to rock briefly. He sucked in a breath, jerked his hand away from her face, and willed his mind to settle.

Grace launched her body at him, sailing through the doorway and straight into him. He caught her in both arms. She hoisted herself up to wrap her arms around his neck, her feet dangling several inches off the ground. He tugged her against him, gripping her sides to press her closer. She flinched and gasped.

He snatched his arms away. "What did I do? Are you hurt?"

She bent her head back and laughed, her voice as melodic as the chiming of tiny bells. "I'm fine. Your fingers were digging into my ribs, dummy."

"Oh. Sorry."

She tucked her head under his chin. He nuzzled her neck, breathing in the clean scent of her. He beat back the urge to scoop her into his arms and whisk her away to some deserted island, a safe place where they could pretend the past year had never happened. He would stir her memories, the ones buried under eight months of amnesia, and then let her tender caresses and fiery kisses scour away his secrets. His nightmares. His past.

Never let her find out.

She clinched him so tight it blew the air out of his lungs. Had she read his mind? Sweet heaven, he prayed she hadn't. He could not stomach watching another person dive headfirst into psychosis, splintered by the ax-like power of mind reading. Watching the madness shatter Grace...

That would kill him.

Her arms squeezed him harder. He smothered the instinct to push her away and gasped through gritted teeth, "What's wrong?"

She let go, dropped onto her feet, and frowned at him. "You were dead. I saw it happen."

"Clearly not." He thumped his chest. "Still here."

Her gaze drilled into his with the heat of a laser beam, incinerating his every thought. The morning sun glittered on the green specks in her pale-brown irises, tiny jewels swimming in a pool of molten toffee. God, she was perfect. From her slender, round-tipped nose to her graceful, narrow feet and even her flawless little toes that wriggled on the concrete.

When she hugged him again, more gently, her auburn hair tickled his chin. The sweet, tropical scent of her shampoo sparked off a surge of intoxicating hormones that swamped his senses, evoking images that only intensified the desire. The shadows of palm trees swaying over a sun-blanketed beach, while they sipped virgin daiquiris from coconut shells. Grace draped across a towel, her bikini revealing acres of creamy, soft skin. The hollow of her hips. The flat plane of her stomach. The swell of her ample breasts. The delicate curve of her neck. His lips burned with the hunger to taste her small, full lips.

She pushed away from him. "Are you thinking about sex?"

"Not specifically." True, his fantasy had screeched to a halt a second too soon for that. But if he'd had more time...

Damn. He was an ass.

"You are thinking about it." She shook her head. Waves of hair splashed around her face. "I thought you died. I watched it happen. And all you can do is fantasize about sex?"

The meaning of her words crashed into him, cold as a liquid-nitrogen downpour, dousing the bonfire she'd lit inside him. She watched him die? Impossible. Yet Grace would not lie. Not about this. And she'd suffered too much, battled through too many losses, to crack jokes about death.

He grasped her shoulders. *Careful. Protect, don't suffocate, remember?* He loosened his grip, uncurling his fingers. "What are you talking about? I didn't die. You could not have seen it happen."

She folded her arms over her chest, thrusting her breasts upward.

He struggled to concentrate, to rip his gaze away from the sight. Dammit, why did she have to be so... breathtaking.

Grace took one step back. "I saw Tesler murder you. It was real."

His thoughts snapped into focus. The heat of desire sluiced out of him, displaced by a sharp chill. "What exactly did you see?"

She scowled, glancing around. "Maybe we shouldn't talk about this. Someone might hear."

"You think the house is bugged?"

"No, not the way you mean."

She slumped her shoulders, one hand rubbing her arm. A cold suspicion itched in his gut. Something wasn't right here. Maybe whatever she'd experienced had triggered the terror that swamped him. Their connection was potent. If his ordeal had stemmed from her, then he marveled at her composure.

He grasped her shoulders, bending his knees to level their gazes. "Tell me what happened while I was gone. Everything."

———

LIE DOWN, GRACE. NOW." DAVID POINTED AT THE BED. HE'D ALREADY folded the quilt at the foot and pulled back the blanket and sheet.

She rolled her eyes. "I need to build a psychic firewall to keep out hackers. You said so. I don't have time for a nap."

He stared into her bloodshot eyes, rimmed with dark circles, and willed her to obey him. He held out no hope she would unless he convinced her of the need for sleep. Commanding her to do anything never worked. Like the dolt he obviously was, he kept repeating the same mistake. Time for a new tactic.

"Please." He cupped her face in his hands. "Please lie down and at least try to sleep. You're exhausted." Which was his fault. A knot pulled taut inside him, but he trained all his focus on her. "I'm begging you."

She gazed at him, impassive, for two heartbeats. Then she laughed, her beautiful mouth splitting into a grin. "Really, David. I've dreamed about you begging me to do all sorts of things, but napping wasn't one of them."

Just like that, everything besides the two of them evaporated. He dropped his hands to her arms and skated them down until he found her fingers, entwining them with his. He said softly, "What have you dreamed about?"

The slight pallor in her cheeks gave way to a delicate blush, and she fixated her gaze on his chest.

He lifted one of her hands to feather a kiss across her knuckles. "You can tell me. I'd like to know."

She aimed her hazel eyes at him. "You're psychic, you figure it out."

"I can't read your mind." He tugged her into his arms, ducking his head close to hers. She smelled wonderful and felt even better. "Sometimes I wish I could hear your thoughts."

"Ditto." Eyes half-closed, she drew in a slow breath. "You want to know my fantasies, but you won't tell me yours."

"Mine are boring." A beach, palm trees, the scent of wild, exotic flowers on the breeze. And her, gloriously naked, while he explored every inch of her soft skin. That was his fantasy. He ought to tell her, if he expected her to confide in him, but shackles wrought from elastic iron restrained him, stretching taut yet unbreakable. He shouldn't have instigated this line of conversation. He fought the urge to strip both their clothes off and act out his fantasy right here, right now, screw the beach.

She traced a fingertip over the neckline of his T-shirt. "You're many things, David, but never boring."

"I'm not sure that's a compliment."

Her arms snaked up to encircle his neck, her fingers massaging the nape. "I'm not sleepy, but I'd be happy to lie down for you."

Her tongue slipped out to moisten her lower lip.

Every nerve in his body screamed for him to kiss her. When she smiled, slow and sexy, his chest tightened. "Are you trying to seduce me?"

"Yes."

The hunger smoldered inside him, relentless and inescapable. He stroked his hands up and down her back, closed his eyes, and reveled in her aura. *Love her, show her, let it all go.* But he must hold back, despite his selfish desires. Her powers had grown day by day, a fact he sensed even while she denied the truth. The last time they'd made love, the act had affected them both on a metaphysical level. Their telepathic bond, nearly destroyed by her amnesia and his secrets, had strengthened in that moment, fueled by the love they conveyed with their bodies. If he touched her again, he had no idea what it might do to her powers. Bind her to him? Forever?

The thought coursed a thrill through him, and he nuzzled her cheek, hungry for contact. If he told her about his suspicions, she'd vow she didn't care what happened. He knew her too well to expect any other reaction. He could not let her risk it. After what he'd done already, things he could never tell her, he didn't deserve even the latent connection they shared. He'd betrayed her—unwillingly, but that was no excuse. He should've been stronger, fought harder.

Sacrificed his life for her.

Grace raised onto tiptoes and nipped his chin. "Is my evil plan working?"

Her hips wriggled against him, exciting parts of him he was desperately struggling to calm down. Hell yes, it was working. "I can't remember you ever doing this before."

"What? Seducing you?" Her voice had gone sultry, whispery, irresistible.

"Yes, that." He growled the words. "Please stop."

"Why?"

"Because—" While she raked her nails up the back of his scalp, he battled to retain his wits, but her exquisite torment wore him down second by second. "We can't do this. You're exhausted."

She was worn out from more than their late-night escapade, he knew that. She worked too hard to support them both. He clenched his jaw. What if she got sick from perpetual exhaustion, all because of his failures? "Former psychic research subject" didn't fit well on a resume, and he had no other explanation for where he'd been for the past two and a half years. Besides, he had to focus on Tesler. For Grace. He prayed one day she'd understand why.

Excuses. Pathetic, half-assed excuses.

Grace tugged his head down, her lips closing in on his.

He summoned every ounce of self-control he possessed, took hold of her arms, and pushed her away.

She winced.

His fingers sprang open on instinct. "Did I hurt you?"

A heavy sigh deflated her. "Not physically."

But he had hurt her. *Dammit.* How long could he keep doing this to her before he bled dry her willingness to forgive him? Maybe he should end this and set her free. He couldn't.

Because he was a selfish bastard.

"I'm sorry." It was all he could manage to say.

"Yeah, I know." Her defeated tone scraped at his heart. "I am tired all of a sudden."

She scuffled to the bed and climbed onto it to lie on her side, hands clasped to her chest, knees bent. He crawled from the foot of the bed up to lie beside her, face to face. She looked so tired, so fragile, that he wanted to wrap his arms around her. After the way he'd just rejected her, he doubted she'd appreciate the gesture.

A big yawn overtook her.

Though glazed with fatigue, her gaze sharpened on him. "Why do you think Tesler hasn't come after me again? It's been six months."

The question he'd dreaded. The one he had no answer for. Although he harbored suspicions, he must not share them with her. She suffered enough anxiety without piling on more that might well be unfounded. Instead, he reminded her of things she already knew, praying to distract her tired mind. "That's why we moved from Texas to Ohio and rented a house under false names, to hide you from Tesler."

"Then why do you keep looking for him? Isn't that kind of like wrestling an alligator? Sooner or later, it'll turn around and bite you in the ass."

He flipped onto his back, staring at the ceiling. "Go to sleep, Grace."

"But—"

"We have more pressing concerns. And you need rest in order to deal with them."

"Fine." The word blew out on a deep sigh. "I can't relax like this, with you way over there."

Six or eight inches separated them, but he knew what she meant. He'd withdrawn. With good reason, he thought. But he owed her a little solace.

He rolled toward her, wriggling closer until their noses touched. With one hand, he tugged the sheet and blanket over them both. She moaned, a contented sound, her eyelids drifting shut.

She murmured to him as if she were half asleep. "I love you."

"I love you too." He kissed her forehead. "Rest. I'll be here."

"Mmm…"

And then she fell asleep. He watched her body go slack, her breathing shallower. But more than that, he sensed her mind sinking into a deeper, more tranquil place. He brushed the hair from her eyes, trailing a fingertip down her cheek, his touch so light she didn't stir.

He would never let Tesler harm her. Never.

Edward McLean, her grandfather, swore the fake IDs he'd provided them with would shield them from Tesler—for a while. How long, no one could say.

Grace believed his quest was for vengeance, against the man who'd destroyed his life. He let her believe it. To protect her, he must deceive her.

As he studied her face, counting the lashes on her eyes, weariness settled over him. No, he could not sleep. Not here, with her. He always waited until she drifted off, then headed into the living room to sleep on the sofa. Since he woke before her every day, he'd sneak back into bed before she roused. All to keep the truth from her. Yet another secret, wedged between them.

His lids grew heavy. He fought the slumber as long as possible, but finally, it swallowed him.

A whimpering noise woke him.

Grace was gone. He sat up, searching the darkened room for signs of her. Dark? Had they slept the whole day? Unease crawled over his skin. The shadows were too black, too oily. "Grace? Where are you?"

Whimpering. Coming from… everywhere.

His heart thumped hard and fast. He leaped off the bed and spun in a circle, but still saw no one.

She was dead. He'd hallucinated coming home, talking to her, holding her.

No. He was in their bedroom. Head gripped in his hands, he fought to wring comprehension from his brain. He had returned, which meant—

"Is this what you're looking for?" Tesler's voice echoed from within the darkness creeping in around the bed.

David froze.

Grace stumbled out of the shadows, tears rolling down her cheeks. Tesler emerged after her, one hand clamped on the back of her neck, the other wielding a gun jammed into her temple.

"Well?" Tesler said. "Is this what you want?"

The scientist hurled the gun at David.

He caught it, uncertain why. The object lay heavy and cold in his palm, unfurling a frost that leeched into him, infecting his entire body. *This isn't right, this isn't right.*

"Go on," Tesler taunted. "You know you want to."

Grace let out a sharp sob. "How could you do it? I trusted you."

Tesler shoved her toward him. "I destroyed her mind, but you murdered her soul. Finish the job."

David's hand lifted, his finger curled around the trigger. He couldn't control his body, couldn't stop this.

The gunshot exploded.

CHAPTER THREE

GRACE JOLTED AWAKE. BESIDE HER, DAVID THRASHED ON HIS BACK, HIS arms pinned to the mattress as if something held him down. His distress tore into her psyche. It sliced, and it scoured her raw from the inside out.

She jostled him. "David, wake up."

His eyes flew open. They darted from side to side, in search of phantoms spawned from his own fears and guilt. She understood his pain, but not its source, because he refused to tell her.

David shoved a trembling hand through his golden hair, gasping, sweat streaming down his face. His gaze swung sideways toward her, and he grimaced. "I woke you. I'm sorry."

"Stop apologizing and start explaining. Let me help you."

"I don't know what you mean." He mopped the sweat from his forehead with his T-shirt. "It was a bad dream caused by bad memories. A singular event. End of story."

"Uh-huh." The man honestly had no clue. Well, it was time to give him one. "I know you haven't slept in our bed for months, until this little cat nap. And I know about your nightmares."

His body went rigid. His expression blanked.

She tucked her hands under her cheek, depressing the pillow. "Come on, David. What part of telepathic bond do you not get?"

He cleared his throat.

She poked him with her knee. "I can feel when you leave the room, and no matter how far away you run, I can also feel when you're having a nightmare. The same way you felt my panic."

David settled a hand on her hip, squeezing. "I didn't realize you felt it when I leave. I should've guessed." He pulled his hand away. "I am sorry."

His head rotated toward her, those gorgeous eyes focusing on her.

She stretched, draped one leg over his, and combed her hand through his hair. He was unharmed and oh-so-alive, which meant her vision of his death had been a mistake, it must've been. If he wouldn't talk, then she'd settle for nonverbal communication. "I'm feeling refreshed. How about you?"

"No, Grace."

"What?" She let her hand fall to his cheek, her thumb brushing the corner of his mouth.

He bolted upright and patted her hip. "Time to get up. We have work to do."

When will you stop running away? She knew the answer. Not until he got his revenge. She wanted Tesler to pay too, but not at the expense of her relationship with David.

Flopping onto her back, she groaned. "What now?"

"You need to build a wall in your mind."

"May I please pee first?"

"I suppose I'll allow it." A slight smirk slanted his lips. He ripped the blankets away, and cool air wisped over her skin. "You do that, and I'll make us breakfast."

She watched him rise, that muscular body unfurling. The sinews in his back flexed under his shirt as he stretched and yawned. He believed she was oblivious. Yes, she *was* oblivious of many things, hindered by amnesia. Yet she knew he was keeping secrets from her, most likely in the foolish male belief that ignorance equaled protection.

A few months ago, she'd caught him using her computer in the middle of the night. No big deal, she'd thought. But the sight of him had stopped her—the bulging eyes, the parted lips, the blankness beyond his usual stoicism, and the way his hands gripped his thighs. She'd hesitated in the doorway between the hall and the living room, her gaze glued to David, where he hunched in the recliner with her laptop balanced on his knees. The second he noticed her, he'd clapped the laptop's lid shut along with his emotions.

When she'd asked what was wrong, he dismissed the whole incident by saying he'd "stayed up too late trolling the Internet."

Yeah, right.

David strode around the bed, offering his hands to her.

She let him help her up but frowned at him. "What happened to your urgent lead? You know, the one that made us rush to the airport in the middle of the freaking night."

"I told Sean to wait for me and we'll check it out later."

"At one o'clock this morning, it was deathly important."

"Things change." He slapped her bottom. "Go. I'll meet you in the kitchen."

She started for the door but paused on the threshold to glance back. "What changed? What's more critical than your mission to find Tesler?"

Though his expression had shuttered, his eyes burned into hers. In a voice low and steady, he said, "You should know the answer."

He pushed past her, stalking down the hallway toward the kitchen.

———

GRACE SAT CROSS-LEGGED ON THE BED, HANDS ON HER KNEES, EYES closed. A touch danced across her skin, exciting places deep within her. Softening tension. Wiping away fear. She peeked out between her lashes. David perched on the bed's edge, angled toward her, hands resting on the comforter. His gaze trailed across her flesh like a physical touch. He could caress her without moving a finger. That knowledge shot fierce arcs of desire through her.

But when he did explore her body with those hands...

"Concentrate," David said.

Right. She was supposed to be doing that. He slid his gaze over her again, drinking in every inch of her, his sapphire-blue eyes gleaming. *Oh lord.* Her body melted, and she slanted toward him as if he commanded the response from her. The lamplight burnished his short blond hair, transmuting it into twenty-four-carat gold. He sat straight, shoulders square, like a warrior angel meditating before a battle.

David frowned, the expression carving lines into his features. "You're not even trying. Building a psychic firewall won't be easy, so you have to concentrate."

"It's hard to focus when I keep thinking about—" *You kissing me.*

He closed his hand around hers. "I didn't die."

An image punched through her mind. The knife slashing down into his chest. The blood. David sprawled on the ground. She shuddered and wrapped her arms around herself, pining for the warmth, but the frost inside her resisted it. "Tesler stabbed you. I watched it happen, and there wasn't a damn thing I could do."

"It must've been a dream."

"I was awake. And unless you're implying I've gone psychotic, I did not hallucinate it."

"You aren't insane."

He rubbed her arms, his touch banishing some of the chill. A breeze from the air conditioner wafted over her, though, and the frost inside thickened, sweeping through her from her scalp to her toes. David wrapped his arms around her, and his warmth enveloped her. She rested her head on his chest, relishing his heat. *Thump-thump. Thump-thump.* His heart ticked like clockwork.

"Maybe what you saw was real," he said, "but it hasn't happened yet."

"Huh?"

He enfolded her hand in his, massaging the sensitive flesh of her palm with his thumb. "You might've had a vision of the future."

"I don't have premonitions."

"Your powers must've grown."

"What if I don't want them to?"

He shrugged. "Can't fight it. Your brush with the Golden Power might've altered your psychic makeup."

"Great," she muttered.

His lips curved into a smile. "Your powers are the strongest I've ever seen. Who knows what new abilities you might develop."

She'd implored the universe to grant her amnesia about her brush with the Golden Power and yet the memory plagued her to this day. Biting into immeasurable power. Sipping from limitless knowledge. A piece of her buried deep hungered to feast once more.

Never again.

She scooted backward, drawing out a distance between them. "Maybe it was a premonition. In which case, you need to stay home."

"Can't."

"Why?"

"You know why." He traced his index finger down her blouse and over the center of her bra, stopping at the rectangular plastic object tucked inside it. She stroked her tongue across her lower lip, overcome by the notion she could taste him in the air, and her body bent toward him just a little. With his fingertip, he pinned the object to her breastbone. "Still safeguarding our treasure?"

The husky tone of his voice excited her skin, like sparks crackling over her. *Damn him.* He was doing this to her on purpose. The flicker of irritation couldn't overwhelm her hormones.

"Yes, your blasted flash drive is safe and sound." She dived a hand down her blouse, grasped the one-inch-long device, and yanked it out. "You can have the stupid thing."

David folded his fingers around hers, enclosing the flash drive in their hands. His gaze bored into hers with an intensity that fluttered her stomach. A blush fired up in her cheeks, so hot her face must've glowed.

He nodded at their joined hands. "Maybe I should keep this."

The flash drive contained all the research data from Project Outreach, the psychic research initiative her parents and grandfather had run. When a deranged man had bought out ALI, the company that funded the research, her world plummeted into a blood-soaked nightmare. Her parents were murdered. She'd believed her grandfather also died. And a door in her mind slammed shut then, blocking out every memory she had of those events—and of David.

Until he found her again six months ago. They'd reforged their bond, psychic and emotional, but she would've risked her sanity, her life, to regain the rest.

As for the flash drive...

She shook her head. "It's safer with me."

He stared at her for so long she wondered if he'd gone catatonic. Then he dropped her hand, slanting his head. His concern radiated through the air, swirling around her, and anxiety stabbed through her. When he ran off again, she'd have to cope with her psychic intruder alone. Why did she put up with his self-imposed mission to stop Tesler?

A dull ache tugged at her heart. She put up with it because she loved him too much to give up on him without a teeth-grinding, heart-ripping, soul-wrenching fight.

She rolled her shoulders back, shimmying to get a better position. "I need to build a psychic firewall. Before you leave."

He plucked the flash drive from her hand and dropped it down her blouse. It plunked back into her bra. "Then you need to concentrate. And relax."

She settled her hands onto her knees. Closed her eyes. Exhaled. "Where did the crossroads come from?"

"I don't know. Nobody does."

She opened one eye. "How does it work?"

"You know how. You've accessed it."

She drummed her fingers.

He studied her, his face impassive, his posture straight but casual.

"Yeah, but what is it?" she asked. "What's the crossroads made of? Who created it? Why does it work?"

"Like a real crossroads, the sort that carries cars, the metaphysical crossroads acts as a junction. It has many more connecting lines than any physical crossroads has, but the principle is similar."

"But how—"

"For Christ's sake, Grace, I don't know."

His lips had twisted into a frown, and he hissed a breath out his nostrils. Though his strength and composure reassured her, once in a while she craved a taste of the passion simmering below. A kiss would've sated her better, but an annoyed outburst would suffice.

He shook his head, fighting back a smile. "You did that on purpose."

She laughed. "Yep."

He patted her knee. "Back to work."

Grace shut her eyes.

David's voice, calm and gentle, guided her. "Relax and let go of everything."

She relinquished her hold on thoughts, on sensations, on everything. Her body lightened as if floating above the bed's covers.

"Focus," David said. "Think about building a wall."

"Right, a wall. What does that mean?"

"Whatever you think it means."

"Could you be less specific?"

He squeezed her knee. "I don't even know if this can be done. But you need to try."

Letting out a long breath, she unwound her muscles one by one. Her mind drifted into blankness, hovering there. She slithered through the dark tunnel and out into the crossroads. Stars glimmered, yet none beckoned her.

She had no wish to travel anywhere. Strength, power, she coveted those things. The crossroads could slake her thirst.

Vibrations bristled her astral body. She unlocked her mental gates, throwing them wide. The energy cascaded into her, bolstering her powers, chilling her down to the core of her psyche. *Enough.* She'd harvested sufficient energy from the crossroads.

Gathering the new power she'd absorbed, she imagined its glow encompassing her, solidifying, transmuting into bricks that constructed a circular wall. Holes in her psychic structure filled in, imbuing her mind with a new strength.

A ray of warmth prodded the chill inside her. David. Calling her home. She dived through the tunnel. Pressure constricted her mind, stuffing it back into her body.

Claws clamped onto her, wrenching her back out into the crossroads. Sticky, dark power fused to her astral skin.

She grappled with the force restraining her. Its talons dug into her psyche. Her head swam. Pain lanced her eyes. *Let me go.*

"Come back to me."

David's voice reverberated in the chasm. She latched onto it, her life preserver, and kicked at the restraint. The talons slipped, loosening. She plummeted into her body, and her eyes flew open.

Blackness drowned her vision. *Oh no, please no.*

Hands seized her. David's energy poured through her, scalding away the frost.

She hugged their connection and dragged herself up it like climbing a rope. The restraining talons tore at her. She funneled David's warmth into her, firing it at the force that held her. The talons popped free.

She vaulted out into the light, gasping for breath, sucking in blessed oxygen. David stared at her, his wide eyes searching hers, his hands fastened on her shoulders. Why was he so far away? She squinted as if peering through a telescope at an object miles in the distance. His touch anchored her, yet her mind still hovered. Numb. Remote. Separate from everything physical, even the hammering of her own heart.

David shook her. "Come back, Grace. Please, whatever it is, shake it off."

His voice, riddled with tension, chopped through the invisible fog. His words shepherded her out of limbo and back into reality. Air tickled her skin, cool and dry. Humming vibrated her eardrums. The AC had just kicked on. She wiggled her trembling fingers, the nails scraping across her cotton sweatpants.

She blinked once, twice. The world shifted into focus.

David covered her hands with one of his. The heat of his skin bled into her. Warm. Alive. Normal. She hadn't been dragged into a netherworld.

He grasped her face in his free hand. "What the hell happened?"

"I—I don't know. Something grabbed me, it was alive, it… wanted me."

He plowed his fingers into her hair to tilt her head up, bringing their gazes into alignment. "Are you okay?"

"I think so. Yes." She forced a smile. "Whatever it was, it's over."

His eyes narrowed, and his lips compressed.

"David, I'm fine, I swear."

If she told him about the talons, and the oily energy, he'd realize it might be connected to the Golden Power. She was tainted, forever. How could he want her if he knew? Then again, if he accepted it, he'd worry about her, about what was happening to her. The distraction, in the middle of his quest for Tesler, might get him killed.

She drew his hand out of her hair, feathering a kiss over his palm. "I get anxious about using my powers, you know that. Probably all this was. Anxiety."

His shoulders slumped a little, his lips relaxed, and he nodded. "Okay. We'll chalk it up to stress affecting your powers—for the moment. Did you at least try building a firewall?"

"Yes." She rolled her shoulders back and straightened. "I'm not sure what I did, but I think it worked."

"Good."

David's phone chirped. He wrestled it out of his pocket.

Grace leaned forward to read the caller ID, spotting a name she knew. Sean Vandenbrook. David's sort-of protégé.

He gave her a little shove. "Stop snooping. I have to take this."

"You know what he wants."

"Uh-huh." Tapping the touch screen, he grunted a greeting. His expression blanked. "I'm on my way. Don't move until I get there."

David jammed the phone back in his pocket.

She clasped her hands on her lap, quelling the lingering tremors. "You're leaving."

"Yes," he said. "I ordered him not to, but Sean traced the lead we got earlier today and he thinks he found another of Tesler's facilities in Montana. If I don't get there quickly, he'll go in alone."

She sighed, her shoulders deflating. He was right, but she still itched to throttle him, to burst into tears, to scream, to implore him to stay. Instead, she spoke in an even tone that demanded all her self-control to achieve. "Sean's even more obsessed with finding Tesler than you are. He could get himself killed."

The teenager needed adult supervision. Sometimes she thought David did too. Both he and Sean pursued every lead, no matter how lame, to track down Tesler. How many times had they stumbled home with bruises and cuts? She'd lost count. There was nothing she could say to stop them. Right now, she could've strangled the pair of them, one with each hand.

She anchored her hands on her hips. "Besides, even when you're here, you're not really here. I get more attention from the mailman."

"Grace, don't do that."

"What?"

"Don't retreat into your fortress of sarcasm."

The anger boiled off in an instant, dissipating into the air. He was right, again, and she hated herself for being such a bitch. "I'm sorry, I don't mean to do it. Stuff sort of bubbles out of me. You better head out, help Sean. I can call Grandpa if I need anything."

David scrunched his eyebrows, the only crack in his unreadable expression. "Are you sure you don't mind if I go?"

Of course she minded, dammit. But what else could she say? She'd deal with it. Like a mature adult.

Rats. She hated being a grown-up.

"Sean needs a rational adult to rein him in," she said. "I insist you go."

He nodded and then strode out of the bedroom. She pursued him down the hallway to the front door. A stoic mask cloaked his face, revealing nothing but those glittering eyes.

She bit her lip. "Remember, just because Sean can heal you doesn't mean you can take crazy risks. I expect you to come home in one piece. Don't make me have to rescue you again."

His features tensed, darkened by a reaction that baffled her. What had she said?

"I'll be careful," David said. He spun away and grasped the doorknob. "Are you sure you're okay with this?"

"Yes." The word burned on her tongue, but she had to say it. He needed to hear it.

He yanked the door open.

Humid air whispered over her, cloying and hot. Her socked feet slid across the wood floor, heavy and stiff, unwilling to let her lift them even while she closed the distance to David. Her hand lighted on his arm, and she soaked in the heady warmth of him. Her fingers caressed the firm ripples of his muscular body, tracing the lines up his arms and onto his back. Before he left, she yearned to etch him into her memory.

Fear crunched her heart in its icy fist. The vision. Tesler. Blood slicking her hands. Pain searing her chest. His pain. His blood.

He might not come home this time. *Remember.*

She explored him with both hands, relishing the contrast between hard muscle and tender flesh. As the fabric of his shirt rasped across her palm, a shiver vibrated through her. Even through the barrier, his heat spread into her palms. It poured into her body, dousing the tension, snuffing out the fear.

"Go," she murmured. "I'll be okay, and Sean needs you more than I do right now."

His body tensed. His muscles undulated, igniting a tingle in her hands. It unfurled through her body in a blistering, aching wave that tightened something deep inside her. *Oh God.* She gnawed her lip, battling the urge to drag him into the house. Slam the door. Jam the deadbolt. Fall on her knees and plead with him to stay here, with her.

David whirled around and crushed her against him.

His kiss consumed her in a fiery torrent that scorched away reason and doubt. Her body wilted against him as his lips sparked firecracker explosions inside her. Every ounce of his passion and anguish rushed through her mind and body, a gift of sensation that stole the breath from her. The world gyrated around her. A delicious ache washed through her body. Her legs quivered, on the verge of buckling. Heat flushed her skin, her chest heaved with every breath. *Oh David.*

He pushed her away and stomped out the door.

CHAPTER FOUR

THE DOOR BANGED SHUT. GRACE SAGGED AGAINST THE WOOD, TEARS streaming from her eyes. Sobs shook her body from head to toe. Her legs quivered, and breaths gasped out of her, spiking pains through her chest. She'd done what she must. She'd let him go. As the psychic gift David had granted her sluiced out, a deep chill numbed her heart and mind. The sizzle of living energy that had sparked between them fizzled out. Their connection crackled inside her, yet an emptiness cleaved her soul.

She sank to the floor, knees bent in front of her, back against the door. If he survived his quest, he would come back to her. Either way, she prayed she'd done the right thing.

Her head thunked into the wood as her eyelids drifted shut. So hard to force them open again. Why bother? Everything she'd fought for was yanked away from her. David. Her parents. At least David was alive.

For how long?

She hugged her knees, letting her head fall forward onto them. Life offered her two choices. Cower here bawling and wallowing in self-pity, or hoist her ass up off the floor and charge back into the fray.

Her body whimpered for a rest. Her eyes burned with fatigue. Her mind tumbled into a web of half-complete thoughts that tangled around her. Lying here, she might shut out the world. Disregard the drama. Relinquish control.

Get up, dammit. In all her life—at least the part of it she remembered—not once had she resigned control. Would she give up now? Weep and moan and bitch?

Hell no.

She jumped up, wiped the tears away, and tromped across the living room to her corner office. How could she help David? At this moment, she had no clue. Getting back to work, earning a little money to support them both, that would bolster her morale. And lord, did she need a boost.

Pangs sliced into her eyes. A vise cinched tight across her forehead. She slumped onto her desk chair, massaging her temples. Pain throbbed behind her eyes, spreading through her brow and down into her jaw. She snatched up a box of breath mints and popped one into her mouth. The soothing flavor of peppermint trickled down her throat, and still, her stomach churned.

The sunlight beaming in through the windows speared into her brain.

Damn. She should've known better than to tap into her powers twice in one day. The crossroads had leveled its penalty in the form of a migraine.

Shutting her eyes, she rubbed them with the heels of her hands.

Lights pulsed behind her lids. The room tilted and twirled.

She stumbled down the hallway and into the bedroom. Her stomach heaved. She bolted for the bathroom and collapsed in front of the toilet, draping her arms over the bowl. Seconds ticked by as she clung to the toilet seat. The sourness of bile tainted her mouth.

An engine rumbled outside, growing louder.

The nausea relented. She leaned back, inhaling long breaths of cool air. The chemical scent of toilet-bowl cleaner assaulted her senses. *Yuck.*

The rumbling ceased.

She kneaded the knot in her neck, but still, the migraine pulsated through her skull. She slapped both hands on the sink's lip and levered her body off the floor. Light glanced off the mirror, straight into her brain. She ducked her head. To avoid the brightness, yes. But mostly to avoid glimpsing her face in the mirror. Good thing David had left. Every woman dreaded being seen with red eyes and pale lips. And she couldn't forget the gonna-vomit-any-second look on her face.

The doorbell buzzed.

Wonderful. A visitor.

She splashed water on her face, pinched her cheeks for a little color, and trotted to the front door, ducking into the bedroom along the way to snag her revolver. The doorbell rang again. She peeked through the peephole. A gray-haired man stared back at her.

Who the hell?

Holding the gun in her right hand, behind her back, she swung the door open to the limit of the security chain and pasted on a generic smile. "May I help you?"

The man met her gaze head-on, with an expression of detached interest on his clean-shaven face. "Ms. Powell, my name is Roland Wickham. I've come on behalf of Gabriel Amador."

He spoke with an English accent, his words enunciated with precision.

Bracing her hand on the door, she eyed the man's polo shirt and khaki pants. "I don't know any Gabriel Amador."

"Yes, well, you may not recognize the name. But you've had contact with him." Wickham clasped his hands behind his back, rocking forward on his toes. "Quite recently. And in a rather… unusual manner."

Grace stared at him, her jaw slackening. Her tongue probably stuck out too, but she didn't care. Unusual manner. What the blazes was this guy talking about?

Wickham screwed his mouth into an uncomfortable expression. "Gabriel understands why you ignored his text messages, and why you're blocking his communications altogether. He asked me to call on you in the old-fashioned manner."

"I haven't blocked any texts or phone calls."

"Not telephone calls. You've blocked his… metaphysical contact."

A shiver tickled her spine. He meant the brain hacking. This man's employer—or friend, or whatever—was taking credit for the psychic assault that robbed her of any security she'd scraped together over the last six months. Gabriel Amador had hacked her mind. And now he dispatched this polite Englishman to smooth out her feathers. Did he honestly believe this would placate her? *He must be insane.*

Amador might've taken credit for the attack, but she had no way of knowing whether he actually was the psychic intruder, or how much he knew about paranormal powers. Better play it safe.

She locked her gaze on Wickham's green eyes. "I don't know what you mean."

"I believe you do." He inched toward her, stopping near enough that she tensed, but far enough away that she could bang the door shut in his face, if necessary. In a flat whisper, he said, "Gabriel understands your predicament. He's been there before. Give him a chance to explain, and I'm certain you will realize why he intruded on your privacy."

Grace dropped her hand to the doorknob. Intruded on her privacy? Was he joking? The psychic assault had torn through her innate defenses, exposing her innermost self. No permission. No warning. *Wham.* And her world imploded.

She adjusted her grip on the revolver behind her back. "Why didn't your pal pay me a visit himself?"

"He believed an intermediary would prove more helpful in easing your concerns. It's his way."

"Sure, sending his lackey fosters lots of trust."

With a curt nod, Wickham stepped back. "You have an open invitation to visit Gabriel's home, at the address he provided to you. I assure you he wants to help."

She rolled her shoulders back, lifting her chin. "Tell Mr. Amador he can take a flying leap off a very tall cliff. And I hope he lands face-first in a pile of cactus on top of a fire ant mound."

"I'm sure that will amuse him."

She grunted. "I'm thrilled."

Wickham extended a hand.

Grace shoved her free hand into her pants pocket.

"If you change your mind," Wickham said, withdrawing his hand, "our door is always open."

He rotated on his heels and marched down the concrete path to the driveway.

She poked her head out to watch the man as he tromped to the silver Jeep Cherokee parked in the driveway. She waited until the vehicle disappeared down the street, and then she shut the door. *Click.* The lock engaged. She clutched the gun to her stomach, its cold weight a mild comfort. Locks and deadbolts, even the revolver, couldn't protect her from telepathic spies.

Amador had resorted to sending his minion to deliver his message. If he was the psychic intruder, then her mental firewall worked. Nobody could break in.

Thank you, David.

Her pulse quickened. Had David arrived in Montana yet? No, he couldn't have. He'd just left. Their link assured her he was alive and un-harmed, for now. She itched to tap into her powers and remote view him, to see for herself nothing had happened to him. The impulse throbbed inside her. *Do it. You'll feel better.* No, she must not invade David's privacy the way Amador crashed through hers. When David uncovered another lead or stumbled onto Tesler's facility, he'd call her. *Patience.*

Crap. She'd never been good at that.

If she tracked down Tesler, then David would come home. But how might she locate the scientist? She sometimes employed her remote viewing, sort of a combination between astral projection and GPS-like tracking, to check on David, but she couldn't use it on anyone else. Without an intimate connection to the other party, her psychic GPS failed. No one she knew or had read about possessed the ability to locate another person simply by thinking about them.

There must be another way. She'd find it, dammit.

Back at her desk, she struggled to concentrate on work. Her latest client, who'd promised his self-help book would be "easy-peasy" to design, had way-laid her yesterday by insisting on adding complicated tables and charts. Green tea and chocolate sustained her for fifteen minutes or so, but then she flagged, cradling her forehead in both hands, elbows on the desktop.

The doorbell buzzed.

She heaved her body off the chair and trundled to the door, pulling it open with the security chain in place.

A bald man smiled at her, his hazel eyes sparkling a slightly darker hue than hers.

Grinning, she unhooked the chain and swung the door wide.

Edward McLean spread his arms in invitation, and she flew into her grandfather's embrace. He smelled of Old Spice and black coffee. His hand patted her hair, and the tension cramping her muscles, her heart, eased a bit. She ushered him into the living room and parked her butt on the sofa, slouching into the cushions. He sat in the recliner. David's chair.

She tore her attention from the chair's chocolate-brown fabric, evading the memories it evoked, and focused on her grandfather's face. "David called you."

"From the airport, yes. He's concerned. We both are."

"I'm fine." She folded her arms over her chest. "I don't need a babysitter."

He propped one ankle atop the other knee and clasped his hands over his belly. "You had a premonition."

"It's nothing, I'm okay."

With a sharp shake of his head, he frowned at her. "Grace, you have to stop downplaying these things. You had a terrifying experience, believed David was dead for hours, and you never called me."

She grunted. "Wake you up at an ungodly hour to tell you... What? I had a panic attack after a bad dream?"

"It was no dream, we all know that. And you do not panic. Not without extreme provocation."

The air rushed out of her as a loud sigh, and she flopped her head back against the sofa. "I have to do something. David will get himself killed if I don't—" She thumped her fists on her thighs. "Gah! I can't just sit here pretending life goes on as normal. Nothing about my life is normal."

Edward rose and shuffled to her, perching on the coffee table. His hands wrapped her fists. She flinched at the sudden warmth, unaware of how cold her hands were.

His eyebrows wrinkled, lifting into a V over his nose. "David told me about your visitor."

Her head snapped up. "What?"

David couldn't know about Wickham's visit. Could he?

"Yes," her grandfather said. "The mental assault must've been disturbing, more than you're willing to let on."

Ohhh, *that* visitor.

She shrugged. "It won't happen again." She wrested a hand free of his and tapped her temple with one finger. "Like a fortress."

"I heard. But the text messages—"

"Were creepy, yeah." She sat forward, laying her hand over his. "Frankly, there's not a damn thing you can do to protect me from telepathic stalkers. So please, trust me to handle this my way."

"Grace, I know you're strong and capable. David and I are simply trying to—"

"Protect me. I got the message." She stood and stomped to the window that overlooked the front yard and driveway. "I appreciate the sentiment, and I love you both for it, but honestly, I can take care of myself."

"You asked me to trust you." He came up beside her, hands in his pants pockets, eyeing her sideways. "But you won't trust us—me and David. Why?"

She leaned against the window frame and scrutinized a tiny crack in the glass. "I'm sorry. Please believe me, I'm trying, but I got used to handling things myself when I had amnesia and you guys were in California."

He bowed his head, shoulders sagging. "We shouldn't have left you alone in Texas. Keeping you in the dark was my idea, not David's. If you need someone to blame, it's me, Grace." Despair crept into his voice when he said, "I failed Christine. I can't bear to fail you too, Grace."

She threw her arms around him. In a tone as fierce as her hug, she told him, "Mom wouldn't blame you. I don't blame you. Please don't worry about me." She pulled away, blinking back stray tears, and straightened. "I'll be okay."

Whether he believed her or not, she couldn't say, but his mood brightened a bit, and by the time he departed, she thought he was moderately convinced she wouldn't die today. The best either of them could hope for these days. As she watched his car roll down the street, she shut and locked the front door.

Two visitors in one day. She preferred the second one. Roland Wickham had been polite but unforthcoming.

A thought bubbled to the surface of her brain. Gabriel Amador had contacted her at the exact time when Sean and David caught another lead on Tesler and his new undertaking. Coincidence? Reason said yes, but the gnawing in her gut warned her no. Once again, outside forces conspired to corner her. In this go-round, she refused to twiddle her thumbs and wait for David to guide her. If he chose to run off in search of his demons, then she would grab hold of the reins in her own life. David might find answers, or this "mission" might derail like all the others.

They needed outside support. *She* needed support.

Wickham had told her Amador wanted to help. Could she trust either man?

Hell no.

Her vision replayed in her mind. David on his knees. Tesler wielding a knife. Blood. Agony.

No, no, no. She must do everything in her power to prevent the premonition from coming true. But how? She lacked the one tool she needed. Information.

It granted power, right? Well then, she better steal some. Or wheedle it out of Amador.

A cold fist clenched around her heart. *Bad idea, this is a very bad idea.* She'd exhausted her options over the last six months. Maybe her vision wouldn't happen, but she refused to wait and see. Time to risk a new tactic.

Amador schemed to use her, though for what, she had no clue. Why not use him right back?

David would kill her for this. And for a psychic, that meant he didn't even have to come home to do it.

You've got to end this once and for all.

Time to investigate on her own.

CHAPTER FIVE

A CHILL WIND SIZZLED THROUGH THE TREETOPS AS DAVID CROUCHED behind a jack pine for shelter. He shoved his hands in his jacket pockets. Despite his clothing, olive-green camouflage, he preferred to hide behind the tree while scouting the location. He must enact every precaution, not just for himself, but for Grace too.

He never should've left her.

Stop thinking about it. You're here now, focus on that.

He exercised caution for someone else besides Grace. He did it for Sean.

The teenage boy crouched behind another tree, an arm's length from David. At seventeen, Sean fancied himself a man, yet David had trouble thinking of him as anything other than the cowering boy he'd met while interned at the facility in California's remote Mojave Desert. Tesler and his cronies at ALI had exulted in tormenting anyone with paranormal powers, whatever their age. The memory of his first encounter with Sean replayed in his mind—the boy curled up in the fetal position on his bed, a blanket lumped on top of him, cocooning him from head to toe. That had been less than a year ago.

Today, Sean crouched behind a tree dressed in camouflage, his red hair shaved into a buzz cut and his expression stern, the portrait of a commando wannabe. Sean might've shed his outward fear, but David sensed it lurking underneath, like a pond cloaked in ice.

The wind gusted, shaking the trees.

Panic flashed across Sean's face, blanching his fair skin. His freckles stood out against the pallor, like stars in reverse. Sean locked his green eyes on David for a second. Then the boy shrugged, twisted his mouth into an annoyed expression, and swung his gaze back to the object of their investigation.

David leaned sideways to peer around the tree. There, about a hundred feet away inside a clearing, hunkered a metal shed about ten feet square and eight feet tall. High above, a satellite dish clung to the trunk of a towering tree, mounted near the top. Nothing else hinted at the presence of anything more sinister than squirrels. Still, he and Sean needed to keep an eye out for the wildlife, as well as security personnel. If this was the new facility, then it would have security, of the covert kind.

David glanced at Sean. The boy pointed at his eyes with two fingers and then shut his lids. It was a signal they had developed. It meant one of them should remote view the location in question. Sean opened his eyes and pointed one finger at his chest.

David shook his head. He indicated his own chest.

Sean slumped his shoulders and rolled his eyes, his way of saying, "I'm not a baby anymore, you overprotective dork."

David supposed teenagers didn't say "dork" anymore. Whatever the derogatory phrase associated with it, the expression conveyed petulance. Sean wanted to take a more active role in their investigations, but David clung to his overprotective instinct. Besides, he was better at RV'ing than Sean was.

And the boy knew it. That was part of the sentiment behind the eye-rolling.

Closing his eyes, David let his mind go blank. He soared up into the crossroads, hunting for the path that would lead him into the facility, if the metal shed concealed a facility. A star in the crossroads pulsed, and he latched on to it, letting it pull him ever downward, spiraling through a dark tunnel.

He hurtled out into the real world.

Light blinded him. He winced and flung up a hand to shield his eyes. Though no one else could see him, and he had no physical body when remote viewing, he always envisioned himself in a physical form. So far as he knew, all travelers experienced it this way. The human mind, even when disconnected from its body, fought to make sense of its surroundings. That was his theory, at least.

He stood in a corridor. The glare of white lights swallowed details. With every second that ticked past, his vision acclimated to the light. After a moment that felt like forever, but must've eaten up no more than thirty seconds, he discerned more of his surroundings.

The brilliant glow emanated from bulbs recessed into the ceiling. He shuffled down the corridor, past closed doors set into the walls at regular intervals. White paint coated everything except the floor. Even the doorknobs were white. His phantom shoes traveled over the pale-gray linoleum in silence. He spotted no markings on the first two doors. As he strode deeper into the facility, he watched for signs of life, or at least an actual sign to clue him in to what function this place served.

The doors did bear markings, he realized, though none that made sense to him. Alongside each door, at waist level, raised figures—dots, lines, and squares—designated each door with a unique code. It looked like Morse code or a strange kind of Braille. He reached out to finger the markings, but of course, with no physical body, he couldn't touch them. His fingers met emptiness.

The ventilation system hissed overhead. He crept down the hall, glancing at each doorway he passed, spotting nothing that might alert him to this building's purpose. Another facility? Another hellhole where Tesler tortured psychics? He clenched his jaw, grinding his teeth. He must thwart the scientist, whatever the cost. Tesler must never get his claws into Grace or Sean or anyone else.

David rubbed his forehead. He'd essentially left Sean alone outside this building. The boy longed to expand his powers. Would he attempt more advanced feats of psychic ability while David was distracted in here? He hoped he'd taught Sean better than that, but the boy's impulse to grab more power was strong. A couple of weeks ago, he'd told David, "I want to manifest. That would be so cool."

"You can't."

"Why not?"

David had shrugged. "You're not Grace."

"But I'm strong too. Why can't I manifest like she does? Why can't you?"

"Because we are nowhere near as strong as Grace is." He'd laid a hand on Sean's shoulder. "We can't manifest without her help. Accept it."

Naturally, Sean balked at the suggestion. The truth was irrefutable, though. David knew of no other travelers who could manifest. He'd heard rumors, but nothing concrete. As far as he knew, Grace alone possessed the ability to manifest a physical body, for herself or others.

A thwapping reverberated down the corridor, from around a corner twenty feet ahead. David froze. The noise grew louder and louder, nearer and nearer. He backed up, staying close to the wall, and locked his gaze on the corner. *Thwap, thwap.*

Murmuring. Nearby. Getting closer. The thwapping sharpened into *clomp, clomp, clomp.*

Two men dressed in white lab coats traipsed into view. They paused at the intersection.

David hesitated twenty feet away. He pressed his body into the wall, a human pancake on a vertical skillet. He knew the men couldn't see him, since he had no physical body, but the instinct to conceal himself tugged too hard. He'd given up trying to rationalize the urge a long time ago.

"I know what the boss wants," the older of the two men said. He ran a hand through his rim of gray hair and over his bald crown. "It's a bad idea."

"We do what he tells us," the younger man said, "no matter what we think of it. That's called doing our jobs, Yellen."

"Even JT couldn't contain her. How the hell are we supposed to?"

The younger man shook his head, tousling his shoulder-length chestnut hair. "We do whatever we have to do."

Yellen snorted. "That's easy for you to say, Evans. You won't be involved in the containment process. If she lashes out, I'll die, but you'll be safe and sound in your office."

"She won't lash out. The boss will keep her under control."

Her. She. A double-edged blade of fear and realization sliced through David. They couldn't mean…

No, God, please.

"I don't like this induction program," Yellen said. The crow's feet around his eyes deepened as he tensed his features. "Don't care if Jackson Tennant himself dreamed it up, he was a lunatic after all."

"The boss isn't." Evans adjusted his black-rimmed glasses with one finger. "If he wants the girl, then we help him get her. If his methods don't work, then we use our well-tested induction procedures to bring her in. It's our job."

Yellen's shoulders deflated, accentuating his flabby physique. He scowled at his fit colleague. "I know. But I heard she blew up our best facility."

"JT did that, not the woman."

"Well, whoever did it, we still haven't recovered from the loss of data and materials. Besides, I don't care to be blown to smithereens, not even in the pursuit of knowledge and scientific advancement."

Evans snickered. "You think that's why we're doing all this? Scientific advancement?"

"Why else?"

"Power, man. Power." Evans leaned closer to Yellen, as if sharing a secret. "Whoever controls these freaks and their powers has the potential to control the world. If we do what the boss wants, then he might let us share in the spoils, get it?"

Yellen harrumphed.

The younger man sighed. "We do what the boss wants. Nothing more, nothing less."

The older man studied the floor for a couple of seconds. Then he raised his head and nodded. "You're right. We execute our duties, no matter what. Doesn't mean I have to like it."

"Induction works, dude."

Yellen jerked his head in a curt nod and grimaced.

Evans lifted his angular chin. "One way or another, either willingly or by force, we will bring in Grace Powell."

David jerked as if Evans had punched him in the gut. Pressure that originated deep inside him pulverized his heart. This was what he'd feared for six months, the impetus for his obsession, and yet he hadn't believed, deep down, that it could happen. Until now.

His insides crystallized into ice. His heart thudded in his chest, and although he knew it wasn't a real heart, the pounding ached no less than the genuine article. This must end. Today. This instant.

But first, he had to warn Grace.

Anguish tunneled straight through his heart into his soul. He collapsed to his knees, the imagined bones hitting the floor in silence. How could he have abandoned her, knowing about her vision and the telepathic intruder? What if the brain hacker obeyed Tesler's orders? This was all his fault.

So save her, jackass.

He snapped upright. Last time, she'd rescued him from a facility much like this one. But this time around, he would rescue her. He'd strap on his macho and gun down anyone who got in his way. No one would hurt Grace. No one.

Holding his position inside the facility, he stretched out his powers to connect with Grace. To contact anyone else, he'd have to retreat into the crossroads. With Grace, he required nothing more than to think of her. To fully contact her, to ascertain her whereabouts and communicate with her, he must strengthen the connection. Feed power into it. Widen the pathway.

A shock jolted through him. Everything around him spun. His mind whirled out of control. Pain, sharp and hot, gored him on a metaphysical level. His lock on the facility frayed. He struggled to link with Grace, but the shock walloped him again. His RV grip on the facility disintegrated. His mind shot upward, through the tunnel, into the crossroads. He twirled and twirled, like a top set loose on a smooth table. Lights blurred around him. He couldn't latch on to one light, couldn't grasp any connection that might guide him out of here. Every time he flailed for a hold, his mind pitched backward as if it bounced off—

A wall.

Shit. Grace had built a psychic barrier so strong nothing could ram through it, not even him.

His mind tumbled out of the crossroads, spiraling downward. He punched back into his body. For precious seconds, he struggled to breathe, to see, to untangle the sensory input overwhelming his brain. The surroundings blurred and mingled. His head pounded, his chest ached, and his head throbbed. Cradling his head in his hands, he forced his lungs to draw in deep breaths. Grace endured headaches after using her powers. He didn't. The amount of energy demanded by traveling drained him, yes, but it triggered no pain.

Until today.

The world around him coalesced into recognizable shapes. Trees. Bushes. Grass. The stench of sweat permeated the air. A breeze chilled his chest through his damp shirt. Between his fingers, he glimpsed Sean staring at him. Eyes wide. Face pale. Lips parted. David's stress must've shown on his face. He worked to erase the pained expression. He must've succeeded, because the color returned to Sean's face, though he still gaped as if David had grown a pair of horns. Just to make sure, David palpated his head. No horns.

Sean whispered, "You looked like you were dying."

"I'm fine," David said in an equally soft voice.

He did feel better. The pounding in his head had dissipated, although intense fatigue blanketed him. Sweat dribbled down his temples. He swiped it away with the back of his hand.

Grace's firewall blocked him, and yet, before leaving the house, he'd gifted her with his emotions in a last-ditch effort to reinforce their connection, even as he recognized the need to temper it, for her sake. She'd built her new psychic defenses before that. Their link wasn't severed, merely dampened. Maybe he could get through if he calculated it just right and—

No time to think about it.

Grace was in danger. Tesler's minions had zeroed their sights in on her. They would storm the house and capture her, if they hadn't already.

His throat tightened. He clenched his hands into fists, the nails digging into his palms. Pain sparked in his flesh. To warn Grace, he'd have to resort to old-fashioned, purely physical means.

He dug out his phone. A text message wouldn't do. She might not heed his warning unless she heard it from him directly. But if this facility boasted the kind of security he'd encountered at the Mojave Desert location, then the system might detect voices outside. He couldn't risk talking loud enough for Grace to hear him over the phone. But he must warn her.

Screw it. If a security squad lassoed him, so be it.

David caught Sean's attention by waving his hand. Then he risked speaking in a louder, though still hushed, voice. "Get out of here. I'll meet you at the car."

Sean shook his head.

David mouthed, "Go."

Sean glared at him for a second, but then rose into a semi-crouch and trotted back the way they'd come. His footfalls whisked against the grass and dirt, barely audible. David prayed no one else heard Sean's movements.

He tapped the phone's touch screen, dialing a programmed number.

Sean's silhouette vanished from sight. His footsteps faded into silence. With any luck, the boy had reached a safe distance.

The call transferred to Grace's voicemail. Her cheery voice instructed him to leave a message at the tone. His gut churned. Acid soured his tongue. How soon would she retrieve her messages? *Dammit.* He'd assumed he could catch her and deliver the news as close to face-to-face as possible.

A long beep rattled his eardrums. He had a minute, maybe two, to convince her before the blasted voicemail cut him off.

"Grace, it's me," he said. "Please listen carefully. Tesler's men are coming for you. Do not stay at home. Do not use your cell after this. Hang up, ditch the phone, and get the hell out of there. Your psychic firewall is—"

Click. The line went dead.

A low battery warning flashed on the screen.

David jumped to his feet. He must get home. As fast as possible.

Sean stumbled out of the woods straight ahead of David. The boy scowled, his shoulders slumped. "I'm sorry. I tried to get away."

"Away from what?" David eyed Sean through slitted eyes. The boy held his hands behind his back. David slouched forward, knees bent. "What's wrong? Are you injured?"

Two figures traipsed out of the trees behind Sean. The burly men wielded semiautomatic handguns, both trained on Sean. A third man emerged from the woods to David's left. The newcomer targeted his weapon at David. All three men wore camouflage outfits with military-style boots and two-way radios clipped to their belts.

The closest man, the one fixated on David, said, "You're coming with us."

David attempted to look confused. "We were just out for a hike. Didn't mean to cause any trouble."

The man shook his head, an unfriendly smile on his lips. "We aren't that stupid. And besides, we know who you are. David Ransom and Sean Vandenbrook. Ain't facial recognition software awesome?"

David exhaled a long sigh. What energy he had left flooded out of him. He must've talked too loudly, or for too long, on the phone with Grace's voicemail. And he'd gotten Sean wrapped up in his mess.

"Take me," David said, "but let the boy go. I'm the one you want."

"Nice offer," the stranger said. "But I don't think so."

The man shoved a hand into his jacket pocket, pulling out a nylon zip tie.

David surveyed the area for an escape route. He spied more human-shaped figures in the woods, encircling them like wolves homing in on their prey. David grabbed for his gun, berthed in a shoulder holster under his jacket.

One of the men behind Sean jammed his gun into the boy's temple.

The other man, the only one who'd spoken so far, told David, "Make it easier on both of you. Don't fight."

He couldn't fight, not with so many of them versus him and Sean. In any other situation, he might've tapped into his powers to barge his way out of this mess. Since he'd emptied his energy reserves in the failed effort to contact Grace, he had nothing left to fight them with.

At least Grace would know of the danger to her. Getting captured was worth any torment that might follow if it meant Grace would be safe.

David dropped his gun.

Tesler had won this round.

CHAPTER SIX

OWN A HALLWAY THE TWO OF THEM MARCHED, SINGLE FILE, WITH Roland Wickham leading the way. Grace stared at the back of his head since closed doors barred her view of the rooms on either side of the hall. Though Gabriel Amador had invited her to his home, clearly he did not care to expose all his secrets to her. Thoughts of what might lie beyond the doors bounced around in her brain, tickling her curiosity.

Wickham halted at a door and knocked. A voice inside invited them to enter, and Wickham swung the door wide, motioning for her to go inside.

She hesitated.

A thirty-minute drive down increasingly desolate roads, followed by a tooth-jarring trip up a long, two-track driveway, delivered her to this house. She'd opted to come here. Yet a quiet voice in the back of her mind warned her against it even now. Maybe it was David's voice, borne of memories.

Wickham waved his hand again.

She faced the room and swallowed. *Just do it, coward.*

Grasping her purse strap, she inched across the threshold.

The musky smell of leather washed over her, mixed with a lightly floral aroma. The combination peaked her senses.

The door clicked shut behind her.

Across the room, on the opposite side of a massive wooden desk, a man lounged in a leather executive chair. Gabriel Amador waved toward one of two leather chairs, smaller than his, positioned on this side of the room. Grace took a step and froze. She chewed her lip. Amador had probably hacked into her mind, for pity's sake. And what, he expected her to just sit down and strike up a conversation?

She scuffled backward a step, snaking her hand behind her back to grasp the doorknob. When she twisted, the knob turned. A coil of tension slackened inside her. Not locked in, at least. She dipped her fingers into her purse just far enough to touch the cold metal of her .357 revolver. The weapon granted her a modicum of security, but only that much.

Heaven almighty, when David found out about this, he'd chain her to the sofa to keep her at home. She knew she shouldn't have come here, but she couldn't sit at home watching chick flicks while David and Sean gambled their lives on a frantic search for a boogeyman. Her psychic wall blocked out everyone except David, as far as she knew, but she still needed to confront *her* boogeyman.

Amador flicked on a lamp. Sun-bright light glanced off the white walls, piercing her eyes. The remnants of her migraine throbbed behind her temples. She squinted and threw a hand up to shield her gaze.

"I won't harm you," Amador said, his voice seasoned with a light accent. "Take a seat, please."

Grace glanced at the nearest chair. Pursed her lips. Tapped her toe. Good or bad, crazy or sane, whatever his motivations, Gabriel Amador was a stranger to her. She thought. At times like this, amnesia really sucked. She might've met Amador last year and not remember it.

"If you mean no harm," she said, "then why did you hack into my brain and scare the holy living shit out of me?"

"I apologize for that, truly. But hacking seems an exaggerated description. A telepathic intrusion was the most expedient way to test your reaction."

Intrusion. He made it sound almost genteel.

She tilted her head, squinting at him. "Test my reaction to what?"

He shrugged one shoulder. "Me. Those things that we share in common. Our special connection."

Yeah, she'd heard this spiel before. From the only other person who ever hacked her brain. A man who believed he shared a "special connection" with her. *You are mine, golden girl,* he'd proclaimed. JT had battered his way into her mind, thrusting those words inside. Never again would she allow an assault like that.

She swallowed hard. "We don't have a connection, special or otherwise. Having the same powers doesn't make us soul mates."

Amador leaned forward to rest his elbows on the desktop. His expression faded into something inscrutable, halfway between curiosity and annoyance. He steepled his fingers and propped his chin on them. "I am not Jackson Tennant. I have no delusions that you and I share a psychic bond or that your blood will grant me your powers."

Jackson Tennant. The name blustered through her mind like a hurricane wind, propelling the memories of six months ago to the forefront. Acid rose in her throat. It tainted her tongue with a sour, almost metallic taste. Like blood. But the tang rose from her memories, not her stomach. Snapshots flashed in her mind, bits of memories she'd regained six months ago.

A car flipping end over end. A sickening crunch. Steam hissing. A voice wailing.

Gabriel Amador lowered his hands. His eyes widened a touch. "I'm sorry. I reminded you of something terrible, didn't I? Something Tennant did to you." He stood halfway, pointing to the chair. "Please sit. You look pale."

Was that concern in his voice? She dropped her arms to her sides. And for reasons she couldn't comprehend, words tumbled out of her mouth. Maybe she needed to say them, to sweep the memories away again. "JT murdered my parents. He caused the car accident that killed them and then—" She snapped her jaw shut and sucked in a deep breath. "Can we talk about something else?"

"Of course. My apologies for dredging up bad memories. I know how painful that can be."

The tight coil inside her unwound a little more. *Crap.* She did not want to like him. She shouldn't like him. He'd stalked and terrified her. Right now, though, she needed answers from him.

What had Wickham told her? *Gabriel understands your predicament. He's been there before.* Been where? She needed to know. Amador might have information that would help her. With Tesler's goons on her trail, she must take risks to survive. She needed to do this. She *could* do this. Alone.

Squaring her shoulders, she strode to the chair and settled her butt onto the cushioned seat. Perched on the edge, she plunked her purse onto her lap. Hands folded over the bag, she locked her gaze on Amador's dark-chocolate eyes.

He smiled, flashing neon-white teeth lined up in perfect rows. His cinnamon skin darkened a shade in the brilliance of his dental work. Oh yeah, no way those were natural teeth. "I've anticipated this meeting more than you know."

"How flattering." There she went again, mouthing off when she really wanted to cry or scream or bolt for the door. David called it her fortress of sarcasm. Not complimentary, but so true she winced even thinking about it. Today, she could use a fortress.

Amador folded his hands on his lap. "I do apologize for my intrusive methods. I hope you can forgive me."

"Forgive you?" She arched her eyebrows. "How about you try convincing me not to shoot you."

"Oh, you won't shoot me."

The utter certainty in his tone bristled her temper. She bit back a smart retort and instead asked, "How can you be so sure?"

"You avoid violence and do harm only when absolutely necessary."

"You don't know me. Maybe I'm a ruthless killer."

He chuckled. The accompanying smile tightened the crow's feet around his eyes and the lines around his mouth. A faint scar on his cheek danced. She couldn't blame him for laughing. Her statement sounded ludicrous even to her. Grace Powell, assassin for hire. Yeah, right.

"You are far too refined to be a murderer," Amador said. He rocked in his chair, aiming a faint smirk at her. "I am so pleased you've accepted my invitation. And may I say you are even more beautiful than I imagined. Quite stunning, actually."

She stared at him, her lips twisted into a half scowl. Flirting? Was he serious? If she threatened to stab him, maybe he'd propose marriage.

If David had spoken the same compliments, she would've blushed. Here, now, with this man, no such heat bloomed in her cheeks. Her stomach grumbled, but she doubted that had anything to do with Amador's flirtation. Something about him scraped at her nerves. She trusted her intuition, and it warned her to take care in dealing with Amador. She pulled her purse snug against her body. The hard lump of her gun pressed into her flesh.

"I'm here," she said. "So can we cut the crap and get down to business?"

"I do enjoy your directness. It's refreshing and immensely appealing."

She doubted her fiancé would agree. *David, where are you?* "I'm not trying to appeal to you, Mr. Amador. You're the one who invited me here. Time to prove I should stay."

"Of course."

"You claimed you could help me. What exactly did you mean?"

With one finger, he traced swirling lines on the smooth desktop. "I can help you understand your psychic abilities and use them to better effect. I know you suffer from debilitating migraines anytime you use your powers for more than a bit of remote reconnaissance. I can teach you how to set your powers free, so you will no longer suffer because of them."

She clenched her fists around her gun's outline. How the blazes did he know so much about her? Would he have risked insanity merely to read her mind and gain tidbits of knowledge about her?

Risk insanity? He must've tipped that boat a long time ago. No sane person would burrow into her mind, rummage around a bit, and then invite her over for a cozy chat.

Grace drummed her fingers on her purse, on the gun hidden beneath the vinyl. "Your offer sounds great. What's the catch?"

His brown eyes targeted her gaze, like a radar-guided missile zeroing in on its target. "You will need to drop whatever psychic shield you've erected."

"Mmm… no. What else have you got?"

A frown flickered across Amador's features, evaporating in the space of a heartbeat. "If you allow me to help you with your powers, then I will use all the money and influence at my disposal to help you find Karl Tesler."

Her heart skipped a beat. "Who?"

"Dr. Karl Tesler. The scientist David is searching for as we speak."

"I have no idea who that is."

He burrowed a hand through his black hair. "Please, Grace, I know you're lying. It's time we told each other the truth. I am not your enemy."

Right. Not her enemy. He was her new best friend. With fangs, venom, and a rattling tail.

Searing pain skewered her heart. She gasped. The pain spiked through her again, deeper, tearing into muscle and sinew. She clutched the chair's arms, panting, whimpering. *Jesus, no.* Tentacles of power lashed at her.

The agony dissolved into a yawning emptiness that ached in her heart.

She knew this ache. Not physical pain. A psychic shock. And it radiated to her through a connection so intimate, so alive, that it smacked into her with physical force. She squeezed her eyes shut as a silent sob wrenched her body.

David was hurt. Screaming. Bleeding. Dying.

Behind the ache, an oily energy roiled. Its tentacles flailed, striving for purchase.

This was not from David. Someone, or something, was laying siege to her defenses. Her fears tricked her into believing the agony originated with David.

Boiling agony scorched her veins. Blades ripped her flesh.

She toppled forward.

Amador snared her in his muscular arms.

And she passed out.

CHAPTER SEVEN

THE GUARD SHOVED DAVID THROUGH THE DOORWAY INTO A SHAD-
owed room. The guards wore no name tags, and so he had no idea what
to call them. "Assholes" came to mind, but he figured they wouldn't appreciate that.

David rubbed his shoulder, where the cretin had punched him when
he protested at being separated from Sean. Another bruise on his forearm
was blossoming a nice shade of plum. That one he received for blinking, or
maybe breathing. The guard hadn't specified.

He scuffled deeper into the room. His shoes scraped across the concrete
floor. At a dozen feet wide and long, at most, the space pressed in around
him. It reeked of sweat and blood and fear. A single bulb recessed into the
ceiling spilled flickering light into the center of the room, but the sickly
glow petered out before reaching the corners. A narrow wedge of brighter
light from the corridor sliced through the gloom. David squinted. He still
couldn't make out much besides the square shape of the prison cell.

And that's what it was. No bed, no chairs, nothing to provide a modicum of comfort. He kicked his toe into the bare concrete, catching it in
a pit.

The guard kicked the door shut.

A locking mechanism chunked into position. David trudged further
into the room. Halfway across the space, he stopped. A humanlike shape
huddled in the far corner, masked in shadows and motionless as a boulder.

He had a cellmate.

The man's ebony skin blended into the gloom. Indirect light glimmered
off his clean-shaven scalp. When he lifted his head to gaze at David, the
whites of the man's eyes almost glowed. A trick of the dim light, David
knew. Still, the sight of the pure white of the man's eyes, with inky disks at
their centers, made David hesitate.

At the Mojave Desert facility, the scientists had locked him in a cell outfitted like a hospital room, without the windows. His captors kept the door sealed at all times and, toward the end, they sedated him into unconsciousness. Here in Montana, without JT at the helm, Tesler clearly had adopted a new tactic for imprisoning psychics, something closer to the way prisons operated. At least the guard removed the zip tie from his wrists before dumping him into the cell.

A spasm wrenched his entire body. Electric shocks ripped his flesh.

He staggered into the wall, gasping, his chest racked with pains. His spine contorted as if a wire threaded through it was yanked taut. Sweat rolled down his temples, and blackness dotted his vision. He slumped against the concrete wall.

This pain. He'd endured it earlier today. It came from Grace.

Her firewall prevented him from contacting her directly, anyway. He must try the indirect route, via emotion.

Grace had teased him into an outburst earlier because she recognized his worst weakness. The inability to express his feelings. The irony of emotions being his only psychic path to her might've given him a laugh under other circumstances. But at this moment, afflicted with her suffering, he found no humor in it.

"Are you ill?"

David jumped away from the wall. He'd forgotten about his cellmate.

His new friend sat unmoving, turning only his spooky eyes to keep track of David. The man did not watch with wide eyes, however, but with a curious gaze. His mouth held a neutral position, not a smile but not a frown either. With his back to the wall, angled into the corner, he had his knees bent in front of him and his forearms resting on his knees with his hands dangling. The man appeared relaxed, yet David sensed a tension beneath the surface, coiled within the man's core like a serpent that might spring out to attack at any moment.

If his cellmate morphed into a werewolf, even that wouldn't stop him from what he needed to do.

"I'm fine," he muttered, to satisfy the other man.

Then he fixated his gaze on the far wall, unleashed his mind from his body, and soared up into the crossroads. No traveling this time. He dragged in as much energy as he could withstand, consolidated every drop of passion and longing and adoration for Grace he possessed, and fired the missile down at her wall.

The projectile splintered.

White-hot shards punctured his mind, and he slapped his palms on the wall, swallowing a cry. Force wasn't the way, he should've remembered it from the first time he tried to contact her after she raised her defenses. When he'd shared himself with her before leaving the house, it had been more subtle, more intimate. The fact she'd been in his arms then, completely open to him in body and mind, must've eased the way.

He tried again. This time, he avoided the crossroads and stayed in his body. Instead of attacking her wall, he concentrated on sending her another gift, wrapped in the intensity of his love and concern for her. A single message, conveyed in emotion.

I'm okay.

It slid through, he felt it. Her fear, her pain, it melted away in the heat of his message. She was asleep, he sensed, yet she relaxed out of the torment.

"You don't look fine," his cellmate said, and now David realized the man had an accent.

David pulled himself up straight and forced a smile. "I'm good. Why should you care? We're strangers."

"The smell of decaying flesh bothers me. I'd prefer you don't die until the guards return."

"I'll keep that in mind."

David shuffled into the corner opposite the man. He seated himself at a forty-five-degree angle to the room, mimicking his cellmate's position. David stretched one leg out in front of him and bent the other so he could rest one arm atop his knee. The other arm he let hang down, with his hand on his thigh. He too could feign relaxation.

David nodded at his new friend. "I've never had a roommate before. Not sure what the etiquette is." He leaned his head back against the wall. "My name is David Ransom. What's yours?"

The man stared at him for several seconds, the whites of his eyes gleaming. Then he let out a small sigh. "I am Nkosi Uba."

"Where are you from?"

"South Africa. Johannesburg, originally."

"I'm from Wisconsin." The words tasted strange. He hadn't spoken of his home in years. Though he'd told Grace about his childhood, those conversations happened during the eight months she no longer remembered. So essentially, he hadn't mentioned his home to anyone in a very long time.

Nkosi studied him in silence.

"Wisconsin is in the United States," David said. "It's north of—"

"I know where it is."

David shifted position, his pants scritching on the concrete floor as he moved out of the corner to lean against the flat wall. "How long have you been a guest in this luxurious resort?"

A trace of a smile played across Nkosi's face, but it faded swiftly. "I have been here for two months. I know this only because my watch tells me the date. Otherwise, I would have no answer for your question."

"They don't mind cruel and unusual punishment at these places. I imagine you haven't seen the outdoors in two months either."

"I have not, except for a blade of grass that fell off of a guard's boot."

David grunted. "I'm sure they believe that counts as seeing the out-doors."

Nkosi watched David intently, as if measuring up the man before him, and David wasn't quite sure if Nkosi liked the result.

"If they have sent you," Nkosi said, "to befriend me in hopes I will give them what they want, then you may inform them it will not work."

"Why would my befriending you get them what they want?"

"It is their way. It didn't work the four times previously, and it will not work this time either. If they burn you, I will not give in. If they slowly cut off your hand, still I will not give in. If they—"

"I get the idea." David felt a lump hardening in his stomach, like a meal he'd eaten too fast. He knew Tesler salivated at the prospect of tor-turing psychics, but this was the first he'd heard of burning or cutting off hands. Tesler favored cleaner methods that involved no messy fluids, other than tears. Seeing people cry and listening to them beg for mercy, that was Tesler's pleasure.

"Does your arm hurt?" Nkosi asked.

"What?"

Nkosi waved at David's left arm. "You've been rubbing it as if it hurts."

David glanced down and saw he was rubbing his arm. Old habits, he supposed. The bruise might have healed, but the memory lingered. He'd been strapped to a less-pleasant version of a dentist chair, veins combusting with a novel mixture of drugs meant to boost psychic powers and render the subject compliant. Tesler hunched before him, expressionless except for the glittering in his dark eyes.

"Who is Janet Austen?" Tesler demanded.

He slanted over David with one hand on each arm of the chair, pinning his already restrained arms to it. The pressure of Tesler's grasp triggered a dull aching in his arms that spread down into his hands. David winced, but said nothing.

Tesler pressed down harder. David gritted his jaw so hard he thought his teeth might shatter. He would never tell this man what he wanted to know. Never.

"I know it's an alias," Tesler said. "Tell me Janet Austen's real name and the pain will stop."

Grace. Her name flitted through his mind, soft as a breeze. Beautiful Grace. Sweet Grace. His gut wrenched. He couldn't betray her even when his own life depended on it.

"Have it your way." Tesler stepped back, releasing the pressure on David's arms. A sigh rushed out of him unbidden, like the release of air when a vacu-um-sealed container was torn open.

Tesler nodded to one of the guards posted near the door. The man strode over to David's chair and unhooked a billy club from his belt, which he of-fered to Tesler. The scientist took the club, slapping it on his palm.

"Tell me," Tesler said.

David shook his head.

Tesler slammed the club down on David's forearm. He stifled a cry as pain shot through his arm, into his hand, convulsing the tendons. The agony seared his muscles, rushing through his body in a wave that annihilated his thoughts. His ears rang. Darkness licked at the edges of his vision.

Kill me. The thought came from nowhere, it seemed. He didn't want to die, and yet he did not want to betray Grace, not even accidentally.

Tesler studied David with a look of detached interest. He might as well have been observing a baboon in a cage.

"I don't know who she is," David said.

Tesler pursed his lips, thumping the club on his palm. After a couple of seconds, he shrugged and tossed the club to the guard. "Ah well, perhaps the drugs will work better. You may have masochistic tendencies, after all."

Then the scientist had left the room.

"How did it happen?" Nkosi's voice broke David out of the past. "Your arm. How did you injure it?"

"Wrestling with a snake."

Grace compared his mission with wrestling an alligator. She was right, his foolishness had whipped around to bite him in the ass.

He scrubbed a hand over his face, but the stain of guilt was embedded too deep to wipe off so easily. If Tesler captured Grace, he'd get answers from her no matter what it took. If she denied him, he might even overcome his aversion to messes and unlock fresh, more agonizing methods of convincing her to cooperate.

All because of me.

"Now you seem angry," Nkosi said. "You must have troublesome memories."

"Troublesome." David laughed, though not with amusement. To his own ears, the laughter sounded harsh and bitter. "You could say that."

Nkosi's eyes narrowed. His lips flattened.

Metaphysical energy tickled at his brain. He winced. Nkosi was attempting to touch his mind without his consent. Only Grace had permission to poke him this way, though from her, it came through with subtle, nearly sensual tenderness. He batted away the mental feather irritating him.

Of course, if Nkosi resolved to get inside David's head, he could batter down the gates without much effort. Every human mind boasted a built-in barrier, not quite a wall, but more of a curtain. Grace's firewall, erected with conscious purpose, blocked out everything. The natural curtain impeded curious travelers. Anyone with a serious interest in mind reading could rip away the veil with little expenditure of energy.

Nkosi prodded him once more.

"Are you sure you want to do that?" David asked. "Maybe you enjoy the occasional psychotic break, but I prefer sanity."

"The risk is only to me."

"I still don't want you ransacking my brain." David relaxed against the wall. "Besides, I don't care to have a lunatic for a roommate. I'd rather not have to clean up after you when you lose control of your bowels."

Nkosi arched an eyebrow. "I thought it was speculation that mind reading caused such dire side effects. You've seen the results before?"

"Yes." David met Nkosi's gaze. "Trust me, you don't want to risk it."

Nkosi squinted for a couple of seconds, then nodded. "I have decided to trust you."

"Thanks." David supposed he should feel grateful, but he hadn't decided yet whether he trusted Nkosi. The man might be a plant, using the very techniques he claimed their captors used on him with his previous cellmates. David couldn't know for sure.

He sighed and said, "So you're from South Africa. I had no idea the induction program had gone global."

"Induction?" Nkosi's confusion seemed genuine.

David still had to play it safe. "How did you get here?"

The other man shrugged. "I was backpacking with my brother when men raided our camp. They wore black clothing and helmets that covered their faces. These men attacked while we slept, and by the time we knew what was happening, they had already tied us up. Once they determined our identities, they shot my brother in the head."

David jerked his head up and stared at Nkosi. The man stretched his fingers out, then clenched them. His upper lip curled in disgust.

"He was of no value to them," Nkosi said. "They wanted me, not my brother. I watched him die before they injected me with something that put me to sleep. I woke up in a place much like this, but in Siberia. I didn't know where I was at first, and only later discovered how far they had taken me from my home. Then two months ago, they shut down the Siberian facility and brought me here." Nkosi shut his eyes. "They killed everyone at the old facility—except for me. I don't understand why I lived when so many others died."

Nkosi's pain seemed real enough that David felt like a heel for doubting the man. Still, he must doubt. He must be suspicious, of everyone. He knew of just one person in the entire world who he trusted with no reservations or doubts.

Grace.

He had to get out of this place and get back to her.

David studied his cellmate for a moment. Nkosi had opened his eyes, but he stared down at the floor. His shoulders drooped. He did not move, except for the rising and falling of his chest as he breathed.

"Tell me," David said, "why do our hosts want you so badly?"

"They want me to give them something, but I don't understand what it is."

"What do they say to you?"

"They speak of Golden Power and transference of psychic energies. They force me to watch as they torture my cellmates, all the time demanding I help them acquire this Golden Power they crave. Only when my cellmate dies do they relent."

David knew he had to ask one question, even at the risk of exposing the depth of his suspicion. "Why do they torture your cellmates and not you?"

"They tried in Siberia. It did not work." Nkosi gave him a weary look. "I am not stronger than other men. I simply do not know what they want me to tell them. They used several means to encourage me to cooperate, but I could not. If I had the information, I would've given it to them. Believe me. I am not a superman."

The shame in his voice and on his face triggered a wave of sympathy in David. He knew what it felt like to struggle against Tesler's methods. In his case, however, he would die before talking. If he broke, Grace would be the one to suffer for his weakness.

Nkosi had endured the torture not out of moral conviction or love for another, but simply because he knew nothing about the Golden Power. Assuming he told the truth. Assuming he hadn't cracked. If David believed the man's tale, Nkosi let his cellmates die because he had nothing to give his captors, no way to save the others' lives.

If David believed him. If he could trust anything or anyone in this place.

Nkosi had just tried to sneak into his mind after all.

The other man twisted around to lean sideways against the wall. A beam of weak light flashed over his head and neck, revealing a network of thin scars that slashed across his throat. In a tired voice, he said, "They always leave us alone for a few hours, then they return to begin the questioning."

David glanced at the door. A few hours. He must get out of here before then. Under no circumstances would he betray Grace again, wittingly or not. But if he died…

He would not leave her alone. Some way, somehow, he must get back to her.

GRACE ROUSED IN STAGES. FIRST, THE COOLNESS OF THE AIR-CONDItioned environment kissed her skin. She wiggled her fingers, and her nails scritched across the chair's leather. Next, she tasted sour acid and sniffed spicy cologne. Finally, she parted her eyelids and blinked away the bleariness. Dim lighting eased her vision out of sleep, into awareness.

Amador crouched in front of her, his face creased with lines of worry. "Are you feeling better? What can I do?"

She recalled the suffering, the soul-rending certainty David was dying. Then, after she passed out, a warm serenity flowed into her, carrying with it reassurance and… love. The kind she luxuriated in whenever David drew her into his arms. Real, pure love.

David had penetrated her psychic fortress. For a few long seconds, she wondered how he'd done it. But of course, he accomplished the same feat earlier today, when he poured his emotions into her with an all-consuming kiss hotter than any they'd shared before. Though her firewall must've prevented him from traveling to her, it permitted him empathic communication.

"You are smiling," Amador said. "The pain is gone, then?"

She touched her lips, which were slanting upward. David's phantom embrace lingered around her, and a ghost of his lips tantalized hers. She cleared her throat. "Uh, yes. No pain."

"Are you injured or ill?"

"Neither. It wasn't physical pain." But it sure as hell shredded her insides like the real thing. "I'm fine, I swear."

Amador eyed her for a moment, lips tight, and then settled a hand on her knee. "You do look less pale than before you passed out. Perhaps I should call Wickham and have him fetch a doctor anyway. To be certain."

"No-no, I'm fine." She noticed he hadn't carried her to a bed or a sofa to make her comfortable, or waved smelling salts to awaken her, or dabbed a cool cloth on her forehead. So far as she could tell, he'd knelt there staring at her until she revived on her own. *Creepy.*

Without getting up, he grabbed the phone off his desk and dialed a number—an extension within the house, most likely, since he dialed just three digits. "Wickham, please bring some juice and a small snack for our guest. She's feeling peaked."

He hung up, plunking the phone back into its cradle. His attention centered on her once again.

She fidgeted, the solace David imbued her with diminishing. He might've communicated his okay-ness to her, but she needed confirmation. She dug her phone out of her purse, flipped it open, and frowned.

"Is something wrong?" Amador asked.

"No signal. I need to call David." An edge of panic sharpened her voice. *Damn.* She hated sounding weak in front of Amador, but she couldn't help it.

He snatched the receiver from his desk, offering it to her. "Please use my phone. I insist."

Of course he'd insist. He probably recorded every phone call made from his home, or at least the ones made by guests. He could've jammed cell signals too.

She must hear David's voice.

Her shoulders hunched as she accepted the phone. "Thanks."

Amador nodded. He did not back away to grant her privacy.

After dialing the number for David's cell, she clutched the phone to her ear. One ring. Two. Three. She drummed her fingers on her thigh. Four rings. Five. Six. His voicemail picked up the call. She hung up and dialed her own cell to retrieve any messages. One voicemail awaited her, time-stamped twenty minutes ago. Her fingers trembled as David's anxious voice spoke to her from the past. The tension in his tone infected her, and she gripped the phone tighter. Her frantic mind processed his words in snippets.

Tesler. Coming for you. Get out. Your psychic firewall is—

The message cut off. Ringing deafened her. Numbness tingled down her scalp, into her face. She hauled in a breath, and then another. The ringing and numbness faded, but a frozen ball of panic congealed in her gut.

Her psychic firewall was what? Working great? About to collapse?

She redialed David's number and got his voicemail again. "David, please call me as soon as you get this. I heard your message and—" Amador was scrutinizing her, no doubt paying rapt attention to her words. She performed a quick mental edit of what she wanted to say. "I think we should discuss the possibility before taking any action. I'm away from home, so call my cell. Love you, honey. Bye."

The last part she'd added for Amador's benefit. His hand still warmed her knee with a discomfiting familiarity. A niggling at the back of her mind compelled her to remind him she was taken.

She started to hand him the phone but froze. *Grandpa.* He was clueless about the danger. "May I make another call?"

"As many as you like."

And he'd observe and eavesdrop on every single call. Stifling a grumble, she dialed her grandfather's number. He answered on the second ring.

"Grace, I'm glad you—"

"Hi, it's Grace Powell. I'm afraid we'll have to cancel our meeting for this evening. Something's come up."

A pause. A gruff sigh. "You're in trouble. And you're not alone."

"Uh-huh. I'm sorry I have to flake out on you. The house is being fumigated, so I don't think we'll want to be in there for a few days at least."

"Fumigated?" He repeated the word slowly as if puzzling out her meaning. "You mean it may be bugged."

"Worse than that. Some kind of black fungus is invading the place."

"Black—Holy heaven, Grace. Are you talking about Tesler's commandos?"

"Yep. Don't put off your vacation on my account. We can catch up next week."

He said nothing for a few seconds. "I will not leave town without you. Tell me where you are, and I'll come get you."

"No." She nearly shouted the word, and Amador's mouth quirked in confused amusement. "I mean, uh..." She floundered for a way to convince him without Amador catching on. Oh screw it. "Please do as I ask. Please."

"Grace…"

"*Please.*" She made no effort to conceal her pleading tone. "I promise I'll make our next meeting."

"All right. I'll go to our backup location. But if I don't hear from you by morning… I don't know. I'll find you somehow."

"Thank you." She disconnected the call. He would be safe, which gave her one less worry to gnaw at her gut.

Passing the phone back to Amador, she scooted sideways in the chair. Her butt had started to ache despite the cushioned seat. Though she'd fainted moments ago, energy pulsed back into her, on both a physical and psychic level. Her connection to David hummed in the background, easing some of her tension.

Amador's hand caressed her knee.

She gripped the arms of the chair. "Tell me how you know about Tesler."

Amador observed her for a moment, eyes half-closed. Then he bent forward, resting his elbows on his knees. "I know of Tesler because I've met him. I spent time at a facility in Siberia where Tesler detained a number of travelers. It was not an enjoyable time."

Grace couldn't decide whether to believe him or not. The tightening of his features, the slight frown on his lips, the hunching of his shoulders, those things suggested the memory distressed him. Yet she didn't know him well enough to distinguish between real pain and great acting.

"The Siberian facility is shut down," Amador told her. "I managed to escape before the guards murdered me, as they did all the others."

Time for a strategic revelation on her part. At least she hoped it was strategic, and not plain stupid. At some point, she had to reveal a little to test his knowledge.

"I have some of JT's files," she said, "from the Mojave Desert facility in California. They name the travelers held at all the sites. Your name is not on that list, Mr. Amador."

"My friends call me Biel."

"We're not friends."

"Not yet."

He spoke with such complete certainty about the promise of their future friendship that she almost laughed. Almost. His certainty also struck her as arrogance, a trait she never trusted in anyone. "Whatever. The point is, your name appears nowhere in the database of travelers' names."

"I adopted a pseudonym, as you did." He arched an eyebrow. "Unless your true name is Janet Austen. I hope not, though, because Grace describes you far better."

"How do you know about Janet Austen?"

"I also have some files that once belonged to JT."

"Where did you get them?"

Dark glee colored his smirk. "I stole them. From the Siberian facility."

Liar. The word flared in her mind, but she struggled to keep her expression neutral. She guarded the sole copy of JT's private files on Project Outreach, on the flash drive tucked into her bra. JT had told her it was the one and only copy, and she believed him—considering the number of people he'd murdered in his zeal to reclaim the flash drive from her. Even a psycho wouldn't waste that kind of energy on a task unless it was vital. When JT had blown up his own facility, that act had also destroyed the computer system and those precious files. Amador could not have the same information.

Unless someone else, like Tesler, secretly copied JT's files.

Amador's extensive knowledge about her chilled her entire body, from her skin straight down to her core. He knew things JT hadn't known about, as far as she knew.

"Please," Amador said, "I speak the truth. You must believe me."

"You've been spying on me," she said. "In my bedroom. You RV'd me in my private space, and that tends to annoy me. So no, I don't have to do anything for you. Especially not believe you."

"I have already apologized. I did not realize you were alone in your bedroom until after the excursion began."

The hairs on the back of her neck stiffened. In Project Outreach, the scientists called the RV sessions excursions. Something about Amador's use of the term bothered her, an indefinable off-ness she couldn't describe.

"Will you trust me?" he asked.

She tapped her fingernails on her purse in a fast rhythm. Trust Amador? No way. But if she wanted to learn how much he knew, and what he really wanted, she had to take a few risks.

Lips pursed, she zeroed in on his dark eyes. "I'm not letting down my psychic wall just yet. First, you need to prove to me you're on the level." Snowballs and brimstone popped to mind. She kept the analogy to herself. "Show me everything you have on JT, his companies, Tesler, the facilities, everything."

"Of course."

He retreated around the desk, flipped open his laptop, and tapped keys on the keyboard. The tickety-ticking of the keys was the only sound in the room, except for the thundering of her pulse in her ears. Nobody else could hear that, though. She hoped.

After a moment, Amador spun the laptop around to face her. "Here it is. Everything I have on anything remotely related to Project Outreach. You may view it here, or I can copy it onto a DVD for you."

"How about I take a peek right now and you give me that DVD to take home."

He nodded. "I'll have Wickham prepare it for you before you leave."

"Thank you." She scooted her chair closer to the desk. Eyes on the screen, she asked, "What pseudonym did you use?"

"John Mendoza."

"Who knew your real name?"

"Only Jackson Tennant. He hungered for psychic power and strived to harvest the abilities of travelers. And he harbored a bizarre fixation with blood."

A shiver ran down her spine as a memory replayed in her mind. JT grasping a syringe. About to suck the blood from her veins forcibly. His expression wild. His desire for power palpable. He had honestly believed that by injecting himself with the blood of a psychic, he could acquire that person's abilities. Well, at least one part of Amador's story matched up with what she knew.

If he had JT's files, though, he might've learned about the blood thing that way. She hadn't read all of JT's files, since they were extensive, which meant the notes on his blood theory might await her somewhere deep inside the data. Amador might've found it first.

"I'm acquainted with JT's obsession," she admitted.

"He gave up on many travelers when he realized the blood types were incompatible. He never gave up on you, though, did he?"

"No." She clenched her jaw. "Not until I made him give up."

"Yes," Amador said, his tone contemplative. "You killed him, didn't you?"

She froze, her fingers over the keyboard. Without looking up, she asked, "How do you know that?"

"Postcognition."

She snapped her head up to squint at him. "Post what?"

"Postcognition. I'm sure you know that precognition allows one to see future events. Postcognition is a term my captors used to describe an aspect of remote viewing that allows one to see past events. It doesn't always work, and it can be quite difficult to control. My only successful attempt occurred when I tried to replay JT's death. I know you shot him."

"Why would you want to replay his death?"

"To know that he was truly gone." He offered her his hand, palm up. "And to thank the person who rid this world of a vile human being."

She glanced at his hand, knowing he wanted her to take it. She didn't move.

He curled his fingers shut. "You may not trust me yet, but know this. I admire you—your strength and determination, your loyalty to those you love, and your incredible psychic talents."

She focused on the computer screen, double-clicking to open a database file.

"I can help you get him back," Amador said in a soft voice. "If that is what you truly want."

Head bowed, she turned her eyes to glance at him. "Get who back?"

"David. Your beloved." Amador leaned over the desk, placing his head inches from hers. He smelled of the outdoors, fresh and clean and masculine. "Together, we can find Tesler and stop him. Then David will have no reason to abandon you anymore."

"My relationship with David is none of your business." She drummed her fingernails on the desktop. Through gritted teeth, she said, "How the hell do you know so much about me, anyway?"

He shrugged. "The files. And my remote reconnaissance of you and your associates. I needed to know as much as possible about you before I risked exposing myself to you."

She grunted. Yeah, his rationale made sense. She didn't like it, and sure as hell didn't trust him. At the moment, however, she needed him to think she might.

Forcing herself to relax, she said, "Thank you for sharing your information with me. But my relationship with David is off-limits."

"As you wish. Nevertheless, I will help you find Tesler." He glanced down at her left hand and the diamond ring on the third finger. "But in the process, you will learn things about your beloved that you may not like. Do you still wish to proceed?"

"Yes."

Amador settled back into his chair. "Then we shall find Tesler. I hope you are as prepared for the truth as you believe."

"I am."

Was she prepared? No clue. She had to proceed. For her, there was no choice anymore. To save David, she must risk losing him. To save the world from Tesler and his cohorts, she must risk everything—including her own life.

Tesler was coming. For her. Now.

Chapter Eight

GOOSEBUMPS PRICKLED HER SKIN. TESLER. SHE'D NEVER MET THE man, yet she knew from David's reaction to the very mention of Tesler's name the scientist was a sociopath at best. He tortured people in the name of science. What Tesler practiced bore no resemblance to real science. It was a dark perversion of a scientific experiment.

Why had David called her on the phone? In emergencies, he relied on their telepathic line, not the cell phone network.

David's final words echoed in her mind. *Your psychic firewall is—*

Her throat tightened, and her mouth went dry. She knew why he used the phone, and what he'd been about to say in his message. Her psychic wall, the one he encouraged her to build, must've blocked him from contacting her. No one, not even David, could breach her defenses.

She must lower the barrier.

No, she couldn't. Not with Gabriel Amador scratching at the wall. He wanted in too, and she had no intention of admitting him. But David...

He hadn't asked her to lower the wall. He must not want her to, or else he would've said so. Unless the message cut off before he got the chance.

Dammit. For the time being, she must keep the barrier intact.

Where could she hide? Where would Tesler and his goons not think to look for her?

Her foot tapped the floor in a frenzied rhythm. This wouldn't be the first time she'd gone on the lam, but no. She refused to flee and cower in some dank hideout. Going home wasn't an option either. Even she wasn't pigheaded enough to waltz right into an ambush.

She pushed up off the chair, muttering a rapid string of curses under her breath. "If you'll give me that DVD, I should be on my way."

"Of course." Amador rose to his full height, a good six inches taller than she was. "You are welcome to stay the night here, of course. I have spacious guest quarters."

"Thank you, Mr. Amador, but I have to be going." *Where to, dummy?*

"You will never assent to calling me Biel, will you?"

"It's doubtful." Realizing the statement sounded rude, and wary of poking a dragon, she added, "Sorry. It's just that I don't know you."

"Not yet. But you will." Again, his utter certainty rankled. He picked up the phone on his desk, punched buttons, and waited for the other party to answer. "Yes, Wickham, please bring the DVD for Ms. Powell. She is ready to leave us. No, forget the snack. She has urgent business to attend to."

As he hung up the phone, she said, "Thank you for sharing your information with me."

"It is a pleasure." He extended a hand to her, and she settled her palm into his. He brushed a light kiss across the back of her hand. *Weird.* He did not release her hand when he spoke. "We will see each other again very soon, Grace. I look forward to it."

His hand was warm and soft, like the skin of a man who rarely deigned to perform manual labor. His gaze, locked on hers, sent an odd shiver through her. Not desire, like with David. Not fear either. Something else she couldn't place.

"Who are you?" she asked.

He laid his other hand atop hers. "Gabriel Ricardo Amador, president and founder of Catalan Enterprises." He encased her hand in his strong fingers. "And your friend, I hope."

"I need to go, but I may have questions later."

"Naturally. Call or stop by anytime. Wickham will provide you with a number where you can reach me." He lifted her hand to his lips again, his flesh skimming over hers. "I am at your service, always."

He freed her hand. She stepped out into the hallway, shutting the door.

Wickham rounded a corner ahead of her. He held a DVD, sheathed in a hard plastic case. Grace met him halfway, accepting the disk from him with a thank-you and a smile. He pointed out the business card tucked inside the DVD case, assuring her she could reach "Biel" at any time if she called the number on the card. Then he escorted her back to the front door, smiling and wishing her a good day as he opened the door for her. When the door closed behind her, she let out the breath she'd been holding.

She still had no idea what to think about Amador. Maybe it didn't matter, since she planned on avoiding him whenever possible. Contact only when necessary to glean more info from him. Simple. Clean.

Then why did razor-wire butterflies flap in her stomach?

First up, she needed to compare the information on his disk with the data on the flash drive. Viewing the DVD's contents on her own computer seemed ill-advised. Sure, Amador presented himself as an amiable, if cautious, fellow. But she couldn't risk contaminating her computer or the flash drive, if Amador's disk turned out to contain a virus or worm.

She pressed two fingers to the valley between her breasts, pinning the flash drive to her sternum. David thought it was silly to keep the flash drive there. Today, with her home compromised, she was damn happy about her paranoia. Before she could consider viewing Amador's DVD, she had to accomplish another feat.

Track down a safe place to stay while evading Tesler's goons. Piece of cake.

Steel-reinforced concrete cake. And all she had to cut it with was a plastic knife. Well then, she'd forge herself a new blade. *No more running.*

She marched to her car, each step buoyed by a renewed purpose.

———

GRACE DROVE TO THE BANK AND WITHDREW THE ENTIRE BALANCE of her checking account. A visit to an electronics store netted her a new laptop, since she'd left her computer at home, and a clean cell phone, prepaid and untraceable to her. She stowed the Pontiac in a covered parking structure downtown, and then hitched a ride in a taxi, heading for an old house on the outskirts of town. A nice old lady sold her a beat-up, though well-maintained, Dodge Ram pickup. With her purse at her side, and the revolver berthed inside it, she drove along the interstate in search of a motel.

Maybe David was wrong about her developing a new ability, because if she could see the future, then she would've brought her computer with her. Then again, maybe not, since it might've been bugged or hacked or something. If she'd foreseen this trouble, she most definitely would not have let David run off to Montana.

Her vision of Tesler murdering him had been real, but for the vision to be true, she must've developed precognitive abilities. Maybe using her new power required a deliberate effort. Nice theory, except the first time she'd stumbled onto her precognition without any intent to do so. She rubbed her neck, squinting in the sunlight streaming through the windshield. She couldn't test the boundaries of her abilities right now. Too much risk. Too much unknown.

What if Gabriel Amador was stalking her again?

Calm down, you're safe. Her psychic barrier thwarted everyone, including David. If he couldn't break through, despite their telepathic bond, then Amador sure as hell couldn't tap into her brain.

Her thoughts circled back around to the dark presence clawing at her when she built her firewall, and the freakish incident earlier, when for the second time in one day, she'd believed David was in mortal jeopardy. Something—whether a human mind or a presence beyond her comprehension, she didn't know—still wielded the strength to manipulate her mind, with more vigor than any psychic mentioned by David or in JT's files.

David found a way into her mind through their emotional union. Six months ago, JT forced a link with her by injecting himself with enough drugs to boost his latent powers into the stratosphere. What if another someone discovered a new way to tap into her brain? A method too strong for her firewall to withstand?

She had to shove the possibility aside and keep moving.

The Ram carried her to a motel thirty miles outside of town, a dingy place with ten rooms and a heavily tattooed clerk with rings in his nose and lower lip. He wore a T-shirt that looked like a souvenir from a heavy-metal rock festival. A name tag pinned to his T-shirt identified him as Tag. She almost laughed, but suppressed it for the sake of politeness.

"Is that your real name?" she asked, in as un-sarcastic a tone as she could muster.

"Yeah," he said, with a Chicago accent. "It's actually Taggert, but I go by Tag most of the time. Specially when I'm at work. It makes the customers wonder."

"About what?"

"Whether I'm too high on drugs to remember my own name."

And then he smiled. A wide, welcoming smile that she couldn't help but reciprocate.

Tag chuckled. "I ain't, by the way. High, that is."

He tapped a small round button pinned to his shirt. She hadn't noticed it before, and she leaned forward a little to read it. The button, rusty and scratched, featured the slogan "Just say no."

"I got this when I was a kid," Tag said. "Kept it ever since. A motto to live by."

"It sure is."

He sighed. "You didn't come here for my anti-drugs lecture, though. What can I do ya for?"

"A room."

"Just you?"

"Yes." Just her. Alone. On the run.

Life sucked. Life as a fugitive amnesiac sucked like a Godzilla-size vacuum cleaner.

He nodded and turned to the PC on the counter. "Name?"

"What?"

"Your name. I need to enter it into the computer."

"Oh." She hesitated, wringing her brain for an alias. "Christine Marcus."

Combining her parents' first names was all she could think of at the moment. Tag seemed satisfied and pecked at the computer keys with both index fingers.

Five minutes later, he handed her the key to Room 8, and she walked out of the office. Room 8 lay at the far end of the one-story building, on the side facing the road. At least that meant she'd have a clear view of the office and the parking lot, to keep watch for any suspicious characters. These days, she didn't know exactly how to differentiate suspicious types from regular people. The clerk, Tag, had seemed threatening until he spoke and smiled. Gabriel Amador seemed friendly and upstanding, yet he kept secrets and spied on her. Damn, she really wished the bad guys would wear black hats so she could tell them apart from everyone else. It was rude of them to blend in so cunningly.

Inside the room, she shut the door and moseyed over to the bed, dropping her purse and her new computer on the table situated beside the double bed. The outside of the motel looked dingy. Here, though, she found a clean room with the usual amenities.

She returned to the bed, flopping onto it with all the delicacy of a dog jumping into a pond. Her eyes were gritty, her tongue cottony. A heaviness overwhelmed her as if she'd gained fifty pounds in the past hour. Her brain ached from the pressure of thinking. She needed a plan. She needed information too. She needed help, dammit, but instead, she got more trouble. Would Tesler himself show up to bag-and-tag her, or would he send his goons?

A memory snapped into focus in her mind. A man in a black outfit reminiscent of military fatigues. His head shielded by a black, full-face helmet. A large gun in his hand, aimed at her. The sound of his sneering laugh echoed in her mind.

The man had been called Battaglia. He neglected to share his first name when he captured her during her attempt to break into the Mojave Desert facility. He'd treated her like an animal. To Battaglia, psychics were nothing more than freaks of nature, not human beings, just wild beasts in need of putting down, or at least containing. Battaglia was nasty, but nowhere near as bad as Tesler because, underneath the bravado, Battaglia was a coward. She remembered his choked voice when he begged her not to shoot him. Since he'd been tied up at the time, and no longer a threat to her, she let him live. His commando buddies must've rescued him later on, after she and David fled the ruins of the facility.

Battaglia was still alive. Had he stuck with Tesler? Would he show up to hunt her down?

She wiped her slick palms on her pants. Sucking in a deep breath, she shut her eyes and exhaled slowly. No more fear. She must not let Battaglia or Tesler spiral her into a full-blown panic over the mere possibility of running into either of them. She'd stopped them before. She could do it again.

This time for good.

Rubbing her eyes, she yawned and stretched. She dragged her new computer off the bedside table, down onto the mattress beside her. The brief look she'd gotten at the files earlier, while Amador kept an eye on her, revealed nothing she didn't already know from the data on the flash drive. She popped Amador's DVD into the computer's disk drive and browsed the list of files it contained. The data was organized into dozens of folders, each of which contained multiple subfolders. She clicked on a folder called "Profiles." Within it, she found subfolders identified with abbreviations that she recognized. They were codes for the various types of psychic abilities—RV for remote viewing, AP for astral projection, TK for telekinesis, and on and on. The list included abbreviations she'd never seen before, like PRC and PTC. The letters TP undoubtedly referred to thought projection, and MR must indicate mind reading. Despite the dangers of mind reading, the scientists employed at ALI after the takeover by JT and his minions had coerced some psychics into attempting to use the ability.

The abbreviation on one folder stopped her: "GP."

She'd seen the abbreviation before. At the time, she hadn't understood what it meant. Since then, she'd learned the letters GP referred to the Golden Power.

Biting her lip, overcome by a dark sense of dread, she opened the GP folder. It contained two files, each labeled with a name. The first file was called "Janet Austen." Finding her alias listed in these files didn't surprise her. The second file was called "John Mendoza." Okay, so the name Amador claimed was his alias appeared in these files. He could've altered the data, though, to make her think he spent time in an ALI facility, or John Mendoza might not be his alias after all, but rather the name of another man interned at the Siberian facility. This proved nothing.

She opened the Mendoza file. It gave his basic description in bullet points—height, weight, hair color, eye color—and listed his psychic abilities as "high level." His powers included remote viewing and astral projection. That meant he could spy on anyone he liked and project an image of himself to whoever he liked as well. Manifestation was not listed as one of his gifts, but then she hadn't yet seen that ability listed as a separate power in any of the ALI files. Creating a physical body while astral projecting involved, from what David had told her, a combination of other abilities, including thought projection and telekinesis. Maybe ALI hadn't considered that to be a separate power. In common terms, astral projection was manifesting. In reality, however, manifesting a physical form required a massive amount of psychic energy as well as a connection with another person who could serve as a kind of conduit for the process. David could manifest only with Grace's help. Their combined powers made it possible.

And he'd assured her no one else possessed the ability.

She searched her brain for the memory of what David told her when he explained psychic abilities to her six months ago. She'd learned a little more on her own, by experimenting with her own powers, but his lessons still formed the basis of everything she knew about paranormal abilities. The truth, according to David. She trusted him, and yet she wondered sometimes if he'd disclosed everything to her. Amnesia surely affected their relationship, but he might have other reasons for holding back with her. More immediate reasons. Things he kept to himself because...

What? He didn't trust her? No way. What else might explain his reticence? She must figure out the reason. She couldn't accept that the man she'd admitted into her life and her heart—not once, but twice—didn't trust her. Their faith in each other had saved their lives.

She browsed the remainder of Amador's profile. Nothing of much interest there. A listing of excursions he'd taken under Tesler's direction, or that of another scientist. During an excursion, a traveler remote viewed a target location to demonstrate the extent of his or her powers, while the scientists measured their accuracy in describing the target. Her perusal of the files on the flash drive hadn't yet turned up a description of Tesler's methodology. Grace didn't know the specifics of how the experiments worked. She ought to find out. To do that, she would need to ask David or Sean.

Or Gabriel Amador.

She closed Amador's profile, if indeed the profile belonged to him. He might've been Amador, or he might've been a child. The data left her to assume Mendoza and Amador were the same person.

Next, she opened her own file. A knot tightened in her stomach as she looked at the profile. No photo in this file either. She hadn't actually expected to see one since her parents had done everything they could to shield her from Tesler and JT. The profile described Janet Austen in the vaguest terms, though it included her height, weight, eye color, and hair color. Strangely, it gave her hair color as blonde and her eye color as blue. The height and weight were correct. Had she worn a wig? Or bleached her hair blonde? She would've noticed the roots growing out even after she dyed it auburn again because matching her natural hair color precisely would've proved difficult and time-consuming. She must've worn a wig and colored contact lenses. Why? To confuse anyone trying to find her, she guessed. Hiding her weight and height would've proved next to impossible, but masking her hair and eye color wouldn't take much effort.

It had taken JT a good while to track her down. Her parents took every precaution to hide her from him. In the end, they died for her.

Tears burned in her eyes. Her throat constricted, and her breath shuddered with a silent sob. Crying would not help. Neither would guilt.

The tears rolled down her face anyway.

"Dammit," she hissed, and swiped the tears away with her fingers. She hated crying. It solved nothing and accomplished nothing except to make her eyes red and scratchy and puffy.

Her parents sacrificed their lives to preserve hers. If she hadn't gone to the Mojave Desert facility, if she'd stayed home, they might still be alive.

Six months ago, when David had found her again, he explained how she'd visited the facility while on vacation, to see what her parents did there. They received permission to show her everything, and on a lark, she participated in a test to determine psychic aptitude. The results had shocked everyone, he said, because they demonstrated she not only had psychic abilities, but they were "off the charts."

Her parents shielded her with a false name, but her file remained in ALI's records, and that was how JT learned about her. Why didn't they delete her file? They couldn't have guessed what horrors would ensue. No one could have. They kept her file because it was part of their research.

The text on the screen blurred, her eyes too weary to focus. She rubbed her neck, rolled her head in a circle, and gave her body an invigorating shake. No time for sleeping.

She backtracked through the DVD's folders, located a file that looked promising, and double-clicked to open it. The file was a report of a meeting between Tesler and JT, written by the scientist. Tesler outlined every boring detail of the meeting, from their decision to repaint one of the conference rooms to their disagreement over what type of ballpoint pens to buy. Toward the end of the report, she spotted something that grabbed her attention.

"JT insists it is my fault," Tesler wrote, "that the boy won't cooperate. He believes if the boy knows the truth, then he will stop fighting us. I assured JT it won't work, and I have no intention of ever acknowledging the mewling mutant. The child has no discipline, no self-awareness, and worst of all, no spine. No one will ever know he is my grandson."

Grace froze, her fingers hovering over the keyboard. Grandson? She had trouble visualizing Tesler with a family of any kind. Was the "boy" sadistic like his grandfather, or merely an innocent victim of his own genetic lineage? Even the worst parents on earth could raise a decent child, through no doing of their own. Or maybe the kid's mother or father fled from Tesler.

Either way, this changed things. She didn't know how yet, but it had to. Tesler's grandson had psychic abilities. Maybe that explained why the man seemed hell-bent on tormenting psychics in order to capture their powers. She couldn't quite figure out how his tactics related to his grandson, but she sure as hell wanted to find out.

Tesler's notes called his grandson "the boy," without giving any details about the kid's age. The term boy might refer to a five-year-old or a nearly full-grown teenager.

Or even a man. To a sixtyish cretin like Tesler, even a man in his twenties might seem like a boy in comparison to himself. Without knowing the identity of Tesler's grandson, she had no way of knowing whether she'd met him or not.

Amador claimed if she kept on her current path, she'd learn things about David she wouldn't like. Had he meant this? Would she find out David was Tesler's grandson? No, he couldn't be. The idea was ridiculous. She knew David better than anyone else in her life.

Did she really? She knew he kept secrets from her.

Not this one. He could not have any familial ties with Tesler, the man who tortured him for months. Until she identified Tesler's grandson, however, she lacked anything close to certainty, about anything.

The truth might await her on the DVD.

She clicked on a folder designated "AP" for astral projection. It was one of David's main powers.

There it was. A file labeled "David Ransom."

A shiver swept down her spine, and she hesitated with her finger over the enter key. She needed to know. She feared what she might find. The truth usually came with strings attached—in the form of razor wire.

Suck it up, woman.

She hit the enter key. The file opened on-screen.

At the top of the document, she saw a photo of David. He looked serious, as usual. Serious and beautiful, in a masculine way. A warrior with the face of an angel. Below the photo appeared the same kind of bullet points she'd seen in the other profiles, and below that, the list of his psychic abilities. Astral projection, thought projection, remote viewing. She scrolled down to see more of the document. A single line of text, printed in large red letters, rolled into view.

Her heart thudded. Fear exploded through her, cold and sharp, like a thousand microscopic blades tearing through her flesh from the inside out. No. She wouldn't believe it. *No, no, no.*

The line read, "ALERT: Extreme caution advised, subject has killed before."

Her ears rang. The room whirled around her. With a start, she realized she'd stopped breathing. As she hauled in long, slow breaths, she scrolled down to the next line of text in the file. Her breath caught in her throat, and a single word burst out of her. "No."

The document said, "During his stay at this facility, David Ransom murdered another traveler in cold blood."

Chapter Nine

GRACE HUNCHED ON THE BED, HANDS GRASPING THE LAPTOP, HER gaze nailed to the screen. David's profile contained no further information about the traveler his captors asserted he had killed. She'd spent the better part of an hour scouring through the records on the DVD in search of details, but found none.

He must've killed the other traveler in self-defense or to save an innocent life. He was no murderer. Hell, she'd killed men before. Gunshots fired by her hand snuffed out the lives of Jackson Tennant and his right-hand man, Xavier Waldron. Not that she celebrated the fact. Not that she didn't occasionally suffer a twinge of guilt. But overall, she knew she'd done what had to be done. Both men were evil, and she didn't apply the term lightly. Together with Tesler, JT and Waldron conspired to abduct, torture, and murder countless human beings simply because they displayed psychic abilities. Their deaths improved the world just a bit.

She knew why she'd taken lives. Now she needed to understand why David had. To find out, she must ask him. Would he answer? Would he bare his secrets to her at last? Despite his secrets, despite his collusion in concealing the truth from her last year, she trusted him with her heart, her life, her very soul. He'd seen her through a horrific time in her life, and he had opened up to her when she needed him to the most.

Please, David, do it for me again.

Why did this revelation about David appear nowhere in JT's personal data collection? Had Amador faked the file to upset her? With his agenda a big freaking question mark, she lacked the vital information necessary to decide. Vetting electronic data, especially the stolen kind, was not her forte.

The keys clacked beneath her fingers as she executed another search of the DVD. It coughed up no more information about John Mendoza. Combing through every file on the disk might take days, and she had a creeping feeling she didn't have that long.

Before she took any further action, though, she had to talk to David.

Snapping the laptop's lid shut, she slid the computer across the quilt, out of her way. Sitting cross-legged, she rested her palms on her knees and closed her eyes. Ghost images of the computer screen danced behind her eyelids for a few seconds. She took slow, deep breaths as she urged her body to relax and her mind to clear of all thoughts and worries. It was harder than it sounded. Thoughts ricocheted in her mind, gouging out bits of her self-control.

David killed someone.

Tesler is coming for me. Is David safe?

I have to do something.

Should I trust Amador?

Can I trust my own powers?

Lord almighty, she'd never get anywhere this way. The chaos in her mind threatened to drive her bonkers. She sucked in the deepest breath she could, held it for two seconds, and released the air slowly as she concentrated on counting out the seconds. Her shoulders relaxed. Her jaw loosened. The rest of her muscles followed suit, the tension melting out of them as she let go of more than the air. She let go of everything. Everyone.

Her physical body retreated from her awareness. Darkness replaced the light seeping in through her eyelids. She floated in the blackest night, alone, at peace.

With a swift determination, she soared through the crossroads to a pulsing star that was David and tumbled out into a twilit world.

For a few seconds, she wavered there, blind and numb from the trip. Then she spotted David. Seated on the floor, wedged into the corner of the room. Body slumped. Eyes closed. Mouth twisted into a frown. And he wasn't alone.

Another man sat in the opposite corner. His eyes were open. He stared at David without expression.

Grace looked around. Concrete walls and floor. No furniture. No windows. It was a prison cell.

She hurried to David, kneeling beside him. "Hey."

Though she knew the other man could neither see nor hear her, she still found herself whispering. David did not move or respond in any way. With her psychic wall in place, she couldn't feel him the way she usually did. The connection trickled through her instead of flowing like a stream. Being so disconnected from him gave her a strange queasiness.

She said a little louder, "David, it's me. I'm here."

He cracked one eye open to peek at her. "I know."

"So why are you ignoring me?"

The other man said, "What do you know?"

David pushed into a more upright posture. To the other man, he said, "I don't suppose you'd agree to plug your ears and close your eyes for a few minutes."

"Why?"

David scrunched his lips and huffed a breath out through his nostrils. He was thinking, she knew—thinking and annoyed. She recognized the signs. He must not fully trust his new friend.

He closed his eyes for a second and then looked at the other man. "Someone is here to see me."

"Ahhhh," the man said. "I understand. I will do as you ask."

The stranger jammed a finger into each ear and shut his eyes.

Grace studied David. The stoic mask slipped over his features.

"I'll do most of the talking," she said. "I need to ask you a question."

"Fine."

"Well, several questions, actually."

"Get on with it, please."

His flinty tone stopped her for a second. "Are you okay?"

"Yes." The syllable hissed snake-like, rife with impatience.

His state of okay-ness wasn't the main question plaguing her. She ached to ask the real question, but every time she formed the words in her head, her stomach twisted into knots.

"Go on," David said. "Whatever it is, ask it."

"Okay." She clamped her hands over her knees. "Have you ever killed anyone?"

His expression went blank. "Why would you ask me?"

"I—I came across a file that said you're dangerous because you killed someone at the Mojave Desert facility."

"Where did this file come from?"

"The man who lives at 1325 Meroz Road. Gabriel Amador."

He stared into her eyes with such intensity that she wanted to look away, but recognized she mustn't. "Your telepathic stalker."

"Right."

"And you went to his house? Alone?" Hisses and growls punctuated the words. "Are you insane?"

"Possibly." Anger flared inside her, but she clamped a lid over it and lifted her chin. "I didn't have much choice, since you took off on another mission."

"Didn't you get my message? Tesler wants you."

"I'm staying at a motel, and I ditched my old phone and car. I'm safe."

"For the moment."

She slumped, resting her hands on her thighs. "Amador offered to help me. He says he was a prisoner at another facility, in Siberia. I get the feeling he hates Tesler as much as you do." She dug her nails into her knees. "Amador said I'd learn things about you I wouldn't like."

David clenched his jaw. "Naturally, you believe everything your stalker tells you."

"No, of course not." She practically spat the words at him. "I am not an idiot, you know. That's why I'm asking you if it's true or not. Did you kill someone?"

"You shouldn't have to ask."

"Which is not an answer." Since he glared at her without speaking, she said, "We're engaged to be married, David. You say you love me. But you won't let me in on whatever secrets you're holding in. Why are you so afraid to confide in me?"

"You haven't been eager to do the same."

"I have amnesia. Hello, stress alert. What's your excuse?"

He slumped deeper into the corner.

She longed to reach for him, to draw him closer. How had they spiraled so far away from each other? She trusted this man more than she'd trusted anyone else in her life. He was right, though. She withheld certain facts from him, just as he held back from her.

Amador might be aiming to drive a wedge between them. He needn't bother. They were fashioning their own wedge.

David raised a hand as if to touch her face but then, realizing he couldn't, he dropped his hand to his thigh. His eyes glimmered less blue somehow, less vibrant, as if the color had drained away along with his anger.

"You're right," he said. "I have no excuse for the things I've done to you. I've put you in danger over and over, without intending to, but intentions are meaningless. I betrayed your trust."

"No, you haven't. Why would you say such a thing?"

"Because I—" He shook his head with a vehemence that ruffled his hair. "You have no idea what I've done, and it doesn't matter anymore."

His guilt and misery overwhelmed her, escalating her own. A tear dribbled down her cheek into the corner of her mouth. Bitter salt oozed over her tongue. She scuttled toward him and fell to her knees. "Please, David. Tell me what you think you did. If you hurt someone, I'm sure it was self-defense—"

"Don't." His brow furrowed, and his mouth twisted into an agonized expression. The look flitted across his face, vanishing within seconds as the old stoicism cloaked him.

And David the warrior angel returns.

She sank back onto her heels. David the distant angel. Unknowable, unreachable, untouchable.

Footfalls pounded in the corridor outside the room.

"Leave," David said. "Right away."

A command, not a request. She planted a hand on her thigh and bent forward. "I will not. I can help you escape."

"No." He snapped his back straight. "You'll only get in the way."

"Excuse me?"

"Go away."

The footsteps ceased outside the door.

She gaped at him. The anger in his voice. The stoic mask on his face.

Of course. Why hadn't she noticed earlier?

"You're lying," she said. "I can feel it, David. You're pushing me away out of fear. But of what?"

His eyes turned toward her, though he didn't face her. "For once in your life, could you not be so goddamn stubborn? Curse me, hit me, yell at me. But don't be understanding. I'm breaking up with you, Grace."

She inched nearer. If she'd had a genuine body, her kneecaps would've bumped his thighs. With her face a breath away from his, she waited until he grudgingly met her gaze. "I don't believe you. And I will not allow you to break up with me. We have to fight for each other, not run away."

"This isn't the time or the place to discuss it."

"I agree." Weakness rippled through her as her psychic energy dwindled. She wished like hell she could grab him by the arms. Throttle some sense into him. Instead, she glared into his gleaming blue eyes. "This conversation is not over."

She released the tether between their minds. As the crossroads dragged her back into the tunnel, she swore he mumbled, "Forgive me."

Then she was gone.

—

DAVID BLINKED AT THE EMPTY SPACE WHERE GRACE HAD BEEN A second earlier. He couldn't get the image of her out of his mind. The solitary tear dribbling down her cheek. The confused expression that morphed into sorrow, and finally, mutated into exasperation.

He'd expected tears. Dreaded them, yes, while knowing they must come. But frustration? It made no sense. Why didn't she rail at him?

Because she knew he was lying.

He cracked his fist into the floor. Pain shot through his hand, up his wrist, and straight into his forearm. He winced, grunting. He deserved the pain. After what he'd done to Grace, he deserved far worse than this. She'd loved him when no one else would. She trusted him. And how did he repay her faith? With a string of betrayals.

Nothing had unfolded the way he'd planned. Someday, maybe she'd understand and forgive him.

We have to fight for each other, she'd urged him, not run away.

Fight for her? He'd crawl naked through a jungle of poison thorns to revel in her warmth again. If he could guarantee her well-being. Which he'd destroyed in the first place.

Why couldn't she let him break up with her? He hadn't fought her refusal with much vigor. He let her have her way because…

He shoved both hands into his hair. He gave in because he didn't want to end their relationship. She was his weakness and his strength. He needed her. She had no use for him, though she would deny it. His incompetence forced her to track him down, and her very presence here jeopardized her safety.

If anyone realized he could communicate with her psychically, then Tesler would manipulate their connection to get to her. He didn't know how. He couldn't risk finding out. The wall she'd constructed around her mind ought to shield her from the worst of it. If Tesler tortured him, she might sense it but not experience it the way she would without the barrier. At this moment, he was glad of that. She must keep away from him until he escaped from this facility. Any attempt at contact endangered her. As much as he burned to see her—to hear her voice and feel her, psychically and physically—it was out of the question.

He was right back where he started two years ago. Alone.

"Has your woman left?" Nkosi asked.

David glanced sideways at the man. "What?"

"I assume you were talking with your woman, from the way you were so protective of her."

"You listened in?"

"No. I meant the way you ordered me not to listen or watch. That was protective."

"Oh." The explanation was quasi-plausible. And since David could use the help of a coconspirator to get out of here, he may as well give Nkosi the benefit of the doubt.

He would never, under any circumstances, admit to communicating with Grace.

"No worries," Nkosi said. "I don't expect you to confirm what I believe. She must be quite something for you to shield her so."

A mechanism thunked. The door swung inward.

Karl Tesler walked into the cell.

David stood up. Nkosi stayed on the floor.

Tesler halted just inside the doorway. He glanced from David to Nkosi and back again. A smirk tugged at the corners of Tesler's mouth. "Welcome home, David."

"You can torture me all you want," David said, "but I won't tell you anything."

"Torture you? No, I won't do that." Tesler swept one arm through the air to point at Nkosi. "I'll torture him."

David envisioned death rays shooting out of his eyes to scorch holes through Tesler's chest. Wouldn't do any good. The man had no heart. He probably wasn't even human.

Nkosi pushed up off the floor, favoring sore muscles, and rose to his full height, a good three inches taller than David. "Don't worry, my friend. Neither one of us will give this… person what he seeks."

Tesler made a sound somewhere between a growl and a chuckle. "Such bravery—and camaraderie. We'll see how long it lasts once we get you into the fun house."

Two guards trundled into the room. Both held stun guns at the ready. One guard herded Nkosi out of the cell and down the hallway out of sight. The other waved his stun gun at David, gesturing for him to exit the cell. David complied. There was no point in arguing, at least until he'd figured out a plan of escape.

As David walked past Tesler, the scientist murmured, "How is your golden girl?"

David stopped. He narrowed his eyes and glared straight into Tesler's. "You will never get your hands on her. She's tougher and smarter than you or any of your thugs."

Tesler smiled like a wolf baring his teeth before pouncing on his prey. "We'll see about that."

"JT failed, and so will you."

Tesler tsked. "Jackson Tennant was ill-prepared and stark-raving mad. I have a clarity of purpose he never found. And I have a plan that doesn't revolve around a harebrained hypothesis that blood contains the essence of psychic powers. I plan on extracting them directly from the source."

A chill ran through David because he suspected he knew the answer before he asked. "What source would that be?"

"The human brain, dear boy. The human brain."

David couldn't muster a response. His every thought centered on Grace and a terrible image of Tesler drilling into her skull to tap into the source of her power. A sharp pain in his chest blossomed, until it devoured his entire body, tearing through muscles. *God no.* He would never, never, never allow the image to become reality. Whatever the price to spare her, he'd pay it without hesitation.

Tesler chuckled again. "Do you know what the greatest prize of all is?"

David ground his teeth.

"The brain of a traveler with the Golden Power," Tesler said. "The pretty pink brain of your darling girl."

If he had to die for Grace, then he was dragging this bastard down with him.

Chapter Ten

GRACE LAY MOTIONLESS ON THE BED FOR SEVERAL MINUTES. NIGHT had fallen, and the harsh glow of sodium-vapor lights leaked in between the curtains from the parking lot outside. A horn blared out on the interstate. The draft from the air conditioner rustled her hair.

David had said awful things to her. Although she realized he'd spoken out of fear, his words hurt anyway. One day soon, he would explain himself. What happened then…

She thrust the question aside. Drained in body and mind, she could spare no energy on fretting over the future. David could have his way, for the time being. She'd leave him alone.

But not for long.

Gabriel Amador had offered to help her, and she might have to accept his offer. First, though, she wanted a little more information about the man. Since the DVD provided nothing of value, she must search elsewhere.

She called the front desk.

Tag answered on the first ring. "How can I help you, Ms. Marcus?"

"Uh—" He was calling *her* Ms. Marcus, she realized just in time, before she told him he must've confused her with someone else. She almost forgot her own alias. "Does the motel have Wi-Fi access?"

"Sorry, no. We're still living in the Dark Ages here." He paused for a second, then said, "You could use the office computer if you want. It's got DSL."

"Won't you get in trouble for letting me use it?"

"Nah," he said, his tone utterly dismissive of the possibility. "Nobody'll find out, but even if they did, they wouldn't care. This dog's leash is pretty loose, ya know. Come on down and I'll set you up."

"Thank you. I really appreciate this."

"Ain't nothing."

She hung up, grabbed her purse, and headed for the motel's lobby. The big neon sign at the edge of the parking lot declared "Stay-A-Night Motel—Vacancy." As the lobby's door swung shut behind her, Tag greeted her with a big smile and a sweeping gesture meant as an invitation for her to come around behind the desk. She returned his smile, ducking behind the desk. When she reached the computer, she saw he already had a web browser open on-screen.

"Have at it," he told her.

"Thanks."

She watched Tag pick up a pile of unopened mail and carry it to the far end of the desk, about six feet away from her. The computer monitor stood at an angle on the desk which meant he couldn't see the screen from his position. Still, she must assume the computer had some kind of tracking software on it that let Tag's employers keep tabs on his activity—a keystroke logger or similar application. Maybe she was being paranoid again, but paranoia seemed prudent when she had Tesler's goons on her trail.

Okay. She'd keep this brief and vague.

Navigating to a search engine, she typed in two words: Gabriel Amador. The search results came up with links to Facebook pages and Twitter accounts for various individuals named Gabriel Amador. None of them matched the man she'd met. She tried Gabriel Ricardo Amador, with no better luck. Next, she typed in "Catalan Enterprises." The top results had nothing to do with Amador's company but were instead links to informational pages about the Catalan people of northern Spain. She scrolled down to see more results.

Eureka.

She clicked on a link for "Catalan Enterprises: Venture Capital, Investment Services, and More." The website loaded in a few seconds. She skimmed the text on the home page, learning the company provided seed money for new businesses, ran an online stock-trading service, and owned a number of banks and other financial institutions around the world. The company was, predictably, based in the Catalonia region of Spain. She browsed the rest of the site but found no mention of Gabriel Amador. The site didn't name any of the company's officers or the board of directors, and it supplied nothing more exciting than gobbledygook-filled explanations of how venture capital worked and how to apply for it.

Maybe that was the point. Amador gave her his company's name because he knew it would lead her nowhere.

"You feel that?" Tag asked.

She glanced up at him. He surveyed the small lobby which consisted of a coffee table and three chairs situated in front of the desk. He held an envelope in one hand, and a letter opener in the other, as if he'd frozen in the middle of slicing open the letter.

Grace shut her eyes, letting her paranormal senses kick in. She felt something too, though it was vague. The nape of her neck tingled.

Her pulse shifted into overdrive. *Someone's watching.* She scanned the room, trying to listen through the pounding of her own heart. No use. She couldn't hear anything else. The sharp scent of Tag's coffee wafted into her nostrils, and she could almost taste the bitter brew.

"What was it?" she asked Tag.

He shrugged. "Weird feeling. Like a ghost walked through me or something."

A ghost. She'd never heard of a traveler walking through someone, but she didn't know everything about psychic abilities. Since travelers didn't have physical bodies, they could walk through solid objects—people too, she imagined. She hadn't tried it herself, though she'd seen David walk through walls. But walking through human beings? The thought of it made her queasy. Sure, in her astral form she was essentially a ghost, but still…

Walking through walls and people? *Ew.*

She surfed back to the search engine and typed in John Mendoza. A boatload of results popped up, and though she tried to sort through them for relevant information, she got bogged down by the myriad John Mendozas in cyberspace. Everyone had a digital footprint these days. Everyone except Gabriel Amador.

Out of curiosity, she searched for David Ransom. The results numbered in the millions. A listing for a yellow-pages website announced "268 David Ransoms in the United States." *Oh jeez.* Seriously? One David Ransom was all she could handle. Hundreds of them running around out there sounded like an awful lot of stoic, pigheaded men.

A ridiculous image unrolled in her mind. Hundreds of tiny Davids trotting around on a map of the United States. One little Grace struggling to herd them all with her lasso.

She couldn't help the chuckle that tumbled from her lips.

"No fair," Tag said. "You gotta share the funny emails."

"Oh, it's not an email. I had a weird thought, that's all."

Movement flashed in her peripheral vision. She glanced at Tag, but he held the same position as before, having moved only his head to look at her. The movement she'd spied seemed quicker than he would've moved his head. She must've imagined it. Or else it was a bird.

"Something wrong?" Tag asked.

"I thought—no-no, it's fine."

Tag shrugged and went back to sorting the mail.

Grace stared out the glass doors of the lobby. A few cars occupied spaces in the parking lot, scattered along the length of the motel. Although the establishment sat next to the interstate, it lay on a side road at the end of an off-ramp. She couldn't see the traffic whizzing by on the interstate. The occasional car exited the off-ramp, driving past the motel.

The movement she swore she'd seen had come from closer. Much closer.

If she could sense other travelers, then maybe she could sense normal people too.

Beyond the glass doors, the glow of the streetlights tinged everything with a jaundiced yellow. Focused on the light outside, and the beat-up cars bathed in it, she relaxed and cleansed her mind of thoughts. The crossroads tugged at her, but she resisted. Instead, she expanded her mind to sweep the vicinity like radar. Nothing. Nothing. She hit a blip when she scanned over Tag. Then nothing. Nothing. Nothing.

Blip.

She jerked. Was the blip a person? She locked onto the signal—a feeling really, impossible to define but definitely there—and aimed her remote-viewing sense at it. The wall barred her view, of course. She was psychic, for crying out loud. Walls didn't matter to her. She itched to shut her eyes, to block out all other stimuli, but she couldn't afford to limit her natural vision. A voice in the back of her mind warned this might be a trap, set by a traveler in league with Tesler or Amador, or both. She must keep her natural vision available even as she switched over to remote viewing. Sure, piece of cake.

You can do this. Concentrate.

The walls faded into semi-transparency as she tracked the blip back to its source. Her inner vision zoomed in on the target, flying through the ghost image of the wall. She panned left, toward the junction of the lobby wall and the rest of the motel that jutted out from the office and lobby section. There, in the shadows cast by the overhanging roof, she caught sight of a figure crouched against the wall. The person wore black military-style fatigues, black boots, black gloves, and a black full-face helmet. He had a radio clipped to his belt and gripped a big automatic weapon in both hands.

Her heart thudded in her chest. She swallowed against the lump in her throat as a wave of cold dread crested over her. A commando. The black-suited man was an ALI goon.

They were here.

She pulled back from the commando and resumed scanning the vicinity. Nothing. Nothing. *Blip.* Nothing. *Blip, blip, blip.* This time, she had no trouble peering through the walls to identify the blips. Four more commandos had spread out along the outside of the building. As she followed the contours of the structure, she found two more commandos inside a plain white van parked behind the lobby.

Oh shit.

How in the hell had they found her? She'd ditched her credit cards, her car, everything except her cash, her new computer, and her purse with the gun inside it. Even as she watched the commandos with her remote vision, she reached for her purse to pat the hard outline of the .357 revolver inside. Sliding her hand into the bag, she curled her fingers around the gun's grip.

"You okay?"

Tag's concerned voice broke her concentration. The walls snapped back into view. Her head spun a little. As she grasped the edge of the desk for support, she realized she'd stopped breathing. No wonder she was woozy. She sucked in a couple of deep breaths and, steadier now, pushed away from the desk.

Out of the corner of her eye, she noticed Tag taking a step toward her.

She held up a hand to stop him. "Um, I can't explain this, but some very bad people are trying to kidnap me. They're in the parking lot. I imagine they're about to storm in here and take me by force. I don't want you to get hurt."

"I can handle myself."

His expression had turned hard, and suddenly he reminded her of a hitman in one of those mafia movies Hollywood loved to make. He probably could handle himself. But against seven armed commandos?

Dammit. She hadn't intended for Tag to get caught in the middle of her nightmare. She didn't want him to suffer or die because of her, and yet she could not let Tesler capture her. Remaining free offered the sole hope of stopping the mad scientist.

"There's a back way out," Tag said, hooking a thumb toward the door behind her.

"Bad guys have a van out back."

Tag frowned, working his lips as if thinking hard. Finally, he said, "Take the side door. It opens off the back of the office, onto the sidewalk on the far side of the building."

"Okay. Thanks."

"I'll keep 'em occupied while you beat it."

He waved toward the office door.

She tugged her purse tight against her, the bulk of her gun jostling inside it. If she let this man cover for her while she fled, Tesler's minions would hurt him—or worse, if he failed to cooperate to their satisfaction. Tag's blood would stain her hands too.

No more deaths because of her. *Stand and fight.*

Trouble was, Tag wouldn't back down. Despite meeting him a few hours ago, she understood a basic truth about him, about men of his ilk, the noble warriors. They fought for what was right, without fail. She knew this because she loved just such a man.

David wouldn't abandon her in these circumstances. Neither would Tag.

Unless she urged him into it.

When she'd set out on a cross-country odyssey to free David from the California facility, he'd knocked her unconscious to slow down her progress, in the vain belief she might give up when she woke. Fat chance. If she could replicate his technique, then she might keep Tag out of harm's way without hurting him.

Much later, she'd asked David how he gave her a psychic mickey. He'd told her, "With a small, controlled burst of telepathic energy empowered by my fervent need for you to sleep. The subject must be willing on some level to succumb. That's how thought projection works. Desire coupled with power."

But if she employed too much power, she could damage Tag's mind.

Did Tag want to submit to her will? She'd given in to David because, though it chagrined her to admit it, deep down she liked surrendering to him. A little bit. On occasion.

Tag was a stranger. This might not work at all on him.

She'd once tricked an old man into believing a twenty-dollar bill was five thousand bucks. Putting a guy to sleep should be easy.

Tag urged her toward the door with a large, but gentle, hand on her arm.

Another door, behind him, caught her attention. "What's that?"

He looked where she pointed. "Closet."

Three, two, one…

With her gaze glued to his, she summoned a ball of psychic energy and blew it into Tag. His eyes widened. She beamed a fervent wish into his mind. *Get in the closet, sit down, sleep.* She repeated the command over and over until she felt his will softening.

He shuffled to the closet, swung the door open, and tromped inside. She kept up her inner chant, afraid he might snap out of it if she stopped. He sat cross-legged on the floor of the closet, leaned against the wall, and promptly fell asleep.

Thank heavens.

She kicked the closet door shut. The latch clicked into place.

A quick telepathic pass confirmed he was undamaged. If she interpreted things right.

She whipped the revolver out of her purse and peeked into the office. A door on the left must open onto the rear area. Another door led out the back of the office. The stale smell of dust drifted out of the air-conditioning vents. She wiped her clammy hands on her pants.

Tag had told her to take the side door. She hustled over to check it was unlocked, then retreated to the lobby, closing the office door.

From her position behind the reception desk, she reached out again with her psychic senses. The walls turned semi-transparent once more. It was strange, peering through the ghost image of the walls, seeing through solid matter but knowing she couldn't walk through it, not in her corporeal state. She spotted the commandos outside the lobby doors. As she observed them, they surged forward and headed straight for the doors, storming through them with guns raised. The doors banged open, and the commandos' boots thundered across the floor.

Her vision reeled back to the normal, and the seven helmeted, armed men arrayed in front of the desk. She held the revolver muzzle down, her arm slack, the weapon hidden behind the desk. Her finger hovered over the trigger, separated from it by millimeters of air.

One commando, apparently the leader, detached from the group to approach the desk.

"Grace Powell." He sounded far too pleased with himself. "Gotcha, sweetheart."

A glacier hardened in her chest, expanding to scour out her soul. That voice. The way he said "sweetheart" with a slight snarl. *Holy shit.* She swallowed hard and said, "Battaglia."

He removed his helmet and tucked it under his arm. The sneer was familiar too, and it triggered a flashback of him tackling her, threatening to stab a syringe into her neck. Her trigger finger itched to pull.

Six bullets. Seven men. Bad odds, even for a crack shot. Which she wasn't.

Battaglia sniggered. "I'm tickled pink you remember me, honey. Maybe this time you'll show me why so many guys are after your sweet little ass."

"Tesler wants me undamaged." She hoped.

"Yeah," Battaglia said, his leering gaze traveling down to her breasts and back up to her face. "But I can do lotsa things without causing permanent harm."

A legion of phantom insects skittered over her skin as she muttered, "You're just as crazy as JT."

"What was that, sweetheart? Didn't quite catch it."

She raised her voice. "Go to hell, you sick son of a bitch."

His guffaw echoed in the small space. He slashed one hand through the air, gesturing toward her. "Cuff her, boys."

Oh hell no.

She must lead them away from the motel, away from Tag. How long he'd slumber, she couldn't gauge. If Battaglia decided to check the closet…

No one else would die for her.

Raising her gun, directing it at Battaglia, she aimed a nasty smile at him. "I wouldn't do that if I were you."

Battaglia shook his head and sighed heavily. "You really are a dumb bitch."

"So come and get me."

She bolted into the office, thwacked the door shut, and locked it.

The knob jiggled.

Battaglia bellowed, "Unlock it or I'll blow it open."

With her inner radar, she did a quick check of the motel's vicinity. The two commandos in the van had not moved, and no others had shown up to join the operation. She withdrew her psychic senses, snapping the walls back into solid form, and ran for the door at the back of the office. Twisting the knob, she flung the door inward and fled outside. Her footfalls clapped on the sidewalk and echoed off the building as she tore down the pathway, past the closed doors and curtained windows of the motel rooms. No one so much as peeked out between the curtains.

The air whooshed over her. A gust of wind snatched up gravel and dirt, flinging it into her face. Grit stung her eyes, pebbles pinged her skin, and the earthy taste of dirt infiltrated her mouth. Her leg muscles burned hotter and hotter with every step she took, screaming for a rest. She pushed her body to run faster.

A gunshot boomed behind her, inside the motel office. Voices shouted, but she couldn't make out the words. The rushing of her own blood in her ears, the huffing of her breaths, and the smacking of her footsteps obscured the words of the commandos.

Just short of the end of the building, she swerved left to race across the parking lot toward the scrubby woods beyond it. The sickly light from the parking lot streetlights petered out at the edge of the woods. Her heart pounded so hard and fast it made her head swim, but she couldn't stop. Her feet left the pavement, landing on dry, rock-hard ground and parched grass. She kept running.

The shouting drew closer. She glanced back.

Commandos streamed out of the office.

Run. The thought spurred her body into more speed. In the instant she refocused her attention on the woods ahead, a shot detonated behind her. A projectile sliced across her arm, setting off a scorching pain that lanced through her, knocking her off balance. She stumbled, nearly fell, and caught herself a second before she hit the dirt. Her arm burned, but she refused to look at it. Not now. Not yet.

She pushed her legs to pump harder. Muscles cramped in protest. She ignored the pain, the sweat stinging her eyes, and the scrambling and thumping of boot-clad feet behind her. Another gunshot boomed. She ducked into the trees. Bark exploded from the tree she'd just passed. On and on she raced, panting so hard her chest ached, fighting for each breath.

Her toe caught on a tree root. She tripped, sailing face-first onto the ground. Her body struck the earth with such force it knocked the sense out of her. She couldn't breathe. Couldn't move. Couldn't think.

Branches cracked. Dry grass rustled. Boots clomped.

They were coming.

Snap out of it.

She sucked in a breath, pushed onto her knees, and glanced over her shoulder. Black silhouettes, distant but moving closer each second, headed straight for her. No time. She must do something. The only thing she could think of would come at a hefty cost.

No choice.

She disengaged from her physical body. Her mind soared upward, a balloon cut loose in the wind. Her mind flew into the dark tunnel, up and up. Bursting out into the crossroads, she halted with an abruptness that would've snapped her neck if she had a body. Pain radiated from the base of her skull, down into her neck. Floating there, she extended all her psychic faculties and reaped as much juice as she could from the energy matrix around her. The stars pulsed and swelled. Power, searing and molten, cascaded into her.

She plummeted downward, bursting out into the world and back into her body with a suddenness that stunned her. Every nerve in her body twanged, the psychic pain as sharp and real as the throbbing in her neck and the stinging in her arm. She focused her newly acquired power on one objective.

Destroy the commandos.

Wind erupted in front of her. In a wall of gyrating current as strong as a hurricane, the wind swept away from her toward the commandos. The gale uprooted small trees, drawing them into its eddies. Chunks of dirt and rocks twirled up from the ground, whirling on the currents of the wind.

The commandos ran straight into the maelstrom.

Someone shouted, "Jesus Christ!"

Male voices screamed in pain as rocks and airborne trees socked them. Still the wind spun, traveling forward at breakneck speed. The maelstrom hefted the commandos off the ground and hurled them through the air. Their bodies smacked down with wet thuds.

Nausea swelled inside her. She choked back the bile rising in her throat, tasting the bitter acid.

The screams ended.

She released the air. Saplings, rocks, and dirt rained down onto the ground. As the ruckus settled into silence, she bent forward and vomited.

Wiping her mouth on her shirt, she finally looked at her arm. Blood trickled over her elbow and down her forearm. It originated from a wound on her upper arm, a couple of inches below the shoulder. It looked like a deep scrape. A bullet must've grazed her. The wound still smarted, and she dabbed at it with her fingertip. Pain shot out from the wound. She gasped.

Her stomach hurt. Her head pounded as if a metal spike had been shoved straight up her spine into her skull. Every muscle trembled. She struggled to stand, but her knees buckled. She flopped onto her butt on the ground. Tears spilled down her cheeks, driven by sobs that racked her body, triggering sharp pains in so many places she lost count.

Hot shards pierced the backs of her eyes. The first signs of a migraine.

Shit. Considering how much power she'd funneled through her mind and body, she wouldn't have much time to get to safety before the migraine disabled her. She rose onto all fours.

Her right hand crunched an object.

With two fingers, she picked it up. Her cell phone. Demolished by a large and heavy booted foot.

Tossing it aside, she stashed her gun in her purse and crawled through the debris from her whirlwind. When she discovered the first body, she halted. The commando lay motionless, eyes wide and dead. She checked his neck for a pulse anyway. Nothing. She noticed the radio clipped to his belt, but that wouldn't help her. Not unless she wanted to chat with the buddies of the men she'd killed.

She bowed her head. She'd killed… how many men?

Don't think about it. They would've killed you in a heartbeat.

With trembling hands, she searched the man's jacket pockets for something, anything, that might help her. What dragged on like hours, but probably had been seconds, ticked by before her unsteady fingers closed around a hard object in the man's hip pocket. She jiggled the thing until it popped free of the pocket.

A cell phone.

Relief flooded through her. Tears flowed anew, streaking down her cheeks as she dug in her purse for the card Roland Wickham had given her. Finding it, she held the card up to read the text. Tears fogged her vision. She sniffled and wiped them away. In the few seconds before new tears emerged, she read the number on the card and dialed it. The phone rang once, twice, three times.

"Hello?"

She almost burst into sobs again at the sound of Gabriel Amador's voice. Her own voice rasped when she said, "It's Grace. I need your help."

"What happened?"

"I'll explain later. I'm pinned down behind the Stay-A-Night Motel, just off the interstate."

"I know where it is. Stay out of sight until I arrive."

"Okay." Despite her best efforts not to, she sniffled.

"Hold on, Grace," Amador said, his tone authoritative. "I am on my way."

He hung up.

She dropped the phone. He hadn't even asked what she meant by pinned down. He didn't seem surprised at all that she needed help. In fact, she could've sworn she detected a note of triumph in his voice—faint, but there. Probably her paranoia rearing its head again.

Either way, help was coming. If she could evade the remaining commandos until then.

A twig cracked.

She pulled the gun out of her purse. Hold them off, that was all she had to do.

For how long?

CHAPTER ELEVEN

G RACE CLAMBERED AWAY FROM THE BODY AS FAST AS SHE DARED
move, and as fast as she could manage, taking the dead man's phone
with her. Despite worrying about the commandos' ability to track their
buddy's phone, she decided the benefit of keeping it with her outweighed
the risk. At least she hoped it did.

The pulsating in her head strengthened with each passing minute. She
started out waddling on all fours, but when her arms crumpled, she resorted to belly-crawling. The parched earth, cracked and jagged, clawed at her
flesh. Her injury impelled her to adopt a limping belly-crawl that favored
her wounded arm. The effort of hauling her body over the uneven terrain
while hampered by a blinding headache, a wounded arm, and spry commandos on her tail drained her beyond exhaustion. She longed to collapse
under a nice shady tree. She didn't dare stop for even one second, for fear
she might never rouse herself again.

So far, she'd kept ahead of the commandos. Maybe they got distracted
by the bodies of their comrades. The memory of their lifeless forms jolted
her, yet she was fresh out of guilt. *They* shot *her*.

In the wake of her own deadly action, she realized one fact. If David
had killed anyone, he must've done it in self-defense. She knew him, and she
understood through far too much experience that sometimes a person was
provoked into taking another's life. Her gut still churned from the desperation
of choosing between her survival and the innate inhibition against killing.

Most people operated under that inhibition. Some did not. They were the
ones who compelled people like her and David to enact deadly measures.

Please, David, just tell me the truth.

She prayed he heard her plea, even through the wall blocking off her
mind.

The phone in her pocket vibrated.

Catching her breath, she paused to pull out the appropriated phone and glanced down at its screen. The number on the caller ID was familiar. She pressed the button to take the call but didn't dare say hello.

"Don't speak," Amador said. "I am at the motel. Leave this line open and I will track you."

Oh great. If he could track the phone, then her pursuers might be closing in on her too.

As if he'd read her mind, Amador said, "I don't think Tesler's men are tracking the phone. They seem to be setting up a perimeter to begin an organized hunt for you."

Could he read her mind? David swore trying to read minds led to insanity, but he might be wrong about that. Amador could've thought of the same thing at the same time she did by coincidence. Whichever it was, the answer hardly mattered right now.

"I have your signal," Amador said, in a hushed voice. "Hold on, Grace. I will mute my phone and come for you. Do not hang up."

The line seemed to go dead. He must've muted the call on his end.

She huddled there, on her belly, propped up with one arm and gripping the cell phone in one hand, her gun in the other. As she tilted her head to listen, she also scanned the woods with her eyes—her physical eyes. All her psychic senses were hollow, emptied of power. She could do little more than lie there, squinting from the migraine pain and struggling not to vomit again.

She yearned to curl up in a ball and sleep for days.

Would her psychic barrier stay in place if she slept? She hadn't taken so much as a nap since building the mental barrier, unless passing out earlier counted as rest. It felt like days had elapsed since she sat on the bed with David, both of them trying to figure out how she might erect a psychic firewall. She checked the display on the dead man's phone. It gave the time as 11:02 PM. She flipped the phone facedown in her palm to hide the glow from its display.

Even the fragile moonglow hurt her eyes.

Her eyelids threatened to close. With a gargantuan effort of will, she kept them open.

David, I need you.

He wouldn't come. He couldn't. Besides being held hostage at the Montana facility, he most likely couldn't track her down because of her psychic wall. Lowering the barrier would let him reach her, but it might also let in enemies. Soon she might not be able to fend off sleep any longer, and her psychic wall might become a moot point.

Rustling. Behind her.

She rolled onto her back, raising her gun.

Gabriel Amador stepped out from behind a bush.

She nearly keeled over right then, out of sheer relief. Her arm fell to the ground, and the gun tumbled from her fingers. White lights flickered in her vision, a signal her migraine had worsened. The pain swallowed her head, fractured her mind, and vacuumed every last ounce of strength from her body. She tried to push up onto her elbows, but her arms gave out. She toppled to the ground.

Amador crouched beside her. He plucked her gun from the dirt, shoving it into her purse. Her tight throat strangled the words she tried to speak. So tired. Sleep beckoned to her, though she battled against it. Keeping her eyelids open got harder and harder. They drooped half-closed. She peeked through her lashes, her gaze intersecting with Amador's.

His expression was pinched.

She tried one more time to speak but eked out nothing better than a moan.

And then, like a hero in a movie, Gabriel Amador scooped her up into his arms and lugged her out of the woods. David had carried her this way once, in a similar situation. In his arms, she'd enjoyed safety and warmth. Cradled in the arms of Gabriel Amador, she suffered an odd mixture of relief and tension.

The pain and exhaustion brought on by her migraine overpowered everything else. By the time they reached Amador's vehicle, an enormous SUV, she gave up the fight.

Her lids fluttered shut as she sank into a deep slumber.

———

AVID SCUFFLED TO A STOP A FEW FEET INSIDE THE DOORWAY OF THE twenty-foot-square room. Fluorescent lights recessed into the ceiling cast quivering light onto the white walls and concrete floor. The far wall housed a two-way mirror that would, undoubtedly, allow Tesler's fans and cohorts to observe his sessions with travelers. Nkosi staggered in behind David, coming up on his left, an arm's length away. Armed sentries guarded them, one to Nkosi's left and one to David's right. Both their gazes were riveted to the sight in the middle of the room.

A metal chair hunkered there, padded with meager cushioning. The seat resembled a dentist's chair, though without the cozy atmosphere. In the chair—strapped down with restraints around his wrists, ankles, and forehead—huddled Sean Vandenbrook.

The boy's green eyes glittered with anger. He lifted his chin high, his lips compressed.

David tipped his head to Sean, and the boy almost smiled. In the past six months, Sean had labored to become a man, bolstering his body and mind through sheer force of will. To Sean, achieving manhood meant never crying or showing weakness. David tried to explain showing emotion didn't make a man weak, but it sounded hypocritical coming from him. He didn't exactly excel at sharing his feelings.

Which explained why Grace was angry with him.

He flashed back to his last conversation with her when he'd told her to leave because she'd only get in his way. On the surface, she'd been frustrated, but underneath she nursed a wound he had inflicted. Even now, her anguish congealed as a hard lump in his chest. He'd wanted to drag her into his arms, kiss her senseless, and vow to never leave her again. That was selfishness talking. Being with him brought her more pain, more danger, more of everything bad. The worst things in the world trailed behind him wherever he went. Grace deserved better. Maybe if he told her...

No. He had revealed the whole truth once and look what happened. Her parents were murdered, and her grandfather was imprisoned. David should've stayed away from Grace after that, but he'd given in to his need to be with her. Not this time. From here on, he safeguarded her above everything else.

He wouldn't burden her with the truth.

Please, David, just tell me.

Grace's voice murmured into his psyche, subtle as a breeze. He must've imagined it. His desire to confess everything to her led him to fantasize she was begging him to do exactly that. The psychic wall she'd built prevented him from touching her mind. But she could contact him, so maybe...

Wishful thinking.

David, I need you.

This time he knew it was her, without a shred of doubt. Her pain and fear walloped him in the gut. He breathed hard as if someone really had punched him. He tried to contact Grace without leaving his body, but the barrier knocked him back.

With less force this time. Her wall had thinned.

It signified either of two things. One, Grace had decided to let down her psychic defenses in order to contact him. Or two, she was sick or injured and couldn't maintain the wall any longer. Neither option neutralized the acid churning in his gut. He fisted his hands at his sides. If he tried to travel to her, through the crossroads, his body would be undefended. Tesler might notice his vacant expression, and punish him, or worse, he might punish Nkosi or Sean. David would not let that happen.

Damn Tesler. Damn himself for getting captured. He could either go to Grace and help her as she'd practically begged him to or stay here to protect Nkosi and Sean.

Shit, shit, shit.

He stretched out his psychic senses, gently, staying rooted in his body. Using this method, he couldn't see or speak to Grace, or determine her exact circumstances and condition. But he could get an inkling. As he snaked out his paranormal senses, feeling for Grace, he kept an eye on the room around him. Tesler had yet to arrive. David knew the bastard would come eventually once he thought they'd accrued enough anxiety to feed his hunger.

Grace. There. Her fiery aura sparkled in the cold void. Her barrier had weakened, though not disintegrated. It pushed back against him, with the gentle compulsion of one magnet repelling another when their opposite poles faced each other. He discerned enough to tell Grace was alive, not badly injured, and felt safe enough to sleep. He also detected another presence nearby, the vacant sensation of a non-paranormal human.

The door to David's right opened. He withdrew his psychic faculties, returning all his attention to the room around him.

Tesler strolled through the door, shutting it behind him with a sharp click.

David watched the scientist stroll to the chair that restrained Sean. Tesler patted the boy's arm in a gesture that seemed threatening rather than comforting, and then he confronted Nkosi and David.

"I will discover what you know," Tesler said. "The only choice is how I do it."

Nkosi watched Tesler without expression.

David bit his tongue to keep from uttering a sarcastic reply. He wanted to bash in the heads of the guards and Tesler. Smash his way out of here using all his psychic faculties. But what then? He didn't have Grace's power. Simply getting out of this room would probably drain him. To escape the facility demanded greater energy than what he, Nkosi, and Sean could muster combined.

A muscle in his jaw twitched, and he stifled a growl. He'd needed Grace to break him out of the Mojave Desert facility.

"Here's your choice," Tesler said. He waved at Nkosi, and then at Sean. "Which one of them do I torture to death first?"

David clenched his teeth and hissed. "None of us will talk. You're wasting your time."

"Oh really? I disagree. Your darling girl is nearly in my grasp as we speak. So perhaps you'd rather I wait until she arrives and torture her for the information I seek."

"You're lying. You don't have Grace." He'd noticed another presence near her, a non-paranormal human. Could Tesler have captured her already?

A bead of sweat trickled down his temple.

Tesler clucked his tongue, wagging a finger. "Cling to that notion as long as you like, dear boy. Moments ago, my men surrounded her. She has no place to hide."

If Tesler was telling the truth, then everything David had fought for was lost.

No, not yet. He still had a chance to save her. She was asleep or unconscious, injured, and exhausted, both physically and psychically.

David threw a sideways look at Nkosi. He deliberately spoke in a monotone. "I'm sorry. I have to sacrifice you to keep Tesler from getting what he wants."

"I understand," Nkosi replied, his voice filled with a level of certainty and understanding that surprised David. He hadn't expected the man to accept his fate so easily. Nkosi nodded at David and then looked at Tesler. "I will be the first."

"Excellent," Tesler said, almost crowing.

He thought he'd won. And in a way, he had. But David would make sure no one—not Tesler, not Amador, not anyone—would get their hands on Grace. Saving her might kill him. It might also cost Nkosi and Sean their lives. He hoped they understood the necessity of this. He couldn't explain, because he couldn't connect with them telepathically, the way he could with Grace. He might inject a thought into their minds, but even doing that wouldn't guarantee they'd get the message. Thought projection relied on the power of suggestion rather than the power of will. He couldn't force them to accept the thoughts he inserted into their minds. To coerce them into hearing the thoughts required far more energy than he dared expend.

Tesler glanced over his shoulder at the two-way mirror. He gave a quick nod before turning back to face Nkosi and David.

The door opened, and a technician entered the room pushing a cart loaded with tools. Sharp, nasty-looking implements. Syringes filled with liquid. Shiny needles. And, of course, a baseball bat.

David flexed his fingers slowly, then curled them into his palm, the nails scraping flesh. All three of them would, in turn, suffer and die to protect the rest of the world from Tesler and his cohorts. Sean, at least, recognized they also sacrificed themselves to protect Grace. And he would've volunteered for the pain because he cared for her too.

The technician parked the cart near Tesler and left the room. The door clicked shut.

Deep in the walls, something buzzed. The noise was familiar, yet he had no idea what it meant.

No time to wonder. He must go now.

Keeping his eyes open, David cut his mind free of the shackles that bound it to his body. He rocketed upward.

And crashed headlong into a barricade. Hot currents tore through him. He pushed against the impediment, but it stung him harder, hotter, sharper. The pain lanced his mind and sliced into his body. His muscles convulsed.

His mind crashed back into his body. Ten thousand volts of agony arced through him, and he doubled over from the force of it. What the hell was this? His muscles convulsed again, driving him to his knees, contorting his back. A million electrified needles stabbed deep into flesh and sinew. He let out a strangled cry. His entire body curled up as if the muscles had shrunk. He collapsed onto his side, coiled in the fetal position, and rode out the last wrenching wave.

He'd hit a wicked barrier. Not Grace's wall. This obstacle was designed to kill, or at the very least immobilize. Besides, he hadn't even gotten into the tunnel that preceded the crossroads. He got nowhere near Grace.

Tesler walked closer to look down at David with a faint, unpleasant smile on his lips.

David couldn't speak this time. He could do nothing more than scowl at the man.

"Ah," Tesler said, sounding pleased, "I see you've met my new toy. Can't have you skipping off to help your darling girl, now can we?"

From behind Tesler, where David couldn't see, he heard Nkosi say, "What have you done to him?"

Tesler chuckled. "I made a cage for your minds. The engineers who designed it call it an electromagnetic containment field." Tesler sneered, like a tiger admiring its wounded prey. "You see, we discovered quite by accident that EM fields of the right strength and frequency inhibit psychic abilities. Of course, we are risking cellular damage, but I think it's an equitable price to pay for the power you can help us achieve."

With his arms for support, David tried to sit up. His arms shook but held, for now.

He hissed out three words. "We'll fight you."

Tesler shrugged. "Go ahead and try. Inside this room, you are as vulnerable as any normal human being."

David felt weak and vulnerable. He felt... normal.

Tesler strode back to the chair and the cart beside it. He selected a syringe, tapping it to remove bubbles.

"Hmm," Tesler said, "I believe David should go first."

"No," Nkosi said, taking a step toward Tesler. "I am first. You said we choose, and we did."

The two guards grabbed hold of Nkosi's arms, hauling him backward toward the wall. They pinned him there, each keeping one hand clamped on one of Nkosi's arms while in their other hands they grasped their guns.

David's arms gave out. He collapsed onto his back on the floor.

"No," David said, meeting Tesler's gaze. "I'm first. I always have been."

Tesler walked toward David, kneeled beside him, and lowered the syringe to his arm. David winced as the needle pierced his skin. He would die in this room. The realization hit him as the liquid from the syringe heated his veins. He would die, and Grace would fall into Tesler's hands.

He prayed the man had lied. He prayed for more than that, though.

Please, God, spare Grace.

Chapter Twelve

Grace shifted her arm but kept her eyes closed. Something cool and smooth brushed her skin. She tried to roll over, but her nose smacked into a barrier, one that yielded under the pressure from her body. She inhaled a musty scent. Not a bed. Not *her* bed, for sure. A chill shimmied down her spine. Where was she?

She pried her lids apart. A brown, shiny surface filled her vision. Her face was pressed into a leather backrest. She pushed up into a sitting position. *Crunch.* She slid her legs over the sofa's edge, planting her shoes on the floor. *Crunch.* Nothing under her feet. She scooted forward. *Crunch.* The leather protested yet again.

Leather. Metal. Wood. Oh hell, she knew where she was. She'd called him, so of course, he had rushed out to rescue her. *Crap.* She'd needed rescuing? Oh yeah. Men with guns. Hunting her. Pain. Blood. Screams. Not hers, though. Theirs. She shuddered.

Gabriel Amador had saved her. She must be in his home.

The flash drive. She slapped her shirt, right over the breastbone. The flash drive cut into her skin. *Thank God.* Amador hadn't stolen it.

He might've borrowed it, though, while she was asleep. *Cripes.* She couldn't worry about everything. Anxiety over David ate up enough of her brainpower.

The weight of fatigue still blanketed her, almost suffocating in its intensity. Yawning, she peered into the near darkness. A lamp on the desk chased away the shadows, but its glow petered out after a few feet. She rubbed her neck. *Wake up.* Her head ached, though not with the throbbing pain of a migraine. No, her nap had obliterated the worst of the headache.

Her stomach growled. The ache of hunger battled with butterflies in her gut, creating a queasy mixture. Every muscle in her body screamed for more rest. Heaving her body off the sofa, she shuffled over to the desk.

The scent of leather and dust wafted over her. She inhaled a deep breath, and another scent, spicy and earthy, infiltrated her senses, erasing the scent memory of gun powder, damp earth, sweat, and blood. A shiver rattled through her. This place smelled like Gabriel Amador.

She brushed her palm across the slick wood. Polished to a brilliant shine, the surface glimmered in the ambient light. The laptop computer was gone. The phone stood upright in its base. Chewing the inside of her lip, she stared at the receiver. She ought to call the cops. Or her grandfather. Someone. Her arm trembled slightly as she stretched it out toward the phone.

Pow.

She gripped the desk. Her pulse roared in her ears.

Pow, pow, pow.

Panic knifed through her. The explosions had issued from somewhere outside. She rushed to the French doors. *Pow.* She peeked out between the curtains. There, maybe a hundred feet from the house, Roland Wickham stood with legs spread, arms raised in front of him. Black earmuffs protected his ears. He grasped a gun in both hands, homing in on a target mounted on a metal post. *Pow.* His hands jerked a hair as he fired the weapon.

Target practice? He was a butler or something, she'd thought. Maybe his job involved a lot more than opening and closing doors.

Click.

She spun around just as the door swung open.

Gabriel Amador strode into the room and flicked a switch on the wall.

Light burst from the desk lamp. She struggled not to squint. Her stomach flip-flopped.

Amador left the door ajar as he crossed the threshold, halting several paces beyond it. Muscles flexed beneath his gray slacks and long-sleeve dress shirt. The pinstriped white fabric hugged his torso. Two open buttons at the top let the collar drape outward, revealing cinnamon skin sprinkled with dark hairs. His brown loafers glistened with a high-wattage sheen. One of his hands dangled casually at his side. The other dipped into his pants pocket.

"You look better," he pronounced, aiming a genial smile at her. "That must have been a terrible migraine."

"Yes, it was." She leaned her buttocks on the desk, clamping her fingers on its edge. "Um, thanks for coming to—" The words *rescue me* popped into her head, but she dismissed them. "—help me out. I had a little trouble with Tesler's men."

"So I gathered. You may stay as long as you wish. I promise you will be safe here."

His vow bristled, like a stiff hairbrush grated across her nerves. She frowned at him, folding her arms over her chest. "You can't promise that. I don't even know how Tesler's men tracked me down. They might find me here too."

"No," he said, in his tone of absolute certainty. The tone that ticked her off big time. Then he added, "I have taken precautions against all varieties of surveillance."

"All varieties? Come on, there must be some type of surveillance you haven't thought to guard against."

He shrugged, his smile mutating into a smirk. Did he actually think he'd guarded his home against all possible surveillance technologies? And what about the non-technological kind?

"If a traveler attempts to breach this house," Amador said, "I will know. I will sense it. Would you not sense it as well?"

Once again, she had the skin-prickling feeling that he'd read her mind. Yet he didn't look frothing-at-the-mouth insane. Maybe he simply had excellent intuition.

"Yeah," she said, trying to sound more certain than she was, "I'd sense it if another traveler came on the scene."

"Of course."

A quivering spread from her knees into her calves and thighs. She glanced around the room. Her purse lay on the floor by the sofa, a few feet from Amador but farther from her. He watched her with a noncommittal expression, though his eyes darted to follow her gaze when she looked at the purse. With the jelly squiggling in her legs, she doubted she could run over there to grab her purse before he snatched it away.

Sighing, she lowered herself into the nearest chair. The same damn chair she'd sat in the day before. Or earlier today. Whenever the hell it was. Time had twisted into a Mobius strip, with no end and no beginning, everything turning in on itself.

Yesterday. She met Amador yesterday.

She rubbed her arm. The fabric of her shirt was crusty. Realization tingled over her skin. Her gaze flew to the spot on her arm and the blood dried onto her shirt sleeve. She shoved up the fabric to expose—

Unmarked flesh.

Amador chuckled, a light, airy sound. "Ah yes. I bandaged your wound in the car, but when I checked it later, it was gone. You healed yourself, no?"

A sick feeling sloshed in her stomach. She'd healed her own injuries before, six months ago, but hoped it was a fluke. *Nope.*

He plucked her purse from the floor, hooking one finger under the strap. Then he approached her and held the purse out as if he wanted her to take it.

Her mouth fell open a bit.

"Yes," he said, "I know you have a firearm in your purse."

"I have a concealed carry license."

He gave her a tiny smile. "I don't mind that you have a pistol, Grace. Why do you think I'm offering it to you willingly?"

She looked at the purse, dangling from his grasp at her chest level. The purse swayed a little as he adjusted his grip. She lifted her hand, fingers outstretched to take hold of the strap. At the last second, she pulled her hand away.

"Why do you hesitate?" he asked, thrusting the purse closer to her. "This is an act of trust, Grace. Take the purse, and you will feel safer because you have your pistol. I'm trusting you not to shoot me although, of course, you will be quite able to do so if you wish."

Well, when he put it that way...

She nabbed the purse. Cradling it on her lap, the gun's hardness under her palms, she regarded Amador. "Thank you."

He gave a dismissive wave of his free hand. "As I told you yesterday, I don't believe you would shoot me. I may not know you well, but I can see that you aren't a murderer."

A lump hardened in her throat. She ducked her head to stare at her hands. A murderer. That's what she was, though Amador had no way of knowing it.

Withdrawing his hand from his pocket, Amador dropped to one knee in front of her. His gaze landed on her with a palpable weight that commanded her attention, and a shiver swept through her, lifting the hairs at the nape of her neck. She did not flinch or avert her eyes from his.

"I killed a man today," she said, her voice flat. "Six months ago, I shot and killed both Jackson Tennant and Xavier Waldron. This evening, I killed at least one other man, maybe more. So you see, I am a killer."

Amador's brows knit together. "I saw a dead man in the forest when I came for you. He had a gun and was likely the one who shot you." He shook his head. "You defended your life against men who would have done grievous injury to you."

"I know." She leaned back, though she didn't break eye contact. "I said I'm a killer, not a murderer. You shouldn't be so cocksure I won't shoot you if I feel the tiniest bit threatened."

"Of that, I have no doubt. But I mean you no harm." Amador lowered his left hand leisurely onto hers. His flesh scalded her skin. She hadn't realized how cold her hands were. He slipped his right hand into his pants pocket, hesitating there, and then pulled it out to rest it on top of her free hand. Almost in slow motion, he coiled his fingers around hers. All the while, his eyes tracked hers, and she discovered she couldn't divert her attention. Those dark eyes trapped her. When he began to trace circles on her palms with his fingertips, the touch triggered a warm tingling in her hands that spread, inch by inch, up her arms and into the rest of her body.

He raised one hand to brush his knuckles across her cheek. "You are no killer, Grace. Tennant and Waldron deserved to die, and they left you no choice but to take their lives in self-defense. I saw it through postcognition, remember? I know."

"Right. I forgot." She should've shaken his hands off, but her muscles had liquefied. Her voice came out dreamy too. What was wrong with her? "I appreciate the reassurance, but it's not necessary, Mr. Amador."

"Biel."

"Huh?"

"Please call me Biel." His fingers kept sketching circles on her palm. With his other hand, he cupped her cheek. "I am on your side, Grace. I would never abandon you."

Like David had. Although Amador refrained from saying the words, she knew what he meant.

Amador stroked her cheek with his fingertips. "If you will allow me, I would take care of you."

His caress made the tension in her unwind and scattered her thoughts. Was this man manipulating her psychically? This morning, she would've thought it impossible. Tonight, she'd lost her unerring faith in her firewall.

It should've been David comforting her. If he sensed her anguish, he would've come to check on her. The fact he hadn't pointed to one of three things—he couldn't feel her anymore, he was unable to come to her, or he didn't want to come to her. He had ordered her to go away and proclaimed she got in his way. The memory of his words, and the hardness in his voice, conjured a pain in her chest that made her wince and suck in a shallow breath. Her heart had calcified, cold and brittle and no longer capable of beating.

David had been terrified, though of what, she couldn't figure out. His callous actions, his harsh words, they stemmed from his fear. If only he'd talk to her...

Unlike David, Amador had no trouble expressing his feelings. He also hadn't dismissed her with all the tenderness of a cat throwing up a hairball.

Gabriel Amador was attractive. And attentive. And he rescued her when she needed it.

He ran his fingers down her cheek.

She cringed inside. However attractive and attentive he was, Amador harbored a secret agenda.

And she loved David. No one else tempted her.

She tensed her hands, preparing to yank them free of his.

Amador released her hands and rose. Towering over her, he combed his fingers through her hair. "Even if you cannot or will not trust me, I will help you in any way I can. That is my vow to you."

She nodded. "I appreciate that."

He turned and headed for the doorway.

"Thank you again," she said. It galled her to need his help, but she did. So she opted for a strategic concession. "I'm very grateful to you... Biel."

He froze mid-step, and for a couple of seconds, he neither moved nor spoke. Then he twisted around to face her and flashed the first genuine smile she'd witnessed on his lips. "No, Grace, thank you. Together, we can accomplish incredible things."

"I'm sure you're right."

"Come, you must be hungry." He gestured toward the door. "I will have Wickham prepare something for you."

He waited for her to stand and then headed out the door. She trailed after him, walking slower than usual. At least she wasn't limping. Amador bounded down the hallway with a light step. He maintained a discreet, but distinct, gap between them. The prisoner led to the execution.

No. He would not harm her.

Yet.

"How long was I asleep?" she asked.

"All night."

A modicum of relief filtered through her. When she'd peeked out the French doors at Wickham, she had caught sight of the morning sun halfway over the horizon and worried she'd slept for days. All night was bad, but better than days. She couldn't afford any lost time, not with David held captive and Tesler on her trail.

Amador veered right, into a dining room.

When he pulled out a chair for her, she eased into it. The table gleamed in the ever-brightening daylight filtering through the windows. She rested her hands on the wood. Cool. Slick. Dark.

Smiling, Amador seated himself opposite her. He folded his hands on the tabletop, interlocking his fingers. "I am so pleased to have you here, Grace."

Unease trickled through her. Befriending Amador might prove her best chance of survival, yet it burned her soul like a betrayal.

David.

Circumstances winnowed her choices down to bad and worse.

Amador sneaked a hand across the table, slipping it over hers. Warmth tingled through her hand and wrist. It seeped up her arm, throughout her body, and into every crevice of her soul. The urge to yank her hand away flared white-hot inside her. What the hell was happening to her? The wrongness of it screamed in her head, frantic yet indistinct, like a voice from another room. If he was doing something to her, influencing her psychically...

But how could he? Her psychic wall blocked everything. Even David.

She couldn't be sure of that.

Gotta play along. Find out what this creep knows. She resisted gritting her teeth, exhaled slowly to relax her muscles, and aimed a tentative smile at him.

And then the heat swallowed her whole.

"I'll get that breakfast for you," Amador said.

"Huh?" His words vibrated her eardrums, but their meaning failed to register. Quicksand sucked at her thoughts, hauling her downward into oblivion.

Amador patted her hand and ambled out of the room.

Her heart thudded. Cold sweat broke out on her forehead. Conscious but numb, immobilized and breathless, she wrestled for control of her own mind.

And realized she'd already lost.

———

THE GUARD PITCHED DAVID INTO THE CELL. HIS BODY HIT THE FLOOR with a dull thud, his chin smacking into the concrete. Pangs radiated through his jaw. The pain failed to register as more than a background ache, driven aside by the fire searing his veins. The fire ignited by the drugs.

David struggled to push up into a sitting position. His arms collapsed under him. He whumped back onto the floor and groaned. What the hell had Tesler injected into him? Not JT's formula, for sure. Every cell in his body burned and throbbed. His muscles sagged like wet rags clinging to his bones. And Christ, how his bones ached.

The stench of sweat and blood permeated his clothes, his hair, his skin. He rolled onto his side. His head spun, fast as a tornado. His gorge rose in his throat, but he gulped it back. No vomiting. No passing out. Signs of weakness would please Tesler and embolden him to switch to phase two. David knew all too well how Tesler's methods progressed. First, drugs. Second...

Physical pain.

He clenched his jaw until the whirling subsided. His head rested on the floor. His shoulder, slumped beneath him, forced his head to lie at an angle. Discomfort tugged at his neck muscles. He raised his head, grimacing from the effort, and surveyed the damage.

Sweat soaked the fabric under his arms. Dots of blood spattered his T-shirt. Whose blood? He palpated his scalp, neck, arms. No injuries. He lifted the collar of his shirt to peek inside it at his chest. No wounds there, either. He inhaled, and the metallic scent of blood filled his nostrils. With one finger, he explored his nose. Dried blood caked around his nostrils. What kind of drug caused bleeding from the nose?

Maybe it hadn't been the drugs. He'd fought damn hard to break through the electromagnetic barrier blocking him from contacting Grace. His mind bounced off it with enough force to wrench his physical body. The power of the EM blockade might've overtaxed his brain, triggering a nosebleed. He'd seen similar things happen to other psychics. Never before had he experienced this kind of side effect.

If anyone could breach the barrier, it would be Grace.

Her face hovered before his mind's eye. Her auburn hair glowing in the sunlight. Her hazel eyes sparkling. A glorious smile enlivening her features. If Tesler got his hands on her, the tactics he'd used on David, Sean, and Nkosi would pale compared to his plans for Grace. Tesler's voice reverberated in David's head.

Do you know what the greatest prize of all is? The pretty pink brain of your darling girl.

David ground his teeth. The grating noise vibrated through his skull. Tension rippled through his body, tightening muscles that screamed in protest, and he choked back a gasp. *Please stay away, Grace.*

Trouble was, he knew her better than that. She would come for him. She would risk her own life to rescue him. Her stubborn determination, her willingness to endanger herself for others, those were two of the countless reasons he loved her.

But dammit, he should've been the one rescuing her. What kind of man couldn't manage to safeguard his most precious treasure, the woman he loved? Somewhere between his imprisonment at the Mojave Desert facility and his obsession with hunting down Tesler, he'd lost sight of what mattered most.

Grace.

Was it too late to rectify his mistakes? Could she ever forgive him? Only one way to find out. He must escape from this place. He needed to free Nkosi, Sean, and any other hostages. And then he must track down Grace before she barreled into this facility to find him. He would save her this time—from her own reckless, if well-intentioned, actions.

God, he loved her. More than anything in this world or the next. If he must make the ultimate sacrifice for her, he'd do it without hesitation. He would die for her.

The door burst inward, banging into the wall.

David thrust himself up off the floor. Seated there, he glowered at the man standing in the doorway.

"Nap time is over," Tesler said. "Time to play twenty thousand questions. I believe you remember the consequences for refusing to answer."

"Torture me all you want. I won't tell you a damn thing."

Tesler sniggered. "You don't have to." He hopped closer, bending over to meet David's gaze. "I'd venture to guess that Sean knows everything you do, or close enough to everything. I'll torture *you* until *he* cracks."

The scientist flicked his wrist. Two guards tromped into the room, seized David's arms, and dragged him out of the cell. As they rounded a corner, heading down a different corridor than before, David racked his brain to formulate a plan. No way to RV the facility to plot out an escape route. He'd have to rely on his mundane senses and his intellect. His limbs refused to acknowledge his commands, instead hanging limp.

Half dragging, half carrying him, the guards tossed David through an open doorway into a room much like the previous one where Tesler had administered the drugs. But this room contained three chairs. Sean and Nkosi sat strapped into two of the chairs. The middle one stood empty. Waiting. For David.

Two men in white lab coats hauled David into the chair. Yellen and Evans, the men he'd watched when he RV'd the facility, secured the straps around his wrists, ankles, and forehead. Evans buckled the chest restraint.

A long table nestled against one wall held devices of torture. Scalpels. Things with serrated edges and sharp pincers. A wooden paddle with holes in it. And that damn baseball bat.

Yellen scuffled toward the doorway. "Must I watch this, Dr. Tesler?"

"If you can't stomach it, then wait in the corridor."

Yellen rushed outside.

Tesler strolled into the room. He picked up the bat, thumping it on his palm.

Sean whimpered.

David glanced at him sideways. Tears streamed from the boy's puffy, red eyes. His face was pale and gaunt. On the other side of David, Nkosi sat with chin lifted, jaw set, eyes clear and fixed on Tesler. A gash cut a red line across his cheek, and a clump of bruises purpled his neck.

David glared at Tesler, willing the man to burst into flames. Even if his psychic faculties had been at peak levels, he'd never possessed the power of pyrokinesis. Too bad. The bastard deserved to burn, if not in hell, then here on earth.

Tesler raised the bat. His eyes focused on David, but he spoke to Sean. "Tell me, son, where is Grace Powell?"

Sean sniffled. His voice emerged as a trembling whisper. "No."

"Then you leave me no choice."

Tesler swung the bat at David.

Chapter Thirteen

Grace wolfed down the last bite of her breakfast. Omelet, toast, and sausages, with orange juice on the side. No point in starving herself. She'd need all the strength she could muster to accomplish her goals, which included getting the hell out of this house ASAP. That moment of possibility wouldn't arrive until she had milked Amador for everything she could—information, tricks of the ESP trade, and anything else she could think of.

When Wickham had brought the food, she suffered a bout of panic. What if her breakfast was poisoned? Or drugged? But then she flashed back to her reaction when Amador touched her, and she knew. He required no drugs or poison to control her. Regardless of whether she'd finally toppled over to the dark side, her mental state provided him with all the leverage he needed, without chemical assistance.

Unless he'd drugged her while she was unconscious.

She had no clue what was going on anymore. With herself. With David. With any of this. She no longer enjoyed the luxury of choosing her allies. Amador had selected her, and Tesler's men drove her into Amador's corner.

Her hunger sated, she leaned back and endeavored to seem relaxed, despite the tension crackling inside her. Amador lounged in a chair on the opposite side of the wooden table. He had also eaten, though food remnants littered his plate. Her plate was empty. Eggs had never tasted so good before.

Amador pushed his chair back and stood. "Please excuse me. I must attend to some business. It won't take long, though, and I believe we should talk afterward."

"Okay." *Whatever.* She had no plans to flee yet since she had nowhere to go.

"Wait here for me." He ambled out of the room.

The door lock engaged with a click.

Guest or prisoner? Question answered.

Well, at least he hadn't laid his hands on her again. Yet.

A shiver skittered down her spine. Amador's skin on hers had infected her with an eerie warmth and a disturbing slackness. The first time she met Amador, he had kissed her hand, and she felt nothing. This morning, similar contact knocked her off balance and nearly thrust her into a tailspin. Worst of all, the one person she could've talked to about this was incommunicado.

She missed David, so badly.

Was he still alive? Their connection buzzed between them, albeit with far less strength than usual. She tugged on the link. Nothing. No reciprocal pull from his end.

Leaning her head back against the chair, she closed her eyes and tugged harder. Zippo. No tautening of the link. No glowy warmth from their constant, low-grade connection. No sense of his physical or mental state, good or bad. Their bond persisted, but David seemed unable or unwilling to tap into it. Even if he'd stopped caring about her, which she'd believe on the day the sky turned pink, he would've permitted their link to pulse back to her a signal of his status. Injured, safe. Alive, dead.

The connection fed her zilch. This was bad. Very bad.

A chill sparked in her gut, blossoming outward into her entire body. The hairs on her arms and neck stiffened. Goosebumps pebbled her skin. A bitter taste oozed over her tongue, the sourness of bile rising in her throat. A tugging, wrenching pressure tore through her gut. Not physical pain. It originated from her soul.

David, what have we done to each other?

She needed to ascertain why they'd lost contact. She thought of one reason, but pushed it away, unwilling to let it linger in her mind. It couldn't be. He wasn't—

No. His death would've wrenched her inside out. He was alive, somewhere.

Her hands clenched the chair's arms. She worked on releasing the tension in her body and mind with slow, deep breaths. It took far longer than she would've liked, but at last, numbness drove out the world around her. She barreled into the crossroads and scanned the stars around her. Not a single star reacted to her presence.

An icy chill, transmitted throughout her body, mutated into a subzero shiver.

He wasn't dead. She refused to believe it. Until she witnessed his body, lifeless and bloody, she would never believe it.

Come on, David, show me the way.

An echo of power rippled through the crossroads to caress her mind. She latched onto the intimate feel of the familiar energy, scaling up it inch by inch.

A force hurled her away.

She plummeted back into her body. Unable to slow the descent, she hit so hard her body convulsed. Her jaw clamped tight, and pains shot through her head.

A hand enveloped hers. A finger massaged her palm, tracing ever-widening circles in her flesh. Warmth infected her skin, and then her muscles. The tingling swelled and expanded through her body. Her mind switched into a new mode, a cross between total relaxation and pure alertness.

Her eyelids flew open. Slumped in the chair, she jerked upright. Her heart pounded. She gaped at the man kneeling before her.

Gabriel Amador caught her gaze with a serene expression. His finger drew circles on her palm, sending out pulses of heat that intensified the tingling in her body and melted her brain. She couldn't hold on to a thought. Couldn't shake the connection unfurling between them, a tether that cinched tighter each second. This was wrong. The tether slithered deeper into her, alien and cold.

The impulse to jerk free of him flared inside her, but her muscles ignored her commands. Her voice came out breathless. "What are you doing to me?"

"Helping you to relax."

Run. This instant. Go, run, get away.

Go where? Her inner voice offered no answer. She was trapped. The realization whipped her out of the fog, into the harshness of her new reality. Trapped.

No, goddammit. She'd escape if she had to claw her way through the house's foundation to do it—after she mined Amador for what she needed.

Gritting her teeth while feigning nonchalance demanded a serious effort. Either her efforts paid off, or Amador simply didn't care she was deceiving him. "Are you relaxing me by psychic means?"

His lips tightened into a frown. "No, Grace. I am not employing any psychic powers. This is a purely mundane method." He reached for her hand. When she clasped it to her belly, he sighed. "No one can breach your psychic barrier. Yes?"

She shrugged. "As far as I know."

Amador's frown morphed into a knowing smile.

The urge to gnaw on her lip itched inside her. She resisted. Although she was far from reassured, letting Amador glimpse her unease struck her as an incredibly dumb idea. *Pet the dragon, don't pinch his scales.* "You're right. I'm sorry."

He rubbed his palm over the back of her hand.

She bit the inside of her cheek, an action hidden from his view. "I'm ready. For whatever ideas you have about my powers."

"Excellent." He released her hand. "My first suggestion may sound extreme, but please consider it carefully before refusing."

Nothing good ever followed a statement like that. But she told him, "I will."

"I would like to administer a serum."

Panic surged through her, jolting her pulse into overdrive. Her knuckles ached from gripping the chair's arms.

Amador laid a hand on her arm. "Please, don't be afraid. It's a drug my company has been working on. The serum is designed to foster a sense of calm and relaxation that will, I hope, enhance a person's psychic abilities."

A hard shiver rushed through her. "Is this JT's formula?"

He shook his head. "I wouldn't do that to you. His formula was barbaric and inhumane. My company strives for safe, gentle formulations."

"Your company? I thought you ran a venture capital thing."

"I do. Through a shell company I own other interests, including a pharmaceutical research firm."

He sounded reasonable. Even lunatics could pull that off sometimes.

At least the heat in her body had dissipated. She felt almost normal again.

Frowning, she eyed Amador. "Is this what you meant when you said you could help me with my powers? That you'd give me drugs?"

"No. I thought it couldn't hurt, though."

As much as she loathed admitting it, she needed help. *His* help. If he could do what he claimed. Her firewall blocked his psychic intrusions, but if he could teach her a few tricks then maybe, just maybe, she'd shed the migraines. For good.

Her feet wiggled, urging her to escape this place.

Rebelling against every fiber of her being, she said, "If you have some other, non-pharmaceutical way to help me use my powers without getting horribly sick from it, then I'm listening."

He opened his mouth to speak.

"No drugs," she said. "That's my rule, and it is nonnegotiable."

"I understand. We'll employ other means. What psychic task may I assist you with first?"

He uttered the phrase in a tone reminiscent of a customer-service guy answering a phone call.

She brushed aside the mild humor of that. "I need to find David. Fast."

Amador nodded. "Let's get started."

He dragged a chair closer to her.

She prayed he could help her because if he couldn't... No. David was alive, and she would find him.

"Close your eyes," Amador said. He clasped her hand in his. As the warmth infiltrated her body, spiraling her into oblivion, he told her, "Free your mind from thoughts. Hear only my voice. Feel my touch. Let it anchor you on your flight into the crossroads. Do not try. Simply be."

Thoughts fled. The weight of her own body, the firmness of the chair beneath her, the scent of leather, the ticking of a clock, everything drifted away from her until she floated in a void, numb and disconnected. Two things penetrated the emptiness.

Amador's skin pressed to hers. And his voice, deep and soft.

"Are you there?" he asked.

"Not yet." Her voice murmured from a distant galaxy.

His skin stroked hers.

She soared, like a cloud in the wind, up through the dark tunnel. No pressure. No struggle. She glided out into the crossroads.

"Yes," Amador said. "You are there, aren't you? Don't think. Don't fight. Let your mind do your will of its own volition."

A vague thought reared its head. His instructions made no sense. Her mind *was* her will. To effect her will, she must think.

"No," he murmured. "You are trying to implement your desires, aren't you? Stop. Empty your mind. *Feel* what you wish."

His hand. Warm. Smooth. Real. She relaxed into his touch, letting her mind go vacant. She floated there, among the glittering stars, overcome by a seductive sense of belonging. This place knew her. It hungered for her. And she for it. The energy of the crossroads, of its hidden reaches, tantalized her with the promise of boundless power.

"That's right," Amador said in a throaty whisper. "You understand now."

A star beckoned her. A connection. A human mind.

David.

Grace rocketed toward the light, through it, beyond it. Wild energy excited her psychic senses. She drank it in, her mind swimming, as the thirst for more burned inside her.

The tunnel expelled her into a gray fog, whirling her downward.

She smashed headfirst into a granite wall.

Agony stripped her nerves raw. Lightning gored her astral body. Psychic energy spewed out of her, sucked her dry, and cast her aside. She smacked into the wall.

And screamed.

CHAPTER FOURTEEN

THE REAL WORLD BESIEGED HER AT ONCE, A LANDSLIDE OF INPUT THAT overwhelmed her senses and contorted her body. She bellowed, hugged her knees to her chest, and buried her face against her thighs. Wheezing, she rocked in the chair.

How would she track down David without their link?

I lost him.

Not yet she hadn't.

A hand caressed her hair. For a second, she imagined it was David. Then reality collided with her fantasy, shattering the illusion. She shook free of Amador's hand and lifted her head just far enough to peek at him over her knees. Tears blurred her vision, though they no longer streamed down her cheeks. She swiped at her eyes, sniffling.

Amador touched his fingertips to her cheek, then pulled them away. Concern tightened his features, and his lips parted in an unformed question.

"I'm fine," she said, though she felt nothing close to fine. Her eyes burned. White lights danced in her vision. Sharp pains crackled in her head, slowly coalescing into a throb that lurched her stomach. A migraine. *Dammit.* She could not afford this, not with David a hostage somewhere in Montana. If he was in Montana. She had no clue, really. Tesler might've transferred him elsewhere. Despite the wild uncertainty about everything else, she could not deny one fact. Tesler would pummel David until he cracked and exposed both their secrets.

He'll die first. She might've become an outsider in David's life, but she understood one basic truth about him. He was noble.

Amador leaned closer, his face pinched, as if he were in pain too. "What happened? Are you all right? Please tell me what I can do."

Nothing, she almost said. But the truth was, he could do something for her. As much as she despised asking him, she must. Desperation was a snarling bitch. "I need to find David before Tesler kills him." She slid her feet onto the floor and sat up. Muscles in her neck stretched. Hot pain spiked up her neck into the base of her skull, and she winced, swallowing a gasp. "The psychic method of tracking him down did not work. I need another way. Do you have any suggestions?"

The tension smoothed out of Amador. He hopped up and gave a quick nod. "I may have a way. If you will be all right by yourself, I'll see what I can do."

"I'll survive." She'd lived alone for so long, even after David barged back into her life. What did a few more minutes matter? Besides, she needed a break. His voice stabbed into her brain, each word a red-hot, acid-tipped needle. The sound of her own breathing hurt her ears.

"Can you provide any clues as to David's whereabouts?" Amador asked.

"Montana. That's it, I'm sorry."

"It will be enough." He marched to the door, then hesitated on the threshold. "You may not believe this, but I wish no harm to David. And I will do everything in my power to locate him."

She didn't know whether to believe him or not. "I appreciate that."

He studied her over his shoulder, lips scrunched in concentration. "If your goal is to eliminate your migraines, then you must uncover the reason for them. I suspect you are hindering your powers, unconsciously, for some reason. Root out the reason, and you will free yourself—and your mind."

"You may be right."

"Try to rest. And I will search for David."

She forced her lips to form a weak smile. "Thank you, Biel."

He flashed her a quick, tight smile. And then he left.

The door clicked shut.

Free her powers. Free herself. Sounded great, but how the hell was she supposed to do it?

Root out the reason. Amador had a point. Although he knew nothing of her motivations, he sensed she throttled back her abilities. Until he spoke the words, she'd pretended not to realize the truth. She must acknowledge her fears, and sort them out.

To save David. To save herself.

At full power, with no migraines to saddle her, she might just save the whole damn world.

She buried her face in her hands. Pangs ricocheted in her head as her gut roiled with nausea. Too weak to stand, she curled up in the chair, rested her head on her knees, and shut her eyes.

Some savior she was.

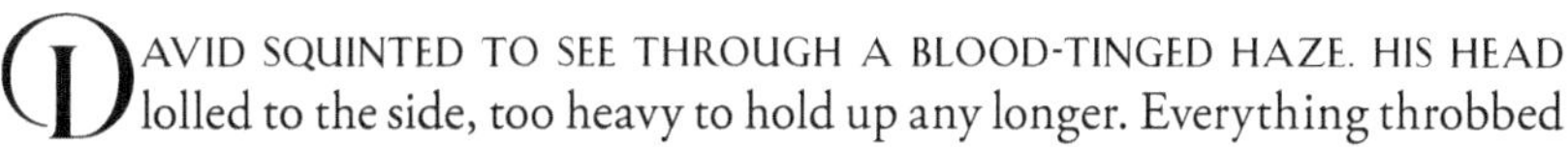

D AVID SQUINTED TO SEE THROUGH A BLOOD-TINGED HAZE. HIS HEAD lolled to the side, too heavy to hold up any longer. Everything throbbed or burned, from his scalp down to his toes. Tesler stood before him, legs spread in a confident stance, tapping the baseball bat on his palm.

"Shall we go again?" Tesler asked. "Or is one of you ready to talk?"

Spitting out blood, David hoisted his head upright. Pain lanced up his neck straight into his skull. He gritted his teeth. "Nobody wants to talk to you, Tesler. Your conversation skills leave something to be desired."

The scientist harrumphed. "We'll see how you feel when I start in on Sean."

David wanted to look at Sean, mostly to assure himself, but feared his beaten and bloodied appearance would terrify the boy more than Tesler had already. Sean was okay. In the past six months, he toughened up more than any boy his age should have to, but everyone had their limits.

At least no physical harm had come to Sean—yet. David had served himself up as Tesler's punching bag. Or batting practice. The bastard packed a mean swing.

Unease trickled into him, the sensation strange and… external. He focused on the discomfort, struggling to name it. To trace its source. The unease burgeoned inside him, like a leaky balloon filled with ice-cold water, slowly disgorging its contents into him. The chill sharpened and mushroomed out. Fear knifed into his heart.

Grace.

The sensation crumbled away as quickly as it had bloomed. His connection to Grace dwindled back to a whisper, one he could discern only if he concentrated all his psychic energy on the task. Had she broken through the EM screen for a second? *No, Grace, don't.* Could she even hear him? Or feel him? Conflicting desires warred within him. The need to sense her, to feel her, to know she was all right. And the lightning-bright fear that she would reach out to him. Connect with him. Share his experience.

Suffer his torture.

Tesler pointed the bat toward Nkosi. "Perhaps you care more for your new friend." He strode one step closer to Nkosi, raised the bat, and sneered. "Well, David? Shall we try this one on for size?"

David's nails rasped on the metal as he gripped the arms of his chair. A lacework of pain burst out from his knuckles to spread into his wrists. He choked down a gasp, denying the agony its outlet. Tesler would never see him grimace or hear him cry out. Never.

"No?" The scientist ambled past David, to Sean. He spun on his heels, facing the boy. Sean muffled a whimper. Tesler waggled the bat in the boy's face. "Will you tell me now, son?" He glanced at David, then back to Sean. "Or must I beat you to hurt your savior?"

"If you need to feel like a man," David hissed, "then make your statement on me. I'm the one you despise. I'm the one who ruined the plans you and JT cooked up together."

Tesler chuckled, his eyes gleaming with pleasure. "It was your darling girl who laid waste to those plans, not you."

He stepped in front of David, straddling the chair, and leaned forward to grind David's left wrist beneath his hand. Agony ripped through David's hand and arm, but he quashed it with gritted teeth.

Tesler smirked. "You are a worthless specimen undeserving of being called a man. Your lover had to rescue you how many times? Perhaps she only stays with you out of pity."

The truth in his words stung like a smack to the face. David fought not to wince. Grace had saved him. Repeatedly. He wasn't much of a man. He couldn't argue with Tesler on that point.

Did Grace pity him?

Of course not. She loved him. Her passion and affection nourished him during his worst moments. And yet, a sliver of doubt lodged itself in his psyche. Tesler had jammed the sliver in there. He knew this. But he could not silence the voice whispering into his brain.

How could she love you when you can't even protect her?

If he couldn't shield her from Tesler, then what good was he? Escape no longer seemed like a viable option. As long as he lived, he posed a threat to Grace. Tesler had been right about that too. He was leverage.

Protecting Grace meant saving her from her misplaced, pigheaded loyalty to him. He had one choice left. If he died, she wouldn't need to search for him.

At last, he had a plan. Stop Tesler. Save Sean and Nkosi.

Sacrifice himself for Grace.

Tesler poised the bat for a swing, zeroing in on Sean.

He froze. His brow furrowed, and his mouth warped into an expression of... Was that anguish?

Stunned, David could only stare.

Tesler let out a frustrated growl. He tossed the bat aside. It clattered on the concrete, spun across the room, and bumped into the wall.

This madman never held back his torture. And yet, he just had.

With a flick of his wrist, Tesler summoned a guard to his side. He snatched the semiautomatic handgun from the holster on the guard's hip. A snarled command sent the guard scuttling back to the doorway.

Tesler leveled the gun at David. "Last chance. Where is Grace Powell?"

David raised his chin. "Go to hell."

"No," Tesler said, his expression turning to mock gravity. "I won't be the one to make that journey tonight."

A gunshot cracked through the room.

CHAPTER FIFTEEN

GRACE TWISTED THE KNOB, SURPRISED WHEN IT ROTATED IN HER hand. Amador had left the door unlocked this time. *Hmm.* Forgetfulness, or purpose?

She eased the door open a couple of inches, peering into the empty hallway. Somewhere in another room, a grandfather clock chimed. A cool draft filtered through the opening, tickling her bare arms. She must go out there. Sitting in the dining room, alone, with the door shut was triggering her latent claustrophobia. A squirmy itch in her brain compelled her to action.

Maybe the closed door had nothing to do with it. She might feel trapped because, well, she was. Tesler's men had cornered her. She escaped only because she wielded her powers, and because Amador rode to her rescue.

He was no knight.

Now David she could envision galloping up on a white horse, armor glistening in the sun, those blue eyes gleaming with the fire of purpose. Even in a T-shirt and jeans, he was sexy as hell. Dressed up like a knight, he'd sweep her off her feet literally and carry her away on his steed.

Oh brother. She ought to be formulating a plan to save David, not fantasizing about playing dress-up with him.

Pulling the door wide, she tromped out into the hallway. Her head swung left and right as she debated the choices. *Pick one, for crying out loud.*

She swerved right, heading deeper into the house, away from the front door. The hallway housed six doors, three on each side, spaced at staggered intervals. Straight ahead, the corridor dead-ended at a blank wall. She veered toward the first door on the left, tried the knob, and found it locked. Back and forth she moved, testing each door. Left. Right. Left. A bizarre urge to goose-step cropped up in her brain, but she shook it off. All the doors were locked, except the one leading into Amador's office. She'd already seen that room, though. Since his computer no longer sat on the desktop, the office held nothing else of interest to her. She ducked inside just long enough to try the file cabinet drawers.

Locked, of course.

At the end of the hall, she hesitated. To her right, a short corridor led into the kitchen. She saw, through the open doorway, a refrigerator and gas range. To her left, a stairway descended into darkness.

A lot of houses had basements, but she had to wonder what a man like Amador did with his subterranean space. A wine cellar, maybe. Or a place to hide things he wanted no one else to see.

Grace tiptoed to the stairs. Half a dozen steps penetrated the shadows congregating at the base of the stairway. There, half masked by the gloom, stood a windowless metal door. She gulped against the tightening in her throat. Her breaths came shallow and fast. Why should a door frighten her? It wasn't the door itself. Her psychic senses crackled with the cold awareness of danger.

You've got to see what's in there.

She sidled down one step. Held her breath. Listened. Sidled down another step.

Thump.

The noise originated on the other side of the door.

A shiver skittered down her spine. Her attention telescoped down until her vision encompassed one object—the door.

She halted at the base of the stairs. Tilting her head, she opened her mouth a little, focusing on sounds. The hiss of the AC. The beating of her heart. The distant rumble of an airliner passing by overhead. And something else. Something familiar, yet alien. Muffled by the door.

She inched closer, settling her ear against the chilled metal.

Whimpering. She heard an animal whimpering, inside the room beyond the door. The pitiful sound escalated in volume, crescendoing with a sharp cry.

Every hair on her body stiffened.

Not an animal whimpering. A human being.

One instinct urged her to flee. Another warned her she'd better uncover the truth before it lashed out of the shadows to sink its teeth into her neck. Whatever Amador concealed in the basement, it involved a human being in pain.

She wrapped her hand around the doorknob and, with deliberate slowness, twisted. The knob refused to budge.

Behind the door, footfalls clapped on a hard floor.

Her heart thudded. She spun around and clambered up the steps. Her foot slipped. She flailed for a handhold, and her palms met slick, painted walls, sliding down the surface. Her toe, balanced on the edge of the step, flipped out from under her. An "ow" burst from her lips as her chin smacked into the concrete step. Agony shot through her jaw. White lights exploded in her vision.

The door lock chunked. The knob swiveled. The latch clicked. And the door swung wide open.

Prone on the steps, she twisted to face her enemy. Pain sparked in her neck. Wincing, panting, she gaped at the figure looming over her.

Gabriel Amador frowned. "What do you think you are doing, Grace?"

"Um…" Questions fired up in her mind, but the dark tension rippling through Amador warned her not to ask what she really wanted to know. "You said I could look around the house. I tripped on the stairs."

"No." He shook his head, his expression regretful. "You heard the girl's pain. You likely sensed it too. I should've guessed you would." He knelt before her, laying a hand on her shoulder. "But I wish you weren't quite so curious, or so determined. I had hoped to keep this away from you."

Terror ripped through her like hot lava, searing her down to her core. Her voice constricted to a hoarse whisper. "Keep what away from me?"

He stepped aside, revealing the doorway and what lay beyond.

Inside the dark, windowless room, a single overhead bulb drove a wedge of brilliant white light down on a teenage girl huddled on a wooden chair. Ropes bound her ankles. Her hands were behind the chair, suggesting ropes secured her arms too. A red liquid dribbled down her face from her scalp, dripping onto her white tank top.

It was blood.

The girl lolled her head to the side and back. The light streaked across her face where a purple bruise surrounded her swollen eye. The good eye, dark and bloodshot, fixed on Grace. A sob erupted from the girl.

Grace's gut clenched. *My savior is a psychopath.*

She couldn't move. Her thoughts reeled and bounced off each other, like pinballs in a machine. The world tilted and rocked. The acrid taste of bile infiltrated her mouth as she choked back her gorge.

Someone had to stop this man.

Why me? her inner voice asked.

"Please," the raven-haired girl implored. "Please help me."

The pain radiating from the girl's tone stung Grace. She took a shaky breath.

Why me? Because nobody's riding to the rescue this time. She heaved herself off the stairs, onto her feet. Squaring her shoulders, she gritted her teeth. *It's me or no one.*

The terror ended right here, right now. Time to fight, with every ounce of courage and psychic power inside her. For the girl. For David. For everyone.

She whirled on Amador. "Let her go."

"I'm afraid I can't. If you'll allow me to explain—"

With a burst of psychic energy, Grace flung him backward into the wall.

He hit with a thud and a crack. His body slid down the wall, his knees buckling. Slumped on the floor, he shook his head. "I'm sorry, Grace."

She bolted into the room, straight to the girl. Fingers trembling, she wrestled with the knots binding the girl's feet.

"Wickham," Amador shouted, "push the button."

She hesitated in the middle of her struggle.

Inside the walls, a mechanism buzzed.

She spun around. From his position inches outside the threshold, Amador blocked the doorway with his body.

The buzzing echoed in the concrete room, hushed but menacing, like a horde of wasps holed up in the walls.

Grace balled up her power and slung it at Amador.

The energy ricocheted back to her, slugging her in the chest. She toppled over backward. Her skull whacked into the floor. Lightning bolts slashed in her vision as roiling pain hauled her toward an ever-darkening abyss.

Amador towered over her, his expression something like sorrow. "I didn't want to do this, Grace, but you've left me no choice."

She clawed her way out of the abyss, back into consciousness. Her head throbbed, her entire body ached, and the room seemed poised on the head of a spinning top.

Crouching beside her, Amador jabbed a sharp object into her neck. His voice murmured into her ear. "I need you, Grace. I've come too far to turn back, and my plans will fail without your power. It pains me to say this, but I cannot let you go." He pressed his lips to her forehead. "Rest. I will explain all of this when you wake."

She tumbled down and down, into the abyss of unconsciousness.

———

DAVID STRAINED TO OPEN HIS EYES. HIS EARS HAD STOPPED RINGing, and the muffling effect of the gunshot had subsided. His body had grown strangely numb. A bad sign.

His eyelids parted no more than a sliver. He peeked out through a bleary haze.

Tesler stood ramrod straight, hands balled into fists, shoulders hunched. Rage ignited redness in his face. The gun, smoking faintly, wobbled in his fist. He dropped his hand to his side.

David pried his lids further apart. Moving only his eyes, he surveyed the damage. No gunshot wound. Not on his body. He flinched. Not on *his* body.

He rolled his eyes to the side, catching a glimpse of Sean. The boy's lower lip quivered, but he appeared unharmed. David glanced in the other direction, toward Nkosi. A red stain had blossomed on his shoulder, soaking through his shirt.

Nkosi managed a tight, pained smile. "I will survive. Believe me, I've had far worse injuries." He glanced at Tesler, and his lip curled. "There will be retribution for this."

David tried to lift his head, but it felt as heavy as an iron bowling ball. His arms and legs seemed glued to the chair. His eyelids drooped, and he longed to let them drift closed, easing him into a deep slumber.

No, dammit, don't give in.

He breathed in and out slowly. A little of the fog cleared, though traces of it lurked around the edges, ready to swallow him.

Tesler stomped his foot. The concussion reverberated through the concrete room.

Nkosi flinched. Sean gasped.

"Wake up," Tesler said. "I'm through playing games with the three of you. Someone will tell me how to find Grace or—" He trained the gun on Sean's head. "—I pull the trigger. You have until the count of ten." He curled his finger around the trigger. "One, two—"

David floundered for a plan. His notion of escaping had sounded good, but he'd failed to come up with a viable, concrete scheme to realize his goal. His psychic energy was drained. Worse, he was disconnected and fuzzy-headed, numb and sleepy. He recognized the danger of giving in to the exhaustion but resisting got harder and harder every second.

Tesler counted down. "Four, five, six—"

Nkosi muttered words in another language. Maybe he was praying.

Sean had ceased trembling. He stared straight ahead without expression.

David drew in one more deep breath, and then he released the last thread of hope. "I'm sorry. I thought we could beat this, but we can't. Whatever happens, we must never give in to Tesler. Never."

Nkosi nodded. "Never."

When Sean spoke, his voice was stronger than his demeanor. "Never."

Tesler swung the gun to his right and fired.

Nkosi slumped. Blood oozed from a wound on his chest, right over his heart. The life disappeared from his eyes.

The EM field constrained David to this room, so he couldn't access the crossroads. Despite that, he'd managed to separate from his body when he tried to contact Grace—and rammed into the EM barrier. But still, he had used his powers in a small way. Any bit was better than nothing.

Targeting his gun on Sean, Tesler locked gazes with David. "One down, two to go. Whether you tell me what I want to know or not, I will hunt down your beloved. And when I find her..." He jerked the gun as if he'd fired a shot. "Bang. She will die. Her brain is all I need, after all."

I'll rip your heart out, you bastard. Anger and grief blasted through David, sharp and hot and electric, fueling his powers, re-energizing his body. Adrenaline heightened his normal senses and kick-started his thoughts. The boost wouldn't last, he knew. The fury amping up his energy, both physical and psychic, might grant him one last attempt.

Save Sean.

He pummeled Tesler with a telekinetic blast that flung him through the air backward. The scientist bounced off the wall, rolling across the floor. The gun skidded toward Sean's chair.

The EM field zapped into David. Pain coruscated through his head, but he focused all his residual energy on one final task.

Sean's restraints popped open.

The boy's eyes bulged. He whipped his head toward David.

"Go," David said, his voice hushed and raspy.

The boy leaped up, snatching the gun from the floor.

Drained, in every way possible, David let his head fall back onto the chair.

The guard threw a wide-eyed glance at David, then at Sean. The man bolted out the door. His footsteps beat out a frantic rhythm as he fled down the corridor.

Crumpled on the floor, Tesler moaned.

Sean hesitated in the doorway. Gnawing his lip, he cast a questioning look at David. "I can't leave you."

"Yes, you can." Mustering his last reserve of strength, David infused his next words with the finality they demanded. "I'm a lost cause, Sean. Grace is the only one who can stop this nightmare. Find her. *Run.*"

Sean ran.

Tesler pushed up onto all fours. Glasses askew, he puffed out an angry breath.

David relinquished his hold on... everything. As he sank ever deeper into nothingness, Tesler spewed a parting shot.

"You are a pitiful failure. Your darling girl will suffer unspeakable pain for days until the moment I finally terminate her miserable life."

Goodbye, Grace. Please forgive me.

Chapter Sixteen

Grace perched on the edge of the cot, her feet planted on the concrete floor of the basement room. Since waking up several minutes ago, she'd sat here immobile, her thoughts muddled by the sedative hangover. How long had she been unconscious? What had Amador done to her during that time?

Where was the dark-haired girl?

The wooden chair was gone, the girl too. Besides Grace and the cot, nothing else occupied the room. The overhead light sliced a circle out of the darkness. The white glow petered out before reaching her toes. Her cot, wedged into the corner of the room, creaked when she adjusted her position.

Her gaze was drawn to the center of the lighted circle. There, a dark stain had spread across the floor.

The heavy scent of blood permeated the room.

Had Amador killed the girl? Grace shuddered. She'd been a fool to come here alone, hunted by Tesler's goons. Amador could easily hand her over to the mad scientist.

Unless she agreed to whatever plans he had in mind for her.

His words replayed in her mind, searing her soul. *I need you,* he'd said, *I've come too far to turn back, and my plans will fail without your power.* Of course. Like every other nutjob out there, he coveted her psychic talents. His offer to aid her was a trick, to gain her trust. She should've seen this coming, should've steered clear of Amador. Instead, she let him guide her metaphysical endeavors, took his advice about her powers, and… believed him when he urged her to stop being afraid. His assistance had been a ruse, and she fell for it out of a reckless compulsion to liberate her mind from the shackles of amnesia and post-traveling migraines. She was as obsessed with her own quest as David was with his.

She should've listened to him.

The door pivoted inward.

Amador traipsed straight to her, carrying a tray of food. He deposited the tray at her feet. Crouching before her, he laid a hand on her knee. "How do you feel?"

His expression revealed nothing. His hand warmed her skin through her jeans when he squeezed a little, his mouth crooking into a ghost of a smile.

She resisted the impulse to slug him.

"I'm fine," she said. "Where's the girl?"

"Gone."

Her gorge surged up into her throat. She clutched the cot's edge.

Amador huffed out a breath, and his face scrunched with annoyance. "The girl is not dead. She needed a break, so I transferred her to a room where she may sleep for a time. I have no desire to kill her."

She grunted.

He shook his head. "I am not your enemy, Grace."

Words tumbled out of her mouth, despite her efforts to contain them. "Great, you won't kill her. But torture is acceptable? And how about drugging me? That's okay too, right? I thought you were sincere about wanting to stop Tesler, but you're just as bad as he is."

His head drooped. He lunged both hands up to clasp them at the base of his neck as he puffed out sharp breaths and rocked on his toes.

She reached out to touch his shoulder, then yanked her hand away. Why the hell should she want to comfort him?

An ache started in her forehead, this time from annoyance and drugs, rather than power usage. She stuffed her hands under her thighs. "What have you done to me?"

He lifted his head a smidgen, enough to meet her gaze. "You were terribly upset. I sedated you for your protection."

"Uh-huh." Arguing the validity of his claim seemed irrelevant right now. "I meant before that. Every time you…" She bit her lip. Saying too much afforded him an advantage, but she must know the answer. *Risk everything to save the world, right?* "Every time you touch me, I get confused and I feel weirdly limp. I don't feel like myself, and it's freaking me out."

He studied her for so long she wondered if time had skidded to a halt. Finally, he planted his hands on her knees and said, "You are correct. I administered an experimental serum designed to encourage compliance. I hoped it would relax you and help you overcome the fear of your own powers."

"How did you give it to me? In the food?"

Grimacing, he turned one hand over. "The serum works best when absorbed through the skin." He dived his hand into his pocket and brought out a small glass vial, holding it between his thumb and forefinger. "I place a small amount of this on my fingers, then I… touch you."

He tipped the vial, and the pale-yellow liquid sloshed inside it.

"If you had it on your skin," she said, "how come it didn't affect you?"

Amador replaced the vial in his pocket. "I gave myself a counteracting agent. It does not last long, but I didn't need much time." He returned his hand to her knee. "I regret the serum was necessary."

"I said no drugs."

"After I'd given you the serum."

"You drugged me again after that."

He exhaled a long, exasperated sigh. "That was for your own good, Grace."

"Bullshit." She sprang off the cot, jumped to the side, and flattened her back against the wall. The door looked so far away. "What the hell do you want from me?"

"Cooperation."

She barked out a derisive laugh. "This is how you think you'll get my cooperation? You're insane."

"Please understand. My priority, my sole purpose in life, is to end the horrific reign of Karl Tesler." He inched closer, but when she gave him a warning look, he backed off. "I need you fighting at my side, at full strength, not hobbled by migraines."

"Cut the crap. You've been manipulating me from the beginning, and I want to know why. What exactly do you expect me to do for you?"

"Fight. In ways I cannot."

She flexed her fingers against the cold wall. Her gaze flicked to the door, then back to him. A hard pit bounced around in her stomach, set off by a slithering suspicion she knew what he wanted from her. "No."

"Think about it." He strode toward her, grasping her shoulders in his big hands. "It is the only way to defeat Tesler. You are the one person in all the world capable of handling this task."

"I said no."

He squeezed her flesh and let go, squeezed and let go, in a gentle rhythm probably meant to lull her. Instead, it pissed her off. Oblivious, he kept up the rhythm, his fingers massaging deeper with each squeeze. "You must make use of your greatest gift. You must employ the Golden Power."

She glanced at the door and then down at his hands that restrained her. The sedative's aftereffects, coupled with dizzying fear, weakened her in every way. The last time she accessed her innate powers, a force had snapped her mind in two. The Golden Power was far more dangerous.

Why had her powers failed her?

She'd crashed into a barrier, like the one she had constructed to barricade her mind. Had the psychic firewall gone haywire?

No. The instant before her powers imploded, Amador shouted for Wickham to "push the button." Then the buzzing started. And her powers went kablooey.

When she tried to contact David, her mind had struck a similar blockade.

Her fingers curled slightly, and she tapped them on the wall. "You put up some kind of psychic dampening field, didn't you?"

Shuffling backward, he lowered his gaze to the floor. "You left me no choice."

"There's always a choice, and you made yours." Anger simmered inside her, but a solitary spike of ice punched through it. Not the cold of fear. The pacifying influence of reason. *Listen to his words. What is he really saying?* His statements replayed in her mind in rapid succession.

I need you. My plan will fail without your power. He referred to more than the Golden Power, which wasn't hers, but borrowed energy. *I spent time in a Siberian facility.* He carefully avoided calling himself a traveler or a prisoner. And when she chastised him for RV'ing her in her bedroom, his response had, once again, been carefully phrased. *I did not realize you were alone in your bedroom until after the excursion began.* Why not say "after I traveled to you" or "after my excursion began"? He was distancing himself from the action, misleading without lying outright.

The truth rippled through her in a chilling wave. Of course. She'd gotten everything wrong. Confronted with Amador's claims, and so intent on unmasking her psychic stalker, she hadn't bothered to consider another possibility. He was lying, yes. But about more than his motives or the fact he'd imprisoned and tortured a young woman.

She pushed away from the wall, narrowing the gap between them, and stabbed a finger into his chest. "You don't have any psychic powers, do you?"

His body jerked. Lifting his eyes to hers, he winced. "No. I do not."

A horrifying thought surfaced, and she prayed it was not true. But she knew it was. "That's why you abducted the girl. She has psychic abilities, and you tormented her, probably with drugs, until she broke down and agreed to do your bidding. You made her stalk me with RV. You made her assault my mind. That poor girl was your psychic puppet." Grace jabbed her finger harder into his chest. She recognized the folly of her anger, of letting it show, but the fury flamed too hot and wild to contain it. "You are a monster, just like Tesler."

Amador shook his head violently. His mouth hung open, his lower lip trembling. "No. Grace, no, please understand—"

"Shut up." Spittle sprayed from her lips. Her stomach roiled, and her thoughts whirled. Terror and rage melted into one swirling, scorching mass in her gut. This man conspired to torment her by enslaving and brainwashing a child. He was a monster. The impulse to throttle Amador mushroomed inside her, made her body go rigid, and consumed common sense. Through clenched teeth, she snarled, "Turn off the goddamn dampening field, or whatever the hell it is. Shut it down. *Now.*" She stomped one step closer, her face inches from him. Her breaths huffed in his face, reflecting onto hers. "Do it, or I will rip you apart molecule by molecule. You know I can. You've seen what I'm capable of. Remember the woods, and those commandos I eliminated without lifting a finger?"

The shame and anguish on his face converged into an indefinable expression. He stared at her for several seconds. Then, his features contorted, and a single tear rolled down each cheek. "I am sorry, Grace. I never intended to—I believed we could—" He hauled in a long breath, exhaling slowly. The pained look washed out of his face, replaced by the impassivity she'd witnessed on him before. "I had no choice, believe me. I needed you alone, and there was no other way to draw you out. Your affection for David is too strong."

Her hand twitched, anxious to slap him.

Get a grip. She watched him for a moment while she collected her wits. It took some time since her wits had scattered to the four winds. The fury dwindled to a bed of coals, radiating heat without setting fire to the landscape. Sweat sheathed her forehead, and she wiped it away with the back of her hand. "Most people introduce themselves with a handshake, not a mental assault."

"We are not most people."

"I am nothing like you." She took a breath, but her stance remained rigid. "You don't know me. We met yesterday. I appreciate how you lent a hand last night, but if you try to keep me here against my will, I'll find a way to escape. Or I'll die trying."

He raised an unsteady hand and let it hover near her cheek. "I have no wish to harm you. As long as you are under my roof, Tesler will not touch you. You have my word."

She snorted. "This from the man who swore he could help me with my psychic abilities."

"I did try to help you, no? I may not have abilities myself, but I have experience in counseling those who do."

"Is that what you call what you did to that girl? Counseling?" His lips parted, but she cut in before he could respond. "You lied about having powers. You used an innocent child to spy on me. Pardon me if I have trouble trusting your word."

He nodded in resignation. Bending over the cot, he began to fluff the pillow with a deliberate gentleness, so intent on his task that his lips pursed. "There is more you should know. If you are to trust me, then I must reveal everything to you. I see that now."

Grace caught sight of the doorway out of the corner of her eye. She edged sideways toward it. "Fine. Tell me."

"It's about Tesler." He smoothed the wrinkles out of the pillowcase. "I placed a tracking device on the DVD I gave you. Tesler's men found you at the motel because I alerted them to your location."

His admission stopped her in her tracks. Suddenly paralyzed, she watched him peripherally. "But you took me away from Tesler's men. You gave me shelter. Why would you do that if you called in the goons?"

He ran his hands over the sheet covering the cot, straightening it with a light touch. "I needed to isolate you, to drive you to me. I knew you would escape Tesler's men. And with David away, you would have nowhere to go." He straightened, turning to face her. "It was a gamble. I hoped you would call on me for help. If not, then I had plans to stumble upon you wherever you decided to hide."

"That's a pretty crappy plan." She shuffled toward the door, one inch at a time. Her shoes scraped across the floor. The walls buzzed faintly. Her pulse beat fast, and she fought to remember to breathe. "I didn't have the DVD with me anymore. You had no way to track me then."

"Cari did." He raked a hand through his dark curls. "The girl. She could've tracked you."

Wonderful. He'd conscripted a child to be his psychic GPS tracker. She tried not to think about what he'd done to the girl, but images flashed in her mind. Drug injections. Physical torture. Amador had a bizarre idea of what constituted noble behavior.

She must get out of here—with the girl.

The dampening field, or whatever it was, seemed confined to this room. If she got past the doorway…

Grace bolted for it.

Wickham leaped in front of the doorway.

She halted so abruptly her feet slipped. Her arms flailed. Her body tumbled backward.

And she stumbled straight into Amador's embrace.

His hands gripped her under her arms, suspending her fall. He eased her onto her feet and let go.

Breathing hard, she tugged her shirt hem down to cover her midriff. Wickham had planted himself just outside the doorway, jaw set, arms crossed over his chest. He must've jumped out from alongside the door, outside the room.

A memory unreeled in her mind. Wickham firing a handgun. Hitting the target with each shot. His deadly accuracy suggested he was more than a butler. He was Amador's enforcer.

The scent of Amador's cologne, spicy and musky, lingered on her skin and clothes, even in her hair. If she ever hoped to get out of this house, she needed a real plan.

"Please, Grace," Amador said. "Allow me to finish explaining."

"Apparently, I have no choice." She angled sideways to both men, keeping watch on them peripherally. "If you want to have any hope of earning my trust, then you need to make a show of good faith."

"In what way?" Amador asked.

"Shut down the dampening field. Or whatever it is you're using to block my powers."

"It is an electromagnetic field."

She braced her hands on her hips. "Turn it off."

Amador strode up to the wall, plucked a small remote-control device out of his pocket, and punched a button on it. A rectangular section of wall sunk inward, sliding out of the way to expose a doorway. Beyond the threshold, she spotted electronic equipment.

He entered the room, leaned over a console, and tapped keys on a keyboard.

The buzzing fizzled out.

Her powers bloomed inside her. Energized. Alive. Ready.

Agony slammed into her. She gasped, staggering backward. The pain ruptured her from the inside, blistering hot, razor-sharp, driven deeper and deeper each second. A strangled cry escaped her.

David.

Another surge battered her. She crumpled to her knees, weeping, overwhelmed by sheer terror. Her connection to David pulsed with pain and anguish. And guilt. Its gravity towed her down into an obsidian whirlpool. His last thought blasted through her mind.

Please forgive me, Grace.

Dammit, he did not get to abandon her again. Not like this. Not forever.

She launched up into the crossroads, barreling through the darkness toward a single blindingly bright star. Her mind crashed into the light. Dived down the tunnel. Exploded out into the world. She collided with the barrier, but her mind bounced back, reeling toward the crossroads.

No.

With every iota of energy left, she latched onto David's location. If she couldn't reach him directly, maybe she could anchor herself to the facility. The EM field surrounding David shoved her away. She clawed at it and scrabbled around the edges of the barrier. Trapped in the pitch dark, she couldn't make out shapes.

But she heard voices. Indistinct. Nearby.

Zeroing in on the sound, she catapulted toward it—and vaulted out into a control room.

An alarm screeched. Technicians banged their fingertips on keyboards at computer workstations, their movements furious and panicked. Two men in white coats stood behind the techs, arguing in loud, angry voices. The workstations faced a window that filled the wall's entire width and half its height.

"Where the hell did he go?" someone shouted.

Grace trotted to the glass. Please, God, let David be alive.

The window overlooked a larger room constructed from bare concrete. In the center of the room, three chairs hunkered. One was empty. The other two held human beings, though all she could see was the tops of their heads. A dark, bald scalp belonged to no one she recognized, at least not from the crown of his head. But the instant her gaze fell on the other head, covered with blond locks, her gut twisted and her head swayed with internal motion. She'd recognize that head anywhere, whether she could see his face or not. She'd run her hands through that hair and kissed the top of that head.

David.

Neither of the men stirred. Dread burrowed deep into her and crystallized into spikes that punctured her soul, shattering hope.

He wasn't dead. She would not believe it until she touched him.

But how? The walls and windows vibrated, evidence of the EM field's existence. Her mind pulsed with pains triggered by her link to David. Despite the barrier between them, part of her reached out to him constantly. She'd relied on that bond far more than she realized. She'd counted on it to always be there. Even now, her mind sought his—and bounced off the EM field.

An invisible vise bore down on her forehead. Starbursts flashed in her vision. How much time did she have before the migraine snapped the tether grounding her to this place?

Not enough.

She rushed to the nearest technician, a young man with dark eyes and tawny skin. Computer-code gibberish unfurled on his monitor as his fingertips fluttered over the keyboard. Sweat dribbled down his temple. His tongue protruded between his clamped teeth, and his breaths puffed fast and sharp.

One of the white-coated men barked, "Where's Dr. Tesler?"

Grace's attention snapped to the speaker. A name tag sewn onto his jacket declared the older man was "Dr. Yellen."

"Don't know," the young tech in front of Grace said, panic constricting his voice into a whine. "I lost track of him when he ran out into the corridor."

"In which direction?"

The tech shrugged and flapped his head from side to side, emitting tiny gasps of confusion and desperation.

"Dammit," Yellen said, "somebody find Sean Vandenbrook."

Sean had escaped. Good. But David…

Drawn by an inevitable need, her gaze veered to the concrete room. Tentacles of ice coiled around her heart.

Focus. She bent close to the tech's ear—and hesitated. The first time she'd exploited this aspect of her powers, the guilt over what she'd done haunted her for months. Using it again, on the motel clerk, had made her queasy. Regret lurked inside her still, an amorphous tumor on her soul. She'd had no choice those other times, and she had no other options at this moment either.

And so she gathered her courage, stifled her conscience, and adopted the most commanding whisper she could muster. "Destroy the EM field. Hurry, before it explodes and everyone dies."

The tech went still, from his furious fingers to his panting breaths. His eyes were aimed straight ahead, but unfocused.

She had no clue whether EM fields could explode, but that hardly mattered. Shutting off the field might not be good enough. Someone else could flip the switch to turn it back on. She needed the barrier gone. Permanently.

"Do it," she commanded, using her astral voice to inject her wishes into his brain. "Destroy the EM field. Save everyone."

His eyelids fluttered.

"Hurry," she insisted. "It's going to blow any second. You can feel the pressure building. Dismantle the field."

The tech's eyes closed.

She'd done this before without really trying. But today, when she needed her powers at full throttle, when lives depended on her ability to—

The man's eyes flew open. His fingers descended on the keyboard, typing with such speed and ferocity she expected the keys to smash apart.

The buzzing ceased. The pressure in her head let up a smidgen.

It had worked. A frenzied laugh bubbled out of her but died in an instant.

Giving the tech an imaginary pat on the shoulder, she told him, "Good work, but shut off the blasted alarm."

Keys clicked. The alarm silenced.

Yellen scampered to the tech, leaning over his shoulder. "What the hell did you do? Saints in heaven, Toby, you disabled the EM field."

Looking dazed, Toby muttered, "I did?"

"It'll take hours to get it back online, if we can do it at all."

The bickering of the men and the clacking of computer keys faded into the background. The world around her dimmed, like a TV screen with the brightness cranked down to the lowest setting. Something inside her dimmed too.

Her connection to David.

It hadn't died, not yet. But it had weakened into a thread, frail and tattered, ready to disintegrate at the slightest pressure.

Faster than a clock tick, she shot into the concrete room to stand before him. A sob tore out of her, rupturing the tomb-deep silence of the concrete vault.

No one could hear her, not even David. He no longer heard or saw or felt anything. Restraints pinned his limp body to the chair. Blood oozed from his nostrils and lips. His head sagged onto his shoulder.

And his eyes. Another sob jarred her body. His eyes were glazed and vacant.

Her knees folded under her, striking the floor.

David had sacrificed his own life to defend hers. Despite lacking any knowledge of what transpired here, she recognized what he had done for her. The truth of it ruptured her heart, smothered her breaths, and pumped the life out of her.

He had died for her.

"No!"

Her cry reverberated in the room. She scrambled to her feet. They had not conquered amnesia and psychopaths, clawing their way back to each other, for everything to end this way. The universe owed her a debt. It had ripped her parents away from her, stripped her most precious memories of David, and thrown her into a flaming pool of psychic trauma and unending danger. She was supposed to keep fighting alone? Like hell.

The universe would pay up. Now.

She rocketed into the crossroads. Hurled out tendrils of her power. Latched onto the limit of the crossroads. Tunneled into it. She split a hole through the fabric of the metaphysical plane, propelling her mind beyond the limits of psychic faculties, straight into the essence of the universe.

She seized the Golden Power.

And gorged on it.

Chapter Seventeen

ENERGY SURGED THROUGH DAVID AS HIS EYELIDS FLUTTERED OPEN, vanquishing the remnants of pain that pinched his body. Brilliant light drenched him. He squinted and squirmed in his restraints. Something was off.

The truth roared back to him in a surround-sound memory of gut-wrenching proportions. Gunshots. Blood. Torment. And a blessed numbness right before the world spiraled away from him, replaced by nothingness.

He had died.

The realization chilled him from the inside out. Cold certainty burgeoned in his heart, spreading outward, freezing his veins. Nkosi was dead too. But Sean, thank God, had gotten away. He would find a hole to slip through and flee the facility. The boy knew how to sneak around places like this.

Warmth trickled into David, the blood pumping through his body once again. He still couldn't see much, his vision blurred by the shock of the bright light and... whatever had revived him. The energy flowing through him simmered with a familiar flavor. Sweet. Sharpened by electric pulses. It tingled on his skin and saturated him to his core. His mood lightened, buoyed by an external source, as a cocktail of relief and bittersweet bliss flooded into him.

Grace.

Her love infused his entire being, borne on the energy she funneled into him. She had resurrected him. Which meant only one thing.

The Golden Power.

Jesus, no. She shouldn't have risked it. Not for him, or anyone.

He sensed her nearby, her presence radiating over him like sunlight. The facility had gone eerily quiet. The hairs all over his body stiffened. The wrongness he detected a moment ago lingered in the air, almost palpable. He blinked furiously until his vision cleared and he glimpsed *her*.

Grace stood several feet from his chair. A breeze he could not feel stirred her dark-auburn hair so that it billowed around her face in a silky curtain. Her fair skin seemed to glow from within. Her eyes, focused on him, glimmered with a golden light, the hazel irises bright as faceted jewels. A cool smile curved her lips.

She looked… stunning. He gulped against a lump in his throat. A ghost of desire flitted through him, but it fizzled out the instant she spoke. Her voice echoed from a distant void. "How do you feel?"

"Normal." He stared at her. He couldn't help it. She was beautiful beyond words, ethereal, and more remote than the stars. "Are you all right?"

"Yes." She flicked one finger, and his restraints evaporated. "But we should go. I trapped the scientists and security guards in another corridor. They'll find a way out soon."

Someone moaned. David jerked his head left, toward the noise. Nkosi's chest rose and fell. His eyes drifted open, at first unfocused, then zeroing in on David.

Nkosi sat forward, scratching his head. "I thought I was shot, but I must've hallucinated it."

"No," David said, his tone calmer than the emotions churning inside him. "You died. We both did."

Nkosi cocked his head, his gaze traveling to Grace. "This must be the darling girl Tesler mentioned. The one you spoke with in our cell?"

"Yeah." David waved a hand toward Grace, though he kept his gaze nailed to Nkosi. The energy spinning out from her licked at his psychic senses and bristled an intuition buried deep. "She, uh, saved us. Long story."

"I believe you." Nkosi's eyebrows arched as another wave of power gusted over Grace and her hair fanned out around her. Nkosi threw a sidelong look at David. "The story must be quite interesting."

The man wanted to know, but he wouldn't press. David appreciated that. He hopped out of the chair and inched toward Grace, struggling to ignore the cold fist clenching his heart.

Her luminous eyes rotated toward him, and a shiver sidled down his spine.

An arm's length from her, he halted. "What happened, Grace?"

She blinked in slow motion.

That fist choked his heart. She was lost in another place, somewhere between the here and now and the crossroads. The last time she'd exercised her powers, to build her psychic firewall, an unknown force attacked her, intent on dragging her into the abyss. Could he coax her back this time?

Did she want him to?

Yes, dammit, of course she did. He raised a trembling hand toward her face, but she backed away. "Grace, talk to me. Please."

"I'm still in Ohio. At Amador's house." She turned away from him and glided toward the door. "I'll explain everything later."

As he trailed her out of the room, a memory replayed in his mind. Six months ago, when he'd tracked Grace down in Texas, she demanded answers from him. And he'd promised to explain later. Standing on the other side of that statement today, he finally understood why it infuriated her back then. Starved for answers and suffused with dread, he needed her to talk to him. Yet she refused, with a coolness that terrified him.

With Nkosi close behind, David let Grace lead him down the maze of corridors. She strode around corners, through doorways, and down more corridors with a purpose and certainty beyond anything he'd witnessed in her before now. Grace always possessed an inner strength, more than even she realized, but this was different. The tendrils of her power snaked out around her, invisible, yet palpable to him. Slippery, viscous tongues of energy. They swirled around him, but never touched his psyche.

She was shielding him. From her power.

Hope burgeoned within him. If she maintained enough control to steer her energy away from him, then he still had a chance to drag her back from the void and free her from the Golden Power.

Once, he'd encouraged her to utilize the power. What a fool he'd been. Grace feared it, and now he understood why. He prayed it wasn't too late.

Grace halted before a set of massive steel doors. She raised a hand. "Stay back."

David scuffled backward a few yards, thrusting out an arm to block Nkosi from proceeding further.

She swept both hands up, palms to the ceiling, and threw her head back.

The doors groaned.

Energy assailed her. The outskirts of it sideswiped David, knocking him off balance. He stumbled backward. Nkosi seized his arm. David righted himself and gaped at Grace.

White light pulsed out of her in glittering curtains.

"What do you see?" Nkosi asked.

David tore his gaze away from Grace long enough to frown at Nkosi. "Don't you see it? White energy coming out of her. It's everywhere."

"I see nothing." Nkosi fisted his hand and rubbed his thumb over the knuckles, his mouth tight.

The light kissed David's flesh, filled his psyche, caressed his power. Dizziness crashed over him, reeling him backward. If not for Nkosi's hand on his arm, he would've tumbled to the floor. Passion and adoration streamed into him, tainted with desperation. The sheer magnitude of the power overwhelmed his psychic senses, and pains shot through his head. His knees buckled, striking the floor hard. Nkosi hefted him to his feet.

David's voice emerged in a strangled whisper. "I have to stop her."

"Perhaps I—"

"No. Has to be me."

Nkosi nodded.

Hunched over, David staggered toward Grace. The energy ripped into him with ferocious force. His hand trembled as he stretched it out to grasp her shoulder. Scorching desire bolted out of her into him, and his knees threatened to crumple again.

The steel doors burst open.

Beyond them, crimson bulbs lit a tunnel carved out of the earth.

The light extinguished. The power pouring out of Grace dwindled from a raging torrent to a forceful stream. The pressure on David released with a near-physical rebound. The pain in his head faded. A trickle of desire wended its way through him, a faint tickle compared to the heat that had incinerated him seconds earlier. How she could think of sex while channeling the ultimate source of psychic energy baffled him. Questions bounced in his brain, but he ignored all except one.

He tugged her shoulder. "Are you still with me, Grace?"

She turned toward him inch by inch. Her eyes glowed with less intensity, more like the luminescence brought on by harnessing normal psychic abilities.

Normal. He never dreamed he'd use that word to describe psychic faculties.

"I'm here," she said, and relief flooded into him at the sound—the normal sound—of her voice. Her gaze latched onto his. "Why are you sweating?"

David swiped at his face. His hand came away damp. The sweat oozing from his pores hadn't registered before. Her energy had consumed his every thought and swamped his senses. Grasping her shoulders, he searched her burning hazel eyes for some sign she'd come back to him.

Then it hit him. His hands gripped her flesh. *Physical contact.*

"You manifested," he said, unable to quell the shock in his voice, "and you're not curled up in a ball, riding out a migraine." In fact, she glowed with a preternatural vitality. He tugged her closer, desperate to spur a reaction from her. He got nothing. "Grace?"

"Yes, I manifested. So what? It's easy." Her breezy tone set his nerves on edge, but she charged ahead. "I have to get you three out of here quickly. The distraction I arranged won't keep Tesler or his men busy for much longer."

"Where are we going?"

"Somewhere safe. Trust me."

He trusted her without reservation. But with the Golden Power influencing her, he didn't know if he should.

She spun away from him, toward the steel doors.

"Wait," he said, seizing her hand. She glanced back. "Us three? It's only me and Nkosi."

A knowing smile curved her lips. "Just wait. I sent him directions."

"Who?"

Bang.

David whirled around. A ceiling panel had popped out, clattering to the floor. A pair of sneaker-clad feet dangled through the opening. Sean plopped onto the corridor floor, knees bent.

"Him," Grace said, and she marched out the doors. "I retrieved Sean for you."

Stunned and immobile, David watched her backside retreat from him. No psychic he'd ever encountered commanded enough power and control to perform two tasks at once, much less three. From what Grace told him, though, he suspected she had. Locating and directing Sean. Setting up a distraction for Tesler and his minions. Freeing David and Nkosi. And she resurrected them too.

Make that *four* tasks at once.

Sean trotted past him. Casting a glance over his shoulder, he said, "Why do you look like your best friend died? We're escaping."

David tried to speak. Nothing came out.

Nkosi hurried after Sean and Grace. "We must go, David."

An eerie sensation prickled the skin at the base of his neck. Grace had amassed more psychic power than anyone should command. If he hadn't run out on her for the umpteenth time, she would never have needed to tap into the limitless power she'd feared for six months. The energy boost empowered her, for sure. But it also altered her on a fundamental level.

It was his fault. He must cleanse her of this... infestation. Whatever happened, he would not give up on her without a fight. He'd rather die—again.

His top priority had always been, and always would be, her. From this moment forward, he must prove that fact to her. He'd save her, dammit, whether she liked it or not.

Squaring his shoulders, he took off down the tunnel.

It dead-ended at a much smaller set of double doors, constructed from steel and buttressed with concrete. The doors hung ajar, their edges warped. Grace must've unlocked both sets of doors at once, employing the limitless energy granted to her by the Golden Power. A frigid current trickled through his veins. *Five* tasks at once. *Holy heaven.*

They pushed the deformed doors aside and clambered out into the night. Grace guided them onward, with a purpose and conviction that did nothing to alleviate his unease. She knew precisely where to go—down to the inch, he realized. Left at this tree, right at the next one, straight down a gentle grade and across a clearing. Their breaths condensed in the chilled air. He should've checked the weather forecast before waltzing out here on his half-assed mission. Nothing except his desperate quest had stuck in his brain, not even Grace's warnings and her silent pleas for his help. He was such a fool. And a total ass.

Goosebumps riddled his arms, but try as he might, he couldn't dismiss them as a side effect of frosty air on his bare arms. The fabric of his T-shirt protected him somewhat but left his arms exposed, since the guards had confiscated his jacket. Nkosi wore a long-sleeve T-shirt, and Sean had opted for the ultra-cool layered look with a long-sleeve shirt underneath his short-sleeve tee, granting him more protection than David had without his jacket. Both Sean and Nkosi rubbed their arms off and on, but neither shivered noticeably. David's teeth had begun to chatter, so he clamped his jaw tight. But as with his goosebumps, his clenched teeth stemmed from more than an attempt to ward off the outward chill. Another, deeper cold infiltrated his being.

And it centered on Grace.

He lost track of the minutes as they, with David in front, trailed Grace through the woods. East, west, north, south, he gave up trying to sort out the directions. Despite the gloom of night, pierced by only the occasional shaft of pale moonlight, their guide had no trouble navigating. The longer they trekked, the less David noticed the cold. His goosebumps disappeared, but the hairs at the nape of his neck remained stiff. Sweat beaded on his brow. The air chilled it within seconds, drawing the cold across his brow like a damp washcloth.

They broke out of the trees, heading down a hill into a clearing. A log cabin hunkered at the hill's base, near the other side of the clearing. The house was dark, more a shadow in the night than a beacon of hope and safety. Since Grace brought them here, though, he'd trust she knew what she was doing, even if he couldn't grasp the logic of it. They should've run as far as possible. Then again, how far would they get before Tesler's men caught up? This cabin must offer security, or else Grace would never have led them here.

At the cabin, they halted. A dirt two-track drew a line through the moon-lightened field, terminating at the roofed porch of the cabin. A stack of cut firewood, partially covered by a brown tarp, occupied one end of the porch. David saw no vehicles, no lights, no signs of habitation. Given the weeds and grass dotting the two-track, he surmised no one had visited the cabin in months, maybe longer.

Grace, positioned a few feet from the porch steps, waved a hand toward the front door. "You can hide here until morning. By then I'll have a plan to extract you."

Nkosi eyed the cabin with raised eyebrows. "Won't our enemies track us here?"

"No." Grace sounded far too certain, which scraped a steel file down David's spine. "I've obliterated our tracks and planted false clues to lead Tesler's men away from here. I've also permanently disabled the facility's electronics, as well as the mobile devices of everyone there tonight."

"Cool," Sean said, his tone rife with teenage wonder. "Can you teach me how to do that?"

David laid a hand on the boy's arm, urging him toward the cabin, and flashed Nkosi a look he hoped conveyed the import of his words. "You two go inside. I need to talk to Grace."

Sean balked, in typical rebellious-boy fashion, but Nkosi grasped his upper arm and, with a gentle hand, guided him up the steps and across the porch. At the front door, he paused. "Perhaps we should gather some wood first?"

Grace shook her head. "There's enough inside to start a fire and keep it going for tonight. There's also a generator, but it's out of gas."

Nkosi gave a curt nod and twisted the doorknob. It turned in his hand, unlocked. He did not comment on the open door, despite the curious twitch of his lips. Easing the door ajar, he entered first, with Sean close behind. Once the door clicked shut, David strode toward Grace, until inches separated them.

The whites of her eyes glistened in the moon's glow. Her expression conveyed such innocence and sweetness that, for a few ecstatic seconds, he forgot all about her shocking power and the dread coiling in his gut with each new feat she accomplished. In that fleeting moment, he gazed into the eyes of the only woman he'd ever loved. His true better half. His soul mate.

Then her psychic energy pulsed into him, electrified by the Golden Power, and shattered his serenity. Her love still warmed him, transferred into him by her telepathy, but the old chill resurfaced with a sharpness that scraped his nerves raw.

"You unlocked the door," he said.

"That's right." The disturbing calmness in her voice had faded, but not vanished. "I took care of everything. You'll be safe tonight."

He cradled her face in his hands. "You do these things without even a hint of discomfort. No migraine. No anxiety. Nothing." He ducked his head close to hers, their breaths mingling. "It's the Golden Power doing this to you. But why aren't you afraid of it anymore?"

"Because I understand it now. It's a part of me, always has been, and I've accepted that."

The woman he knew would never accept it. "It's changing you. I can feel it."

She shrugged.

"Please, Grace, listen to me." He stroked her cheeks with his thumbs, marveling at how she felt so warm and normal on the outside when oily darkness roiled within her. "You have to let it go. Stop channeling the Golden Power before it changes you forever." His nose bumped hers, and his lips grazed her mouth. "Come back to me. Please."

"I am here."

No, she wasn't. Not fully. Her body brushed against his, her skin heated under his hands, but the part of her he cherished most lay smothered beneath her newfound power. Words failed to crack the granite-hard wall of psychic energy shielding her mind, her heart, her soul. *No, dammit.* He wouldn't surrender this battle.

He claimed her mouth in a possessive kiss as he thrust his hands into her hair, grasping the back of her head, slanting it up to press his lips harder into hers. Her soft lips opened for him. He forged deep inside, lost in the silky sweetness of her mouth, the answering strokes of her tongue. Her body arched into him. He glided one hand down to splay his fingers across the small of her back and yanked her snug against him. She rasped her nails up and down his chest. They scratched over his T-shirt, a rough tease on his flesh.

The world dropped away. They plunged into a private pocket of reality where the only sounds were their frantic breaths and hungry moans, and the only sensation was the rubbing of their bodies against each other and the hot, slick dance of their tongues. The passion blazing between them disintegrated guilt and fear and inhibition. The darkness fled from their psychic link, conquered by a scorching desire and a fierce love.

He felt *her.*

The essence of this woman. Beautiful, supple, sweet as honey, but underpinned by strength and vitality. Joy blossomed within him, its petals fashioned from her, drawn open by the radiance of their indestructible bond.

They peeled their lips apart, so slowly he swore he tasted every cell in her skin. Their chests heaved in unison, her breasts mounded against him. Condensation billowed out from their mouths, but the cold barely registered on his skin.

"David. Wow." She murmured the syllables against his mouth, her eyes half-closed. "I had no idea you could kiss like that." She raked her nails down his chest to the waistband of his pants. "Do it again."

Words caught in his throat, constricted into a groan.

She rocked her hips into him.

Hunger coursed through him, arousing every part of his body. He fought the impulse to sweep her into his arms, carry her into the cabin, and drop her onto the first padded surface he found so he could make love to her all night.

The moonlight burnished her golden eyes and ignited the emerald flecks. He wanted to capture her bottom lip between his teeth to suckle her flesh.

She ran her tongue over her swollen lips, curving them into a shy smile. "Thank you."

"For what?" At least she seemed normal, but he couldn't shake the sensation of impending doom.

Her smile turned bittersweet. "You saved me."

His heart thudded, and relief rushed through him, flushing out the desire. Well, most of it.

"I was lost," she said, "and you found me. I gave in to the Golden Power but..."

Tears trickled down her cheeks. She veered her gaze down to the ground. Her shoulders slumped, bowing forward, and he knew, the way no one else would have, that she was trying to curl up in a ball while upright, to disappear into herself. What she'd done, absorbing the ultimate psychic power, had left her ashamed. The link between them hinted at it, but his intimate knowledge of her confirmed it.

His heart ached for her, his arms too. He enfolded her in his embrace and tucked her head under his chin. While he reassured her with his words, promises he wasn't sure he could keep but he'd damn well try, she relaxed into him. Even knowing this wasn't her real body, but a manifestation created by a process neither one of them fully understood, he still relished the warmth and softness of her body against his. Her hair smelled of coconut and vanilla, from the conditioner she used. How on earth a manifested body could smell like anything amazed him, and he briefly wondered whether his manifestations gave off any scents.

He caressed her hair, rewarded by her nuzzling his neck. "Why did you seek out the Golden Power?"

She lifted her head to squint at him. When she spoke her voice conveyed great patience and a hint of disbelief. "I did it for you. I came to find you and—" Her voice faltered. She raised a trembling hand to his face, etching a line down his cheek with one fingertip. "You were dead. I had to do something."

He shut his eyes, shocked by his own stupidity. Of course she'd done it for him. He remembered dying, recalled the pain and then the numbness, and he should've understood the moment he awakened. Reviving him from the dead, as well as resurrecting Nkosi and all the other incredible things she'd done, demanded a steep cost. To acquire that much psychic energy, she had no choice but to plug into the source she'd feared since the day six months ago when she first stumbled onto it.

Back then, she'd inadvertently harnessed it. Today, she sought it out and welcomed it into her mind, her body, her soul. Could she expunge it on her own? Could anything rid her of its influence? He wanted to believe his passionate kiss, his total commitment to her, expelled it. He'd seen too much in the past few years to delude himself.

She was back. She was his again. For how long?

He rested his forehead on hers and scrutinized her gaze for any remnants of the otherness he witnessed earlier. All he saw was her. "I'm sorry. I should've listened to you and stayed home. If I had, none of this would've happened."

"Sean would've charged headfirst into danger, and into Tesler's hands. Neither of us could live with ourselves if we let that happen."

"It's my fault. I..." He had no clue what to say, how to explain, how to rectify the mess he made.

She kissed him, a sweet and lingering touch imbued with sorrow, affection, need, and hope. He hadn't imagined the last one could've survived after her ordeals. And yet the hope flowed down their connection, a gleaming, unbreakable thread.

"I'll see you again," she said, "soon. Wait for me."

"Wait where? Here?"

"Yes." She backed away from him, her face glowing with tenderness. "The last time we talked, I told you the conversation wasn't over. It still isn't. So don't go dying on me again, at least until we've finished our talk."

"I'll try." He could promise no more, and she knew it. "Be careful. Please."

She nodded. "I love you."

Her manifested body winked out of existence as her mind retreated from him.

Gone.

Wind gusted over him, blowing grit into his eyes. He blinked it away and stared at the spot where she'd been a heartbeat ago. "I love you too."

Chapter Eighteen

GRACE GLIDED BACK INTO HER BODY, NO PAIN, NO PRESSURE, JUST A gentle slide back into herself. David's final words, a warning to be careful, replayed in her mind, bouncing off the empty spaces inside her, the holes left behind by his absence. Their connection resonated in the background, but without direct contact, it diminished to a distant echo. She sensed his presence in the world, nothing more.

An ache sprouted in her chest, deep and spiritual, rather than physical. The ache built into a heart-rending throb, tearing her hard-won composure to shreds. *I miss you, David, I'm coming for you soon so please wait for me, please.* Would he hear her promise and her plea? No. Not with their connection reduced to a trickle. But she'd done all she could for him.

A weariness blanketed her, with almost suffocating pressure. She sank to her knees, then reality burst into her mind, sharp and bright and agonizing in its abruptness. The basement. In Amador's house. She slumped on the concrete floor, shoulders hunched, pangs webbing out through her knees from their collision with the hard surface. Amador knelt before her with his lips parted, his wide eyes fixed on her, face warped by panicked emotions she preferred not to decipher.

He stretched out a tentative hand to touch her arm, but pulled it back at the last instant, hovering his hand a few inches from her. "Are you… unharmed?"

She made a rude noise. "Yeah sure, I'm great. You suppressed my powers with your EM doohickey, drugged me into unconsciousness, held me against my will, and led Tesler straight to me. Your concern is touching. Thanks a bunch."

Amador flinched and lowered his hand. "I understand you hate me, and you should, but I have done these things to protect you, in my own way." He bowed his head, draping a hand across each knee. "You may leave this place whenever you wish. No one will stop you. However, Tesler's men are still hunting for you and I cannot call them off."

"I figured." She sat back on her heels and sighed. "I need to get to Montana, fast."

His head popped up, and his eyes were bright with curiosity. "You found David?"

"Yes." She'd keep the details to herself, though his desire to know crackled in the air. The Golden Power might've deserted her, thank heavens, but it deposited a trace of its energy within her, something she could neither erase nor explain. Amador's emotions slipped inside her, wending their way past her defenses and into her psychic essence. His need and desperation scratched at her, but she suffered no confusion over whose emotions were whose. "Can you provide transportation?"

"Of course. It is the least I can do, to make up for… what I've done."

Sorrow burned. Regret pinched. She shoved aside the invasive feelings, and the urge to chastise him for daring to suggest he might make amends so easily. It'd take a hell of a lot more than a ride to Montana. "I'd appreciate that."

He rose, towering above her. "I'll have Wickham arrange for my jet to take you wherever you need. You may leave within the hour."

With that, he strode toward the door.

"Wait." She heaved her body up off the floor, against the wishes of gravity and exhaustion. "I want to see the girl. Cari."

A muscle in his jaw twitched. His hands clenched, then slackened. Squeezing his lips into a tight smile, he said, "Of course. Follow me."

She marched out the door behind him, up the concrete steps, and down the hallway to a closed door on the left. He dug a key ring out of his pocket, jangling the keys as he selected the appropriate one. The grandfather clock she'd heard earlier bonged from somewhere nearby, muted by the walls. Amador shoved the key into the door's lock with a chunk.

Then he hesitated, casting her a sidelong look.

Her newfound heightened intuition kicked in, warning her with a tingle on her skin. He didn't want her to see the girl, which she'd already known, but now she realized why. She clamped her jaw tight against the anger burning inside her and balled her hands into fists, but the inferno blasted away her self-control.

"She's broken," Grace said, squeezing the words out between her teeth. "You pushed her so hard for so long she snapped. I've met others that's happened to. But they were tortured by Tesler and JT." She stomped one pace closer to him. Her hot breaths ricocheted off his cheek. "You did this to her. Admit it."

His expression fell. His lower lip trembled, and moisture glistened in his eyes. "She is damaged, but not insane. I admit I abused this girl for my purposes, and I have no excuse for it except to say I had no notion my tactics would harm her so terribly."

"But even after you knew, you kept on using her." The words fired from her lips, harsher than she'd ever heard her own voice sound. Grace shut her eyes, sucked in a deep breath, and exhaled slowly. *This isn't me, it's the Golden Power, it's not me.* Despite believing, praying, she'd shaken off the Golden Power's hold on her, the truth gnawed at her gut. *It's still inside me.*

She heard the click as Amador unlocked the door and opened her eyes. He pushed the door inward, stepped across the threshold, and moved aside, motioning for her to enter.

I'm not me anymore. The thought ricocheted in her brain, louder and louder with every concussive burst of repetition. How long would the Golden Power influence her? Did it control her even now, in ways she hadn't grasped yet? Questions flared in her mind, but above all the others, a single fear lanced her heart.

Can David love me like this? Can anyone?

Amador stared at her, his face blank. "If you still wish to see the girl…"

Grace stalked past him into the small bedroom. Cari lay on her back on the four-poster bed, hands folded over her belly, eyes shut. Her chest rose and fell in a gentle rhythm. Her dark hair fanned out over the white pillowcase, the strands draped over her shoulders. Grace perched on the bed's edge, alongside the girl's hips.

Cari peeked out between her lashes. Her body went rigid. A pallor lightened her cinnamon skin, and her lips too.

Waves of anxiety rolled out of Cari, crashing into Grace. She gripped the bed's edge to steady herself against the onslaught. What had Amador done to this girl?

Grace settled a hand on Cari's arm. "I'm getting you out of here. You'll be safe."

Amador scuffled into her peripheral vision. "Grace—"

She flashed him a scowl.

He clapped his mouth shut.

"Cari is coming with me," Grace told him. Then she looked back at the girl, offering her a consoling smile. "You've been in my mind, watched me, experienced who I am. You know I won't hurt you, and I'm not with him." A hint of fiery anger singed the last phrase. That wasn't the Golden Power. This anger steamed straight from her own heart. "Will you trust me?"

Cari swallowed, hard. Her wide eyes flicked to Amador, triggering a massive breaker of panic, but then she switched her attention back to Grace. Cari bit her lip and nodded. "I know you won't hurt me."

A mild Southern accent lent her sweet voice a melodic quality. Grace imagined Cari singing, her voice as glorious as a choir of angels. How in hell could Amador torture a lovely girl like Cari and yet claim to be nothing like Tesler? His motives, though noble to his mind, were twisted and cold.

No, not cold. Hot with desire—for power, and for something else she had yet to puzzle out. His emotions tangled up in an ever-expanding mass, confusing her attempts to sort out what he felt, much less what he craved deep inside. A shiver frosted her nerves. Maybe she didn't want to know his innermost desires.

Hopping off the bed, she held a hand out to Cari.

The girl grasped it fiercely. Once Grace helped her stand, Cari said, "I want to go home. Please. I want to see my mom and dad."

The plea in her tone made Grace's heart ache for this girl in a way she couldn't describe, gripped by a frantic desire to rescue her from Amador and shield her from Tesler. She slipped an arm around Cari's shoulders.

Amador hunched at the foot of the bed, impassive.

"We're taking her home," Grace said. "And then I'm taking your jet to Montana." She hugged the girl a little tighter. "I suggest you stay the hell away from both of us."

"I will arrange everything. Please wait in the living room." His shoes scuffed across the floor as he exited the room. Without looking back, he said, "I know you can never forgive me, but I hope one day you will come to understand my actions."

He disappeared down the hall.

Cari buried her head against the hollow of Grace's shoulder and wept, her body quivering with each sob.

Damn him. Amador must pay for his crimes. She must make certain of it.

But first... David.

Chapter Nineteen

Washed in the sulfurous glow of the streetlights, the front door of the stucco cottage swung shut behind Cari. Grace gulped down the lump in her throat and rubbed out the tears stinging her eyes. Amador had sworn Tesler knew nothing about Cari, and he'd assigned three men from his private security force to watch over her. The girl was safe.

As safe as any psychic could be with Tesler on the loose.

The big black SUV pulled away from the curb. Hands gripped on the steering wheel, Amador fixed his blank stare on the street before them. The headlights pierced the false twilight of the streetlights, punching a path into the night. Amador had insisted on driving her to the airport, and she'd been too exhausted to argue.

"Floor it," she said, refusing to dampen the acid in her tone. "No dillydallying just to keep me around longer. I'm not interested in whatever wacko scheme you've cooked up."

His fingers clenched tighter around the wheel, but his voice remained eerily calm. "I know I've destroyed any chance I had of gaining your trust, but I hold out hope you will assist me, once you understand the purpose behind my actions."

She snorted, not minding in the least that she sounded like a dog rooting through garbage. "You're delusional. I've had it up to here with your machinations."

"I understand you, Grace. We've both suffered at the hands of JT and Tesler."

"And how precisely have you suffered?"

His shoulders flagged, and his expression did too. When he spoke, his voice flattened into a monotone. "I saw a photo of you, read your file, and I knew I had to have you as my ally. So I tried to trick you into helping me. I'm so sorry, Grace, so very sorry for what I've done to you and to Cari. I don't ask forgiveness. I simply need you to understand."

"Then explain." She slanted her head, studying him. "Start by telling me why you lied about having psychic abilities."

"It wasn't a complete fabrication. Though it was my son, Evander, who possessed those talents." Amador's features cinched tight, then slackened. "He was twelve when Tesler took him, tortured him, and finally, when he no longer offered anything of value, slit his throat."

She stared at Amador, unable to glean anything from his face or tone of voice. Tesler had murdered a child? The man knew no limits.

Amador dropped one hand to his thigh, the fingers tensing into claws that scraped on his slacks and routed the flesh beneath. "I altered the data on the DVD I gave you. I changed Evander's name to John Mendoza."

"Why?"

He yanked the wheel, swerving onto another street.

She clutched her arm rest to prevent herself from flying into his lap. Well, at least his bad driving staved off the weariness mounting inside her.

He said nothing for several more seconds, and then he hissed out another breath. "I suppose I wanted to erase the memories by erasing Evander's name from the records. It did not work."

The things he and Wickham had told her before rushed through her mind anew, and this time she grasped the true meaning.

Gabriel understands your predicament, Wickham had told her, *he's been there before.* And Amador spoke of *those things that we share in common, our special connection.* When he had compelled her to share the pain of her parents' deaths, he'd apologized for dredging up her bad memories. *I know how painful that can be*, he'd assured her.

The empathic aftereffect of joining with the Golden Power was waning, yet his grief rolled off him onto her, weakening with each wave.

He'd lied to her, over and over, and she wouldn't condone his behavior. But confronted with a truth she had never expected, she needed to reevaluate him. Just a little.

Amador veered the car around another corner. The tires squealed. The odor of burned rubber wafted in through the vents. "Grace, please, I need your help to stop Tesler. I couldn't save my son. At least let me play some small part in destroying the man who took Evander's life."

The anguish in his voice tugged at her heart, which was stupid. Why should she sympathize with Amador, a man as dangerous as Tesler? But she couldn't help it. Memories of her parents flickered in her mind. Her gut twisted, and her throat constricted. "I'm sorry about your son, really I am. But that's no excuse for what you've done."

"I tell you this not as an excuse, but merely an explanation."

"Save it. I'm not interested." Except a part of her was, for reasons too confusing to examine, out of fear he might lure her into forgetting his abuse of

137

Cari. Maybe he'd injected her with more of the anti-willpower drug, or maybe she'd lost her mind. Or else her intuition was speaking to her again. Urging her to, if not trust him, at least understand his mindset. *Know your enemy, right?*

A yawn overtook her, and she shook herself to cast off the fatigue, but to no avail. Her eyelids had morphed into lead aprons, drifting ever downward.

Images streaked through her mind, half dream, half memory. David standing rigid as a statue in front of her as she bid him goodbye. His blond hair glowing in the moonlight. The stoic expression on his face. Nothing revealed, nothing shared. Her warrior angel.

David. In the woods. With Tesler hot on his trail. Just like in her vision.

She jerked awake. Her heart hammered, her breaths gasped, and she gripped the cushioned arms of her chair so tightly her knuckles ached. A cone of lamplight enveloped her. A padded seat cradled her buttocks, and the chair's back supported her head and neck with equal cushiness. As she uncurled her fingers from the chair's arms, the velvety fabric caressed her skin. She dragged in a deep breath, letting it out in one long, ragged sigh. Her pulse slowed, though it still raced.

Where the hell was she?

Not in the car. She blinked away the bleariness of sleep, rotating her head back and forth to absorb her surroundings. She sat in a chair bolted to the floor, beside a small window. Outside, she spied clouds scudding by in the milky glow of the moon. A jet engine whined, muted by the insulation of the aircraft.

She must be in Amador's jet.

Her suspicion solidified into certainty when Gabriel Amador strode out of a curtained doorway to her left and took a seat in the chair across from her. He cupped a bottle of water in one hand. A small table, fashioned from what looked like polished cherry wood, separated them. She straightened, smoothed her shirt, and tucked a stray lock of hair behind her ear. Her heart no longer raced, but anxiety rippled through her like an electrical current.

"Why are you here?" she said. "I told you to stay away from me."

Sitting ramrod straight in his chair, he studied her without expression.

Why did men love to give her the stoic treatment?

"You were in no condition to travel alone," he said. "I couldn't wake you, and I will not abandon you on this plane without knowing you will awaken at some point."

"You could've called a doctor."

He shrugged one shoulder. "No physician can heal psychic wounds. Whatever you did to save David, it drained you with devastating effect." He offered the water bottle to her. "Drink this. You should replenish your fluids."

She stared at the bottle, her anxiety surging. Drugged? *Ah, hell.* If he wanted to drug her, he could've done it while she was unconscious. And her mouth was dry. Snatching the bottle from him, she unscrewed the cap and swigged several mouthfuls.

"Thank you. For the water, and for the ride." She watched a slender cloud slip past the window. "Where are we headed?"

"You said Montana, so I instructed the pilot to chart a course for a private airstrip owned by a trusted ally. It's located near Bozeman."

"Close enough." She didn't understand how she knew David's location, and she couldn't recite the coordinates, but she sensed his whereabouts. She'd given up understanding what the Golden Power did to her. At least for now. Once she had David back, and Tesler was dealt with, she'd examine her brushes with limitless power.

Brushes? Maybe that word applied to the first instance. This time, however, she had succumbed to the power completely.

The old anxiety buzzed in her veins, electrifying her skin. The sour taste of acid infiltrated her mouth. She gulped down another mouthful of water, but the acrid flavor lingered. For David, she would risk anything. Even if it creeped her out big time and made her long for a nice dark corner to hide in.

No hiding. With David in the woods, like in her vision, the premonition still might come true. Tesler sought David, and he would stop at nothing to capture him and use him for leverage, to draw her into the open. It might work too. She knew it. Confronted with a choice to save herself or David, she'd choose him.

Amador leaned forward, bracing his elbows on his knees. Hands clasped, he fixed his dark eyes on her. The lamplight ignited paler specks in his irises she'd never noticed before. Dark caramel dribbled onto coffee, that's what his eyes resembled. A silly image, but somehow it suited him.

"How long was I out?" she asked.

"Two hours. We've nearly reached Bozeman."

Her stomach sank as the jet pitched into a descent. She sipped the water, but her insides refused to calm. "When we land, I go alone. You stay here."

"Please, Grace, allow me to help you." He scooted forward to the edge of his seat and eased a hand down onto her knee. "I wish no harm to David. I will do whatever I can to protect you both."

What about Sean? And David's new friend? She bit back the questions, unwilling to reveal any more just yet. Then again, if she intended for all of them to flee on Amador's jet, he'd find out soon enough.

She grumbled out a sigh. "David isn't alone. He has two others with him."

"They are also welcome on my jet." He swept his arm through the air in an expansive gesture. "As you can see, I have plenty of room."

She counted the empty seats aligned in rows and the pair flanking a sofa. A dozen chairs. Yeah, he had room all right.

Goosebumps cropped up on her arms as the hairs on her neck stiffened. Amador's attention, riveted to her, triggered a physical response.

She folded her hands on her lap. "Why did you drug me?"

He sagged into his seat, closing his eyes as he shook his head. "It was a terrible mistake. I'm sorry." He raked a hand through his hair, mussing it. "I hoped the serum would help you with your powers, yes, but mostly I wanted to make you more receptive." He covered his eyes with his hand. "To me."

"You were trying to seduce me?"

"No." He pulled himself up and met her gaze. "I needed you to believe me, to help me. The serum seemed my best option to make that happen. Time is running out, Grace. For all of us."

His words penetrated her soul like pins and needles jabbed into her core. "What do you mean time is running out?"

He exhaled, and his shoulders slumped again. "Tesler. He plans to capture you and mine your brain for the secrets to psychic power. He already knows how to shatter minds and bend them to his control. Once he has what he needs from you..." Amador grasped his knees. "He will create an army of psychics who obey his will and his will alone. The Golden Power will make it possible."

The world lurched around her, though the jet stayed level. She gripped the arms of her seat, hanging on until the spinning ceased. An army of brainwashed psychics. Tesler in command. Her breaths quickened, her pulse too. Heartbeats thundered in her ears, raged through her veins, and scorched out her thoughts. She'd seen what Tesler's methods did to psychics. Andrew Haley, coerced into reading minds, catapulted straight into insanity. And her own brushes with the Golden Power tainted her with a sourness she could not shake. If Tesler mined her for answers, unlocking the secrets of imbuing anyone with psychic abilities and controlling those subjects, then he could rule the world. Literally. Plant a damn jeweled crown on his head and make everyone genuflect before their master.

Hell no.

Grace shot to her feet, hands clenched at her sides. "We have to stop him."

Amador rubbed his forehead. "It will not be easy. He'll fight and claw and destroy anything that gets in his way. Even you aren't strong enough to stop him." Amador eyed her, his lips compressed. "Unless..."

"I use the Golden Power again."

"Yes."

A shudder racked her body, knocking her off-kilter. She dropped back onto her seat. Though she'd vowed never to use the Golden Power again, her sabotage of Tesler's facility wouldn't slow him down for long. He'd hunt down David. Punish him. Leverage him.

And she'd cave in to Tesler's demands.

Which left her one option.

Tap into the ultimate power, no matter the cost. If it meant insanity, fine. If it molded her into something else, something both more and less than herself, then she'd swallow the consequences whole. Even if it choked her.

She glared out the window, into a night as thick and suffocating as a drenched wool blanket. "I'll do it. To stop Tesler, I will tap into the Golden Power."

And if it mutated her into a monster, heaven help the rest of the world. She squeezed her eyes shut and beamed a message out to David, praying he'd receive it.

Kill me, David. If it comes down to me or the world, kill me.

Chapter Twenty

David jolted awake. The back of his head smacked into the wall, radiating pains through his skull. The hammering of his heart shattered the quiet inside the cabin, though only inside his head. *Dammit.* He'd fallen asleep, despite his promise to Sean and Nkosi that he'd keep watch while they slept.

Burning wood crackled in the stone fireplace a dozen feet away. Tongues of flame licked at the air and spilled flickering light into the living room, drowning out the pale moonglow beyond the windows above his head. Nkosi dozed on the sofa. Sean, curled up in an overstuffed armchair, watched David through half-closed lids.

Kill me, a voice begged him inside his mind. *Kill me, David.*

He jerked forward, palms on his outstretched legs, nails digging in. Grace was calling to him. Her energy coursed down their connection, her words a despondent plea. Why the hell would she ask him to kill her?

Amador.

David ground his teeth. The bastard must've hurt Grace. Tortured her. Driven her to the brink of insanity. For no other reason would she beg to die.

With a flourish of power, he reached out to Grace. Her life essence burned like a fireball, blazing into him, around him, through him. He gasped and pulled back from the link, from her. The withdrawal carved out a hollow space nothing could fill except for her—with him, for real this time, not as a manifested entity of shocking power, but as the sweet and passionate woman he cherished.

He snaked out a tendril of energy, testing the waters. *Grace, are you all right?* Her love beamed into him—incandescent, gentle, endless—wringing tears from his eyes. Tears? God almighty, he had never cried before. Never. But bathed in her reverence, he could not stem the flow, because beneath the love simmered a darker energy that clawed for control of Grace. The Golden Power squatted within her, a ghost of limitless power, and it craved more.

Let it go, Grace, please let it go.

"What's the matter?"

Sean's voice, tight with anxiety, shattered the connection, yanking David back to the here and now. Gasping for breaths, he swiped at his eyes. Sean did not need to see him weeping. Aside from the macho reasons for hiding his tears, he knew the sight of them would ratchet up Sean's anxiety.

David cleared his throat and straightened. "I'm fine. Go back to sleep."

Sean slid off the chair and crawled across the bare wood floor to David—crawled because he'd admonished Sean to keep a low profile in the vicinity of the windows. "I can take over so you can rest."

"No thanks." As if he could take a nap knowing Grace was in trouble. Maybe not physical danger, but the psychic variety might prove equally dangerous. The knowledge of her state, of the threat lurking in her own mind, grated on his last nerve. "I'd rather sit up a little longer."

"Me too." Sean scooted backward into the wall. "Can't sleep. Keep thinking about… stuff."

David eyed him sideways. "Tesler won't find us yet. Grace made sure of that. She'll come for us before any bad guys track us down."

"Yeah…" Sean drew his knees to his chest and folded his arms over them. "That's what I keep thinking about. Grace."

"What do you mean?"

"Her power. She's… scary strong." Sean flinched, as if in expectation of a slap. "I like her, you know I do, she's really cool."

But he was afraid of her. Who wouldn't be? David propped one elbow on his bent knee and cradled his forehead in his palm. "I know she was different the last time we saw her, but she's still the same old Grace." He prayed he wasn't lying. "She needs a little time to recover from using the Golden Power, that's all."

Sean stiffened. "She used it? Again? I thought she hated it. Why would she use it knowing what it does to her?"

David sighed, a long and wistful breath. Sean knew nothing about what had gone down in the room with Tesler. About the deaths. About Grace's appearance. He scratched his scalp, his forehead still braced on his palm. "She had to do it to save my life." Which made all of this his fault. He must right the wrong before Grace lost her humanity, her sanity, to the ultimate power. "Tesler killed me and Nkosi. Grace brought us both back."

Sean's mouth rounded into an O, his eyes widening. "Whoa. I didn't know she could pull that off, even with the Golden Power."

"Yes, you do." David lifted his head to look at Sean. "She did it six months ago."

"Noooo, that was way different. We were injured, not dead."

The last thread of David's hope snapped. Sean was right. Grace had gone too far this time, too deep into the psychic realm. How on earth could he bring her back?

An ember of hope hid beneath the ashes. Earlier tonight, he'd coaxed her back from the depths. He could do it again.

How many times would his failures push her to take measures no one should have to resort to? He'd let her down in so many ways. Taking off on Tesler hunts. Abandoning her. Refusing to answer her questions. Ignoring her fears because it suited his needs, his quest for… What? Protecting Grace, yes. If he was man enough to admit the whole truth, though, he had another reason for his obsession with Tesler. He sought redemption.

Did he deserve it? His betrayal loomed between them, a monolithic impediment, one she knew nothing about because he was terrified to tell her.

Sean coughed and rubbed his neck. "You know, since my mom died, you guys are like my family." He fiddled with his shoelace. "So try not to get killed, okay?"

David leaned his head against the wall. "I won't let anything happen to you or Grace."

"Wish I could heal the dead. Can't even heal myself. Is the Golden Power really so awful?"

"You don't want it. Trust me."

Energy rushed through him, hot and sweet and oh-so-familiar. She was here.

David leaped up, tore the cabin door open, and barreled out into the night, toward the one thing in this world that mattered more to him than his own life.

Grace.

———

SHE SPOTTED THE CABIN UP AHEAD, THROUGH A SCREEN OF TREES. HER heartbeat quickened, and her skin tingled with awareness. *David.* Their connection swung wide open, her mind welcoming his without reservation. The energy of him flooded into her, stealing her breath. She stumbled.

Amador seized her arm, steadying her.

She jerked free of him. "Thanks. But remember, the only reason you're here is because I need backup in case Tesler's men find us." She tapped the grip of the handgun strapped to his belt. "You sure you've got the stomach for shooting somebody?"

He bristled. "Yes. If you can do it, so can I."

"It's not a contest. Shooting people is… unpleasant." Memories flashed through her mind, sharp and blinding, but she cast them aside. "If it comes down to us or them, I need to know you can do whatever it takes."

Amador nodded. "I can. I will."

His expression gave away nothing, and a thought flitted through her brain. *Maybe he likes hurting people.* He had tortured an innocent girl. Yet harming a helpless child was far different from firing on well-armed, well-trained muscle men. Would he cower in the face of real danger?

She'd let Amador tag along strictly because she realized he planned on trailing behind her if she rejected his offer to accompany her. Men. Psychotic or sane, they all had macho streaks laced with pigheadedness.

"Shall we continue?" Amador asked.

"Yes." She faced toward the clearing, and the cabin nestled on the opposite side. "When we get there, you do not speak or do anything unless I say so. Got it?"

"Of course." He grunted. "David will not be pleased to see me."

So naturally, Amador sounded smugly satisfied with himself for the future irritation he'd inflict on David.

Grace marched out into the clearing.

The cabin door banged open, the sound echoing off the trees. A figure rocketed outside, headed straight for them. Her heart pounded. Tears spilled down her cheeks.

She bolted toward David.

He swept her up into an embrace so tight it squeezed the breath out of her. She flung her arms around him, burying her face against his neck. Her feet dangled in midair, but she cared about nothing except losing herself in the feel of his hard, warm body. Life surged through his veins, down their psychic link, pouring into her. She sealed her mouth over his, thrusting her fingers into his hair while his hands stroked her back. She savored the spicy taste of him, the delicious friction of his mouth on hers, the unique and irresistible scent of him.

"Oh man," Sean hollered, "you guys need a room so bad."

His taunt barely registered through the fog of desire. David had kissed her hours ago, in her manifested form, but this…

No comparison.

He set her down. His flavor infused her mouth, and she licked her lips. Though she yearned for more, she sensed his mood had shifted.

His hands settled on her hips. "I'd like to finish that conversation we started yesterday."

"Oh, you mean when you tried to dump me?"

He shifted his gaze to the ground. His mouth twisted into a grimace. "Yes. I mean that conversation. You said it wasn't over, and I realized you were right."

"Great. Let's talk on the plane."

"No. We need to talk now. Alone. Please."

Ominous, she thought, but since Amador didn't need to hear her misgivings, she said, "Sure. Give me a minute, though, okay?" She nodded toward her companion. "I need to have a chat with Amador first."

David's mouth compressed. "Why?"

"Because I'm trusting him with our lives, and I need to make sure he knows how angry I'll be if he screws us over. His jet is our ride home."

"I've got a better idea." His lips quirked in a near smile. "Let's tie him up, steal his jet, and chuck him out over the mountains."

"Ha-ha." She skimmed her fingers over his cheek. "Trust me. I can handle Amador."

"Is that supposed to make me feel better?"

"No, it's a statement of fact." She prayed it was a fact and not a self-inflicted delusion. "Wait here."

She turned away from him.

A shiver of knowledge rattled through her.

She whirled on David, seized fistfuls of his shirt, and hauled him toward her. The force of her hold bent him over, his face inches from hers. His fear coursed into her, stronger now thanks to the physical contact. Her jaw trembled. Tears burned in her eyes, tightening her lids.

His face blanched. He knew she knew.

"I can feel it," she said, her voice strained and rough. "Your fear, your anger, your absolute conviction that you're about to do the right thing. Did you think you could hide it from me?"

"No." Emotion roughened his voice too, though his expression was unreadable. "No, I—that's why I wanted to talk to you alone. To explain."

"Explain what?" She tugged him closer. Spittle sprayed his face when she spoke. "That you're abandoning me?"

"I'm not. I wouldn't."

Anxiety rippled through her from all around, not just from David, but from their friends too. Everyone worried when Mom and Dad fought. And weird as it was, that's what she and David had become. The parents of this dysfunctional family.

She released his shirt. Dragged in a long breath. Straightened her blouse. Then she cleansed her face of all emotion and locked her gaze on David's, firing every shred of her anger and terror and adoration into him down their link. His eyes widened a hair, just enough to expose the fact her message had hit him, loud and clear.

"You're not coming with us," she said, careful to speak in a hushed tone, so no one else would hear. "You're staying, to fight Tesler."

"I have to." He matched her soft voice, his face as empty of feeling as hers must've been.

She wasn't calm, not on the inside, but it felt like someone had poured concrete over her to contain her emotions.

"Grace, I'm sorry. I have to stay."

"Okay then."

She tromped toward Amador. David's gaze tracked her, pinned to her back like a ray of concentrated sunlight heating her flesh. She focused on

Amador, and his self-satisfied expression. The bastard enjoyed seeing her and David argue.

"I need you to listen," she told Amador. "Agree with everything I say and mean it. Then I'm going to ask you a few questions, which you will answer without hesitation—and you'll tell me the truth." She barred her arms over her chest. "Do you understand?"

"Yes."

"Good. You're taking Sean and this other guy away from here on your plane. David and I are staying." He opened his mouth, but she raised one palm to silence him. "No questions, no arguments. I speak, you agree. Understand?"

"I do. And yes, of course, I will take your friends to a safe location. I know of one—"

"Uh-uh. You're taking them to my grandfather."

His brow arched. "Edward McLean?"

"He'll protect them." She recited her grandfather's cell number. He was at their backup location—their emergency hideout, an old farmhouse in Kansas, purchased under a false name with cash. Grandpa would take care of them, but he wouldn't trust Amador, a stranger. "Have Sean make the call and do whatever my grandfather says. Got it?"

He nodded. His lips moved as if he wanted to speak.

She dangled her arms at her sides, trying to look nonthreatening. If he needed to tell her something, she probably ought to hear it. "What is it?"

"You should know the entire story. About me." He ducked his head, shoulders quivering. "My wife. She couldn't handle Evander's death. She—" His words were choked off as he jerked his head up, his gaze intent on hers and gleaming with tears about to spill forth. Yet his voice emerged in a hardened tone. "She cut her wrists while I was away on business. After that I..." He clutched Grace's hands, lifting them to his face. His breaths flared over her skin. "I lost my mind, Grace, which I imagine is no surprise to you."

"It's not too late to come back from it."

"For me, I fear it is. Vengeance has eroded my soul."

Vengeance. She gulped back a swell of nausea. Amador was obsessed with the same goal as David—with the same target, Karl Tesler—and his compulsion had toppled him over the edge. If David couldn't relinquish his quest, would he tumble off the same cliff?

Amador and David were different men, with different temperaments. David could survive what had destroyed Amador.

The lunatic in question pressed the backs of her hands to his cheeks, shut his eyes, and sighed. A tear trickled down his face, oozing onto her skin. "I long to be as good as you, as strong and compassionate. But I'm weak." He nuzzled her palm. "Please try to understand. What I've done, I believed these were right things. You've shown me I was wrong."

"You need to understand something too." She took one step toward him, cupping his face in her hands, forcing him to meet her eyes. "I can help you, Biel, if you'll let me. You can reclaim your life."

He shook his head, pulling away from her hands. "No. I've gone too far. After my wife's death, I poured all my wealth and connections into hunting down Tesler. But when I found him, he took me prisoner simply to keep me from reporting what I had uncovered about him." He averted his gaze. "I stole files from the Siberian facility, and that's how I learned of you. I prayed your powers could bring Tesler's world crashing down on his head."

"They still might." She glanced over her shoulder at Sean, Nkosi, and David, whose gaze drilled into her though he watched without expression. Her attention glued to David, she told Amador, "Take Sean and Nkosi."

"You know the other man?"

"Huh?"

"Nkosi. You must know him, since you spoke his name, but he looks at you as if he's not met you before."

"I haven't met him."

"Then how do you know his name?"

The Golden Power. That was how she knew. Tiny blades dug into her heart, nicking and scraping at her soul. "Just do as I say. Please."

"You have my word." He fidgeted, his gaze darting left and right, up and down. Finally, he drew two objects out of his pocket and held his hand to her, palm up. "These may be of some use to you."

A glass vial rested on his palm. It contained pale-yellow liquid.

"The serum you gave me," she said.

"Yes."

She took the vial and poked the other object with her little finger. It looked like a pen with no writing tip and a little button on one end. "What's this?"

"An auto-injector. It holds the counteracting agent. There is a single dose left, and it will last fifteen minutes at most."

"Thanks." The serum might prove useful, somehow. She palmed the auto-injector along with the vial and slipped them into her pocket. "Time to go our separate ways."

"Where will you go?"

David's energy infused her, warm and sweet and spiced with desire. Every iota of her being called out to him. The barest smile curved her lips. "Where I belong."

Grace watched Nkosi and Sean stride off into the woods with Amador. Then she let David take her hand, leading her into the cabin. A fire crackled in the hearth. She inhaled the musty scent of dust and stale air, but the earthy aroma of burning wood overpowered the other smells. David tugged her toward the sofa, an overstuffed number with flower-print fabric. She sank into the cushions beside him.

He scooted away.

"What is wrong with you?" she asked. What if he said he couldn't stand the taint of the Golden Power that lingered in her? What would she do then? What could she do? Wringing her hands, she bit her lip and waited.

The distance between them measured in inches, but it gaped like a vast canyon. She swore she could hear her words echoing back to her. *Do not cry.* An emotion she couldn't puzzle out darkened his expression. She yearned to smooth the lines from his forehead with her fingertips, to brush away the tightening of his lips, to caress the tension out of his shoulders.

He slipped a hand over hers, his arm stretched across the gap between them. "It's not you, Grace. You're... perfect." He sucked in a ragged breath. "But I have to tell you the truth, and you won't like it. I don't expect forgiveness, I won't ask for it, but you need to know the truth."

His voice had quieted to a whisper, his tone bleak and fraught with pain. When he raised his chin, revealing his face, his expression unleashed a torrent of sympathy inside her. Never had she seen him so anguished, so defeated, so repentant. She lifted a hand, desperate to touch him, but pulled it back. Her hands trembled. She tried to rip her gaze away from his, but the connection between them imprisoned her. Their psychic link. It smoldered within them, between them.

His fingers tightened on hers. "You asked if it's true. If I killed someone."

Everything inside her froze. She stared at her fingers, at his laid atop them, at the creases of his knuckles. Oh God, oh God, she'd changed her mind. She did not want to know. David would not commit cold-blooded murder, but what if he'd been forced to kill in defense of himself or another? She could handle that. But what if Tesler had pumped David full of drugs and coerced him into murdering someone? *Suck it up and be here for him, like he's done for you.* Yeah, she could do that. She must do it.

David retracted his hand. In a voice devoid of emotion, he said, "It's true. I am a killer."

"I—"

He pressed two fingers to her lips. "Shhh. Let me finish."

She swallowed, nodded, and tried to smile but failed miserably.

"It was self-defense," he said, refusing to look at her. "Another traveler broke into my room and tried to coerce me into telling him who Janet Austen was. He thought if he found you, and delivered you to JT, then he'd be released unharmed." David withdrew his fingers. Stiff and impassive, he stared into the shadows past her shoulder. "He gave me no choice, tried to strangle me. I grabbed a lamp and hit him over the head. End of story."

She reached for his hand.

He yanked it away.

"David." She slumped against the sofa, deflated inside and out. "It wasn't your fault. Why would you push me away because of that? I don't get it."

"I was answering your question. But that's not the reason I…" He rubbed his hands on his pants as if struggling to cleanse them. "Listen to me. Amador was right. There is something I've done, something unforgivable."

"You don't know what I can forgive."

His eyes had gone glassy, his demeanor so remote she wondered if he'd dispatched his mind to another world. A psychic knew how to literally let his mind wander. She lifted a hand to touch him but drew it back. Foreboding weighed down on her so heavily that it immobilized her.

Then he turned his gaze on her, and she saw the yawning distance in his eyes, their color somehow faded. He spoke with a detachment that chilled her. "You've wanted to know how JT found you. Who told him your real name. Who's responsible for the torment he inflicted on you, and that Tesler wants to continue inflicting on you. You need to know who to blame, right?"

She hesitated. "Yes."

But she wasn't sure at all she wanted to know. Her skin crawled. Her throat went dry. She could not tear her gaze from his, though, or stop herself from hearing what he told her next.

"It was me. I told Tesler who you were and exactly where to find you." He shut his eyes for a second, then opened them again. "I betrayed you, Grace. I am responsible for the hell your life has become. All the people who died because they got in the way of JT capturing you, I'm the one who set him loose on them."

She shook her head, unable to comprehend.

His mouth twisted into a sad, sardonic smile. "Can you forgive me now?"

Chapter Twenty-One

AVID CRINGED THE SECOND HE UTTERED THE WORDS. HE FLATTENED his hands on his thighs, then dropped them to the cushions and dug his nails into the padding. He couldn't breathe, didn't dare glance at her. Adrenaline pumped through his veins, electrifying his nerves, scouring away thoughts. The impulse to drag her into his arms swelled and crashed against his willpower. *Don't touch her, don't do it, let her process this.*

How could she process it? He'd just confessed to betraying her in the worst way and ruining her life. No one could forgive that.

Grace's hand crept across the sofa toward him, her fingers crawling ever nearer. When the tips bumped his hand, she slid her fingers over his skin. He tried to pull away, but she clamped her hand firmer around his. The warmth of her flesh leeched into his skin as her scent wafted over him, and the urge to plunge into her tempting mouth, to bury his pain and fear in her kiss, exploded inside him.

He would not do it. Not unless she gave him a sign she wanted the contact.

She was holding his hand. Wasn't that a sign? It might be pity, nothing more.

When she spoke, her tone was hushed. "I don't believe it. I will *never* believe it."

"You have to."

"No, I don't."

Her thumb caressed his palm, and he longed to accept her reassurance, but he couldn't. Her love pulsed down their connection, warm and gentle and fueled by empathy. A piece of her burrowed into him, overpowering the shame and guilt. He could not let her do this. He could not let her forgive him.

"Go on," she said. "Tell me everything."

Once she knew, she'd hate him. She must. He deserved it.

"I wasn't strong enough then," he told her. "I—I didn't expect what they did to me. The drugs made it hard to focus, and then they'd start in with the cutting and the beating. I could deal with pain, but the chemicals… They messed with my head. I fought as long as I could. It wasn't enough." He slung his head back against the sofa. A tightness in his throat roughened his voice. "I made a horrible mistake, and I wound up giving Tesler and JT exactly what they wanted. You."

Her hand went stiff, but only for an instant. She drew his hand to her chest and clasped it between her breasts while he focused on the carpeting, obsessed with a loop of loose thread.

She kissed his fingertips one by one.

He squeezed his eyes shut. She was so much stronger than he was, so much better, and he loved her with a passion he'd never known before. He would do anything to protect her. Well, not quite anything. Her parents had died to shield her from JT and Tesler. And what did he do? He cracked.

She nuzzled his hand, guiding his fingertips over her mouth. He felt his body lean toward her as his lids opened of their own volition and his head slid across the cushion, ever closer to her shoulder. God, he needed her touch, her kiss, her supple flesh. To lose himself in her. To scrub away the stain inside him. But it wasn't right. He couldn't accept comfort from her after what he'd done.

"It's okay," she said.

"No." He yanked his hand away, straightened, and riveted his gaze to the knob on the front door. "It will never be okay. I should've let them kill me. That's what I swore I'd do, to save you. But I was too damn weak."

A gust of wind buffeted the cabin. Wood creaked. A tree branch grated across one of the windows.

Grace wriggled her butt, jostling the cushions and him. "I don't understand. You've only been acting weird for a couple months. Before that, everything was good, relatively speaking."

"I must've repressed the memory. I had no idea until—" He sank his forehead into his palms. "Until I found the video. Irrefutable proof that I—"

"Wait a minute."

Her voice had taken on the suspicious, no-nonsense tone he knew so well. It usually made him smile. Tonight, he couldn't bear to hear it. Though he raised his head, he watched her peripherally.

She folded her arms over her breasts and studied him with squinted eyes. "The night I found you in the living room, staring at the computer like it was sucking the life out of you. That's when you stumbled onto this so-called evidence."

"It's not so-called. The video is ireffu—"

"Baloney. Videos can be doctored or faked altogether." She silenced his protest before he could voice it, by flashing him a sharp look. "Tell me exactly what you saw. I want the blow by blow."

"Grace."

"Don't *Grace* me. Describe the video, in detail, just the facts."

He heaved himself off the sofa, stalked to the window, and glared out at the darkness. "The file was damaged, I think. There was too much static at the beginning to see or hear what was happening. But then the picture cleared, and I saw... me. Strapped to the old dentist's chair. Tesler was hovering over me, the way he does, gloating about how he'd finally broken me. He thanked me for giving him Janet Austen." He squeezed his eyes shut, ducking his head. "He said JT would be very pleased with me."

He spat the last phrase, but the sourness of it coated his tongue.

From the rustling behind him, he knew she was getting up off the sofa. Her footfalls were light and quiet, almost imperceptible. Her arms encircled his chest, her warm, soft body flush against his back. Her cheek rested on his shoulder, her hair tickling the nape of his neck.

"You don't know what you saw," she murmured. "The file was corrupted, possibly tampered with. If you were drugged, Tesler might've been lying to trick you into exposing me."

"No one else knew your real name."

"Grandpa did."

"He wouldn't betray you."

She kissed his neck, her lips a delicate flutter on his skin. "Neither would you. There has to be another explanation. I will not accept that either one of you led JT to me."

The conviction in her tone buoyed him a little, for a heartbeat, or maybe two. He yearned to believe it.

She set her chin on his shoulder. "This is why you wanted the flash drive. To, what, delete the incriminating evidence?"

"I tried to delete it when I found the video. Didn't work. I'm not as good with computers as you are."

"Then why did you want the flash drive?"

"I don't know." His hands moved on their own to cover hers. "All of a sudden, getting the thing away from you seemed vitally important."

"Guilt makes you irrational. But you have nothing to feel guilty about. Understand?"

"The video—"

"Is crap." She entwined her fingers with his. "I know you. No matter what Tesler did, you wouldn't tell him squat. You'd die first."

He'd always assumed he would. The evidence suggested otherwise.

"Even if you did this," she said, her breaths hot on his skin, "I would understand. Tesler tortured you. Drugged you. I won't let you push me away because—"

"Stop." He wrestled out of her embrace and avoided her tender gaze. "Don't do it. Don't forgive me."

"Or what? You'll dump me again?" She made a soft sound, almost a laugh. "You tried that already. I'm not so easy to get rid of."

"I know." He should've walked out the door, but his feet seemed nailed to the floor. "You can't trust me anymore."

"Of course I can." She moved in front of him to take hold of his shirt and shake him. "Get this through your thick skull, David. I trust you. Whatever you think you've done, it changes nothing. I will never give up on us."

He stared at her, blank in mind and spirit, desperate to believe but unable to accept it.

"Never." She shook him harder. "Not even when we're dead."

"Don't talk about dying. If anything happened to you..."

She looped her arms around his neck, hands linked at his nape. Her fingers traced delicate circles on his scalp and ruffled his hair. His muscles relaxed, even as her body pressed into him. She splayed her fingers through his hair and gently urged him to slant his head toward hers. He obeyed, as always a slave to her tenderness.

Her hazel eyes were alive with passion, the emotional kind. It filtered into him through his pores from her skin, through his parted lips from her breaths that flavored his tongue. Sweet. Electric. More powerful than anything in the universe, it eclipsed even the Golden Power.

"I love you," she said. "No conditions. No qualifications. And I fight for what I love, fight with everything I've got until there's nothing left in me. You should know this by now. You know *me*."

He did. And that was what terrified him. Grace Powell would never give up because she loved him. Her passion flowed out of her whenever their eyes met, whenever their fingers brushed or their lips tasted each other. He'd struggled for so long to restrain his ardor, his devotion to her, his need to unite with her in every possible way. She owned his heart, his mind, and his soul.

At last, he understood what he must do. His mistake had been to shut her out in a vain attempt to divorce their minds and sever, or at least weaken, their connection. Why had he ever believed that would protect her? The solution was right in front of him, entwined with him, caressing him and gazing into his eyes with the gleam of pure love in those beautiful golden irises.

He hugged her tight. "I will never leave you again. We're in this together, until the end." He let his lips skim over hers, and the intoxicating sweetness of her teased his senses. "No more running. I'm with you, forever."

She smiled against his mouth. "I'm with you, David. Forever."

His feet, once rooted in place, lightened, along with the rest of him, until he was sure he must've floated up off the floor with her secure in his arms.

She canted her head, stroking her fingertips down his cheek. The movement of her head streaked firelight across her eyes, making the shadows beneath them stand out against her creamy skin.

He grasped her hands and pulled them down to his chest. "When did you last eat?"

Chewing her lip, she considered the question. "Not sure."

"Grace, 'not sure' is too long." He glanced around the cabin. "I wonder if there's any food around here."

"Bottled water and canned goods in the pantry." She nodded toward a doorway at the far side of the living room. "Through there."

"How…"

She hunched her shoulders. "Limitless knowledge."

Understanding bloomed in his mind and heart. The information she'd gained from the Golden Power persisted inside her.

Not for long. He knew how to save her from ever again having to tangle with the ultimate power source, and the answer was ridiculously simple.

All he had to do was love her.

With passion, purpose, and absolute conviction.

Chapter Twenty-Two

GRACE SAT AT THE KITCHEN TABLE IN A STRANGER'S HOUSE, WHICH she'd appropriated without permission, and scooped up the last forkful of baked beans purloined from the pantry. The rustle of pine needles on the roof, stirred by the wind, lulled her senses. The low purr of the cordless electric can opener lured her attention to the man busily liberating a second batch of canned peaches. *Her* man.

She couldn't recall thinking of him that way before, but tonight she embraced the term. Her man. He was hers, after all, bonded to her by a ring and a telepathic connection. And love. Deep, unfaltering love.

The beany scent wafting up from her fork made her wrinkle her nose. Her stomach protested at the idea of accepting more food, particularly beans. It wasn't a very romantic dinner, what with gas-inducing dishes and eating straight from the cans.

"I'm full," she said.

He half-turned to frown at her. "Fruit has electrolytes or something, stuff you need after overtaxing your powers and your body."

"I'm regular taxed, not over." She waggled her fork. "I'm finishing the beans, and that's it. I'll barf if you make me eat any more peaches."

"Gr—" He'd been about to *Grace* her, but thought better of it. *Smart man.* Instead, he set down the can opener and plucked up a peach slice. Juice dribbled onto the counter. He tossed the slice into his mouth, chewing with vigor.

She wrinkled her nose again when he tipped the can toward her.

One corner of his mouth dimpled downward.

He was anxious, she realized then. About her health and their relationship. About their inevitable confrontation with Tesler. About the future, if they lived long enough to have one.

So she rolled her eyes, shoved the beans in her mouth, and forked a peach slice.

David turned away, absorbed by the task of replacing the can opener precisely where he'd found it, in a holder affixed to the wall. His actions afforded her the chance to admire him in secret. With his back to her, he didn't know she was ogling his tight ass, the way his muscles rippled under his weekend-warrior outfit. Damn, he looked hot in camo.

Done with the can opener, he nabbed a container of disinfectant wipes and set about cleaning up the juice he'd drizzled on the counter.

She thrust the peach slice into her mouth and munched with more ferocity than necessary. The crisp efficiency of his movements as he swept a soft, damp cloth over the smooth counter awakened her body more than she would've expected. She was exhausted. But suddenly, her skin tingled with anticipation and she squeezed her thighs together to squelch a dull throb in her most intimate places.

Oh, to be that countertop, bathed by his deft hands.

Grace averted her eyes to her plate and chewed harder. The owner of this cabin clearly adored beans—the pantry was stocked full of them—as well as canned corn, sliced peaches, and ravioli. Her first meal in more hours than her weary brain could calculate consisted of these items. David had insisted she eat all of it, and just to be more stubborn, he gobbled up his own servings of the odd feast.

She hadn't wanted to eat anything, despite the grumbling in her stomach. Questions battered her mind. How long would her confusion tactics deter Tesler? Was the facility still in the dark, or had her permanent disabling of their systems turned out to be not so permanent? Had Tesler already dispatched commandos to hunt them? What could she and David do to save themselves?

Run. That was their sole option.

Swallowing her food, she dropped her fork onto the table with a clack. They couldn't run. Tesler would hunt them wherever they hid. This ended one way—with a battle, bloodshed, pain, and death.

They must ensure the death was Tesler's.

David snatched up her fork and the empty can of beans, pecked a kiss on her forehead, and strode back to the counter. Damp cloth. Strong hands. Swirling motions of his powerful fingers.

He tossed the used wipes in the trash and took a seat opposite her, one arm draped on the table, one ankle braced atop the other knee. A slight smile relaxed his mouth, and his entire expression. Since his pronouncement he would never leave her again, his demeanor had altered so much her head spun from the shock of it. Tense, distant David morphed into relaxed, determined David. It was like he'd reached some important decision.

His anxiety hadn't completely fled. He'd needed to clean up, after all. But otherwise, he was… different.

Maybe this was the man he'd been before, during those months she still couldn't remember. Whatever the reason for his change, it did things to her. Subtle, sensual things.

He stretched his hand out to lace his fingers with hers.

She had to test this, to make sure he wasn't glossing over his issues for her benefit. The heat of his hand spread into her, though, melting away doubt.

Dammit. She snapped her spine straight and zeroed her gaze in on his, on those gleaming blue eyes. "Do you still believe you betrayed me?"

He flinched, just a tad. His fingers loosened their grip on hers, only for a second, then clinched her tighter. "I did, Grace. We both have to accept it."

She let out a long sigh. "No, David, I'm not convinced we do. I think I can prove whether the video is accurate."

"How? There's no computer here. You can't access the flash drive." His gaze flew to her breasts, right where the device in question lay nestled between them. His lips curved into a hungry slant.

Desire thrummed inside her.

Snap out of it. Her self-admonishment broke the spell, and the idea she'd hatched a little while ago resurfaced in her hormone-drenched brain. "Amador mentioned a power called postcognition. According to him, some people can view past events as if they were there at the time it happened. Kind of like psychic time travel."

His lips pursed. His fingers dug into her palm. "You and Amador have gotten close, I gather."

The acid in his tone burned her, but she wouldn't relent this time. "I barely know him, and no, I do not trust him." She wrapped his hand in both of hers. "This might not work. I mean, for all I know, Amador's full of shit."

David snorted.

She pinched his hand, rewarded by his playful smile. "I'm going to try it. Postcognition."

One of his brows lifted. "Do you have any idea how it works?"

"No. Do you?"

He shook his head. "First I've heard of it."

She shrugged. "I didn't know how to use the Golden Power either, but I did." She leaned forward, her grip on his hand firm. "If the video is real, and you did this, it wasn't your fault. Nothing changes between us. But if you didn't do it, don't you want to know?"

He rubbed his neck and shifted in his seat, grimacing. She massaged the back of his hand with her thumb. When she was about to speak, to reassure him, he abruptly bent forward and his expression switched back into relaxed assurance, as if he'd reaffirmed his mysterious decision.

"All right," he said. "Do it."

"Close your eyes and remember the video."

One corner of his mouth lifted. "Thought you had no idea how to do this."

"I don't, but I have a plan." She gave his hand a light slap. "Shut up and do what I say."

"Yes, ma'am." With his free hand, he saluted her.

She restrained a grin, stifled a laugh, and forced herself to concentrate on the task ahead.

David closed his eyes.

Grace raised her hands before her as if praying, with his hand sandwiched between them. "Try not to freak out at what I'm going to do. Okay?"

"I don't freak out." He cracked one eyelid to peek at her. "I can handle whatever you can."

"This is not a test of your machismo." She rested her chin on their joined hands, her lips grazing his knuckles. "I'm about to throw open the floodgates."

"What are you talking about?"

"Between our minds. I'm going to open the psychic floodgates. I don't know what will happen."

His eyes locked on her with unnerving intensity. "You think I'm holding back with you."

"Aren't you?"

He wiggled his fingers to tickle her lips. "Not anymore."

Something in his tone convinced her he meant it, which shot a bolt of heat lightning through her entire body. David unbridled? She couldn't remember a time when he didn't hold back. Hell, she couldn't remember a time when *she* didn't either.

His jewel eyes glimmered from inside, with the secret fire only a traveler sustained. He was unleashing his powers even now. The tendrils licked at her psyche in an almost sensual way.

"Go ahead," he told her, in a husky tone. "My mind is yours."

Somehow, he turned the statement into an erotic challenge.

He shut his eyes, his expression serene, and spoke in a calm voice. "Whatever you do, Grace, make sure you keep that firewall up."

"Okay." Suddenly, her heart was pounding. She drew in several deep breaths to steady herself, closed her eyes, and knocked down the barriers shielding her mind, her soul, from him—though she kept the firewall intact. These were private floodgates in a channel connecting the two of them, and no one else. Her psychic intruder couldn't sneak in, she knew it, without understanding how she knew. The truth of it resonated inside her.

The essence of David flowed in as she poured all of herself back into him. No hiding anymore. If he could let loose, in mind and spirit, then so could she. Part of her had longed for this, dreamed of it even, the day when they might come together without fears or doubts. This was it.

Their link unfurled, an iridescent thread of blue in the darkness. She took hold and let it draw her in, to a place buried deep in his memory.

Static. Voices.

Pain bit down on her. She wrestled free of it, undeterred from her goal. *Help me see, David.*

White light exploded around her. She tumbled headlong into the brilliance, toward the voices and the static. Without warning, she burst out into the world.

Into the past.

———

DAVID LIES IN A CHAIR, STRAPPED DOWN, SLUMPED, EYES OPEN BUT vacant. The drugs have immobilized him, in body and mind. A bruise, dark purple and blue, covers one entire forearm, and blood trickles from a gash on his head. She senses him there, but too weak to form coherent thoughts. When she reaches out to his mind, her powers bounce back from it. This is the past. She can't communicate with him.

Yet even here, their connection binds them. It's how she's found him. David in the present guided her. David in the past anchors her.

Tesler slouches a few feet from the chair, at David's feet. He holds a syringe in one hand, turning it over and over between his fingers. The syringe is empty. He stares at David, his expression cool, detached.

Behind him, another man waits. He touches his face, eyes wide. "Dr. Tesler? Is he…"

"Alive." Tesler's tone is cool too. "Though perhaps I should terminate him. He's of no use to me anymore."

"Terminate?" The other man pushes up his glasses, clearing his throat. "Uh, is that really necessary?"

Tesler whirls on his colleague. His lip curls as he spits words. "It is if I say so."

"Yes, Dr. Tesler."

"Perhaps he can still be of some use…" Tesler glances over his shoulder at David, who blinks slowly, his jaw slack.

Tesler marches past his colleague, and with a flick of his hand, orders the other man to follow him. She follows too, a ghost in this event. Tesler storms out into the corridor, down the passage, to another door marked as an excursion suite. He flings the door inward. It bangs into the wall.

Inside the room, a startled technician jerks his head up to gape at Tesler. "Sir—"

"Has he told you anything yet?" Tesler says as he barges into the room.

"Nothing, sir."

She freezes. God in heaven.

There, bound to a chair, sits Sean. He's weeping, sobbing, his face streaked with blood that runs from wounds hidden by his hair. Raw, red burns blister his arms.

Detached. She must remain detached. This happened last year. It's horrible, but it's over, and Sean is fine now. She just saw him, walking off with Amador and Nkosi.

She must stay focused.

"What about Ransom?" the tech asks.

Tesler hurls the empty syringe into the wall. "He's with her now, I know it. Yet he resists all my attempts to wring the information out of him. I gave him a stimulant to pull him back from the excursion, but he resists that too." Tesler cocks his head, focusing in on Sean. "Perhaps this mewling mutant can be of assistance."

David is traveling. That's why she sensed a vacancy in him, what she mistook for an effect of the drugs.

He's with her, the her from this moment in time.

Tesler waves the tech away and turns to his colleague. "Get me the serum, Yellen."

The other man shoves his hands in the pockets of his lab coat. "Which serum?"

"The only one there is!" Tesler snarls. "Fetch me Jackson Tennant's personal formula."

"But we're not supposed to use that anymore."

"Bring it here!" Tesler's voice booms off the walls, a deafening assault on her astral eardrums. "And spice it up with a bit of thiopental sodium."

Truth serum? Of course. To encourage Sean to cooperate. The monster thought of everything.

Yellen trots out of the room.

Tesler moves to stand beside Sean. He rests his hands on the chair's arm, no more than an inch from the kid's arm. His gaze drops to the floor, his brows gathered tight.

Head bowed, he speaks in a hushed voice. "She loved you."

Sean is too lost in his agony and terror to hear, to comprehend. Tears sting her eyes just watching his features contort with each sob.

Tesler's hand floats up, toward Sean's face.

He yanks it away. Lips drawn in a pucker, he scowls at Sean. "I did love her once. You may not believe it, but I did. So very much. I wish this could be another way…" He steps back, squares his shoulders, and the icy expression overtakes him again. His voice is equally chilled. "But there is no other way to deal with your kind. I need Janet Austen, and you will give her to me."

Footsteps clap in the corridor.

Yellen scampers into the room and hands Tesler a syringe. "The serum, sir."

Tesler snatches the syringe from Yellen's fingers and lowers it to Sean's arm. He hesitates, his brows pinched again.

With an annoyed sigh, he stabs the needle into Sean's arm, depressing the plunger.

The kid flinches, but tears choke his voice. Sean convulses. His eyes bulge. He sucks in one wheezing breath, then his body slumps in the chair. His eyelids flutter, and his face settles into a dazed look.

Tesler bends near Sean's face. "Now, track David Ransom."

"Can't..." Sean's voice is slightly slurred. "Not my power."

"I just gave you more power than a weakling like you deserves. Track David Ransom."

Sean moans.

Tesler slaps him across the face.

The kid jerks.

"Do it," Tesler hisses. "That's an order."

She feels the shift as Sean departs his body, like a change in a ship's ballast. He's gone for minutes, and all she can do is glare at Tesler. She itches to slug him, throttle him, strap him to an evil dentist chair and pump mind-scorching drugs into his veins.

Sean rouses, his head rolling from side to side. His glassy eyes gaze toward the ceiling.

Tesler grabs the kid's chin and wrenches his head. "Who is she?"

Sean clamps his teeth shut.

"You. Will. Tell. Me." Tesler smacks Sean so hard that his head snaps back and his mouth pops open. "Who is Janet Austen?"

"She... ahhh..."

"Tell me!" Tesler seizes Sean's shoulders and rattles him viciously.

His jaw quivers as tears stream down his cheeks. She sees him battling the drugs, but he can't break free of them. A sharp sob racks him. "Grace Powell."

A sickening grin splits Tesler's mouth. His eyes sparkle with dark glee. To Yellen, he says, "Make sure the boy remembers nothing."

The other man nods.

Tesler sprints out of the room. She flies after him, unbound by physical laws, a spirit in pursuit of a madman. Tesler races into the room where David still sits tied to the chair, though now his eyes are open, if bleary. He glances around as if he doesn't recognize the surroundings.

Tesler stops in front of him and claps his hands. "You, dear boy, have given me exactly what I wanted." Bouncing on his toes, he inclines toward David. "I broke you at last. JT will be quite pleased with this development—and with you, for finally acquiescing."

David stares blankly at Tesler.

The scientist plants his hands on the chair's arms and bends over David, their eyes level. "You gave her to me. Grace Powell is ours."

David shakes his head, slowly at first, then with ever-increasing ferocity. His hands grip the chair with such tension they tremble. He stills his head, and for a moment, his face becomes a stony mask. Then his jaw clenches, muscles twitching, and he sears Tesler with a look of pure hatred.

Tesler rises and casually places one hand in his pocket. "After all your suffering to protect her, you are the one who handed her to us. Waldron is already on his way to her. Thank you, David. JT's plan was floundering, but you saved it."

She feels the moment David gives up. Mechanisms click and whir in his psyche, realigning memories, altering perception. He chooses to forget, and this event recedes into the safe little box his mind manufactures for it.

Tesler begins to hum a cheerful tune and, spinning on his heels, prances out of the room.

David's head droops.

She knows. She understands. This is how they found her.

And this is the true torture inflicted on David.

Tesler will pay. She'll throttle him with her own hands, wring his filthy neck until his eyes pop out of his skull.

He must die.

Chapter Twenty-Three

DAVID'S BACK ACHED FROM HOLDING THIS POSITION—BENT FORWARD, arm outstretched, one hand on the far side of the table—but he did not budge. Not one of his limbs would move an inch until she came back to him.

Her eyes flitted behind her closed lids. REM sleep? No, she wasn't asleep. Her mind had disconnected from her body to travel not elsewhere, but else*when*. Was it even possible? He disbelieved anything Amador told her, and yet…

There was still too much he didn't know about psychic faculties. Especially with Grace. She'd resurrected him from death, for pity's sake. *Death.*

Sean had been right. Her use of healing was different this time. Everything about her powers had altered, escalated, mutated. He winced at his own thought. Mutated? Grace was no sideshow freak. She was beautiful, sweet, intelligent, compassionate, and powerful beyond comprehension.

Did he fear her?

Never. He might worry about the changes in her psychic makeup, but he would never, could never, fear her.

His arm cramped. He bit down on the pain and held still.

Grace muttered, her words indecipherable. Her eyes popped open.

David nearly collapsed from relief. The tension slackened out of him.

A grim, knowing smile stretched her lips. She clutched his hand to her chest as if his flesh moored her mind to the present. He watched her, careful to conceal his abject relief and enduring concern.

"You're back," he said, his tone guarded. "Everything okay?"

"Fine. How long was I gone?" She sounded calm, unfazed.

He didn't believe it for one second.

With his arm pinned to her, he could shrug only one shoulder. "You were gone a minute or two, I guess."

"You didn't experience it with me?"

"No."

She kissed his fingers, one by one. "I saw what really happened."

He ducked his head, shoulders flagging. Once, he would've sacrificed anything to know the truth, but now he wanted to slap his hands over his ears and pretend none of this mattered. Except it did. If he had endangered her, and he saw no other explanation for the video, then how could she trust him? She might've sworn it made no difference, but that was before she traveled back in time to uncover the facts. After witnessing the event in person...

"David, look at me." She waited until he complied, and though he ironed his expression into a placid sheet, he feared his eyes disclosed his sorrow. She rested her chin on his knuckles. "Listen to me. Tesler tried to convince you after the fact that you gave him my name. But it's a lie. The leak didn't come from you. No matter how hard he pushed, you refused to give me up."

Speech, movement, thought, he'd lost his mastery of all those things. So he huddled in silence, unwilling to look away from her, unable to respond.

"It wasn't you, David. That's what matters."

He narrowed his gaze on her. "Who was it? Who exposed you?"

She gave him that world-weary smile again. His fury, contained on the physical plane, must've bristled her metaphysical senses, but she simply pressed his hand to her cheek.

He ground his teeth. "I want to know. I demand to know."

She let go of his hand.

No anger? She hated it when he ordered her to do anything, which he rarely bothered to do because she ignored his commands, anyway. For her to make no snide retort, it set his gut to churning.

He fisted both hands on the tabletop. "Tell me."

"You may think you want to know," she said, "but it won't make you feel any better. For once, let something go. Let this go."

He pounded his fists on the wood. "Whoever it is, I'm going to track them down and punish—"

"It was Sean."

The statement doused his fury in a heartbeat, and ice rushed down his veins in its wake. He jerked backward, making his chair rock. The front legs thumped down again.

"Tesler made him do it," she said. "He gave Sean JT's formula, plus truth serum. Then he ordered him to find you because he was sure you'd come to me. The trick worked. Sean learned who I am, and he couldn't help spilling the news to Tesler. The poor kid was drugged out of his head."

David propped his elbows on the table and dropped his head into his hands. "I know what that's like. They gave me JT's wonder serum once. It's like having hydrochloric acid injected into your veins, and then the world turns into a fun house and your powers get amped up so high it's unbearable. Feels like your skin's peeling off, your brain's dissolving, and at the same time, you can do anything. There's a compulsion to do more, more, more. But it rips you apart from the inside out."

Dammit, why Sean? Why did Tesler have to drag a teenage boy into this nightmare?

It's my fault. And yes, it was. If he'd cracked, then Tesler would've left Sean alone. He wished he could claim he would've done things differently if given the chance, but he knew that was a lie. To protect Grace, he would sacrifice anything, anyone.

Once, he might've thought that made him a monster, like Tesler. No more. The woman he loved, his only family in this world, should come before everything else, even his friends, the world, his own life. His one regret was that it took him so damn long to figure that out.

He raised his head a little to peer at her from between his fingers. His hands muffled his voice. "We can't tell Sean."

"I know." She rubbed her arms.

"You're cold." He jumped up from the chair and held out his hand. "Come on. We need to get you back by the fire."

Without protest, she accepted his hand and allowed him to shepherd her to the living room, to the sofa he'd angled toward the fireplace earlier. At his behest, she plopped down on the cushions. He settled in beside her, one arm across the sofa's back, behind her shoulders. She rested her head in the crook of his shoulder.

The familiarity, the intimacy, of the action and the moment uncoiled a spring deep inside him, relieving a pressure he'd lived with for far too long. The pressure of a secret. The horror of what he believed he'd done. Grace proved he hadn't betrayed her. Though he worried for Sean, the boy seemed unaware of his actions. Ignorance really could be, well, if not bliss then at least a kind of sanctuary.

Grace's head sprang up. Her eyes flew wide, and her mouth slipped open.

He turned her face toward him and searched her eyes for some clue. Their pale-brown depths revealed nothing. "What's wrong? Are you feeling sick?"

"No." She leaned into his touch. "It's not me I'm worried about."

"Tell me. Please."

"It's Sean." She shut her eyes. "I think he's Tesler's grandson."

GRACE SHIMMIED AWAY FROM DAVID. SHE PERCHED ON THE SOFA'S edge, hands gripping the cushions, and fought the urge to look at him.

"I'm sorry," she said. "It's awful, but it makes sense."

While cocooned in David's arms, her thoughts had wandered back to her postcognition experience. Something Tesler had said bothered her. She'd replayed the incident as best she could with her mind so worn out. After Tesler went to Sean, he complained about David resisting his efforts to control him. Then he decided to use Sean instead, and he referred to Sean by an insulting term instead of his name.

"Tesler called Sean a mewling mutant," she explained to David. "I suddenly remembered that, and then I remembered where I'd heard the term before."

David huffed. "Tesler thinks all psychics are scum."

"Shut up and listen." She risked a glance then, and his wry smile pinched her heart. "Sorry. But please, let me finish."

One arm on the sofa's back, his posture relaxed and casual, he looked like a normal guy having a normal conversation with his normal fiancée. If only.

"In the files on Amador's DVD," she said, "I read a report written by Tesler. He mentioned a boy, his grandson, who he would not acknowledge because the kid had psychic abilities. He called his grandson a mewling mutant."

"That doesn't mean anything."

"I think it does." She straightened her spine and rotated toward him, her body twisted at the hips. "Tesler has freckles, like Sean. His hair's gray these days, but it might've been red once, like Sean's. During my postcognition episode, Tesler seemed almost regretful about the need to torture Sean with JT's formula. Then he said the strangest thing."

David's brows rose, then scrunched together. "What did he say?"

"He told Sean, 'She loved you.' And later, 'I loved her once.' I think he was talking about his daughter, Sean's mother."

Much as she'd flailed for another explanation, the facts had bobbed up from the depths over and over, like apples in a barrel of water. Poisoned apples.

"I'm not saying Sean is in league with Tesler," she told David, "at least not willingly. But Amador says Tesler wants to create an army of psychics he can control. Maybe Sean was his first test subject."

"You think he's brainwashed." His tone was flat, and he remained perfectly motionless. Though he'd clamped down on his emotions, threads of them tantalized her mind. He was silent for a few seconds, then he said, "I can't swear he's not. All those months at the Mojave Desert facility, it wasn't Tesler who worked Sean over. It was always his underlings. And lately, I have seen Tesler go easy on Sean, though I didn't understand what I was seeing at first. After what you've told me… I think Tesler might care about Sean, in his own twisted way."

"He didn't torture Sean, did he? When he—" The memory strangled her voice, but she cleared her throat and forged ahead. "When he killed you. He could've hurt Sean to make him talk, but he didn't. I think, on some level, Tesler regrets forcing Sean to out me."

"You may be right. But if Sean is brainwashed, there's nothing we can do about that right now." He leaned forward, his head close to hers. He pressed his warm, strong hand to her back and roamed it over her flesh, separated from his by only the cloth of her shirt. "I want to talk about you. Ever since you showed up here, you've been distant."

"I threw myself into your arms. That's not distant."

His fingertips splayed over her shoulder. "We can feel each other, remember? Even with your firewall, I can tell when something's wrong. You're uneasy, about more than Tesler and how we're going to stop him."

She cocked her head. "We? I thought this was your lone-wolf quest for vengeance."

"I shouldn't have let you keep thinking my missions were about revenge. I was afraid to tell you the truth when I thought I'd betrayed you. I was a selfish prick."

"David, you don't have to explain. After seeing what Tesler did to you and Sean, I understand why you're hell-bent on destroying him."

"No. You don't." With both hands, he grasped her upper arms, and his thumbs massaged in slow, delicate strokes. His voice was quiet and fervent. "This was never about my vengeance. It's always been about you. Protecting you from Tesler. Making sure he can't get his hands on you and turn you into his test subject. I could not stand by and let you be tortured, or worse." He dragged her into his chest, his grip firm, his expression determined and heated. His lips grazed hers with each syllable he spoke. "I would rather die than lose you."

His hot mouth slanted over hers. Hard. Hungry. She tried to catch her breath, but his lips devoured the air.

When he tore his mouth away from hers, he stared straight into her eyes. "Can't you understand? Everything is about you."

The quest for Tesler. Leaving her for days at a time. Risking his life to track down the new facility. He'd done it all for her. He had died for her.

She shut her eyes and rested her cheek against his. Life heated his flesh. The spicy male scent of him surrounded her. She ran her palms up and down his chest, her breasts skimming his muscles with each shift of her arms. Alive. He was *alive*.

Death couldn't keep her from him. Nothing could.

Her lips trembled against his cheek. "Don't die for me anymore. Live for me. Live *with* me. Stay with me."

"There's nothing I want more."

Cheek to cheek, they held still in silence. The fire crackled. The wind buffeted the cabin, creaking its frame.

"Tell me the rest," he said.

"I don't know what you mean."

He took hold of her hair and gently tugged it until her head fell back and their gazes intersected. "Tell me what you're afraid of. And don't say

Tesler. I know there's more." His fingers combed through her hair, his touch light and stimulating. "I won't hold back anymore with you. So do the same for me. Let me in, Grace."

Yes, she did hold back. How could she not?

After criticizing him for keeping her at a distance, now she was pushing him away. And pulling him in closer. Push, pull. Push, pull. No wonder he was frustrated with her, but if he knew… If she revealed all…

The truth didn't matter anymore. She understood what must be done. He'd wanted to save her, but the time had come for her to save him. Again.

He'd hate it. Well, screw his male pride. She'd save his ass a thousand times and never apologize for it.

"Listen to me, David." She bracketed his face with her hands. "You were right all along. Tesler must be stopped, for good this time, and the whole network of facilities has to be shut down. But you can't do that. Only I can."

His hand in her hair froze.

"I have to do this," she said. "I'll tap into the Golden Power and destroy this facility, destroy the remnants of JT's empire and every scrap of Tesler's research."

"No, Grace. I won't let you."

She skated her lips over his, aching for a deep, wanton kiss that would erase her fears and doubts. This wasn't the time for it. If she gave in to the need, she might never stop. "Only I can do this. You have to leave me here, go someplace safe. Promise me you will."

"I won't leave." His fingers tightened on her scalp. "You wouldn't leave me here. Don't expect me to do it to you."

Tears pooled in her eyes, hot and stinging. "David, please, do this for me. I don't want you to see me like that again."

He squinted at her, the expression etching faint lines around his eyes. "Like what?"

"The—the Golden Power. What it did to me last time, when I broke you out of the facility." She bowed her head, and his hand slid down her neck. "Please, I'm begging you, go. This time will be worse. This time, the Golden Power will take me." It had tried before, when she'd gathered the energy necessary to build her psychic firewall. When she accessed the Golden Power again, to save David, it nearly consumed her. "I can't fight it anymore, David. I can't come back from it."

"Yes, you can. You will. I won't let it have you."

The determination in his tone broke the dam, and tears flooded out of her on hiccupping sobs.

He pulled her onto his lap, rocking her in his powerful, tender arms, enveloping her in his heat and strength. She sagged into him, her face buried against his neck. A chill had seeped into her the more she considered what she must do, but his body cradling hers eradicated the cold. His warmth suffused her from her skin down to the core of her being as their link swung wide open, funneling all his love and need into her, heightening her desires until she knew nothing but him, with her, around her, in her soul.

The tears dried up, and a spark ignited, kindling a fire deep inside.

She skated a hand up to his shoulder. "Let me go, David. I have to do this."

"No." He drew her tighter against him, his embrace unrelenting. His chest rose and fell against her breasts. "You don't have to do it alone. And you don't need the Golden Power."

"But a piece of it is still inside me. I can't get rid of it."

He stroked her arm in lazy, provocative circles. "I believe you about Tesler's plans. Earlier, when you broadened our link, I felt the truth of what you said and I felt the Golden Power too, but it's weak. We can sever it from you. Permanently."

"What do you mean 'we'?"

His hand on her arm stilled. He hooked a finger under her chin and, with delicate pressure, persuaded her to lift her head. She moved her hand off his shoulder, up to his neck, and dipped her fingertips into his silky hair. His eyes seemed to glow with an inner fire. She longed to dive into the blaze.

Lightning split the darkness. Thunder shattered the stillness, vibrating the walls and floor.

She jumped and yelped.

David just sat there, unmoving, as if the bomb-like boom hadn't registered in his brain. David the warrior angel. Always calm, always in control. Once it had bothered her, a little, but tonight she gleaned strength from his calm. Besides, he'd exposed his fears to her and shared a part of himself no one else saw. Here, in this moment, she adored the warrior in him.

He rubbed his thumb over her lips. "We can do this together, Grace. Expunge the Golden Power from you and defeat Tesler."

"How?"

"Join our powers."

Chapter Twenty-Four

GRACE FELT HER JAW DROP A SMIDGEN AS SHE GAZED AT DAVID, dumbfounded by his suggestion. Yet liquid heat burgeoned inside her, sizzling in her veins and warming her from the inside out. "Join our powers?"

"Yes." David slipped his thumb between her lips and teeth to tease her tongue. The salty flavor of his skin shot a bolt of desire through her, but she marshaled all her self-control to focus on his words as he said, "I don't know exactly how it'll work, or if we can reverse it. I'm willing to take the risk."

"But I'm tainted. The Golden Power—"

"Is not controlling you." He thrust his hand into her hair, tipping her head back, and lowered his mouth enticingly close to hers. "You are the best person I've ever known. Nothing can corrupt you. Trust me on this, I know you better than anyone, better than I know myself. You are a part of me, Grace, in a way no other human being could possibly understand." His lips claimed hers, stoking her passion to such fiery heights that her head spun. When he withdrew, his mouth lingered a hair's breadth from hers. "Be with me forever. Join your powers with mine, bond with me on the metaphysical plane, give in to what we've both wanted since the day we met."

Breathless, she couldn't wrench her gaze away from his.

He combed his fingers through her hair, trailing them over her scalp. "Each other. Nothing else. That's what we both want. I won't hold back from you anymore, and I will make you my only priority. Will you join with me?"

"Yes." She traced her fingers over the muscles of his chest. "I want you, only you, in every way."

His lips tightened against hers, parted by a smile that crinkled the skin around his eyes. Joy swelled in her heart, and passion blazed deep within. His eyes glittered with love and hunger and a joy rivaling hers. It was hers, in a way. Their bond already blended their emotions. To deepen the connection, to merge her psychic energy with his…

Oh God, it would be incredible.

And yet, doubt pecked at her. Weak at first, but stronger and stronger the more she contemplated their joining. A lump in her throat impeded the words she needed to say, but she shoved them out anyway. "Do you think I've changed? Since the amnesia, I mean."

"You are different."

She nodded and wiped at the damn tears welling in her eyes. *Different.* His words provoked an ache in her chest.

Lightning flashed once, twice, three times. Rolling booms rattled the windows. Hail bombarded the roof, rumbling like a stampeding herd of cattle.

David flattened her palm over his heart. "Being different isn't bad."

"Oh, thanks. I feel all better." She winced, realizing she'd retreated into the fortress of sarcasm again. "I'm sorry."

"For what?"

"Being sarcastic. I know you hate that."

"I don't hate it. Never did." He cupped her cheek in his hand. "But I don't want you to hide behind sarcasm because you're afraid to tell me how you really feel."

His eyes blazed even brighter somehow, like pools of sapphire flame. His inner warmth flowed into her, igniting a new fire that dissolved the cold ball of fear and anger lodged in her heart. Everything inside her melted, from her muscles right down to her soul, and her body quivered with need. She craved him with an intensity that should've terrified her. But it didn't. Not anymore.

"What if," she said, "I've changed too much and I can't remember what we had before. You might get sick of it and leave me."

He grasped her waist and eased her over to straddle his lap. His hands glided up her back and tugged her into him. "One, I asked you to marry me. Two, I'm asking you to join with me on a metaphysical level. What about those two proposals makes you think I have any desire to leave you?"

"Nothing, I guess." She squirmed, suddenly aware of his hard body underneath her. Two needs warred within her—the urge to rip his shirt off, and the panicked impulse to run. "I'm poisoned by the Golden Power. How can you still want me?"

"You're not poisoned." He pulled her closer, her breasts mashed against his chest. The taut peaks tingled, and she burned to tear off her bra to relieve the delicious pressure. "I want you for the same reasons I always have. You're wonderful, beautiful, sexy as hell, and I love you more than life itself."

"Oh. Is that all?" A giggle bubbled out of her. "I, um, think you've gotten me drunk."

He smirked. "On what?"

"You. I mean, your psychic energy and, well, other things." His hunger for her crashed into her again and again, an exquisite torment. "I can feel your passion."

She gulped in air but couldn't get enough.

His smirk broke into a sexy grin, and he chuckled. "I told you I'm not holding back anymore. And I can feel your passion too." His hands drifted up to her shoulders, and his voice roughened. "What should we do about that?"

The weight of her ardor bore down on her, shortening her breaths, flaming over her skin. His eyes transfixed her until she felt herself spiraling down into their depths, but instead of recoiling, she reveled in the sensation. *Join with me*, he'd offered. And oh, did she want to.

His lips explored hers tenderly, savoring her taste just as she savored his. Her body yielded to the ravenous fire, and everything else in the universe vanished from her perception as they plunged into a pocket world of their own.

David scooped her up and carried her into the bedroom. With one flick of his wrist, he whisked aside the plastic sheet covering the bed. It crumpled to the floor. He swept back the quilt, revealing silky, cream-colored sheets.

She ripped her gaze away from his just long enough to take in the hungry slant of his lips. There was no one else for her, only this gorgeous, passionate, courageous man who stood by her no matter what. She'd already gifted him with her heart. Tonight, she would relinquish all of herself to him.

He peeled her clothes off layer by layer, caressing and kissing every inch of her before tearing off his own clothes. When he laid her down on the mattress, his body hovering over her, she raked her fingers up and down his muscled chest, around to his back, dancing her fingertips up the ridge of his spine. He ducked his head close to hers and murmured two words that ignited a bonfire inside her.

"Be mine."

She was his forever, willingly, in every way imaginable.

He claimed her body then, writhing with her, their moans as entangled as their bodies, every breath a promise and every movement a fulfillment. She arched into him, and he cradled her with one arm, stroking and kneading, driving her wild and yet soothing her fears, chasing out the remnants of the Golden Power, leaving nothing behind but the sweetness and power of their minds and bodies united. The pleasure broke over her in wave after exquisite wave, drowned her yet awakened her, scoured out shame and filled her to bursting with a rapturous love. She clung to him until the last swell engulfed her and his own release pulsed within her.

Joined. At last. Hers forever.

The ecstasy of that realization unleashed another burst of pleasure, more powerful than any other, intensified by his hands roving her body and his lips exciting her skin. The doors of her mind blew open, obliterating a wall she hadn't known existed. Memories flared, brilliant and fleeting, vivid and uncatchable.

David smiling. David laughing. Their first kiss. The nights they'd spent entwined in each other, delighting in every sensation. David sharing his secrets. She'd reciprocated, trusting him more than she'd trusted anyone in her entire life. Their deep connection, forged from a shared destiny. Her powers emerging. David patiently teaching her to use them. David loving her. Needing her. Drawing out of her an openness and passion too long denied her.

She floated back to the present, her memories reconstituted, whole again because this man loved her. And with all her being, she loved him in return.

David rolled onto his back, taking her with him. She sprawled over his body, exhausted in the most wonderful way, satisfied beyond measure. He caressed her hair, pecked a kiss on top of her head, and snuggled her against him. With her ear on his chest, she listened to the pounding of his heart as it slowed one beat at a time. She inhaled the smell of his sweat, mingled with the unmistakable scent of him—heady, earthy, masculine.

With one finger, she etched circles on his chest. "I remember."

"What do you remember?"

"Everything."

He froze, his heartbeats accelerating.

She turned her face into his chest and smiled against his skin, too overwhelmed by the revelation of recovering her past to do anything, even look into the eyes of the man she cherished. "It all came flooding back to me. How we met, what we did together, the things we talked about." She tucked her arm around his waist, snuggling into him. "I remember us."

His heart thudded beneath her ear. His chest heaved.

Grace raised her head then and beheld her warrior angel's expression—the tears threatening to overflow, the lopsided grin, the wonder glittering in his eyes. Never had she witnessed this David crying, and yet he teetered on the verge of doing just that.

She feathered her fingers over his cheek. "It's okay. You don't have to worry about me anymore. I'm me again, completely. No more crazy amnesia girl."

He exhaled a long sigh and blinked away the moisture in his eyes. "I'm not worried, Grace. I'm happy."

"Me too. And by the way, you were right. You can strip the Golden Power out of me. You just did it."

His hand skipped down her back to cup her bottom. "That's not all I stripped."

Steam rushed through her at the memory of his hands deftly removing her clothes, his fingers grazing her flesh, his eyes worshiping her curves. "I wish we could stay like this all day, but I don't think Tesler will sit still much longer. Sooner or later, they'll finagle a way to get their systems back online. They've probably got backups, you know."

"I checked right before you arrived. They weren't quite there yet, but I'll check again."

She considered offering to do it herself. Then again, she supposed she ought to let him do something occasionally.

His eyes went distant as his expression blanked. Though his arms held her, she sensed the vacancy inside, left behind by his mind's departure.

Grace tapped one fingernail on her chin and counted the seconds, the pace of her taps accelerating as she passed twenty, then thirty.

Come back to me.

David blinked, drew in a deep breath, and tightened his hold on her. His eyes, bright and mesmerizing once again, fixed on her. "They're still working on it. Won't be long, though."

They both understood what they must do. As much as she loathed breaking away from him, as much as she craved his touch and his kiss, she uncoupled her body from his and rose to a seated position. The absence of his heat chilled her skin. His scent faded, yet the energy pulsing between them filled the void. She would never be without him again, not really, even if continents separated them. Their connection had always granted her a taste of him in his absence, but their newfound bond, forged in their lovemaking, bequeathed her more than a sampling. He smoldered inside her like the missing part of her soul restored.

And they hadn't joined their powers yet.

David sat up and took her hands. "It's time."

"I'm ready."

Chapter Twenty-Five

AVID TIPPED HIS HEAD FROM SIDE TO SIDE AND SCRUTINIZED HER face, determined to ferret out any traces of misgivings in her expression. He found only love and certainty there, but a frozen seed had taken root in his chest. Did she fully understand what merging meant? Did he understand?

To hell with the consequences. Nothing bad could come of letting Grace in, whether that meant into his heart or his mind. She knew his darkest secrets, and he'd vowed to share everything with her from this moment forward. If she perceived his emotions more keenly after the joining, if her psychic GPS expanded into a live television feed from his brain to hers, he was fine with it. Hell, he'd relish every minute. To be with Grace, he'd surrender his privacy and his mind to her.

But should he expect her to do the same?

He coughed, scratching his ear. "Are you sure? We've shared a telepathic bond, but this will be so much more. As far as I know, nobody's done this before. Once we merge our powers, I don't know if it can ever be undone."

"The Golden Power is gone, and I'll never tap into it again. I promise."

His heart sank. If it took the rest of his life, he'd convince her she wasn't corrupted.

Capturing her hand, he fluttered a kiss across her knuckles. "I'm not worried about that. But are you sure you want to shackle yourself to me permanently?"

"You make it sound so romantic." The worry wrinkling her forehead encouraged him to trace his fingers across the skin as if he might smooth out her fears. Her eyes shuttered, and she inclined toward him just enough to rouse his thirst for those soft, pink lips. Through their connection, he experienced the subtle shift as tenderness displaced worry. The lines on her forehead disappeared. She gazed up at him, and her lips quirked in a sly half-smile. "I want to do this. Besides, I'm pretty sure we already started the process."

"That was our bodies merging, not our minds."

"I meant when you helped me shed the Golden Power. We did it together." She rolled her shoulders back and gave a quick nod. "I'm ready, David. Stop stalling."

"Right. Let's do it."

He twined his fingers with hers, letting their linked hands drop. Each of their wrists rested on their respective knees, with their fingers bridging the gap.

Their gazes collided.

Power snapped taut between them. Energy surged through the bond, scorching and seeking, ricocheting from her into him and back again, over and over. Dizziness hurled his mind off balance, but he clutched her hands, her power, for support. Fevered lust swelled deep inside, a voracious need so profound that he gasped. Her eyes rolled shut, her head lolling backward, mouth open, cheeks flushed with desire.

"Look at me," he rasped, breathing hard from the intensity of his desire for her. "Look at me, Grace. *Now.*"

She obeyed. Her hazel eyes flamed with psychic energy and rapacious hunger.

Her powers poured into him. He drove his own powers back toward her in a feedback loop that pumped in and out of him while the essence of her consumed him, transformed him with her sweetness and passion, invigorated him with her laughter and courage. A love more reverent than anyone deserved penetrated him to the core. Her love. His love.

Their love.

His mind settled, the energy dwindling from a torrent to a gentle stream. The ecstasy of melding with her lingered and stimulated his entire body. God, he wanted her. Right now, right here, for hours and hours, damn the rest of the world. He ached to taste her, arouse her, and worship her in the most carnal ways.

Her lips curved into a sensual smile. "I know what you're thinking."

"Don't need psychic powers to know that."

Her arousal vibrated into him, supercharging his own. He sucked in a breath. She was doing it on purpose. "Better stop that, unless you want me to ravish you again."

"Maybe I do."

He chuckled. "I know you do. What I should've said was, we don't have time for me to ravish you again."

She feigned a pout. "You're no fun."

"When this is over," he said, sliding a hand up her thigh, "you have my word I'll make love to you nonstop until you beg me to quit."

A blush rose in her cheeks, though not from embarrassment, from the heat of passion. She was dazzling in her amorous glow, and delicious enough to eat. Maybe just an appetizer…

He jumped off the bed. "Get dressed. It's time to end Tesler's reign of terror."

GRACE CROUCHED BEHIND A TREE, EYES CLOSED. THE TRANQUIL warmth of David's energy suffused her mind and soul, rejuvenating her powers. Her mind soared above the forest to scout the vicinity, and she swooped down low to check out every vague signature of life, determined to rout out Tesler's men before they swarmed her and David. Never before had she been able to detect life-forms this way. Since their merging, though, she discovered she could scent them out, for lack of a better term, with her psychic faculties. Her mind interpreted each scent as a flickering dot in the woods.

Remote viewing had transformed into something more.

A flicker below her brightened. She dived toward it. The single signature separated into multiple lights, a dozen at least. She struggled to differentiate them, to count her enemies. Too many. Heaven above, how would she and David get past them without hurting anyone?

Relax, Grace.

David's voice resounded in her head. No longer did they need spoken words to communicate. His thoughts, his emotions, translated into phrases in her head—more than just words, but his voice speaking them. The intimacy of the contact shuddered a thrill through her. At the same time, it unsettled her. She knew he couldn't read her mind, and his words and emotions reached her only when he chose to share them. Right now, he beamed comfort to her in a soothing wash, like lowering her body into a warm bubble bath.

We can do this, he told her.

Can't hurt anyone, she said.

Except for Tesler.

Cold dribbled into her. *David…*

Relax, no one gets hurt unless they try to hurt us.

Okay.

Grace winced at the sting of his anger, so strong and hot that he couldn't hold it back completely. Still, she knew—despite his loathing for Tesler, his vow to destroy the man—that he would keep his promise to her. No violence without provocation.

She marked out a path to the congregation of commandos, and then she opened her eyes. Adapted to the night, they revealed her surroundings in shades of shadow and pale light. The first rays of the sun trickled over the horizon, spilling out across the sky, squelched by the heaviness of the receding night. To her left, the silhouette of David hunched behind a bush. His eyes fluttered open, exposing the burning blue of his eyes, aflame with the power of his mind.

His hand found hers and squeezed. *Ready?*

No, she would never be ready for war. Tesler had eliminated every alternative.

She nodded.

David scuttled closer, clasping both her hands. She focused on his eyes and let her mind sink into him, embracing the potency of his gifts, granting him unfettered access to hers. His essence swirled inside her, slow and gentle, yet ardent. Her body flashed back to the moments in the cabin when his passion had consumed her with the same sizzling tenderness. His heart and mind, like his body, stimulated her from the tips of her toes to the hair follicles on her head, and way down into the most secret parts of her. She exhaled a shaky breath, and somehow her knees, despite resting on the ground, weakened at the memory of his skin, his mouth, and his hands on her.

She shoved aside the thoughts and commanded herself to focus.

As one, they disunited from their bodies and rose through the crossroads, then out again to materialize in front of the commandos.

The men froze, eyes wide. A few gasped. One by one, they jerked their guns up to target Grace and David.

"You can shoot," David said, his tone low and dangerous, "but you won't hit us."

A figure moved out of the center of the throng to halt a few yards away. "Can't stay away from me, can ya, sweetheart?"

Her heart thudded, and her mouth went dry. "Battaglia."

A wriggling itch crawled over her skin. The arrogant slant of his lips, the oily eyes fixed on her, the massive shoulders hunching as if in anticipation of his next tangle with her... His every gesture awakened a seed of anxiety. It swelled and multiplied until she battled for control of her jackhammering heart.

A wave of empathy from David enveloped her like an invisible hug. The panic dissolved under his telepathic ministrations. *Thank you, my hero.*

Peripherally, she glimpsed his lips twitching into a brief smile. *You're welcome, my heroine.*

She chanced a fleeting look at him. Heroine? She was no savior. He must've been joking, except she'd felt the fervent intent of his message.

"You're astral projecting," Battaglia said, careful in his enunciation of the words. "I know all about you freaks. But we're not scared of you. We won't stop until we find your bodies and blow enough holes in them to shred you to pieces."

Grace latched onto David's calm energy. The bite of anger tainted it, but she'd take whatever she could glean from him. Calm and angry. Only

David managed to hold both in his heart at the same time. She fed a bit of herself into him, praying to assuage his demons for a little longer.

They were in the woods. The fact had not escaped her notice. The vision she'd endured, of Tesler murdering David, had unfolded in a forest identical to this one.

I won't let it happen.

David glanced at her sideways. His question hovered between them.

Oh damn. He'd sensed her state of mind and guessed what she was thinking. He longed to ask if she was okay but couldn't waste any mental fuel on transposing his feelings into words she might hear in her mind, or vice versa. Remote viewing this location demanded every ounce of psychic energy they both possessed, as they combined astral projection, telekinesis, and thought projection into a cohesive image of themselves standing before the commandos.

Battaglia sniggered. "Don't have a plan, do ya? Stupid freaks."

She swiveled her head toward David. His eyes met hers, and the fire in them sparked with a power that crackled between them. *Now.*

They fired their entire arsenal at the commandos, the combined energy of all their powers, consolidated and electrified, fortified beyond anything either of them could accomplish alone.

The commandos twitched. Their eyes rolled back in their heads.

More.

Grace culled all she could from David and dragged in energy from the crossroads. *Not the Golden Power, don't go there,* her own mind warned her. She veered away from the pathway to the ultimate source of psychic power. However much she'd managed to devour from the crossroads, she hauled back down with her.

David stumbled, his eyes bulging.

The power surging between them exploded tenfold. She hurled it at the commandos.

And they crumpled to the ground, unconscious.

The power sluiced out of David, straight through her mind and out into the ether. He vanished, yanked back to his body.

Her mind whirled. Blackness swamped her vision. She slammed back into her body and tumbled sideways. Her head smacked into the ground, bursting stars in her vision as pain wrenched her body, and she curled into a ball, whimpering like an injured animal.

Heroine, my ass. She tried to gulp down the whimpers, to unsnarl her limbs, but she had no control.

David gathered her in his arms. His firm body encased her, yet no heat or comfort leeched into her from him. He rocked her and murmured consoling phrases, but they bounced off her brain, incomprehensible. Shooting stars twirled around her, and she fought to regain her bearings. Up, down. Real, not real. What had she done?

"Not the Golden Power," she croaked.

"I know." David smoothed hair from her face. "It's okay. This is normal power drain. Just relax."

"Normal?" She zeroed in on his eyes, no longer flaming but gleaming in the pastel shades of sunrise. The spinning lessened, and the earth below them rolled out into a flat surface again. "It's not normal. I've never felt like that before."

"You don't have a migraine."

He announced it with authority as if he knew this to be true. Of course he knew. Her feelings, emotional and physical, bled into him. She could restrain the flow somewhat, but in her current state, she lacked the energy.

And he was right. No migraine. For the first time in months, using her powers had not set off an excruciating, nausea-inducing headache.

She twisted out of his arms, her butt plopping onto the ground. "Why don't I have a migraine?"

He smiled. "Because your powers aren't blocked anymore. Whatever happened to free up your memories, it freed your powers too."

When he'd made love to her, that's what had done it.

His smile transformed into a suggestive smirk that instigated a tingling deep inside her. He wrapped an arm around her waist to nudge her closer. "We both know what freed you up."

"Don't get full of yourself. I think it was more than your... prowess that did the trick."

"I know. It was love."

Oh yes. The truth of the statement resonated in her. She loved him more than even she comprehended, and he loved her the same way. Their commitment to each other had shattered the wall in her mind.

David jumped to his feet, hoisting her up with him. "Let's finish this."

A chill whispered over her skin. The worst part was yet to come. "It took everything we both had to knock out those guards. How in hell are we going to breach the facility?"

"We don't need the Golden Power."

"But we barely managed phase one of our brilliant plan."

"Shh." He took her face in his hands and brushed his lips across hers. "We can do this. If you stop being afraid of your powers."

"I'm not. We merged, and I feel great about that." True. But that old worm of doubt, though skinnier than before, writhed in her gut whenever she accessed her powers. The memory of the Golden Power inside her, poisoning everything she was or could be, roused the worm to lash its tail.

"You don't need more power." His nose bumped hers, their eyes close enough the heat from his eyes would've burned her if it were real flames. "Stop being afraid. Let it go. You are wonderful and sweet, the best person I've ever known, and you would never hurt anyone if you had another choice. The Golden Power doesn't own you. No one and nothing does." He moved his hand behind her head, cupping it, slanting it up toward his face. "You belong to me, remember?"

"You said nobody owns me."

"I don't own you. I love you. We belong to each other, now more than ever. Right?"

The mere thought of belonging to him, with him, made her breaths quicken. "But how can we break into the facility, just us, no energy boost from—"

His mouth devoured hers in a kiss so full of passion that it erased every doubt, cleansed her soul, flared so hot inside her that she melted into him. He withdrew, head angled to the side. "Do you trust me?"

"Yes."

"Then trust what I'm about to say, don't ask questions, and follow my lead. Okay?" When she nodded, he dropped his hands to her shoulders. "You and I can do this. We will do this. If we get in there and Tesler has fixed his EM field, then we'll deal with that. You are the strongest psychic I've ever heard of, and together we are unstoppable." He took hold of her hands and laced his fingers with hers. "Let's go end this."

They sprinted through the woods, away from the slumbering commandos, to a spot they'd identified earlier. A shallow ravine shielded them from anyone prowling the woods. Grace sat down at the base of the ravine, her back to the steep wall. David settled in beside her.

Ready? He didn't have to say it. She heard him anyway.

Nodding, she slipped her hand into his. He laced his fingers with hers and gripped her hand.

They sped through the crossroads and back down into the facility, touching down in a corridor bathed in white light from the bulbs recessed in the ceiling. A map of the facility floated in her mind, etched with red lines marking a path. It led in the opposite direction.

Without a word, they both whirled around.

A shadow descended out of the ceiling, dark as the void of space, featureless and human-shaped, a silhouette throbbing with black energy. White disks glittered within its ill-defined eye sockets.

Invisible power snaked out to her, coiling itself around her astral body. She clutched David's hand, but her fingers sailed right through him. *No bodies.* Without manifesting, she couldn't connect with him. The tendrils of power constricted around her like a straitjacket manufactured from psychic energy as ghostly fists pounded at her firewall, to no avail.

David stood immobile, his face blank.

The power collared her throat. "David!"

He stared straight ahead.

She grappled with the thing constraining her, helpless to break free. The thundering of her pulse drowned out her own cries. "David, what's wrong with you?"

His eyes rolled to the side, his focus fixated on her. Fear and anguish steamrolled through her. His fear. His anguish.

The dark power strangled her.

She gurgled, wrestled against her invisible restraints, but gained not one inch. This force, it could touch her, affect her, as if both she and it had manifested physical forms. But she hadn't.

Had she?

The tendrils from the shadow-thing bound her, but her legs were free of it. She stomped her boot on the floor. Pain webbed out through her foot. What the hell was going on? She hadn't wanted to manifest, hadn't tried to, and yet something had forged a physical body for her.

A shiver jolted her entire body. The truth socked her in the gut, and she struggled for breath. The shadow-thing had compelled her to manifest. When its power had entangled itself around her, its will had become real. The thing wanted her in a body, in a tangible, crunchable form.

David, can you hear me?

His eyes never wavered from hers, but he did not respond.

She squeaked out the words. "David, fight it."

The shadow-thing slithered down the corridor toward them. Its amorphous body coalesced into arms and legs and a torso, all corded with thick muscles. The oily surface of its form solidified into dark skin. The eyes flamed as white as the hottest fire, and the bulbs in the ceiling cast glistening rays on the man's bald head and nude figure.

Every hair on her body stiffened, electrified by the recognition careening through her.

The shadow-thing. It was... Nkosi.

He halted a few feet from her. A smile of vicious portent warped his face. "At last, I have what I craved."

Nkosi's fingertips traced the line of her jaw, and though she struggled against the tendrils binding her, they tightened and sharpened. She gritted her teeth, refusing to gasp, repressing the agony that sliced into her flesh and pierced down to her soul.

His smile widened. "The golden girl is mine."

Golden girl. She ground her teeth hard, fending off the memory of the last time someone had called her golden girl. Jackson Tennant's voice echoed in the recesses of her mind, but she slammed the door on it.

Nkosi scraped a nail across her cheek. A streak of pain singed her flesh in its wake. "You don't yet understand, but I will explain. First, however, I must sever you from him." Nkosi threw a blazing glare at David. "His power corrupts yours. I crave your pure, unadulterated energy. It will feed us both and make us one in a way his puny powers could not accomplish."

The energy wafting out of him enveloped her, and she gagged at the acrid taste of it. No, not again. She recognized the taste and the greasy energy seeping into her. She'd suffered this invasion before. Yet it couldn't be. It just couldn't.

"You are beginning to see," Nkosi told her. He seized her chin, forcing her to meet his gaze. The white-hot coals of his eyes seared her mind. "You feel it. But perhaps your lover does not yet comprehend the truth."

David, oh God, David, please break free.

Nkosi aimed a devious grin at David. "I am not this weak human you know as Nkosi. He died long ago when I consumed his essence and replaced it with my own. Psychic powers are more than energy. They are living things inhabiting human bodies." He ducked his head close to hers, and his lips grated over her mouth, his breath hot and fetid. "Tell him."

"No." A choked rasp, nothing more.

"Fine. I will do it." The creature in Nkosi's body hauled her across the floor, until her body pierced the astral image of David, their eyes almost converging. The shadow-thing said, "I am the Golden Power. And your girl belongs to me now."

Energy exploded, rupturing her link to David. Agony wrenched and contorted her body. Power cracked through her. The last thread of her connection to David snapped.

She screamed.

Chapter Twenty-Six

OWER TORE THROUGH DAVID. GRACE SCREAMED AS HE WAS hurled back into his body, far from the facility and Nkosi.

And Grace.

He staggered backward and hit the ground with a thud that echoed through his body and set his nerves on fire. His head pounded. White lights popped in his vision. His muscles twitched and burned. He clambered onto his hands and knees, panting, but when he tried to move, to crawl even one inch, agony contorted him from head to toe.

Grace.

Her scream ripped through his mind, replayed over and over. She'd pleaded with him for help, not with her voice, but with the tormented look on her face and the terror radiating out of her into him. Severing their link had torn her away, stranding him out here in the woods, blind to her anguish, powerless to save her.

"Man, are you okay?"

Sean's voice pierced the haze of agony and anguish. David blinked until his vision shifted back into the physical plane and the blurry shapes around him coalesced into bushes and trees, grass and moss—and Sean and Gabriel Amador.

"What are you doing here?" David tried to scramble to his feet, but his legs gave out. "You were supposed to be on your way to Edward."

"Yeah." Sean jammed his hands in his pants pockets. "We changed the plan."

"Dammit, Sean, you shouldn't be here."

The kid rolled his eyes and scrunched his mouth. "We know what's going down, and no, I wasn't gonna run off in Gabriel's plane. It's a Gulfstream, which is really cool, sure. But you're family."

David clenched his jaw. He understood Sean's decision, even admired him a little for it, but fury ripped through him at the sight of Amador's face, pinched and pale. Grace wouldn't have resorted to the Golden Power if Amador hadn't pushed her, tormented her, scared her into actions she'd sworn never to take again. The bastard had coerced her. *Scared* her. *Tormented* her.

David lunged at Amador. His hands closed around the man's throat.

Sean seized his arm and pulled. "No-no-no! What are you doing? Stop it, he helped us."

David squeezed.

Amador spluttered and choked, eyes bulging.

"Cut it out, he saved you." Sean clawed at David's hands, desperate to pry them free. "He stopped the guards from taking you when you were in transit."

Fingers hard as a vice around Amador's throat, David snarled. "What did you do to Grace? Where is she? Tell me, Amador, or I'll snap your neck right here."

Amador gurgled.

Sean punched David in the side. The blow knocked him off balance, and his hands popped free of Amador's throat. Sean socked him again. David tumbled sideways and whumped to the ground. Pain ricocheted through his ribs and torso. He grunted, rolling onto his back.

"Jeez, you dumb-ass." Sean loomed over David, his mouth twisted into a sardonic expression. "Let people explain before you go all psycho-killer dude on us. You're a real shithead sometimes, you know?"

David pushed up onto his elbows. Sean had never sworn at him before.

Sean plopped onto his buttocks on the ground, knees bent before him. "I know you're freaky protective of Grace, but come on. Get a grip, man. We're trying to help you."

David raised an eyebrow.

The boy snorted. "Don't gimme that look. You're the one being an asshole."

"So now you're friends with the dick who held Grace hostage?"

"No. But he did save your dumb-ass life." Sean screwed up his face and slanted his head sideways to study David. "Did the Golden Power make you stark-raving bonkers or what?"

David heaved his aching body into a sitting position, his legs outstretched, torso braced upright by his shaky arms. Sean had been scared—that David might die, that he might return from his "transit" mentally injured or insane, that the only two people he trusted would be stripped from his life. Of course the boy cursed at David. He was terrified.

"I'm okay," David said, assuming a placating tone. "I'm sorry I lost it there. You don't know what happened in the facility. Nkosi is—"

"A total psycho." Sean's lips warped into a mirthless smile. "We know that already. He convinced us to come back for you guys, but when we found you in that ravine, he tried to slit your throat." Sean nodded toward

Amador, who slumped against a tree massaging his throat. "If it weren't for him, you'd be a meat sack lying in a blood puddle."

Teenage boys had such a way with words. David felt a grim smile overtake his mouth. Had he been like that once? It seemed so long ago and far away. He couldn't remember.

His shoulders folding in, Sean hugged his knees. "We lost her, David."

Blades of ice gutted him and rammed straight up into his heart. *God, please no, not Grace.* His throat cinched tight around the words he needed to speak, but he forced them out one syllable at a time. "What happened?"

"Nkosi and his Nazi pals took her. We tried to fight, but…" Tears glistened in Sean's eyes. "They were too strong, and I'd spent all my energy on saving you. There wasn't enough left."

Saving you. David considered the phrase for several seconds and understanding flared as bright as the sun in his mind. "Nkosi did slit my throat. You had to use your healing power on me."

Sean chewed his lip and nodded.

David narrowed his gaze on Amador. "What did you do, whimper and whine? Why didn't you employ the Golden Power?"

"I—" Amador slouched lower, his pallor deepening, his eyes wild with fear. "Please forgive me, I lied to Grace. I have no psychic abilities."

The rage erupted inside him, but David doused it with a single thought. *Grace is in danger.* He hoisted himself off the ground and offered his hand to Amador. The other man eyed him warily but clasped his hand and accepted a boost in getting to his feet. Amador dropped his hands to his sides, fingers working.

David wiped his hands on his pants. "No forgiveness. I won't kill you, and that's the best offer you'll get."

Amador nodded. "I understand."

Sean scrambled to his feet. "They must've taken Grace back to the facility. How are we gonna rescue her? I'm wiped, and you must be too. We're powerless."

David's nails burrowed into his palm as he fisted his hand tight. He was not powerless. Even without Grace's energy bolstering his, he claimed enough psychic power to do… something. Anything. What?

Save her.

He could do this. He must do it. They shared a connection stronger than telepathy, a bond fortified by passion and commitment—and love. The kind that spawned legends. The kind no amount of distance could weaken. He latched onto that love now, wrapping it around himself like a blanket.

Warmth shimmered inside him, sweet and familiar. It trickled into every crevice of his being. It scoured away the darkness, the fear, the pain, and shrank the distance between them to nothing. The sensation of nearness, of Grace's presence skimming his flesh, flowered inside him. He knew this feeling. But it couldn't be. He'd endured the wrenching pain when Nkosi shattered his connection to Grace, and he'd suffered the aching emptiness left behind. Yet the gentle weight blanketed him, and her warmth filled him, suffused him, altered him, empowered him.

How did he know Nkosi had broken their link? Because the monster told him, that's how. What if the thing that called itself Nkosi had deceived him? He was clutching at phantoms of hope, he knew it, yet the hazy echo of sunlight inside him evoked one thing and one thing only.

Grace.

He threw his head back and laughed.

Exuberance bubbled out of him, dispersing into the air, and he felt sure Sean and Amador must think he'd gone insane. Daylight streamed in through the treetops to bathe him in streaks of gentle radiance. Light, dark. Grace, Nkosi. Human potential versus unspeakable power. The battle had begun. But evil would not win the day because he and Grace wielded the greatest power in the universe. Their love.

David slapped Sean's arm. "Let's go get her the old-fashioned way."

The boy's expression brightened. "With guns and fists?"

"Hmm. We can manage the fists, but as for the guns…"

Sean reached behind his back and yanked out a semiautomatic gun similar to an AK-47, with a long, curved magazine. He reached back again and brought out a much smaller handgun. Offering both to David, he grinned. "Will this work?"

"It'll do." David took the bigger gun, testing its weight. He could handle this. Checking the magazine, he discovered a full complement of ammo. Oh yeah. He could definitely handle this. "Let's get moving."

He called up the mental map of the facility and its environs that he'd compiled before traveling to the facility. The route stretched out before him. With Sean in tow, he strode off into the woods.

Amador toddled up beside him. "I am going with you. This is partly my fault, and I must rectify it."

"Partly?" David halted, struggling to rein in the anger. He fixed his glare on Amador. "I don't have time to talk about your guilt, or how much I hate you and how much you'll suffer if anything happens to Grace. Get out of my sight before I demonstrate for you."

Amador straightened and lifted his chin. "I will come with you."

If he had a rope, he'd tie the bastard to a tree and let the wild animals take care of things. But he didn't have time to argue. "Fine. Just do what I say and keep the hell out of my way. Got it?"

"Yes."

They marched onward. David pushed them to a faster pace until sweat dribbled down their faces and their breaths huffed. Still, he pushed harder, accelerating into a jog, then a run. He hurtled through the woods with a clock ticking in his mind, each second eating away at Grace's life.

Nkosi claimed to be the Golden Power. Was it even possible? Maybe Nkosi had tapped into the ultimate source of psychic energy, but it drove him insane, to the point where he believed he'd become the Golden Power. Andrew Haley lost his mind after trying to read someone else's. Who knew what damage the Golden Power might wreak on a mind too flawed or feeble to handle the influx of energy.

Whatever Nkosi was or was not, he wielded enough power to trample almost anyone who tangled with him. Grace might prove the exception.

Not might. She would.

David stopped to lean against a tree, catching his breath. Sean and Amador did the same. He would help Grace defeat Nkosi. Their link persevered, but Nkosi must've shut the door on it. The thing about doors was, they could be kicked in.

He shut his eyes. Focused on Grace. Latched onto the remnants of their connection. The ribbon of energy joining them led him straight back to her. He couldn't see or hear or touch her, yet the soft, glowing essence of her swelled inside him.

David?

Not a word. Not a thought. A sensation of her mind seeking his, questing for contact.

He had one chance before his psychic energy was spent.

I'm coming, Grace.

With an effort that twisted his gut and seared his brain, he pulled in all the energy left inside him and flung it at the door segregating their minds.

And then he kicked it in.

—⁓—

GRACE'S EYES SPRANG OPEN. HER HEART THUDDED, HER BREATHS gasped, and sweat dribbled down her temples to drip, drip, drip onto the table beneath her. A table? She tried to sit up, but restraints pinned her down at the forehead, wrists, and ankles. Her manifested body was tied down?

Yeah, here she was, strapped to a table. She shot out a burst of psychic energy, intending to crumble her manifestation. The energy ricocheted back to her core. The body Nkosi had stuffed her into retained its form. Trapped in a manifested body and trapped in this room.

As her vision shifted into focus, she caught sight of her surroundings.

Goosebumps erupted up and down her arms.

She lay on a metal table in a square room with concrete floors, a mirror on one wall, and a single door. The dimness of emergency lights spilled over her and permitted shadows to creep in at the corners of the room. The mirror must've been two-way, to allow scientists to observe the goings-on in here. She could see the mirror out the corner of her eye, her prone form reflected in its surface. Did someone watch from the other side?

Her skin prickled. Tesler might be there, studying her from the safety of a hidden room. Or worse, Nkosi might lie in wait behind the glass.

Nkosi.

Grace shuddered. The power he'd exhibited when he controlled her and David simultaneously. The ease with which he fractured their link. Maybe he was the Golden Power as he claimed. She had no other explanation for what he could do.

Heat rippled over her skin. She drew in a ragged breath. *David.* The sensation evoked him, but Nkosi had separated them on the psychic and physical planes. It couldn't be him.

Liquid summer flowed through her mind, into her veins, infusing her soul with a deep longing for what she'd lost. No. She hadn't lost David. He was here, inside her, with her always.

The door to the room banged open.

Grace flinched.

Nkosi stomped through the doorway. He slammed his fists down on the table between her feet. Rage deformed his face and seethed in his eyes.

She tried to cringe, to pull away from him, but the restraints held her in place.

Nkosi took hold of her ankles, his nails digging into her flesh. "You can't be communicating with him. I broke your bond. You are mine."

He knew. He'd detected it the instant she reconnected with David, though the link had lasted only a few seconds.

She clenched her hands and her jaw. "I am not yours."

"You are. You should be." He yanked her legs. The restraints gouged her, and she bit back a cry. "I severed the link. I severed it, I did, I took you away from him, and yet—" He threw his hands up and let out a feral bellow. "How can you still be with him? I am the Golden Power and I commanded you to be mine."

He was insane. Period.

Nkosi moved around to the head of the table. He ran the backs of his fingers across her cheek and gazed down at her with reverence. "You are the key to my liberation."

"From what?"

"The crossroads." He settled a hand on the strap over her forehead. "It keeps trying to pull me back, to confine me in my little corner of the psychic matrix. I don't want to be a prisoner anymore. Your power will free me." His thumb stroked her brow. "This is your destiny, Grace. Only you can access my energy. We are one."

"Oh great. Another psycho who's in love with me."

He gave a low, menacing chuckle. "I'm not interested in your body or your personality. It's your power I crave."

"My power's inside me, which means you need me too."

"I have no use for you." He lowered his face to hers. "I need your brain."

Every nerve seemed to sensitize at once, the air on her skin abruptly sharp, like a thousand needles nicking her flesh. Her brain? How did he intend to…

Realization iced through her. He'd cut it out of her.

But how could he slice out her brain? She was in a manifested form, not her genuine body.

Wasn't she?

Oh shit. For a long moment, she forgot to breathe. Tingling started in her face, paralyzed her lips, and spread out into her limbs. She forced herself to take slow, deep breaths until the tingling faded. Then she spoke with deliberate care. "How did you find my body?"

Nkosi leered at her. "Heat signatures. We used infrared technology to pinpoint your location."

Heat signatures. Infrared technology. Why did someone who claimed to be the incarnation of the Golden Power need infrared to find her? The Golden Power granted limitless knowledge. An omniscient being should not need technology.

"Once we captured you," Nkosi said, "it was simply a matter of eliminating the others."

Others? The meaning of his words burrowed into her and crawled under her skin. Three faces flashed in her mind—Sean, Amador, and David. If any of them had died because of her…

David was alive. His energy reached out to her even now. But Sean and Amador, if they'd suffered because of her arrogance, her blind belief that she and David could conquer the world together, then she'd never forgive herself. Too many people had died for her. People she loved.

No more.

"I give you one more chance," Nkosi said, "to grant me your power willingly. Otherwise, I'll be forced to wrest it from you by whatever means necessary."

"Screw you."

He straightened, aiming a curt nod at the mirror. "We do this your way, doctor."

Footsteps clapped in the corridor, approaching the doorway. A figure waltzed into the room, his gray hair tousled and his white coat dotted with stains. A scrape slashed across his left cheek.

Tesler halted at her feet. His mouth twisted into a vile smirk. "We meet at last."

"Screw you too." If she'd held onto any shred of her wits, she might've cobbled together a better comeback. But her wits had scattered into the ether.

Get them back, idiot.

Nkosi and Tesler exchanged a look she couldn't decipher. Glee, maybe. Or hungry lust for power—of the psychic variety for Nkosi, and of another type for Tesler. What the scientist really wanted, deep down, eluded her. He despised psychic abilities and viewed travelers as freaks, yet he sought the power he believed resided in her brain. Amador claimed Tesler dreamed of controlling an army of puppet psychics. But his endgame struck her as far more complex than the old world-domination gambit.

"Bring in the tools," Tesler called out to the mirror. Then he spoke to Nkosi. "When this is over, I'll have what I wanted, what you promised me. Correct?"

Nkosi nodded.

Grace squirmed in her restraints. No weak links she might exploit. Her bonds were leather and metal, not chain.

The emergency lights lent the room a haunted-house vibe. She squinted at Tesler. "How long will the backup generator last? I know your computer systems are fried, so the generator gives you light and ventilation, but not much more."

He stared at her, blank.

"What have you got left?" she asked. "A couple hours?"

"Shut up." He rattled her ankle restraints. "You're the one tethered to a table, about to be split open."

He had a point. She was helpless.

Like hell.

She commanded more psychic power than anyone else Tesler or her parents or David had ever seen. But she lay there like a salmon caught on a lure. Flopping. Suffocating. Nkosi had commandeered her psychic faculties, right? That's why she was helpless.

No. She'd lost control of her abilities for one reason, and it had nothing to do with the strength of Nkosi's will. He hadn't defeated her. She was helpless because she'd given up. She would never free her mind and body as long as she feared her own powers. David was right.

It was time to stop being afraid.

David beckoned her, his voice a whisper in the darkness.

Let him in.

So she did. Without understanding how, she flung the doors of her mind open, and he rushed in like a hot wind blustering through her. The exhilaration of melding with him again swept into the depths of her being, and she couldn't contain the laughter that bubbled out of her. *Oh, David.* Nkosi had disrupted their connection, but he hadn't broken it.

David's love cascaded into her. No one could sever this bond. No one.

Tesler stabbed a needle into her arm, and the world spiraled into emptiness. His voice growled from far away.

"Hand me the saw."

CHAPTER TWENTY-SEVEN

DAVID CROUCHED AMONG THE TREES, THE FINGERS OF ONE HAND resting on the ground. In his other hand, he grasped the big gun Sean had given him. His eyes were locked on the structure thirty feet ahead. The metal shed that concealed the underground facility.

Grace was in there. Alone.

His fingers tightened around the gun's grip. Metal dug into him, and his knuckles ached from the effort. This was his fault. He'd suggested Grace join her powers with his, and he had talked her into a joint traveling session that put them both at risk. How could he have been so stupid? Of course their psychic journey into the facility had left their bodies vulnerable and exposed. Of course Tesler and Nkosi had taken advantage of the opening to capture Grace. Of course he'd failed her again.

One night of amazing sex had drained the blood from his brain and rendered him useless.

A rustling to his left drew his attention to Sean, who huddled an arm's length away. The boy's eyebrows lifted. Waiting for David to formulate a plan. So he could screw up and get them all killed. No wonder Grace had to rescue him all the time. He was incompetent.

Fingers lighted on his shoulder. He threw a sideways glare at Amador. The other man withdrew his hand but still knelt too close to David. The bastard had no sense of boundaries.

Amador bent his head close to David. "What is our plan?"

Good question. "Rescue Grace."

"That's a goal, not a plan."

The acid boiling in David's gut swelled up into his throat. He hissed a breath out his nostrils, narrowing his gaze on Amador. "Unless you have a brilliant idea, shut the hell up."

In the sulfurous glow from the floodlight on the shed, Amador's self-satisfied expression transformed into a devilish gleam. Or maybe David just really, really hated the man.

The doors of his mind flew open. He swayed on the balls of his feet and sank his fingers into the ground. Energy poured into him in a sweet, steamy torrent that inundated his psyche, his heart, his soul, and…

His libido.

Memories of sensations flashed through him. Grace's body beneath his, warm and supple. Her breasts mashed into his chest. Her panting breaths heating his skin. Her fingers clutching his shoulders, raking down his back.

"Are you okay, man?"

"Fine," he growled, though he dared not look at Sean. The naked hunger overpowering him would expose itself on his face for sure. He battled with his willpower, but the memories kept pummeling him.

"You don't look fine," Sean said. "I've never seen anybody look like that. It's—" He repressed a laugh that came out as a series of snorts punctuated by a hiccup. "Are you seriously thinking about what I think you're thinking about?"

David shoved a hand through his hair and focused all his attention on the shed. And on structuring a plan. And most of all, on quashing his out-of-control libido. He ignored Sean's question, because he'd vowed never to lie to the boy and telling the truth was out of the question.

The desire burned off quickly, reduced to glowing embers. The smoke left behind clouded his mind for a moment, but as the psychic air cleared, a familiar and wonderful presence rained down on him. *Grace.* Their minds had reconnected, bolstering their bond and reinforcing their joined powers. Nkosi hadn't torn her away from him forever. She'd found a way back. *Yes.*

And suddenly, he knew how to save her.

"I have an idea," he said to Sean. "Do you have enough energy to RV the facility and locate Grace?"

"Yeah, I think so."

"Good. What I'm about to do may knock me unconscious, or kill me." He clapped a hand on Sean's shoulder and squeezed. "I'm relying on you to free her."

The boy's face blanched, but then he rolled back his shoulders, straightened his spine, and set his jaw. "I won't let you down."

"I know you won't." David switched his attention to Amador and fought back the urge to slug him. "You're going with Sean."

"But I have no powers."

"You have a gun—and a brain, allegedly. That's enough." He glared at Amador until the other man cringed ever so slightly. "If anything happens to Grace, I'm blaming you. If I die, I'll come back from the grave to haunt you for the rest of your pathetic life. Understand?"

"Yes."

"Don't forget it." David handed Sean the big gun. "You might need this."

Sean accepted it without comment, though his lips twitched downward and drew together in the middle.

David aimed his gaze at the metal-shed facade. Gathering in all the power he dared from Grace, and tapping into the crossroads for an added boost, he fired everything he had at the facility. But not at the shed. Not at the structure beneath it. He shot a wave of psychic fire into the air within the building and watched it race through the corridors, smacking each person it met with a burst of energy so intense it shut down their minds. One by one, like flesh-and-blood dominoes, every human being in the facility fell to the floor, unconscious.

The wave shot back into him in a feedback loop that fried his nerves. Agony scoured him from the inside out, contracting his muscles, and he swallowed a cry, desperate not to give away their position. But there was no one left awake in the facility to hear it. As the feedback convulsed his body, wrenched his gut, and exploded in his brain, he glimpsed Sean and Amador dashing toward the shed. Grace would be okay. He hadn't failed her this time. With his last ounce of mental acuity, he prayed she would forgive him for abandoning her again.

Then he collapsed into blackness.

GUNFIRE SHOCKED GRACE BACK TO WAKEFULNESS. THE BRIGHT lights above her, where she lay strapped to the metal table, stung her eyes, and she winced. More gunshots detonated in the corridor, louder, closer. Her heart raced, though not because of the melee outside this room. Adrenaline burned in her veins, consuming her breaths, because of what she saw inches from her face.

Tesler poised a scalpel above her head. Its blade glistened as he turned it from side to side, his lips pursed, his eyes blurry behind his glasses. His gaze lowered to hers, and his eyes sprang wide. "How are you awake?"

Hell if she knew.

But she did know. David's power, hot and anxious, lingered inside her. He had joined with her again. His will had jostled her awake just in time. But what could she do? Tesler had her restrained, and though whatever drug he'd given her had waned, its aftereffects made her fuzzy in the head.

Stop whining. Start acting.

Nkosi stepped out from behind Tesler. He grasped a saw in one hand. "Are you ready for this yet?"

"No," Tesler snapped. "I have to peel back the scalp first."

A gunshot exploded.

"Shut the door," Tesler hissed, and Nkosi waved a hand. The door banged shut.

Grace shifted in her restraints, hunting for a weakness. "Who's out there?"

Please let it be David.

"I don't know," Tesler said. "Our surveillance cameras are still offline, thanks to whatever you did to them."

She'd done more damage than she'd realized. Celebrating her success seemed a bit premature, though.

It must've been David out there. Who else would shoot up the place to reach her? Sean might, especially if David instructed him to, and Amador... Well, he might. If it benefited him in some way. Or if his guilt proved stronger than she'd estimated.

Tesler laid a hand on her head. "Perhaps I should shave the scalp, though we're in a bit of a rush. It would make for a cleaner—"

Nkosi clobbered the table with his trembling fist. The concussive waves rattled her bones. "Quit talking and just do it, Tesler. No more stalling."

The scientist *was* stalling. Why?

Grace fidgeted some more, but the bindings held. This was the wrong tactic. She lacked the physical strength to snap her bonds, but she wielded another kind of strength too.

Tesler lowered the scalpel toward her head, then hesitated. His lips parted as if he wanted to speak. His dark eyes bored into her, and he mouthed words that she swore were—

Help me. That's what he'd mouthed. Tesler was begging for her help?

The world had just flipped upside down and inside out.

No time to consider the change. She relaxed onto the table, letting every muscle slacken and soften. The release of tension freed her mind. Energy from David plowed into her with tsunami force, and she funneled all of it into the straps pinning her down. The metal buckles split apart. The leather bands sailed across the room to bounce off the walls and splat onto the floor.

She leaped up and flung her legs over the table's edge. Her boots clapped down on the floor. She snatched the scalpel from Tesler's hand, spun toward Nkosi, and rammed the blade into his chest.

He shimmered and vanished.

A manifested body. *Shit, shit, shit.*

Grace whirled on Tesler, seizing his shirt, and raised the scalpel to the hollow of his throat.

His Adam's apple bobbed. The whites of his eyes gleamed in the murky light.

She thrust her face close to his, and spittle peppered him as she spoke. "Where is he? Nkosi is hiding somewhere. Is he in this facility?"

"I—I don't know. I had no idea he was manifesting."

From the shock on his face, she figured he was telling the truth. She needed more answers from Tesler, but another volley of gunfire boomed in the corridor, so close her eardrums vibrated.

The door burst inward.

Sean Vandenbrook leveled a huge semiautomatic gun at her. His mouth dropped open, his eyes bulging, and he lowered the gun to his side. "Grace. Are you okay?"

"Yes. What's going on out there? Where's David?"

"Me and Gabriel came to get you. Everybody's asleep out there except us, but we had to blow a bunch of doors open with bullets." He glanced over his shoulder, and Amador shuffled up behind him, his clothes disheveled and his face darkened by shadows of exhaustion. Sean faced her again but kept his focus on the metal table in front of her.

A chill rippled through her. "Where's David?"

"He, um, stayed outside." Sean meandered into the room, to the table. "He said what he had to do might knock him out or…"

Kill him. That's what Sean couldn't say. David had drawn on both his power and hers to accomplish some feat that rendered everyone in the facility unconscious. It must've required a huge effort and exacted an unknown toll. He wasn't gone. No, no, no, she refused to accept that.

Besides, his presence flickered inside her. His energy. His life.

Tesler shifted, grunting as the scalpel pinched his flesh.

"Wait a minute," Grace said, eying Sean. "If David knocked everybody out, then why are Tesler and I still awake?"

Sean shrugged.

Footsteps clomped in the corridor, and a figure pushed past Amador to stride into the room. "Because I excluded this room to keep you awake."

Her knees buckled at the sight of David. The scalpel tumbled from her grasp, clacking on the floor. She barreled into him, flung her arms around his neck, and lavished him with kiss after torrid kiss. When she let him catch his breath, he brushed his knuckles across her cheek.

"Don't," Sean snapped.

She twisted her head around to see Tesler bent over scrabbling for the scalpel, and Sean targeting his gun on the scientist's head. Tesler stood up, hands raised.

Grace stunned David with one more molten kiss, then turned toward Tesler. David's body buttressed her from behind, his hands on her upper arms, his muscular frame hard against her backside. She asked Tesler, "Nkosi isn't the embodiment of the Golden Power, is he?"

"No. But he is infested with it."

"How?"

Tesler gritted his teeth, curled his lip, and gazed longingly at the scalpel on the floor.

She shook her head. "You begged me to help you. And I did. Now you're in our custody. Don't you think cooperating might benefit you at this particular moment?"

David tensed against her. His fingers tightened on her arm for a second but loosened when she reached up to close her hand over his.

Groaning, Tesler rolled his eyes. "If it will keep me from having to watch the two of you nuzzling each other, I'll tell you anything you want to know."

"Then spill." She leaned into David just to annoy Tesler, and as if he'd read her mind, David circled his arms around her waist to link his fingers over her belly. She reveled in the warmth of him, the vitality resonating from him into her.

"After JT destroyed the California facility," Tesler said, "and you escaped with David and Sean, I sent another traveler to find you."

"Nkosi was that traveler," Grace said.

"He couldn't track you, but in the process of trying to, he encountered something unexpected. When you rejected the Golden Power, it was released into this physical plane, orphaned from its home in the metaphysical realm. It was adrift."

"I didn't set the Golden Power free. A piece of it stayed inside me."

"A piece, yes. But the bulk of it roamed free, like a toxic cloud floating across the ocean on the jet stream. That cloud met Nkosi. He wasn't as strong as you." Tesler glowered at her. "It swallowed him whole. Well, his mind anyway. You are to blame for his condition. You made him what he is."

David lunged toward Tesler but froze mere feet from the man. His voice was harsh and rife with pent-up contempt. "Bullshit. Grace has never hurt anyone." David jabbed a finger into Tesler's chest, and the scientist grimaced. "You created this problem, with your experiments and your insane quest to control psychic abilities. You're even worse than JT was. If anyone is to blame for Nkosi, it's you."

Tesler lifted one shoulder, his expression blasé. "He's your problem now."

A bolt of white-hot rage shot down their connection. Grace clutched her stomach, the breath vacuumed out of her. She stumbled backward a step.

The muscles in David's arms went taut, his whole body tensed for a fight.

She raced to his side and grasped his arm.

Hard as a marble statue, he moved only his eyes to look at her. His hands hung suspended between him and Tesler, the fingers clawing at the air, sinews rigid and ready to strike. He itched to strangle the scientist. His black hatred seethed inside her too and whipped a frigid current through her soul.

This wasn't him. David did not want to hurt anyone.

But Tesler blamed her for Nkosi's condition. David had withstood unspeakable abuse from this man, but he would not stand for anyone, especially Tesler, harming her in any way. He understood the guilt would gnaw away at her if she were responsible, and she understood he would go to any lengths to shield her from it.

"Let it go," she murmured to him, stroking his arm with her fingertips. "He's not worth it. And we don't know whether to believe him or not, anyway."

"He's blaming you."

"I don't care." She flattened her palm on his cheek and rotated his head toward her. Those blue eyes glowed with a secret fire, and she dived into their depths, welcomed him into her at the deepest level, accepting his fear, his anger, his wrath, and most of all his commitment to her. "You have nothing to prove to me, David. You saved me. I'd be missing a jarful of brain cells if you hadn't attacked the facility."

The fire in his eyes softened, and his body followed suit.

She pulled him to her. "*You* saved *me*."

A smile trembled on his lips, strengthening with each passing second, bolstered by the love she pumped into him. He accepted all that she offered him, which was everything.

"How sweet."

The accented voice rumbled behind her.

David stiffened, his face hardening. Grace confronted the man who loomed between them and the concrete wall.

Nkosi chuckled. "You have renewed your love, but I have something far more impressive. Tesler's crowning achievement, at my beck and call. I will return for you, Grace, and the entirety of your power will be mine."

The image of him snuffed out.

Grace scuffled backward until David's body halted her. She looked at Tesler. "What did he mean by your crowning achievement?"

His lips curved into a rueful smile. "I figured out how to transfer psychic abilities into subjects of my choosing. None of them are as strong as you or even David, but they have enough juice to do considerable damage out in the world. They were chosen based on their malleability and programmed to respond to specific visual and auditory cues."

"You brainwashed them."

"To put it crudely, yes." He glowered at the spot where Nkosi had been a moment earlier. "He stole my army."

Amador's intel had been spot-on. Damn.

"What will he do with this army?" she asked.

"The man is insane and infected with a power beyond imagining. Now he commands a small army of psychics programmed to do his bidding." Tesler barked out a hollow laugh. "What do you think he'll do, start a knitting circle?"

Words fled from her mind, dragging all her thoughts with them.

"He wants your power, and he'll stop at nothing to get it." Tesler's lips tightened into a grim smile. "He'll destroy the world to get to you."

David tugged her against him. "How do we stop Nkosi?"

Tesler shook his head. "You can't. Nothing can stop him."

"We will." David dug a zip tie out of his pocket. "I stole this off one of the sleeping beauties. I think it's about time you experienced the delight of being a prisoner."

The acid in his tone scraped at Grace's nerves. She understood his anger, shared it in part, but she doubted she could ever grasp the extent of what Tesler had inflicted on him and the others at the Mojave Desert facility.

David skirted around her, grabbed Tesler's wrists, and secured the nylon band of the zip tie around them. As he ratcheted the tie tighter, the nylon pinched Tesler's flesh, and he winced.

She settled a hand on David's arm. "Easy."

His gaze traveled to hers, sharpened by an angry glint. The hairs on the back of her neck bristled. She swallowed, curling her fingers around his arm. He exhaled a long breath that deflated his shoulders and quenched the searing heat in his eyes. With a swift jerk of the zip tie, he herded Tesler toward the door.

As she trailed behind them, an odd niggling started up in her gut. What would David do if he got Tesler alone? Her vision from two days ago flashed through her mind. David on his knees. Tesler slashing a knife down at his chest. Blood. Death.

It won't come true. We've changed things, haven't we?

That might've been wishful thinking. For the moment, she decided to believe it, but stay vigilant anyway.

Sean and Amador brought up the rear of their little procession as they tramped out of the facility. They departed via the elevator and up through the metal shed, nothing more than a husk to cover up what lay beneath. The trek through the woods, to the vehicle Amador had acquired—rented or stolen, she didn't care anymore—consumed more minutes than her frayed nerves could handle. By the time they parked on the airport runway alongside Amador's jet, she was wringing her hands and chewing the inside of her bottom lip.

David handed his prisoner over to Sean and Amador, who steered Tesler in the direction of the jet's airstairs. Their footfalls created only the barest sound on the asphalt. David positioned himself in front of her and hovered his hands near her forearms without making contact as if he feared touching her. The sun, dimmed by a thin layer of clouds, cast shadows on his eyes but could not hide the tension on his face.

"What's wrong?" he asked. "It's more than what Tesler said about Nkosi."

"Yeah." She hunched her shoulders. "I saw Tesler murder you. And now he's with us."

"Would you rather I kill him?"

Her head snapped back, in sync with the massive thud of her heart. The matter-of-fact way he'd suggested murdering someone...

David drew her closer, their bodies inches apart. "I wouldn't kill him unless he tried to hurt one of us. You know that, or you should." His thumbs rubbed her flesh in vigorous circles. She must've flinched, because he looked chagrined for a split second, then let up on the pressure, the movements mellower and almost sensual. "Don't you know I'm not a cold-blooded killer?"

Less a question than a plea. "I don't know anything anymore."

"Yes, you do." He tucked her into his embrace with his forehead resting on hers. His breaths tickled her skin. "You're blocking our connection, or at least trying not to feel it. Aren't you?" When she gave a tiny nod, he sighed. "Why? What are you afraid of? Is it me?"

"No." She meant it too. "I'm worried about what you might do to Tesler if you get the chance. He—he tortured you. For months. I know you're not a killer, but if Tesler starts taunting you and there's nobody else around…"

"You think I'll kill him."

"I…" She focused on his eyes and the familiar fire there. "I'm not sure. But I don't want you to do it. You'll regret it for the rest of your life, and I couldn't stand to feel that happening to you. So yes, I'm blocking our link."

He shut his eyes, and his hands roved over her back, comforting rather than arousing. She looped her arms around his waist and leaned into him.

"You know me," he said. "You know I would never murder anyone in cold blood. But you're scared, I get it, because Nkosi is out there with an army and Tesler planted a seed of doubt. He made you think what happened to Nkosi might be your fault. Let it go, Grace. Embrace our connection. Invite me into your soul again and I swear you won't regret it."

He was already there, inside her. She'd tried to ignore it, to box it up in a corner of her psyche, but his passion and adoration refused to be contained. It surged through her, a firestorm blustering into every crevice of her being. His mouth descended over hers, and she surrendered to the kiss completely, granting him all of herself in the melding of their lips.

Stop being afraid.

His ardor, infused into every thrust of his tongue and slant of his mouth on hers, vanquished the tatters of her fear. The heat evaporated the cold. It suffused her from head to toe, inside and out, until nothing mattered except him.

"Watch out!"

Sean's scream ruptured their passion. David yanked his head up, his narrowed gaze flying to a spot behind her. His body went stiff.

She pulled out of his arms and spun around to look.

A hunter-green Jeep roared toward the fence that hemmed in the runway. It crashed into the barrier with a clanging *pow* and slashed a hole in the fence. The Jeep plowed through the opening, fishtailed, and rocketed straight toward her and David.

He seized her arm and dragged her toward the jet. "Into the plane. Hurry."

They bolted for the airstairs. Before they could clamber halfway up the steps, the Jeep blasted into the stairs.

The wheeled structure spun sideways. She lurched, flailed for a handhold, and sailed out into open air.

CHAPTER TWENTY-EIGHT

AVID THWACKED INTO THE GROUND ON HIS SIDE. PAIN SHOT through his shoulder and hip, radiating out into the rest of his body. White lights punctured his vision. Behind the glare, he spotted a slender shape slumped on the ground. Auburn hair spilled over a pale face. She lay limp on her side, one leg bent across the other in an awkward pose.

"Grace!"

She did not move.

No, goddammit. He hoisted his torso off the ground and propped his weight up with one arm. Fresh agony wrung his muscles and rooted him in place. He stared at Grace where she lay motionless on the asphalt, near the front wheel of the jet. He saw no blood. That was good, wasn't it?

Go get her, you raging idiot.

His body screamed when he shifted his weight, but he gritted his teeth and heaved himself off the ground.

"You okay?" Sean called from the open door of the jet.

"Yes."

"Engines won't start."

"What?" David's head snapped up. "What happened to the engines?"

"I think somebody fried them."

A psychic somebody. Nkosi's army had begun the siege.

From further down the runway, an engine roared. He stumbled leftward until he could peer around the stairs. The Jeep was back, and it tore across the tarmac straight at Grace.

Damn the pain. He bolted for her and collapsed to his knees beside her slack form. When he carefully pressed a finger into her neck, her heartbeat pulsed strong and steady against it. He palpated her head and neck in a cautious exploration but discovered no open wounds, just a small bump on her head. Her lips fluttered on a muffled moan.

He sank back on his heels, one hand on his forehead. The heaviness of dread whooshed away, and he teetered from the release. She'd be okay. *Thank you, God.*

The Jeep roared.

Lost in his worry for her, he'd completely forgotten about the maniac in the Jeep.

David scooped Grace into his arms and raced away in a direction perpendicular to the Jeep's line of travel. The airstairs had skidded too far from the jet's door, and he couldn't waste time wrestling the contraption back into position. The driver of the Jeep wouldn't sit idle for a timeout. David angled across the runway, toward the hole the Jeep had sliced into the fence. *Get Grace to safety.* The single goal drove him onward, despite the searing pain in his limbs, despite the throbbing in his skull. Up ahead, a gray metal hangar squatted in a wide, empty tract of land, its enormous doors shut. He sprinted for the smaller, human-size door at the building's corner.

The weight of Grace strained the muscles in his arms, but he clutched her to his chest, gasping and grunting. He wouldn't drop her. He would never let her go, no matter what.

The Jeep's engine snarled behind him.

Fixated on the door, he pumped his legs harder, faster, heedless of the pain and the black spots in his vision. *Save her, save her, save her.* Adrenaline spiked through his veins, sharpening his senses until he was certain he smelled the sun's heat. *Save her, save her.* The door swelled bigger and bigger in front of him.

A clanging crash erupted behind him.

He resisted the impulse to look. The Jeep had bashed into the fence again, the driver hell-bent on annihilating the precious cargo in David's arms.

Tires squealed.

At the hangar door, he shifted his hold on Grace just enough to seize the knob and wrenched it. Locked. *Dammit.*

He stumbled backward one step, pulled in a deep breath, and kicked the door as hard as he could. It burst inward, cracking into the wall and bouncing back. He shoved past the door, into the gloom of a deserted hallway, and gave the environs a cursory scan to verify nobody was around. Then he took off down the hall into the unknown.

A shaft of muted sunlight spilled out of a room to his left. He veered through the open doorway into a small office. A chair with a high back faced a metal desk. His legs burned, his chest ached, and his arms quivered around Grace. He dropped into the chair and cradled her limp, soft body in his arms.

She stirred a little, mumbling words he couldn't understand.

His heart leaped at the sound of her voice. She was alive and awake, sort of. Better sort of than not at all. He combed his fingers through her hair, sweeping it away from her face. A whispery moan escaped her parted lips. He skimmed his thumb across her mouth as she snuggled into him like they were napping in bed together.

If only. Instead, they were hiding out from a crazed individual controlled by an evil entity—or energy, or whatever the hell Nkosi was. He should go check on their pursuer, but that obligated him to leave her here.

His hands trembled as he tugged her closer, unwilling to break the contact yet.

The Jeep was still out there. So were Sean and Amador, and Tesler too. He must stop the assault. But he knew of only one way, and it required him to appropriate Grace's power without her consent. She couldn't consent because she was dazed or unconscious. He couldn't tell which. In either case, to stop the Jeep and its driver, he needed an influx of her power.

"I'm sorry," he whispered into her hair.

"Mmm."

Her mumbled noise might've signified consent, or maybe he was so desperate he'd grab onto anything he might interpret as permission. It didn't matter. He must do this.

Please understand.

David untethered his mind from his body and rushed into the crossroads where he commandeered all the energy he could. It wasn't enough. He tapped into his link to Grace and let her power fill in the gaps, until the psychic energy glowed inside him, ripe and ready. Then he plummeted back to the physical plane, steering his mind away from his body. He glimpsed himself slumped in the chair, and Grace cuddled against him.

It's all for you.

His mind flew out of the building.

The Jeep screeched to a halt mere feet from the door he'd kicked in moments earlier. The driver's door swung open. A man in camouflage fatigues jumped out, his boots thumping on the asphalt. His ashen skin, a contrast to his blue lips, shimmered with a glaze of sweat. Psychic energy roiled out of the man to lick at the air with invisible tongues. This man commanded metaphysical power, yes, but a weakened version of it. No match for David.

The man shuffled toward the door. In his right hand, he wielded a gun.

David hurled everything he had at the man. The intruder flipped backward and whacked into the ground on his back. His eyes rolled up in his head. Dead?

He hadn't meant to kill the man. He was a puppet, after all, tortured in ways even David couldn't fathom. But the man looked… No, not dead. David hurried toward the unmoving man, and for the first time, he cursed his inability to manifest. If he had a body, he could render first aid.

Energy infused him, sweet and rich and potent, like… Grace.

His feet touched down on the asphalt. Solid feet. On solid ground. He tested his weight, bending his knees and bouncing a little. Yes, this body was real. He'd manifested, without Grace's direct help.

Yet she had helped him. In her semi-conscious state, she recognized his need and channeled more of her power into him to launch him into a manifestation. She was amazing.

God, he loved her.

David crouched beside the prone man and checked for a pulse in his neck. It thumped against his finger, strong but irregular. The man's skin chilled him, the clamminess transferred onto his flesh. He'd seen a man in this condition before. When Jackson Tennant had pumped himself full of drugs to stimulate his latent psychic abilities, it left him sickly and pale as death, exactly like this man.

Nkosi's army had a flaw.

"Man, that's not fair. You can manifest without Grace's help now?"

David glanced up at Sean. The boy ducked through the gap in the fence to trot toward him. Amador escorted a bound Tesler in Sean's wake. David rose to greet them.

Sean's lips twisted into a teenage frown, rife with disgust at the injustice of just about everything. "Can Grace teach me to do that?"

"No."

"But you—"

"Still need her help to manifest, trust me."

The boy slouched, his mouth tightening into a half-hearted pout. "It's not fair."

He slapped Sean's arm. "Get used to unfairness. That's life."

The boy grumbled.

"Who knows," David said, "one day your powers might expand and you may find yourself manifesting all over the place."

His expression brightened. "You really think so?"

"Sure." David pointed at the fatigues-clad man on the ground. "Keep an eye on him. I have to get back to Grace."

"Sure, man. We got this."

David released his hold on this body, on this location. He spiraled back into his real body, and the weight of Grace resting against his chest anchored him to reality. He nuzzled her hair, drinking in the fresh scent of her. The eyes he cherished opened to focus on him, and he tumbled into those hazel irises.

She smiled with a lazy movement of her lips. "You rescued me again."

"Did I?" He traced his fingertip down her jawline, to the corner of her mouth.

"Yes, honey, you did."

He ran his finger over her lips. "Honey?"

She writhed, trying to sit up. Her buttocks ground into his lap, energizing parts of him that he didn't need to wake up right now.

He hopped to his feet, Grace in his arms, and deposited her on the floor.

She swayed a little, her smile going dreamy. "Would you prefer 'sweetie'?"

"Call me whatever you want." He slanted his mouth over hers, delving deep to savor the taste of her. "As long as you're all right, I don't even care if you call me dumb-ass."

She giggled. "Dumb-ass?"

"I've been hanging around with Sean too much." He cupped her bottom and tugged her into him. "But from here on out, I'm with you."

"Think you'll start talking like me?"

Another voice answered. "I sure hope not. That would be sooooo embarrassing."

David shook his head at Sean but felt his lips curl upward at the corners. Anyone could call him anything and he wouldn't care. As long as he had Grace, nothing else mattered.

And so, right there in front of Sean and Amador and Tesler, he ravished her with a kiss that would've made a sex therapist blush. Just because he could. His quest for vengeance seemed a dim memory, a lapse in judgment he vowed to never repeat. He knew exactly what he had to do to make things right.

He parted his lips from hers long enough to murmur, "Marry me. As soon as possible."

Her smile radiated into him. "Yes."

———

GRACE WRIGGLED, BUT INSTEAD OF LOOSENING HIS GRIP ON HER derriere, David squeezed lightly. She let out a sharp squeak. "David, really."

"Yeah, man," Sean said from behind her. "At least spring for a hotel room before you start mauling her. I'm not old enough to watch porn, at least until September. And I think you're wigging out our prisoner."

A volcanic blush raged in Grace's cheeks. What had gotten into David?

Without relinquishing her, he leaned to the side to frown at Sean. "I thought I told you three to stay outside."

"The puppet dude is out cold, and I mean way cold."

David's fingers dug into her buttocks. "Dead?"

"Nah, but I don't think he's waking up anytime soon. Besides, we locked him in his own Jeep."

The tension eased out of David, and he shifted his hands to her hips. Thank goodness. Maybe her cheeks would cool down without his hands all over her ass. If the rest of her half-melted body would follow suit, she might pretend her fiancé hadn't made out with and fondled her in front of a live audience. She ought to chastise him, but it had felt so good she couldn't muster enough annoyance.

Instead, she patted his cheek. "You saved my life for the second—or is it the third?—time in one day. Feel better?"

"I'll feel better when we take out Nkosi."

He damn well knew what she'd meant. Did he seriously want her to ask "do you feel more manly after rescuing the damsel in distress right here in front of our entourage"? She doubted that, so she let it go. "The guy outside looked half dead. Nkosi's army isn't exactly the Mongol hordes bearing down on us."

He arched a brow. "How do you know what the man outside looks like?"

Oops. She'd assumed he noticed her presence, but clearly not. "I, well, kind of hitchhiked with you on your little expedition through the cross-roads." At his stunned expression, she hunched her shoulders. "I didn't mean to, honey, it sort of happened unconsciously."

Her use of the endearment *honey* dissolved the confusion from his face. "That's how you knew when I wanted to manifest and you shot me up with more of your power."

Sean sniggered. "You guys a couple of druggies or what? She's shooting you up?"

David sighed. "I didn't mean it like that."

Someone behind her cleared his throat. Amador's voice wafted into the room like a spicy, but chilly, breeze. "Perhaps we should concentrate on locating Nkosi. If we stop him, his army will be headless."

David gave a sarcastic laugh. "Headless?"

"Yes, like a snake with its head cut off. No?"

Grace nudged David with a finger in his side, the only spot on his body that wasn't lined with hard muscle. "Amador's right. We need to track down Nkosi."

"I know. But how?"

Here came the part she dreaded. The thing she'd avoided since her last psychic debacle, and the one task that, at the mere thought of it, hardened frost over her from the inside out. "There's only one way. He's too powerful for normal remote viewing to work." She clutched handfuls of his shirt, her fists balled on his chest. "I have to tap into the Gold—"

"No." He growled the word, but it was panic pinching his features. "You don't have to do that. We'll find another way."

"We don't have time." Willing her pulse to slow and her hands to un-curl, she lifted onto tiptoes to level their gazes. "This is the only way."

He pinned her against him with his muscular arms. His eyes, wide and wild, searched hers. His lips parted, but he did not speak.

She flattened her palms on his chest. "There's a catch, though. Since we're, um… bonded on a much deeper level now, I have no idea what this will do to you. The Golden Power might infect you too."

"I don't give a damn what it does to me. It's you I'm worried about."

His hold slackened a bit, and her heels hit the floor. She longed to bury her face in the hollow of his shoulder, but she must remain strong, now more than ever. Swiping the tears away with the back of her hand, she touched his cheek. "I know you're worried. The Golden Power corrupts me, and I—"

"Shut up."

She tried to push away, but he grasped her hips. "Excuse me?"

"I said shut up," he growled. "Nothing can corrupt you. I told you that before, and I haven't changed my mind. It's a fact."

"But you said you're concerned."

He held her face in both hands. "I worry because I know how much you hate using the Golden Power. But I still believe you are stronger than it is. If you can believe that, then there's nothing to worry about."

"David, I'm not that powerful." He grounded her, in mind and spirit, without a doubt. Was their bond truly strong enough to overcome this?

He kissed her, hard and quick. "Can you believe it? Can you believe *me*?"

She studied his eyes, and the truth rippled through her. "Yes. I believe."

"Then do it."

Sean trotted up beside them. "Whoa, are you serious? You're gonna use the Golden Power, right here?"

Grace looked at him. "Maybe you guys should wait outside after all."

The kid stared at her for several seconds, and she could practically hear him chewing on the problem, weighing the risks. But then he nodded, swiveled on his heels, and marched out the door, shouting, "Come on, Gabe, let's go."

In the doorway, Amador was scowling, but whether at Sean's nickname for him or at the prospect of being banished outdoors, she couldn't decide. Finally, he headed out the door.

Sean shouted, "Hey, where's Tesler?"

Amador poked his head inside the room just long enough to say, "Tesler has escaped. We will search for him."

"Wait for us," David said. "We'll worry about him later."

Alone again, she and David stood silent, face to face. There was nothing left to say. They both understood the stakes and had made the decision together.

He enfolded her in his arms, and she nestled her head on his shoulder, against his neck. The feel of his sturdy body against hers calmed the noise inside. She relaxed, shutting her eyes. Her mind shook free of her body and soared into the crossroads, then higher still, beyond the limits of normal psychic power and into the heart of the darkest energy.

She dived into the Golden Power.

Nkosi's voice vibrated in her mind. You've come home, Grace, and you will never leave me again.

Chapter Twenty-Nine

AVID SCUDDED ALONG IN GRACE'S WAKE, THE TAIL TO HER FLAMING comet, as they traveled through the crossroads together. With Grace, every barrier he'd believed existed crumbled into dust. He could neither see nor hear her voice, yet the glowing essence of her ferried him higher and higher into the star field that comprised the psychic crossroads.

A wall. Up ahead.

Pressure constricted his mind, stabbing pains through his metaphysical form. He struggled to draw back from the barrier, but Grace rocketed both of them toward it. They collided with the wall. If he'd had a voice, he would've screamed from the shock of impact.

The pressure vanished.

He hovered somewhere near Grace, bathed in the glow of her energy. Beyond her fire, darkness gaped its maw, hungry for the power it sniffed out in her. Alien thoughts bombarded him.

You've come home, Grace, and you will never leave me again.

Nkosi's astral voice. They must've breached the hideaway of the Golden Power.

He shouldn't have allowed Grace to do this. What kind of coward made his fiancée fight the ultimate battle alone? He was here, sure, but how could he aid her? Liberating her from the facility, and then from Nkosi's puppet man, had depleted his metaphysical reserves. She must feel that.

The darkness closed in around them.

Oily energy slithered through him, seeking cracks and holes in his psyche, avenues by which to sneak inside and break him apart bit by bit. The power would consume Grace. As for him…

It would annihilate him.

Maybe she's better off without me.

He didn't mean it, didn't believe it, but the fleeting thought split open a hairline fracture somewhere inside him. The Golden Power clawed at his soul, pried open the crack, wormed itself into the gap, into him. Slimy, viscous, and putrid, it crept inside.

If it took him, Grace would fall next.

A glistening, incandescent outpouring of love shot down the connection from Grace into him. His own words, the ones he'd admonished her with, echoed in his mind. *Stop being afraid.*

The time had come to take his own advice.

He threw open the gates of his heart and soul and embraced the essence of her. Hope and anguish. Passion and trust. An aching loneliness, at last quenched by his vow to value her above all else. *I won't let you down this time, Grace.* He would sacrifice his very soul for her.

And it was time to live up to the promise.

Summoning all the power he harbored inside himself, he lashed out at the invading entity that was the Golden Power. Slashing. Goring. Spraying black energy into the ether and lapping it up with a ravenous thirst.

Gorged on the ultimate power, he hesitated.

This time, Grace didn't need to taint herself. He'd absorbed the brunt of it for her. And the unbridled knowledge gushing into his mind bestowed on him the one ability he'd failed to master before. The power to deliver her from her darkest fears.

He knew where to find Nkosi.

A wave of anxiety streaked into him from Grace. She sensed the change in him. Her panic begged him to stop, but it was too late.

He raced toward Nkosi.

———

GRACE HURTLED AFTER DAVID, STILL BOUND TO HIM BY THE PSYCHIC tether of their connection. Her mind bucked and scraped across barriers she could neither see nor touch, but that scuffed her raw anyway. The stinging and constriction of repressed sobs wracked her astral body.

Stop, David, please.

What had he done? One second, the Golden Power was pawing at her, with Nkosi's thoughts injected into her mind. The next second, the pressure let go with dizzying abruptness, and a silence deeper than the vacuum of space deafened her. David's energy, once warm and comforting, devolved into a writhing, oily mass of—

No. It couldn't be.

She reached out to caress him with the psychic equivalent of fingers and plunged into the viscous morass. The amorphous thing smothered him, burrowing deeper with each second.

He had absorbed the Golden Power.

Why, why, why?

A sick feeling infiltrated her. She knew why. He'd done it for her.

To save her. To free her. But instead of unchaining her from the tainted lure of the Golden Power, he was dragging her down with him. She'd follow him into Hell, if necessary, but not at the expense of losing him. And she would lose him. Forever. He'd ingested too much of the supreme and insatiable power source, granting it unfettered access to another human body and mind.

This was her fault. He wouldn't have sunk to this level if she hadn't made him feel unworthy. Her nagging, her accusations, drove him to this.

She was going to save him, dammit.

Light exploded around her. She plummeted out into the world, whirling and whirling, without form or focus. David's energy—the warm, sharp energy of him and only him—shielded her from the onslaught. It calmed every nerve and anchored her to the world around them. His arms caught her as she struggled to sort out what she saw.

Trees towered all around them, sentinels that penned them inside a claustrophobic clearing. Green moss squished under her feet. The sun blazed behind the treetops, its rays puncturing the shadows below. A frozen sliver of realization pierced her heart. She'd visited this place before. This was where her vision had unfolded. David died here.

His fingers cinched tight, cutting into her flesh.

She hissed. "Ow."

His fingers dug in deeper.

Grace pulled out of his grasp. Her gaze swung up to his, and her heart stopped beating for an agonizing second.

His eyes. They flared a bright white, the pupils and irises overwhelmed by the terrifying glow that radiated from within. The brilliance expanded, inch by inch, to engulf his body in a sterile aura composed of raw power. The force of it battered her mind. If not for the psychic firewall she'd built, the Golden Power would be breaking through to pillage her mind. The energy roiling out of David scratched at her flesh, inciting a hard shiver.

Her skin. She felt it. His hands had grasped her.

They had manifested. *He* manufactured bodies for them both.

"No, David." The grief rending her heart bled through in her voice. She reached for him, but a wave of sickening power punched into her from him, and she yanked her hand away. "No. David, no, you have to let it go. Please, for us, scrub it out of you and come back to me."

His eyes flashed brighter, tiny stars about to go supernova. The power in him distended, hot and thick and vile, rising toward an outburst of galactic proportions.

She dived into the power envelope that barricaded him. It scorched her skin, scraped at her body and mind, desperate to drag her back into its clutches. *No, dammit, never again, you will never take me and you can't have David.* She seized his face with both hands. Energy seared her flesh and coiled around her wrists, like wires ratcheting tighter. Pain shot up her arms. She bit back a cry and pulled his face to hers.

"It can't have you." Her voice growled as if a feral animal possessed her. Yet it was her voice, her fury infusing her tone and hardening her resolve. "David, goddammit, you listen to me. The Golden Power can't take you unless you give in. Fight it. Scratch and scream and thrash until it lets go." She jerked his head down, their lips touching, her hands clamped to his face. "You're stronger than Nkosi. You can conquer this power and come back to me."

His lips twitched against hers. His body tensed. And in his eyes, a glimmer of blue broke through the screen of white-hot fire.

"That's it," she said, tears running down her cheeks. "That's it, keep fighting. You're mine, remember? Nothing else can claim you." With her next words, the fierceness of her voice reverberated in her soul. "You are mine."

The blue glittered and swelled, annihilating the white brilliance one spark at a time. The darkness seething into her from him weakened. Her heart pounded at the sight of blue fire overtaking the nuclear glow. What else could she say to rouse him, to drive out the alien power?

Nothing. Words were over.

The memory of what he'd done for her surged to the surface.

She crushed her mouth to his, delved her tongue inside, branding him as hers with each swipe and swirl. At first, he held still, his mouth open to her but his entire being oblivious to her wanton assault. Then, with devastating swiftness, the inhuman facade imploded and avid passion combusted between them, ricocheting up and down their connection until she couldn't distinguish his fervor from hers. The whiteness evaporated from his eyes, cast out by the blue bonfire in his irises. The blinding aura around him snuffed out. His arms clamped around her, and his tongue thrust deep into her mouth, demanding more while giving it in return. She let her eyelids shut and basked in the euphoria of their bodies fused.

Their manifestations disintegrated. As one, their minds soared back across the metaphysical distance to their bodies, uncoupling at the last second.

Sean slouched on the desk, perched on its edge. "Back already?"

David pushed away from her, his posture casual, yet with a coiled tension beneath the surface. "I know where Tesler is. Let's go."

His resolve, steel hard and impenetrable, brooked no argument. She would've tried anyway, but she knew it would do no good. The battle was imminent, and he would not be dissuaded from his goal.

Resigned, she let him lead her out to the Jeep.

***

GRACE EYED THE MASSIVE PINE TREE AND REPRESSED A SHUD-der. They'd arrived here, in the clearing where her vision had taken place, a few minutes ago. Sean and Amador had hung back to keep watch. No sign of Tesler or Nkosi. Those facts did nothing to disperse the chill that kept rushing through her every time she looked at the tree.

David kicked the pine's trunk. "He was here, I know it."

"Maybe you were wrong," she said. "We didn't see Tesler when we RV'd this place. You might've been, I don't know, channeling my vision."

"No. He was here."

She grasped his shoulders and turned him toward her. Angry lines carved into his features. Ordering him to chill out, or even begging him, wouldn't work. What else could she do?

Ka-chunk.

David scanned the forest. "I know that sound."

Yeah, she recognized the sound too. It was a round being chambered in a gun.

She stepped away from him and searched the shadows between the trees.

"You won't see them," said a voice colored by a familiar accent. "Not until I command them to reveal their presence."

Nkosi strode out of the trees.

Tesler lurched out behind him, eyes as wild as his gray hair, his cheeks splotched with red.

"Over there," Nkosi told Tesler, nodding toward a thick pine tree.

The world seemed to skid to a halt, and the air caught in her lungs. The tree. In her vision that was where Tesler had murdered David.

She clutched his hand. He was focused on Nkosi, his lips compressed, his eyes narrowed. She tugged his hand.

He turned his head, brows furrowed.

"Please get us out of here," she said. "This is where it happened."

His brows knit tighter.

"My vision." She wound her fingers through his and gripped him with all her strength. "This is where my premonition took place."

He didn't ask if she was sure. He didn't need to. Their link, no longer poisoned with the Golden Power, told him all he needed to know.

The wrinkles ironed out of his brow, and his expression went stoic. "We changed things. It won't happen the way you saw."

"Please, David. Let's get the hell out of here."

"No." He shook free of her hand. "Tesler and Nkosi must be stopped."

"David." The sharpness in her tone made everyone jerk their heads in her direction.

Nkosi chuckled. The sound chilled her to the core and reverberated off the trees. "A lover's tiff? I will gladly give you a moment to mend the rift before I rip the brains out of your heads."

David swelled taller somehow, his stance wide, every muscle tensed and ready for battle. His blond hair glistened in the sunshine, and his eyes glinted with a purpose she'd never witnessed before. Her warrior angel. Her hero.

At that moment, she loved him more than she'd imagined possible.

He hurled himself at Nkosi. A snarl ripped out of him as he tackled the other man and their bodies tumbled to the ground in a blur of motion. They rolled, kicked, clobbered, bellowed. Nkosi's eyes glared white. His lips peeled back, and his crooked teeth sank into David's shoulder. David rammed his knee into Nkosi's gut. The other man convulsed, his face contorted with pain.

David threw a glance at her. In an instant, she knew what he needed.

She poured all her energy into their connection, into him.

He drew his fists back and slugged them into Nkosi's chest. The power gushing through David transformed his fists into masses of energy, and even as his knuckles struck Nkosi's flesh, the energy punched straight to the heart of the other man's power.

Nkosi screamed.

A crack split the air. The power coruscating out of Nkosi shredded and dispersed into the void of the crossroads.

David flung his hands away.

Moaning, Nkosi rolled his head from side to side.

Each breath a wheeze, David clambered to his feet and stumbled backward.

"You fools," Nkosi said, his voice slurred. "Did you think it would be that simple?"

David tripped, flailing toward the ground. Grace hurried to catch him, her arms latching around him so fast he'd barely tipped over yet. He listed against her, and they both stared at the man sprawled on the ground.

Nkosi pushed up onto his elbows. "I was willing. I welcomed the Golden Power. It granted me untold potential, and I offered up my mind and soul to it. You—" He speared the air with a finger pointed at Grace. "You rejected it. I gave it form and purpose."

David trembled in her arms, too weak to move or speak. His body weighed down on her, but she gritted her teeth and held on. No way in hell she'd ever let go of him again.

Nkosi wrestled to his feet and wiped his hands on his pants. "You may have driven out the Golden Power, but I still have plenty of my own psychic energy. Yes, you are the strongest traveler my ally Tesler has ever seen, but I am almost as powerful as you."

"Maybe," she said, "and maybe not."

Nkosi massaged his jaw, one of the places where David had clouted him. "I volunteered for the project. Your parents were weak, unwilling to take the risks necessary for advancement. I was terribly pleased when Tesler came on board, and when he shared with me his vision for the project, I invited him to test his methods on me."

"You let him torture you?"

"Of course." Nkosi grinned with predatory lust. "How else could we discover if the technique would work?"

David stiffened against her, and she hugged him to her. "Technique? You aided in the torture of hundreds of psychics, not to mention the ones who died because of it. You're insane." She shook her head, unable to process the depth of his madness. "You've lost your big advantage. The Golden Power is gone."

"But I still have Digital Prognostics." He took one lithe step toward her. "I purchased JT's company after his demise, which means I own Tesler's files. I own the facilities scattered around the world. You stripped me of my greatest asset, but I hold more cards than you believe."

Like hell. They hadn't come this far, survived this much, to lose the final battle.

She must destroy all the files. There had to be a way. Without JT's secret files, which she still kept tucked inside her bra back in her real body, Nkosi would have nothing if she obliterated Tesler's data. The loss would terminate Nkosi's manic dreams.

But she had no idea how to destroy the data.

Nkosi knew how.

David pushed away from her, though his hand lingered on her back. "No."

"I thought you couldn't read my mind."

"Don't need to. I know you, Grace, and I know how you think. This is not the way to end things."

"I'm afraid it is. If I don't stop him here and now, the suffering will never end."

"Please don't do this. Please."

She kissed him, a light and tender expression of the immortal flame he'd lit inside her.

David's eyes, his beautiful soul, pleaded with her.

I'm sorry. His tiny flinch assured her he'd heard.

She confronted Nkosi. He bared his teeth in a nasty imitation of a smile. She balled her hands into fists, battling the urge to sock him in the gut. Instead, she marched up to him, nailed her gaze to his, and bashed through his mental ramparts.

He wailed. His eyes rolled back in his head. His mind fought her, pushed back, floundered for a weapon to fend her off.

She battered him with the last remnants of her psychic power. His mind splintered under her assault. A crack opened up, and she charged inside.

Not so powerful now, are you, Nkosi?

He whimpered, wailing again, and collapsed to his knees. His thoughts rushed into her, a swirling, seething mass of words and intentions, laced with panic and rage and engorged with a madness beyond comprehension.

Gunshots boomed around her.

David shouted her name.

None of it registered in her conscious mind. None of it mattered. She held a man's mind in her hands, and every thought he ever conceived slithered in her palms. She dived her fingers into the quicksand, digging, hunting, ripping, tearing.

"David, no!" Sean's voice. Distant. Unimportant.

Need, I need, yes, I need this.

She rifled through Nkosi's memories. Tossed each aside. Dug deeper. With one final thrust, she captured the information she coveted and ripped it from his mind without hesitation.

Far away, he shrieked.

A sharp pain jabbed into her neck. Weariness flooded through her, buckling her knees, and she toppled into the void.

Chapter Thirty

David rushed to catch Grace before she hit the ground. His heart jackhammered against his ribs, and the torrent of blood thundering behind his eardrums muffled all other sounds. He lugged her behind the big pine tree, cradling her limp body, with her feet dangling a few inches above the ground. Her head fell onto his chest and the silky strands of her hair feathered across his chin.

Amador and Sean circled the two of them, eyes on the woods, postures tense. Two of Nkosi's human puppets lay dead at the edge of the woods, both shot by Amador. David couldn't believe the man had swooped in to fend off their attackers. He did not want to feel obliged to like the lying son of a bitch.

Amador's gaze flicked to David. "How is she?"

Ah yes, of course. That explained why he'd stepped in—for Grace. For now, David had given up worrying about the man's intentions. "I don't know, she's out cold."

"Care for her. We will guard you."

"Thanks," David said, uttering the word slowly, unable to grasp that he not only thanked this man, but he meant it.

Amador nodded, his attention returning to the woods. Despite the bright sun overhead, a screen of trees cloaked them in false twilight. The gloom hid their attackers, but with any luck, it masked their exact whereabouts too.

David tipped Grace's head back to expose her face to him. He settled a hand on her shoulder and jostled her carefully. "Grace?"

She didn't move. Didn't speak. Didn't stir at all.

His chest constricted. He ran a hand over her forehead, the pale skin cold against his. When he dipped a finger to the pulse point on her neck, the beating of her heart pulsed in a slow but steady rhythm. Relief weakened his knees, but he sucked in a breath and clutched her tighter.

She was alive. For now, that was all he needed to know.

Behind him, inside the small clearing, Nkosi lay crumpled on the ground. His body depressed the thick moss. His eyes gaped wide and empty.

Dead. A chill shimmered through David. Grace had killed Nkosi, without intending to, and she would have no reason for guilt. Nkosi had attempted to kill all of them. He'd imprisoned innocent people and hollowed out their minds to reshape them to his will. How many lives had he taken? One was too many. Grace acted in defense of herself and countless others. When she woke, he'd convince her she did the right thing.

What if she doesn't wake up?

The thought shredded him like an electrical shock. She would wake up, she had to. Her heart still beat, and her psychic energy still crackled through him. She would come back to him. She must.

But he understood what she'd done and the cost it might exact. The look on her face right before she'd enacted her plan, a mixture of determination and intense regret, had conveyed her intentions to him. Their bond compelled him to experience a fraction of what she unleashed on Nkosi, of what she endured to accomplish the feat, and he knew. She'd exploited the one ability he'd made her swear never ever to attempt.

She read Nkosi's mind.

Worse, she tore it apart and rummaged through the fragments to unearth what she sought. David realized what she'd been searching for too, the key to bringing down the entire network of psychic research facilities. The vital piece of information that would serve as the nail she might drive into the coffin of Digital Prognostics, Tesler, and everything both had represented.

David touched her cheek, hunting for some sign of awareness on her face, but detected none. His heart ached with a desperation that burned him from the inside out. He could not lose her, would not stand for it. She owned his heart, his soul, every part of him that was worth anything. Before her, he'd been a zombie, not unlike Nkosi's puppets, devoid of passion or purpose. Grace brought him to life. He owed her more than he could ever repay.

Crunch.

David froze at the sound. It had come from the woods behind him. He bent sideways to peek around the massive tree, careful to keep Grace secure in his arms. Amador and Sean both trained their weapons on the area where the noise had originated. Even the birds no longer chirped, and the breeze had ceased its rustling.

The sharp crack of a twig breaking lanced the silence.

Among the trees, a shadow shifted.

"Who goes there?" Amador shouted.

"Give up," a strained voice replied. "Or die."

Sean sidled toward David, his back to the tree. He said under his breath, "Shouldn't we run or something?"

David shut his eyes and made a quick sweep of the vicinity with his RV senses. "We can't run. They've got us surrounded. At least a dozen people."

"Their master dude's dead. Why are they still doing what he told them?"

"I don't know."

Why? The question plagued David as he surveyed the forest for human-shaped silhouettes. Why hadn't the enslaved psychics abandoned their mission? With Nkosi dead, logic suggested they should stop. Instead, they pushed forward with unstoppable resolve.

And the puppets had guns. Ammo. Knives. He, Sean, and Amador had barely escaped when two of the zombie psychics assaulted them. With a dozen closing in around them…

Grace roused with a faint grumble.

He stared at her closed eyes, afraid to move, to bump her too much and push her back into unconsciousness. She shifted against him, her eyes darting behind the lids. He rubbed his thumb back and forth over her mouth, and at the feel of her warm, alive skin, his gaze flew heavenward. *Thank you.* Her eyes, though bleary, gazed up at him with trust and love. The sun illuminated the green flecks in her irises.

Her lips wriggled under his thumb, then stretched into a smile. He lowered her onto her feet but kept his arms around her until she stopped swaying.

"Are you okay?" he asked.

"Mm-hm." Her gaze rolled toward Nkosi. Her eyes went wide and her mouth fell open. She whipped her head toward David. "Is he…"

"Dead. Yes." David clasped her hands. "You did what you had to do."

"I know." She inhaled, straightened, and gave a sharp nod. "And I found what we need."

"What do you mean?"

"The computers at all the facilities around the world are linked through a secure network. If we destroy the mainframe, everything's wiped out."

Oh hell. Just when he'd given up global quests for justice. "Let's talk about that later. We need to figure out why Nkosi's puppets are still carrying out his orders."

She lifted her fingers to her throat, her gaze distant. After a few seconds, she glanced around as if hunting for something. "Do the puppets have guns?"

"Yes. And clearly plenty of ammo, plus knives."

She fingered the bark on the tree trunk. Her lips compressed, the corners pulled tight. Although she studied the tree, he had the distinct impression she was concentrating on a sight beyond the reach of normal vision. Her psychic senses expanded through him, around him, encompassing them both and fanning out.

Her expression hardened, and her nails scraped the bark. "Tesler."

David moved to enfold her in his arms, but she batted them away. His hands stayed poised near her arms because he didn't quite know what to do with them. "What about Tesler?"

Her hazel eyes glowed a soft, gorgeous green, lit by the otherworldly energy enlivening her mind. "He slipped away from us. He's hiding nearby, though. And he is the reason the puppets are still enslaved. They switched allegiances, and answer to him."

"How? Tesler has no powers."

She shook her head. "Somehow the Golden Power latched onto him too. I didn't notice it before because the energy is subtle and I was focused on Nkosi. Now…" Her expression slackened, as her mind receded from the physical world. Seconds elapsed, each tick of the clock an anvil pounding on his chest. At last, her eyes swam back into focus. "What's left of the Golden Power took refuge in Tesler. I don't understand how, and it doesn't really matter at the moment. To stop the assault, we have to stop Tesler."

Sean and Amador stared at Grace, their faces blank. Thanks to the power boost he'd gotten from merging with Grace, David felt the other men's wariness. About Grace? Or about the Golden Power taking over Tesler?

"Okay," he told Grace. "We go after Tesler. Sean and Amador can occupy the zombie army while you and I track down their new master."

Sean raised a hand, like a kid in a classroom asking for his turn to speak. "Uh, how do we find Tesler? I can't see him, even with RV."

"We can."

"Are you serious?"

David nodded.

The boy's brows lifted. "Wow. You guys are kinda awesome since you did whatever it was you did to each other last night."

Grace flashed a suggestive smirk at David, and he smirked right back. With great effort, he resisted the impulse to haul her into his arms for another super-heated kiss.

"Jeez, you guys." A blush fired up in Sean's cheeks, and he averted his eyes. "I didn't mean—I was talking about the thing where you joined powers or whatever."

Growling resonated in the air. Silhouettes bobbed among the trees.

The puppets were getting closer.

David stripped his attention away from Grace, which was damn difficult considering the way she licked her lower lip. "We'd better get moving. Tesler's minions are getting closer."

Sean scratched the back of his neck. "When you say moving, do you mean literally, or psychically?"

"Have you recovered enough to travel the astral way?"

"Yeah. I'm cool."

"Good. You distract the puppets while Grace and I deal with Tesler."

Amador cleared his throat. "Where does this plan leave me? I cannot… travel as you do."

David squinted at the man, measuring Amador up as best he could. Though pale, with dark patches under his eyes, he stood straight and gripped his weapon with determination. David suppressed a sigh. He might've misjudged the creep a little, but under no circumstances would he forgive what Amador had done to Grace or the young girl he kidnapped. Today, though, he needed the bastard's help.

And the task he had in mind was the only thing he'd trust Amador to do.

"I need you to stay here," David said, "with our bodies. Protect Grace at all costs."

She slapped the back of her hand on David's chest. "He means protect all of us."

"No." David stalked up to Amador and glared into the man's bloodshot eyes. "You protect *her*. Tesler wants Grace's brain, and it's your job to make sure none of his minions get anywhere near her." David leaned closer until his breaths reflected off Amador's face. "Protect Grace. That's your only job. Get it?"

"I understand."

"If you abandon her—"

"You will hunt me down, even after death, et cetera. I've listened to this speech before." Chin elevated, Amador gave him a self-satisfied smile. "I am the one who has never left her to suffer alone."

David swung his arm back, his hand fisted, ready to wallop Amador. But then he glimpsed Grace out of the corner of his eye, and the fury evaporated. He *had* abandoned her. Over and over. Amador was right.

He dropped his hand. "Just take care of her, all right?"

Amador inclined his head. "You have my word."

Right. As if that meant squat.

But he knew Amador would defend Grace.

With two long strides, David bridged the distance to Grace, towed her into him, and planted a quick, firm kiss on her mouth. "Let's go for a ride."

She looped her arms around his neck. "I'll go anywhere with you."

A weight slammed down on him, forcing out a strangled gasp. His head pounded, and a humming vibrated painfully through his skull.

Grace fell into him. The breath exploded out of her. She snared handfuls of his shirt as her eyelids pinched together, almost shut.

Sean doubled over, hands on his head. "Ah! What the hell?"

The pain subsided in seconds, but a pressure compressed his mind in its wake. Not a headache, not anything he could identify. An external pressure. Faint yet powerful.

David rubbed his temple but held onto Grace with his free arm. "What was that?"

Her head snapped up, her gaze intent on his. "Tesler. He just threw an EM shield up around us. We're not traveling anywhere."

"Shit." An EM field, like the one Tesler had employed in the lab. The one that prevented him from contacting Grace. "We're back to the Stone Age, then."

With a sly grin, Sean waggled his gun. "Not quite the Stone Age."

He tossed the big semiautomatic to David and whipped out of his waistband the smaller gun he'd used earlier.

Grace frowned. "Where's my gun?"

Amador reached under the back of his shirt and produced Grace's personal weapon, the .357 Magnum revolver. He lobbed it to her. "I took the liberty of salvaging that from your purse."

"Thanks." She flipped out the cylinder, and even David could see it contained only three rounds. "Please tell me you stole some ammo when you were rampaging through the facility."

"A few extra clips," David said. "That's all the guards had."

"Maybe we can still run," Sean offered.

A twig cracked. Foliage rustled.

Footfalls whomped. Hard. Fast. Homing in.

Before any of them could process it, a dozen mind-controlled men trudged out of the shadows in a circular formation, penning them in.

A second line of jaundiced and haggard men scuffled up behind the first circle. At least a dozen more minions now reinforced the first group.

Grace chewed her lip. "How many bullets have we got?"

David grasped his gun, eying Tesler's puppets. "Not enough."

Chapter Thirty-One

GRACE HUDDLED AGAINST DAVID, HER GUN TARGETED AT THE ground. This was bad. So, so bad. When Nkosi had said he commanded an army, she'd assumed he was exaggerating. No such luck.

David's arm clamped down around her. The gun in his free hand was pointed at the ground.

Sean and Amador flanked them. Every single one of the men in her life looked grimly resolute.

They would fight. They would die.

She would live long enough to have her brain cut out.

A hard shudder jarred her. After everything she'd survived, after the arduous journey she and David crawled through to get back to each other, was this how it ended? Trapped. Helpless. Powerless.

A gunshot boomed.

Sean crumpled.

David and Grace rushed to him. A dark stain was spreading across Sean's left arm, near the shoulder.

"I'm okay," he croaked. "Hurts, but I'll live. Gimme a minute and I'll be good to go."

"Don't worry about that," David said.

Grace waved a hand at Amador. "Get down."

He dropped into a crouch near a tree.

A new sound emanated from the woods—the scraping of feet dragging across the ground. The shuffling of half-catatonic human beings. Tesler's army.

David thrust a hand into her hair. "We have to run, it's our only shot."

"It's too late." She surveyed the trees, counting the silhouettes that approached at a slow but relentless pace. "They're already here."

A voice shouted to them, a voice she knew all too well.

"Drop your weapons," Tesler said. "There's no hope of escape. If you surrender, Grace, I may spare your friends by granting them a quick, painless death. Otherwise, they will suffer along with you."

She would suffer either way. That's what he meant. She'd shoot herself in the head before surrendering to Tesler.

Men shambled out of the shadows to encircle them in an ever-narrowing line of armed and mindless soldiers.

"Shoot them!" David said.

Grace slapped a hand on his gun as he raised it. "Don't bother. There's another band in the woods behind these two groups, at least half a dozen more men. I can see them in my mind. We don't have nearly enough bullets to take them all out."

David's face twisted in anguish. Breathless noises sputtered out of him as if he couldn't quite form words.

Tears stung her eyes, but she blinked them away. In a voice so calm it surprised even her, she told him, "It's over, David."

Their powers were squelched. A small army surrounded them. Yeah, it was all over.

He nodded. The anguish had given way to a bleak resignation, which matched the cold certainty wending through her.

Then his head jerked back, and he squinted at her. "How could you see the men in the woods? The EM field…"

She shrugged. "I don't know. I just did."

His lips parted, and his eyes flared wide for a second. Then his angelic face lit up with understanding. "When Tesler had me strapped in back at the facility, the EM field kept me from contacting you. But I was able to use my powers at a low level, briefly."

She didn't dare think it. Didn't dare hope for it. "The field doesn't shut down our powers?"

"No, it dampens them." He smiled with such brilliant optimism she couldn't prevent her cheeks from dimpling with a matching smile. His hand lighted on her shoulder. "Since we combined ours, maybe we're strong enough to breach the field, or at least slip our fingers through it."

Please, yes, let it be true.

The crashing of footfalls snared their attention. Their heads swiveled toward the clearing in unison.

Karl Tesler stomped out into the open, his back straight, arms at his sides. A ghost of a smile lent him the look of a man supremely satisfied with himself.

His eyes glowed pale white.

Grace swallowed, stepped back, and bumped into David.

Tesler gestured to his minions. "Bring them here."

And so they were herded into the clearing, single file, and their weapons were confiscated. Two minions flanked each of them, one at either side. They halted in the center of the clearing, in a line. The dampening effect of the EM field stifled her as if she'd been locked inside a casket buried six feet under the earth. Could their combined powers overcome the field?

Tesler strolled past them, studying each in turn. His stare flickered unease through Grace, but she noticed a pallor beneath his skin and redness in his eyes.

When he reached David, the last in line, he halted. "Dear boy, did you honestly believe you could keep her from me? I've existed far longer than any human. I am everything."

David snorted. "You're nothing. Just a lunatic who's temporarily holding the remnants of the Golden Power."

"I am the Golden Power."

"Bullshit."

Grace pivoted on her heels to face Tesler. "I drove the power out of Nkosi, and a scrap of it took root in your mind. You are the host to a parasite, nothing more."

Tesler tossed his head. The minions at either side of David seized his arms to haul him toward the big pine tree they'd hidden behind moments earlier. One of the minions whipped a zip tie out of his pocket and bound David's wrists and ankles. Tesler sauntered past the trio, positioning himself between David and the tree, his back to the trunk.

A memory exploded in her mind, a fragment from her horrifying vision the other day. In the premonition, David knelt before Tesler, hands bound behind his back.

The vision was coming true.

Strangling a cry, she tried to run for David, but the men guarding her caught hold of her arms and locked her in place. Impotent, she quivered with repressed rage and terror. *No, no.* This was not happening.

Tesler extracted an object from his pocket. A knife. Long and glistening.

"A gunshot to the head is too clean and quick for you," he told David. "I want you to suffer, while your darling girl watches."

Sean bellowed and jumped, about to bolt for David. One of his captors grappled him to the ground and subdued him on his stomach with a knee in the back. Sean cursed and flailed, unable to break free.

Grace ransacked her brain for an answer. A plan. Some crazy scheme. Anything.

Nothing came to her. Nothing. The blood freezing in her veins crumbled all her thoughts.

Tesler raised the knife. His eyes bulged, his expression wild.

Her heart battered her chest, and her head whirled. No, no, do not pass out. You aren't a weakling. You are the most powerful psychic anyone in this clearing has ever seen. Don't just stand here.

She was powerful. Everyone said so. She'd proved it more than once.

David stared at her, not a hint of emotion on his face. But at the instant their gazes converged, she understood what he wanted her to do.

Shut down the EM generator.

Where was it? The field surrounded them, which suggested the generator was nearby, if not inside the field itself. She had no clue what the contraption looked like.

"I'm going to bleed you," Tesler hissed, "until you beg for mercy, and then I'll make you watch while I cut your beloved to ribbons. Only then will I slit your throat."

She was goddamn sick of listening to this deranged bastard.

As she squeezed her eyes shut, she sank into the depths of her mind, hunting for a spark of the energy she relied on to fuel her powers. Deeper and deeper she dived, searching, pawing, desperate to unearth—

A spark. Tiny but bright.

Its tentacles lashed out to her, eager to latch on and never let go.

Not this time.

She reeled back from the Golden Power. Scrap or not, it tempted her with an easy way out, but the price was too high. She sought out David's energy and gathered it to her heart. Without any conscious decision, she tossed out feelers to locate the EM generator. Its field burned red in the air, from her astral viewpoint, casting the world in a bloody haze.

There. She spotted a box, metal and equipped with a parabolic dish.

She condensed a ball of energy, took aim, and—

Wait. If she knocked out the EM generator, it would unchain the psychic powers of everyone inside the field. *Everyone.*

Including Tesler.

She had no idea whether the field caged the Golden Power, but she could not risk setting it free.

Besides, if Tesler's power was bridled, like hers, then she had a shot.

One shot only.

She opened her eyes. Tesler might be crazy, but he was cunning, especially with the limitless power corked up inside him.

Tesler stood motionless, cloaked in shadow, in front of David. Ambient light glanced off the knife's blade.

Some of the minions lacked weapons. Others held various types of handguns. The one nearest to her wore a semiautomatic pistol holstered on his hip, with a leather strap to keep the weapon berthed in its holster. She might grab for the gun of the man nearest her, but he was eying her as if expecting some kind of attack. She'd have to do this the other way.

When she tapped into David's energy, he blinked and one eyebrow ticked upward for a heartbeat, though his expression gave away nothing. The boost she received from him enlivened her mind and arced through her body, an electric tingle composed of his warmth and stolid nature. It grounded her. Braced her. Strengthened her.

Thank you, my warrior angel.

His lips ticked up then, at the corners, just a touch, before flattening out again. *Warrior angel?* She felt his question rather than sensing his thought. She'd explain that one later.

She used only her peripheral vision to spot their confiscated weapons piled up near a thin jack pine. Her .357 Magnum lay on top. Perfect.

Tesler hoisted the knife above his head. "Time to bleed!"

With a single burst of telekinetic energy, she whisked the gun up off the ground, spun it through the air to her, and clamped her fist around it as the weapon smacked into her palm.

The minion closest to her sucked in a sharp breath.

She slammed the butt of the gun into his head. He crumpled.

"Stop her!" Tesler shouted.

Grace fired one shot at the man restraining Sean, striking him in the leg. He cried out and slumped sideways. Sean seized the chance to snatch the man's gun from its holster and leap to his feet.

Amador broke away from his stunned guards and ran for the weapons pile.

The outer circle of psychic puppets edged inward.

She whirled on Tesler, swinging her gun up to target his chest.

Tesler slashed the knife downward.

Grace pulled the trigger.

The minions roared and swarmed toward them.

Chapter Thirty-Two

THE GUNSHOT THUNDERED IN THE CLEARING. ITS ECHOES BOUNCED OFF the trees in a cacophony that rattled David's eardrums. A red stain blossomed on Tesler's chest as he collapsed to his knees, out of breath, eyes wide.

The knife tumbled to the ground.

David's bindings snapped free, cut by a spurt of power from Grace. He couldn't control telekinetic energy the way she could, and they both knew it.

Tesler toppled forward just as David sprang to his feet.

In unison, Tesler's army stumbled, halted, and the life sluiced out of them with visible effect. Their shoulders wilted. Their heads drooped. Many of them foundered and thumped to the ground.

David raced toward Grace and swept her into his arms.

Gurgling, blood oozing from his mouth, Tesler crumpled.

David saw nothing except Grace. He clinched her tight, and she gripped him just as hard. Their lips found each other's at the same instant, hungry, plundering and being plundered in a brief kiss of such intensity it flared like a supernova, wiping out everything around them.

Not literally, of course.

When their lips parted, and he set her down, they could do nothing more than grin stupidly at each other.

"Uh…" Sean's hesitant query disrupted their afterglow.

David finally noticed Sean and Amador had collected all the weapons from the guards and bound them with their own zip ties. The man Grace had shot sported a bandanna tied around his wounded thigh.

After a quick peck on Grace's lips, David plucked up one of the minions' guns and turned to face Tesler. He lay still, eyes closed, body limp. Blood soaked his shirt.

Grace laced her fingers with David's. "Is he dead?"

"Not sure." He extricated his fingers from hers. "Wait here, I'll check." He took one step.

She seized his arm. "Stop."

David paused, glancing back at her worried face. "What is it?"

"I... don't know." She gestured at the knife that rested inches from Tesler's unmoving hand. "It's too close, he could reach it. And I feel... energy or something, coming out of him." Her fingers sank into his flesh. "Please stay here, for now."

"I could shoot him in the head, and then we'd know for sure."

"I'm afraid that might release the energy again, like with Nkosi." Her gaze darted to Tesler, then settled on David. "Please stay away from him, just until I sort out what I'm sensing."

With a sharp nod, he stayed put.

But his trigger finger itched to blast a hole in the bastard's skull.

Sean and Amador stared into the woods.

"Grace could see other men in the woods," Amador said. "Perhaps the boy and I should see what happened to them."

"Boy?" Sean balked. "I'm seventeen, asswipe."

"It's a good idea," David said to Amador. "But take weapons."

Sean and Amador made their way toward the woods, where the puppet psychics lay motionless in varying degrees of awkwardness.

"Whoa," Sean said, with teenage awe. He bent over to swipe a weapon from one of the minions, a rifle with a pistol grip mounted on its underside and a curved magazine extending down from the stock. "Zombie dude has an AK-47. Sweet."

He swung the muzzle toward a thick tree and pulled the trigger. Rounds sprayed the trunk. Bark pattered on the grass.

Sean's awe morphed into wide-eyed glee. "Full auto. Wicked."

"Fully automatic weapons are illegal," David said.

Grace made an unladylike noise, which only made him want to kiss her again. "Nkosi picked weak-willed people with questionable morals for his army. You're surprised one of them flouts the law?"

He stuck his tongue out at her.

She drew her head back as if shocked.

Amador and Sean headed out into the forest, Sean toting his new treasure, Amador looking aggrieved for being saddled with a rebellious teen. Their footfalls receded into silence.

David brushed his palm across Grace's cheek. "I have to check on Tesler. It can't wait any longer. I'll tie him up." He nodded toward the unconscious minions. "See if one of them has another zip tie."

"David."

He squeezed her hand. "I know you're worried, but we have to secure him."

If we're not killing him. He kept the end of his sentence to himself. The only secured Tesler was a dead Tesler.

She sighed. "Okay. I'll stay here. But I am not searching for zip ties until you've got Tesler in hand. And take a gun. That is nonnegotiable."

They stood sideways to Tesler and the pine tree. To their left, branches bobbed slightly in the wind. The breeze fanned her hair out over her face, and David combed it back with his fingers.

"Deal." He feathered a kiss across her lips, then bent to nab a gun.

Movement flashed in his peripheral vision. He pivoted his head, overcome by a strange slowing of time as if his brain had downshifted. His thoughts lagged behind what he saw, delaying his actions.

Tesler snared the knife. Hefted his body into a crouch. Took the knife in a throwing hold. Bared his teeth.

And launched the knife at David.

Grace flung her body at him, shouting as she threw them both to the ground. The moss cushioned their fall, but they landed askew, her leg under his, their arms entangled.

Her .357 plunked down by his head.

Rational thought disintegrated.

David grabbed the revolver and, still tangled with Grace, swerved his arm to level the weapon at Tesler.

The scientist lunged.

David fired.

Karl Tesler whumped down in a lifeless heap. His eyes gaped, vacant.

This time, David did not wait for Grace's permission. He lifted them both to their feet and marched straight to Tesler. When he found no pulse, no breathing or signs of life at all, he turned to Grace. "He's dead."

"Good." She nailed her gaze to a sight beyond his shoulder.

"What is it?"

Before he could glance back, her mouth fell open on a cry of "no!"

A gunshot detonated.

She propelled her body into the gun's trajectory, behind his back.

He wheeled around.

The impact of the shot flung her backward into him. She gurgled, convulsed, her hands like talons on his arms. Then her whole body slumped, held up by his arms.

Another shot exploded. Then another.

He fell to his knees, cradling her. He touched her face, her neck, her arms, and—*shit*. Her stomach.

Blood. Too much blood.

With one trembling hand, he reached down to palpate the wound, but couldn't make himself touch it. His hand hovered over her abdomen. Rocking her in his arms, he ducked his head near hers. "Grace, no. Why did you do that?"

Her head lolled into his chest. A soft grunt issued from her, muffled by his shirt, and she winced. He stretched his hand out to caress her cheek but pulled it back at the last second.

"Are you shot?" Her voice was weak, shaky.

"No." It was a strangled word, dense with an anguish he couldn't contain. "You took the bullet. Why, Grace? Why? You could've used your powers to stop him."

Her voice was even weaker now, barely a whisper. "Didn't think."

Of course she hadn't. Their attacker allowed no time for thinking.

"There he is!" Sean's enraged voice barely registered in David's ears. "I'll get the scumbag."

The rat-a-tat of automatic gunfire. An infuriated scream. More shots. More yelling.

None of it mattered.

Grace's eyelids drifted half shut.

"Sean, get over here!" David splayed his hand over her cheek. She was cold. So damn cold. "Hold on, Grace. It'll be okay, I promise." He scraped his quivering lips across her forehead. "Don't leave me. I need you."

A torrent of love and anguish, fear and devotion, ripped through him down their connection. The link persevered, even as he felt her slipping away.

"Fight, Grace." His voice trembled with the conviction he mustered from deep within. "Fight for me. For us. Come back to me, please."

Her lids closed. The rise and fall of her chest ceased.

David punched his fist through the moss, straight down to the hard earth.

GRACE COULDN'T MOVE. SHE HEARD NOISES, DIMLY. VOICES? MAYbe. Her dwindling mental acuity turned everything into a radio show playing from a remote speaker. She succumbed to the numbness, to the blessed relief of spiraling down and down into infinity.

"No, goddammit! You do not get to leave me like this."

Was that David? Yes. Why was he screaming at her from so far away?

Drifting down. Weightless. Painless. A brilliant star beckoned to her, its light a promise of peace and fulfillment. She belonged...

With David.

The epiphany hurtled her out of the tunnel, away from the light. *It's not your time.* The statement filled her, awakened her, though it was not her own thought. The words emanated from the beautiful radiance, from the ever-receding star of eternity.

Her hearing returned first. She heard Sean, his voice desperate. "I'll try, oh jeez, I'll try. But if she's dead, I can't—"

"Do it anyway!" David this time. Angry. Terrified.

Physical sensation filtered back into her next. Her body shifted, coming to rest on a bumpy, firm surface. Hazily, she realized they'd laid her flat on her back. Damp moss tickled her nostrils. Voices chattered around her, but her brain couldn't decipher the meaning of their words. *Sleep now,* a voice inside urged.

Warmth penetrated her wound, spreading outward until it encompassed her whole body, tingling with an odd energy. The numbness gave way to a dull ache in her chest, a pain that dissipated second by second. The key to her mind twisted in the ignition, and the engine of her thoughts chugged back to life. The clean scent of earth and grass wafted over her.

She sneezed.

Whoops erupted around her.

Peeling her lids apart, she stared at the three men huddled around her. David crouched by her head, Amador alongside him near her hip, and Sean…

She rolled onto her side to look at him. He'd been kneeling on the side of her opposite David and Amador, with both hands suspended over her wound. The strange energy she'd sensed originated from him.

"Did you heal me?" she asked.

Looking a bit sheepish, he scrutinized a loose thread on his pants, picking at it. "Uh, yeah. David would've throttled me if I hadn't. But you kinda helped out."

"Helped out?"

"Yeah. I felt your power, like, adding to mine. It was cool."

Okay, she'd helped heal herself while she lay dying. *Weird.*

Sean scrubbed his face with one hand, yawning. Dark circles bruised the skin under his eyes, which were red and tinged with yellow.

"You're tapped out, aren't you?" She knew the signs of power drain.

"Pretty much."

She pushed up into a sitting position, with an assist from David, who immediately threw his arms around her and pulled her close, ensconced in his embrace. She hugged him back and then, on an impulse too strong to deny, she crushed her lips to his. He responded with abandon, their passion energizing their psychic bond until it sizzled. Her body did a little sizzling too.

"Gross," Sean whined, though it sounded less than sincere.

With great reluctance, she severed the kiss. "What about the minions?"

"They're unconscious, very weak." David's attention strayed past her, to the edge of the woods. "No sign of the Golden Power since Tesler died." He curled a lock of her hair around his finger, careful to avoid her gaze. "Do you feel it?"

The uncertainty in his voice made her hesitate. Did she feel the oily, alien energy? "No. It's gone—back to where it came from."

"Is it alive?" Sean asked. "Nkosi said it was, but if anybody would know, it'd be you."

Arms linked around David's neck, she craned hers to examine Sean. He watched her with a steady gaze. The kid honestly believed she was the expert on all things psychic.

"Nkosi was full of shit," she said. "The Golden Power is not a living thing. It's energy, pure and simple." She glimpsed the blood on her shirt and her heart skipped. "Who shot me? Did you get him?"

David slid his hands under her bottom to boost her up onto his lap. "It must've been one of the minions. You saw him. That's why you jumped in front of me, right?"

"Is it?" She ran through events in her mind, but cobwebs obscured her memories.

"Can't you remember?"

"It's all fuzzy." Grunting with the effort, she struggled to get up and plopped back down on David's lap. "A little woozy."

He rose and hoisted her up with him. "Can you stand?"

"Think so." When he set her on her feet, she found her legs weren't as wobbly as she'd feared. "So you didn't find the shooter?"

"We assumed he was one of the minions, and they're all out cold."

Sean thumped his new AK-47 against his hip. "I scared him away for sure."

"Did you see a body?" she asked. When Sean shrugged, she turned her attention to David. "You didn't check? RV the area, I mean."

He looked at her as if she'd spoken gibberish. "The EM field is still up."

Ah. Of course. She hadn't gotten a chance to tell them where to find the generator, and so they worked with limited powers.

She pointed across the clearing. "Generator's over there. Behind that tree."

Amador took off at a trot. He disappeared behind the tree and fired his gun once. She flinched—at the noise and the sudden influx of power.

"Woo-hoo!" Sean hopped up and down. "We're back."

She smiled at him and laughed.

Amador returned then, and the four of them trooped over to the nearest clump of limp psychic puppets. Men, she had to remind herself. They were men, not puppets or minions. It had been easier to think of them that way when Nkosi and then Tesler had controlled them, because they'd behaved like zombies. Now, as she studied two of the men, tendrils of empathy unwound inside her. Their lips and skin bore a deep pallor. Saliva drooled out of their open mouths. Their limbs lay in haphazard, awkward positions. Blood had dribbled out their ears, crusting on their skin.

She turned away, her throat tight. Mind control from someone channeling the Golden Power exacted a terrible toll on the victim, worse than she could've imagined. Would they ever wake up? Would they be normal if they did?

Once, she would've blamed herself for this. No more. Nkosi and Tesler, and JT before them, had embarked on a quest borne of sheer lunacy, determined to mine psychic power from her body. She never asked for this. She never encouraged their obsessions. They undertook vile experiments due solely to their arrogance and insanity.

"We have to take care of them," she said.

Amador, standing beside her, settled a hand on her shoulder. "I donate any of my resources you need to treat these poor men."

"Thank you." She patted his hand and did not miss David's tiny grimace when he saw her gesture. She sent a pulse of reassurance down their connection, plus a small hit of raw desire, a preview of things to come. And they would come very soon.

He grinned.

She still hadn't gotten used to him grinning like a... Well, like a normal, happy guy. But the sight awoke pleasant butterflies in her stomach.

Twigs cracked behind them. Brush scraped and rustled.

Grace and Amador whirled around in unison.

Battaglia roared out of the woods into the clearing. He swung up his huge gun, training it on Grace. "You won't cheat death twice, you freaks."

Grace yanked the gun out of Amador's hand and shot three times at Battaglia. His finger twitched reflexively over the trigger of his gun. The rounds flew wild, nicking trees and popping chunks of moss into the air.

He collapsed, dead.

David trotted to the body and checked. "He's gone."

She shoved the gun at Amador, who took it. "Battaglia shot me. I remember seeing him, about to shoot you, and I—Well, I won't apologize for what I did. I'd do it again."

David bowed his head. He stayed like that for so long she worried he was disgusted with her for taking out Battaglia.

Then his head came up, his eyes aglow, and she understood.

"It's over," he said. "I checked out the area and it's clear."

"The people in the facility?"

"Gone. They evacuated."

She nodded. "It's time to destroy the facility."

He walked to her, took her hands, and gave her an amused smile. "I'm beginning to think you're a pyromaniac. Blowing up facilities all over the place."

"Hey." She batted his chest with the back of her hand. "JT blew up the other one."

"Because he beat you to the punch. Your master plan was to torch the place."

She leaned into him, her hand on his chest. "You didn't have a better idea."

"It's okay." He pinched her butt. "Apparently, I'm attracted to pyromaniacs."

"This time is different. I know for a fact destroying this facility will erase every scrap of data related to Project Outreach. It'll finally be over."

"We'll be free." He bent his head toward hers, his lips aiming for her mouth.

Sean made a vomit-like yacking noise.

David pulled away without kissing her.

She could've strangled Sean.

The kid let out a melodramatic sigh. "Are we gonna blow stuff up or what? I want to get away from the creepy ex-puppet guys and the rotting corpses."

"Sure." She locked gazes with David. "Give us a minute."

She and David traveled to the facility, breaking away from their bodies as easily as they changed shoes. They didn't need words. Their minds, along with their powers, operated in perfect synchronization. Thank heavens for Tesler's paranoia, and his need to defend his facility at any cost. They located the right spot, an armory stacked high with boxes of ammo, and set off a spark.

They shot back into their bodies.

A deep boom rumbled in the distance. The earth shuddered.

Project Outreach had been terminated.

Chapter Thirty-Three

AVID WOKE GRACE WITH A FEW GENTLE NUDGES AS THEY PULLED into the parking lot of the private airport near Bozeman, the same strip where they'd battled brainwashed, zombie-like men a few hours ago. A small building, almost a shack, hunkered alongside a control tower. A short distance away, sequestered from the other structures, loomed the hangar. He could just make out the ruined fence.

Amador led them to his jet. The airstairs had been restored to their rightful position, and their group trudged up and into the plane. David, the last in line, paused inside the portal where Amador waited to shut the door.

"About the bodies," he said. "Tesler and Nkosi."

The other man shrugged, his expression unconcerned. "I have already contacted Wickham about all of this."

Yes, David remembered Amador making a phone call during the drive back to the airport. He'd spoken in Spanish—or at least it had sounded like Spanish—most likely to prevent David or anyone else from eavesdropping.

"Wickham will arrange for the remains to be taken care of," Amador said.

Of course he would. "Taken care of" was probably a euphemism for "chucked into an incinerator." The lunatics deserved nothing better, anyway.

David despised relying on Amador to deal with the aftermath. Hell, he despised the man in general. But he had no choice in this case because he lacked the resources to clean up after his own mess. "What about the men they brainwashed and abused?"

"Wickham will have them sent to a private hospital I recently purchased. They will be well cared for, you have my word."

David bristled at the suggestion he should trust Amador's word, but Grace did, so he deferred to her judgment. Still, that didn't bar him from a little scornful suspicion. "You own a hospital? Awfully convenient. When did you buy it?"

The smug look on Amador's face had David's fist itching to connect with the bastard's jaw. "I purchased the hospital during my telephone discussion with Wickham in the car."

Jeez. The son of a bitch could buy an entire hospital in the space of one ten-minute conversation over the cell network. Rather than jealousy, as he might've expected, he experienced a bizarre twinge of appreciation. Wickham was doing the grunt work, but Amador orchestrated things. Both men had earned a little credit for their efforts.

David offered his hand to Amador. "Thank you. We'd be in a heap of trouble if you hadn't stepped in."

The other man accepted the handshake. "Do not thank me. This is the least I could do to begin to make amends."

Sean scuffled up beside Amador. "Whoa, dude, how are you gonna explain all those bodies to the cops?"

Amador arched an eyebrow. "There were only five corpses, including Tesler and Nkosi. The rest are alive. And my colleague Wickham has contacts at the FBI and CIA who understand the importance of glossing over any deaths related to ALI or Digital Prognostics."

Grace wandered up behind Amador. "Why would FBI agents help us cover up this mess?"

"Because they owe us, Wickham and I." His mouth twisted into a somber, yet slightly amused, smile. "We liberated them from facilities elsewhere in the world."

"They're psychics?"

"Oh yes. The FBI and CIA often hire individuals with extrasensory abilities, though they don't advertise for those positions." Amador sighed. "Wickham recommended them for the jobs. He was MI6 at one time and had fostered relationships with several individuals at those agencies."

David stared at the man, his mind sputtering in an attempt to process what he'd said. Gabriel Amador, who had abducted and tortured a teenage girl, had also rescued detainees from ALI facilities *and* gotten them jobs back home? The two types of behavior clashed. Didn't they? A person couldn't torment a young woman to the brink of insanity, then traipse off to be a hero.

"You don't believe it," Amador said, his gaze intent on David. "Do you, Mr. Ransom?"

"Might as well call me David," he said with a resigned sigh. "And no, I can't quite reconcile your supposed heroics with what you did to Grace or the way you treated that girl Cari."

Amador had the sense to bow his head, in imitation of shame if nothing else. He rubbed his neck. "Desperation makes the weak-willed do terrible things."

David analyzed the man's posture—stooped, head down, arms slack—but he wasn't ready yet to accept Amador's shame as genuine. "You're admitting to being weak."

"Yes." Amador's head lifted slightly, enough for him to turn his eyes toward Grace. "I do not ask forgiveness, but please believe me. I will do anything within my power to set right the grievous wrongs I've inflicted on you and others."

"Don't talk to her," David said. "You speak to me."

Grace gave him an exasperated look. "Cool down, cowboy. We're all on the same team, you know. We, all of us together, defeated Tesler, Nkosi, and a passel of mind-controlled, armed men."

Teeth grinding, David glared at Amador.

Grace sidled past Amador and slipped an arm around David's waist, snuggling against him. His body reacted the way it always did, without his consent, curling an arm around her shoulders and relaxing into her warmth and suppleness. The feel of her body against his comforted him more than he'd realized until this moment. Until he'd almost lost her.

But dammit, he wanted to be annoyed. At the man feigning regret. At the scumbag who drugged the woman he loved. He had a frigging right to be pissed.

Her hand slid across his belly, her fingers dancing over his shirt and exciting the flesh underneath. Her every action was directed at him, but she spoke to Amador. "David needs a little time to adjust and accept you're sincere. I'm sure you can understand that."

She injected the last sentence with a faint sternness, a directive for Amador to comply.

"Naturally," Amador said, his head raised to meet David's gaze, "I understand your need to see proof of my intentions. I will demonstrate with actions, not words. One day, I hope you'll see I wish to change." His attention shifted to Grace for a second, and a mysterious emotion flickered over his face. "Grace told me once it's not too late to come back from the madness I gave in to. Her compassion and conviction have persuaded me she is correct. From this day forward, I will commit myself to that recovery."

"How?" David asked.

"By signing myself into the same hospital where the men from Nkosi's army will be tended to." He shoved his hands in his pockets, then pulled them out, reaching up as if to touch his face. He retracted his hand. "There is a psychiatric unit. The doctors are excellent, or so Wickham assures me. I trust him implicitly."

Grace's smile was genuine, if muted. "Good luck, Biel. I hope you find your peace."

"You are far too generous a soul, Grace." Amador's lips curved up but faltered. "If I can achieve a fraction of your goodness…"

David almost smiled. Almost. "Don't set a goal you can't achieve. Nobody will ever be anywhere near as good as this woman." He gave her a quick squeeze. "She's a living, breathing miracle."

She poked him with her elbow and rolled her eyes. "Oh brother. If you lay it on any thicker, I might join Sean in barfing."

The boy snickered. David shot him a glance that shut him up.

Amador managed a sad smile. "No, Grace, David is right. You are a miracle, and I am blessed to have met you. I hope someday to become your friend." He cast a sideways look at David. "A friend to both of you."

"We'll see," David said.

Amador's expression changed subtly, into something akin to gratitude. He gestured toward the sofas and chairs in the cabin behind him. "Make yourselves at home. There is a galley stocked with food and beverages at the rear of the cabin. I will sit with the pilot. He is a good friend and ally."

"Thank you," Grace said.

As he watched Amador meander toward the cockpit, David wondered if the man was hiding out with the captain to give him, Grace, and Sean privacy—and a break from the man they barely trusted. Maybe Amador had some tact after all.

"Hey," David called out, just as Amador reached for the cockpit door handle. The man glanced back. "Good luck with your recovery."

It was the best sentiment he could offer honestly, and Amador knew it. Amador nodded and entered the cockpit. The door clicked shut.

Sean skipped down the aisle—yes, actually skipped, like the kid he denied being—and flopped down onto a cushy sofa a few rows down. Grace clasped David's hand, leading him past the teenager sprawled on a cream-colored sofa, and straight back to the last row. A sofa awaited them there, behind a quartet of chairs arranged around a rectangular table. A long, low table fronted the sofa. The chairs provided a sort of privacy screen, which, combined with the distance between them and Sean, made for a cozy nest.

"I figured," Grace said, "we'd want to be alone for a while."

Yes, yes, and hell yes. They'd won a vicious battle, against human enemies, but also against their own demons. She knew everything about him, and even when the evidence suggested he'd betrayed her, she never gave up on him. This woman fought for him, for their love, without hesitation. He worshiped her. He needed her. He craved her.

"Hungry?" she asked, and waved toward the galley. "Or thirsty? I can get us a drink or a quick bite."

"No thanks." He was starving, but not for food.

The pattering of footsteps drew their attention to the aisle and Sean padding toward them. He rolled his eyes as he moseyed by, on his way to the galley.

"Don't worry," he said. "I'm grabbing a drink. Then you guys can get back to drooling over each other."

He did indeed grab a can of Coke and hustle back to his makeshift bed. A pop and a fizz ensued, then the hushed whine of the engines was the only sound.

Grace moved around the table and eased her lithe body down onto the sofa, wriggling her lovely little butt to scoot backward. She cuddled into the cushioning with a soft, contented moan.

He settled in beside her, with those luscious curves tucked against him and her head on his shoulder. Her silky hair teased his chin. Ducking his head, he inhaled a long breath, entranced by the scent of her. Though tainted with a hint of blood and dirt, her hair still gave off the intoxicating aroma of coconuts. Surrounded by her, he let his thoughts travel back to his fantasy from days ago. Grace in a bikini, on a beach, sunning herself beside him. He'd rub lotion all over her body, starting with her shoulders and working his way down, inch by inch, tracing the elegant contour of her back, the curve of her hips, the perfect mounds of her bottom, and—

"Stop that."

He whipped his head up, startled. "Stop what?"

She tilted her head up, targeting her glorious eyes on him. "You're fantasizing about sex again, I know you are. I can feel you're getting… aroused." Her eyes flicked down, toward his crotch, and then back up. Amusement curled one corner of her luscious lips. "And I feel it with more than my psychic senses."

Right. His pants had grown tighter all of a sudden.

One of her delicate fingers poked into his side. "We can't do anything here, so don't go torturing yourself with erotic daydreams."

"Thinking about you is never torture." He nuzzled her ear and whispered, "You know, we're connected on a much deeper level these days. Maybe we could share a fantasy. I'd love to show you mine."

Her breath hitched. Excitement pumped into him from her, a thrill triggered by his suggestion. *She wants to share this with me.*

A thrill of his own fired through their link, straight into her.

Her sharp intake of breath made him ache in a way that would get him arrested if he acted on it in public. But after a second, she virtually purred her response. "David, I would love to share your fantasy. But can we do that?" A note of anxiety crept into her voice. "I mean, reading minds is bad news, trust me, I've got firsthand knowledge of it."

He'd expected that reaction. After everything she'd been through, extrasensory powers were a boogeyman under her bed. He knew this, but he also knew she possessed more than enough strength to overcome those fears. Her journey toward fearlessness had begun the moment she defeated Nkosi.

Stroking her cheek with one hand, he kissed her earlobe, tugged it between his lips, and suckled gently. Her faint moan turned him on even more. The salty-yet-sweet flavor of her skin whipped his need into a near frenzy. *Take it slow, don't rush her.*

Releasing her lobe, he let his lips tantalize her ear as he spoke. "This won't be reading minds. It'll be more like thought projection mixed with telepathy, and a dash of empathic energy for good measure." He skimmed his hand down her neck and paused with his fingertips at the hollow above her collarbone. "If we get really ambitious, we could astral project somewhere nice and manifest."

Her chest heaved with each breath. She dropped one hand to his thigh and raked it up his jeans until her fingers grazed his swelling erection.

He whisked his tongue across her lower lip.

She clutched his shirt. "That would take a lot of energy. We'd be... exhausted afterward."

"But it would be worth it."

"We'll be home soon. Maybe we should wait."

The light pressure of her fingernails through his shirt pushed him beyond longing, right into raw, hot lust. "Can't wait. I've got to have you *now*."

"David, I... oh." She thrust a hand into his hair as he blew a gentle puff of air onto the tender skin below her ear. Arching her neck, she exposed her slender throat to him, and he trailed kisses down her neck. "David, we shouldn't... please... mmm." Her hand in his hair gripped harder. "Let's do it."

He ran the tip of his tongue back up her throat. "Are you sure?"

"Yes." She groaned the word and cupped his erection through his pants.

David tipped his head up. "A real kiss first."

"Please, yes."

He took her mouth, too famished for her to care how much noise they made. They groped and fondled, devoured and drank each other in, lost in the fervor of skin on skin. It wasn't enough. He needed all of her skin, bare and creamy, ripe for the taking.

They couldn't do that here.

But her lips, her tongue, her fingers...

The jet engines whined dully, but the noise receded, along with the rest of the world, out of the bubble their desire had fashioned around them. He pulled them both down to lie on the sofa, and she clung to him while he grasped her hips, dragging them into him over and over in a frantic, erotic rhythm. She abandoned herself to the kiss, her passion stripping away his control. Their minds touched, melded, whirled out of their bodies into the crossroads.

And still, he felt her slick lips on his, her hot hands on his back. Their minds spun through darkness made of living energy, thrusting out into pure sunshine. The connection to his body waned to a background hum, but their passion joined them as powerfully as ever.

They stood on a beach. Palm trees swayed in a gentle breeze, casting flickering shadows on the golden sand. Crystalline blue water lapped against the shore, and the aroma of exotic flowers whispered over them. No humans in sight. No animals either. Nothing except the two of them, separated by mere inches. Alone. Aroused.

Grace wore a bikini. When that fact finally penetrated his brain, he couldn't stop himself from smirking.

She glanced down at her attire, blushed, and bit her lip. A shy smile tugged at the corners of her mouth.

He was in pants and a khaki shirt, unbuttoned. Naked would've seemed more appropriate, but he'd let her choose his wardrobe—not with words, but with silent permission. She'd given him the same leave, to dress her. Or undress her. That delectable body curved in all the right places, the skimpy bikini more of an adornment than an outfit. Her creamy skin took on a slight flush in the sunlight.

She gazed up at him, her lips parted. "Shall we manifest?"

"Yes."

Psychic energy poured into him, coursed through his entire being, and swept back into her, then repeated in a cycle of exquisite highs and soothing lows. His mind came alive, buzzing with power.

The sun heated his face.

Grace wiggled her toes in the sand. "It worked."

"Of course it did." He hauled her into his arms for a deep kiss. "We're the two most powerful psychics around." He skated his hand up her side, molding his palm to her breast. "Let's see how good we really are at manifesting."

Sure, he'd made love to her while manifesting once before, but this time was different. The bond between them would alter their responses, he sensed that, but how intense it would get remained a mystery. One he intended to solve.

This instant.

Grace dragged her nails down his chest with feather-light pressure. When she reached the waistband of his pants, she raked her nails back up his skin. By the time her fingers hit his pecs, he was throbbing for her. The bikini he'd imagined for her, and manifested onto her body, featured strings for easy removal. He untied them one by one, and her bikini fluttered to the ground. His shirt and pants went next.

They lay on the sand, Grace stretched out beneath him, her skin glistening with tiny beads of sweat. The sight of her—nude, nipples hardened into peaks, her skin damp, her mouth open—stole his voice, his breath, and his thoughts. How could he ever have chosen hunting for a madman over staying with this woman?

A ghost of a frown tensed her features. "You've never been this adventurous before. And you've barely kissed me in the past two months until the other day." With a sharp and questioning look, she nailed him to an invisible wall. "Why go all late-night cable on me all of a sudden?"

"You know why." He lowered a knee between her thighs to ease them apart. "Enough talking."

"Maybe we shouldn't."

His body screamed for action, friction, the ecstasy of burying himself inside her. She crossed her arms over her chest in a gesture that normally indicated annoyance, but her fear trickled into him, tempering his desire. Unable to read her mind, he could only guess at what disturbed her. "Is this about the power merge? Do you think I only want you because I can feel your passion?"

One of her shoulders hunched in a tiny shrug. "You felt my passion before we joined our powers. Our connection was getting more intense even then, but now… Would you have ever wanted me this much if things had stayed the way they were before I got amnesia?"

"Yes." He almost growled the word, infusing it with all his certainty. "I love you. The longer we're together, the closer we get. It's natural and normal, although our relationship has extra oomph."

Amusement sparkled in her eyes and curved one corner of her mouth. "Oomph?"

"Exactly. Our powers are a bonus, not the source of our bond." He ducked his head to touch his lips to hers. "I love you because you're you, end of story."

"But you weren't like this before."

True. He'd been reserved in their lovemaking, afraid to embrace the hunger gnawing at him, desperate to come out and play. Fear of hurting her, scaring her, had restrained him. And, if he were totally honest, fear she wouldn't approve of his fantasies.

Yet she had. He'd offered her the key to his inner sanctum, and she had accepted it. Despite the countless mistakes he'd made, running after Tesler and keeping secrets from her. Despite everything. She never wavered in her commitment to their relationship.

Her love and trust had liberated him.

Elation rushed into him, sweet and warm and tasting like her. He felt the grin that split his lips. A wide, stupid grin borne of the unbridled joy consuming him.

The look on her face—a mixture of adoration, euphoria, and desire—took his breath away. She knew what he felt, though not what he thought. Crazy, silly thoughts that were unmanly in their gushy nature. He had to tell her. The words clamored to get out, and at last, he realized he didn't give a damn if he sounded like a moron.

"You freed me, Grace, you showed me unconditional, boundless love and I couldn't fight it anymore. I love you, I need you, I'm so sorry for the way I've treated you these past months. You're sweet and strong and beautiful and fragile. You make me laugh when I don't want to, you push me to do the hard things because it's right." He took a single, gasping breath. "You changed me. You—"

She sealed his lips with her fingers. "Shh. No need to gush, honey. I know how you feel because you've shown me."

"But all those months—"

"Yeah, I'll admit your standoffish behavior irritated me." Her fingers toyed with his lip, and he ached to suck those little digits. "But I love you, David, and love is never easy or neat. It's messy and difficult and sometimes painful. I'm in for the whole package, whatever happens."

"Me too," he said. Her fingers muffled his words, but she must've understood because she smiled. "Can we stop talking yet?"

She tugged his lip down with her fingertip. "Yes, enough telling. I'm in the mood for some showing."

He sucked her finger into his mouth, and her smile broadened. When he let her finger slide out, she slicked the wet tips over his chin, down his throat, onto his chest. He shimmied down her body inch by inch, relishing the salty tang of sweat, colored with the sweet, rich flavor of her, exploring her breasts, her belly, her hips. When he dipped his head between her thighs, she let out a surprised cry.

"Relax," he said, and peppered her inner thigh with kisses. "You wanted me to show you how much I adore you. So here I go."

And then he did. With all the single-minded focus he'd once reserved for his Tesler hunt, he demonstrated exactly how much he cherished her body, her heart, her soul, by tormenting her with pleasure and driving her wild with the need for release. She thrust a hand into his hair and writhed beneath him, beautiful, ardent, full of life and heat. Her heavy breathing escalated into pants and groans, as her hips bucked and her fingers clutched his hair, the nails scraping his scalp. His passion merged with hers, engulfed him, hardened him, consumed his every thought and fueled his every movement, revved up by the flavor of her desire and the feel of her slick heat against his mouth. Her shuddering climax hit hard, her back arched, her hips fastened down by his hands.

He exhaled a ragged breath against her flesh, and she shuddered again.

"Oh, David." His name emerged as a breathless moan.

Lifting his head, he gazed up at her, his breaths coming hard and fast. The afterglow flushed her cheeks, and her lips, swollen with desire, parted in a plea for a kiss. She was the most magnificent thing he'd ever laid eyes on—and she was his. Every molecule of her delectable body belonged to him and him alone, but more than that, she'd given him the gift of her trust and love.

Her mouth curved into a dazed, lopsided smile. "You've never done that before."

"I know." His grin must've looked wicked since that was how he felt. "I plan on doing a lot of things I've never done before, if my fiancée doesn't mind." He skated his mouth down her inner thigh, nipped her knee, and worked his way back up to her hip to kiss the hollow there. "Does my fiancée approve?"

She nodded and licked her lower lip. "Oh yes. I do, absolutely, no doubt, yes-yes-yes." She hooked one leg around him, rubbing her heel under the curve of his buttock. "I'm ready for whatever you have in mind."

With a naughty smile, she tugged her hand free of his hair to caress his cheek. The sunlight sparkled on the diamond in her engagement ring. Soon she would be his wife. His heart thudded. His wife. The phrase set off a torrent of emotions—happiness, adoration, satisfaction, and oh yes, lust. He drew her left leg up onto his shoulder, rose onto hands and knees, and fixed his gaze on hers. The psychic bond snapped tight between them, coursing her hunger into him, swirling it through his body and mind in an intoxicating mixture that drew a sigh out of him. "Do you feel that?"

"Mmm…" She dived her hands into the sand, fingers curled, and bowed her back. Her breasts heaved upward, the taut nipples grazing his skin. "All I want to feel is you."

For a moment, he gazed down at her in wonder. They lay on a beach, amid the shadow-dappled sand and the glittering sunshine. The tropical vista was stunning, but the breathtaking view beneath him captured all his focus.

He grasped her hips and sank inside her gradually until he'd filled her to the hilt. The exquisite torture of her velvety soft flesh enveloping him nearly pushed him over the edge.

Her fingers clutched his wrists. Her mouth fell open, and a single syllable escaped her lips. "Please."

"I would give up everything to be with you." He ground his hips into her. "Never doubt that again."

He slid out of her, sucked in a breath, and plowed into her glistening folds with one powerful thrust of his cock. He drove so deep the breath exploded out of him, and her hips rocked up to meet him. He plunged in over and over, desperate for her, for this, for everything her body promised and everything she surrendered to him, without hesitation or regret. The pressure mounted with every thrust, every thrash of her hips, every heave of her full breasts and their rigid, mouth-watering peaks. Her body clenched around him, ready to burst, and he lunged into her hard, blinded by need. She cried out as her release pulsed around him, and he exploded inside her, pumping until he was spent.

"Grace." Her name tumbled from his lips, a prayer and a thank-you. He flopped onto the sand beside her, sated more than ever before, and flung one arm around her to pull her close, her head nestled in the crook of his shoulder. "What should we do now?"

"You mean right this minute, or in the more general sense?"

"With our lives. What should we do?"

She traced circles on his chest with her finger. "I still have the flash drive with all of JT's research on it. That includes the location of every ALI facility on the planet and the names of all the people they kidnapped."

"Don't say what I think you're about to say."

"We have to track them down and help them." She lifted her head, those gorgeous eyes studying him. "Remember what Sean was like when you first met him? Terrified and beaten down. There may be others like him and Cari out there, people who need us."

He groaned. "I swore I'd give up insane quests."

"This isn't vengeance or a crazy attempt to protect me." She rolled on top of him, her hair spilling over his chest. "This is a meaningful quest. A good deed. Don't you want to help the powerless?" The weight of her on top of him, and the way she flitted her tongue over his skin, tempted him to do things he couldn't, not with their energy waning and their manifested bodies on the brink of dissipating. Mercilessly, she licked the corner of his mouth. "Say yes."

"To what?" He'd lost all memory of their conversation.

"Saving the world, one psychic at a time."

His mind blanked when she sucked his lip between her teeth and stroked her tongue over it. The second she released it, he sputtered, "Yes, let's save the world."

The craziest part was, he meant it.

"You know," she said, "I won't hold you to that promise. You made it under duress."

As she straddled him, his hips cradled between her shapely thighs, he moved his hands up them to chart their tempting contours. "We both know I would've agreed anyway. This is our destiny. I think it's time we embraced it."

The psychic fuel sustaining them fizzled out, vanishing their manifested forms. They zipped through the crossroads, too lost in each other to notice anything else. Stars streaked by, distant and unimportant, then retreated into the darkness.

The crossroads is never completely dark. Lights glitter there, innumerable beacons lighting the way to the unexplored, the undiscovered, the unknown.

Whether it was her thought or his hardly mattered because the words illuminated a truth he'd ignored until life had forced him to face it. Grace was his beacon. His anchor to the world, to life. She was a part of him, and he was a part of her. The destiny he'd fought for so long had found its fruition in her, and in their future together.

Before he knew it had happened, he was back in his real body, on the plane, with the hum of the jet engines in the background. His arms were still wound around Grace, her body snuggled into him with her face resting against his neck, warm air puffing out of her nostrils onto his skin.

"Wake up, you pervs."

David cracked one eye open.

Sean towered over them where they lay on the sofa, stretched across its length, entwined in each other in so many ways. The boy made a disgusted face. "We just landed in Cincinnati. If you guys can stop psychic sexting for a few minutes, maybe we can get off this plane and go home."

Cincinnati. They were home, almost.

Rousing Grace with a gentle shake, David sat up. "Psychic sexting? We weren't using our cell phones."

Sean snorted. "Maybe sexting isn't totally accurate. Point is, I don't need telepathy to know what you two were doing—and I mean *doing*—back here." He winced, frowning at the floor, and mumbled, "I heard some... uh... moans."

Grace bolted upright. Her hair lashed David's face. With a struggle that wrenched his mind too, she kept her expression neutral, though her embarrassment radiated into him. He laid a soothing hand on her back, drawing circles on her flesh. Her shoulders relaxed.

Oblivious, Sean did what every teenager excelled at. He spouted more blatant observations designed to knock adults off-kilter. "There was a kind of weird energy or something too. I felt it."

Grace's eyes bulged. She'd stopped breathing.

He gave Sean a stern look. "What are you talking about?"

The boy hunched his shoulders, jamming his hands into his pockets. "I think it was, ya know, related to your... activities."

Grace slammed a thought into his brain, and he gritted his teeth. *Please tell me he didn't feel what we were feeling? Is that even possible?* He heard her voice pleading the questions, and her anxiety knifed into him. Sliding his hand down to encircle her waist, he pulled her closer.

She pushed away and swung her feet onto the floor, then braced her elbows on her knees.

He ran a hand through his hair. "Sean, are you saying you sensed our emotions and physical responses?"

Grace lowered her head to cover it with her hands.

Sean pursed his lips, unable to meet David's gaze. "Maybe."

"Oh God." Grace groaned the words with a hint of a whine in her tone.

David cleared his throat. He reassembled his self-control, which had cracked and splintered at Sean's admission, and rose to face the boy. In the most matter-of-fact tone he could muster, he said, "You'll need to learn to control your new power. We'll help you."

"What new power?" Sean asked.

"Empathy. Sensing other people's feelings. It's a natural offshoot of healing."

"Cool!" The boy pumped his fists in the air. "I finally got a new power. This is so incredibly awesome." He aimed a sly look at Grace, who stayed hidden behind her hands. "Don't worry. I won't write any blog posts about your sex life."

Grace peeked at him between her fingers, then shut her eyes and uttered a pathetic, if melodramatic, noise.

David tore her hands away from her face and hauled her to her feet.

She scowled, though a bit half-heartedly. When he smiled, she compressed her mouth into an adorably miffed expression.

He pecked a kiss on those rosy lips. "Let's get married."

Puzzlement intensified her adorableness, and he had to restrain a powerful impulse to give her a no-holds-barred kiss. His lust must've revealed itself on his face, or in their psychic link, because a smile twitched at the corners of her mouth. "So far, David, we've gotten engaged twice. How many more times do I have to say yes?"

"I'm not asking you to agree to marry me. I'm suggesting we do it as soon as possible." He caught her chin between his thumb and forefinger. "We've waited long enough."

"Then let's do it."

He whooped and swept her up in his arms, whirling them both around and around. She laughed, the sound light and airy, full of joy.

Sean bounded down the aisle just as Amador emerged from the cockpit. He slugged Amador's arm and hollered, "I got a new power!"

Looking unimpressed, Amador sidestepped Sean to open the jet's door.

A few minutes later, David carried Grace off the plane, despite her stubborn protests, and to a waiting SUV driven by Roland Wickham. When their group arrived at the house he and Grace shared, he whisked her out of the car and into his arms again, kicked the car door shut, and without a word of goodbye marched up to the front door.

The last ribbons of sunset fluttered across the sky, and the perfume of roses drifted out of the bushes nestled against the house. He heard Sean exit the SUV behind them, saying goodbye to Amador and Wickham, then he jogged up the walkway in their wake.

"I'd pick you a rose," he told Grace, "but I won't risk you getting pricked by a thorn."

"Are you going to be this overprotective forever?"

"Yes." He realized with a stir of heat that she didn't look entirely displeased by the prospect.

Her annoyance reared up, however, when he insisted on carrying her through the front door. Her protests were weaker this time, but her smile was brilliant.

Once the door clapped shut, Sean wandered off to his room. David and Grace lingered at the door, arms around each other, unwilling to let go for one second. The topaz glow in her eyes entranced him and calmed him with the love she exuded from every pore and every neuron. If he gave off half the emotion she did, they were both wrecked.

Her fingers tickled the back of his neck, and he bent down for a kiss, a sweet and innocent one.

"You know," he said, "I used to wish I could lose myself in you. Today I realized I found myself in you, and I'll never forget the gift you gave me."

Then he carried her into the bedroom and laid her on the mattress. Not to ravish her again but to sleep. Lying in her arms all night was a treat he'd denied himself for months. No more. When she snuggled her soft body against his, he let go of wakefulness, succumbing to slumber.

That night, he slept better than he had in years.

Another gift from Grace.

Chapter Thirty-Four

THE AIR CONDITIONER HUMMED, AND A DOG BARKED OUTSIDE, BUT OTHerwise, the house had descended into silence. Grace clamped her hands together to stop her fingers from drumming on the tabletop. None of them had a clue what to say after she'd related what she learned from her dive into Nkosi's mind, because it shed a bizarre light on Sean's grandfather. She supposed this was what people called a pregnant pause.

This pause was having quadruplets.

David closed his big, muscular hand over both of hers. The knot in her gut loosened a smidgen. Seated beside her, in one of four wooden chairs positioned around the oblong kitchen table, he said nothing—but his mind spoke an encyclopedia's worth of words. She was still adjusting to their new, broader link.

Across the table from them, Sean slouched forward and planted his elbows on the wood. His forehead fell into his palms. Rubbing his skin, as if he might squash the information out of his brain, he pulled in a long, quivering breath and expelled it in a rush. Sean snapped straight, his back thumping into the chair. Jaw set, lip curled, he huffed a breath out through his nostrils.

"So," he said, his voice too calm, "Grandpa was a psycho. I can deal with it. Mom was right to get away from him."

Grace leaned forward. The table's edge pressed into her abdomen. "Listen, there's more."

He barked a single, harsh laugh. "No shit? Of course there's more to the Gramps-was-a-serial-killer-who-tortured-me story. That just wouldn't be awesome enough by itself."

"Actually," David said, "Tesler only hurt you one time, when he gave you JT's formula. Otherwise, he steered clear of—"

"The torture sessions? Yeah, it's too bad he missed out on all the really sweet stuff."

Grace stretched a hand out to Sean's, but he folded his arms over his chest. The kid had a ways to go before he'd accept physical affection.

She took David's hand instead, grateful for the warmth and comfort. "Sean, your grandfather made a deal with Nkosi. You see, Nkosi needed Tesler's help to figure out how to create and control psychic puppets. But he had to promise Tesler something in return."

His gaze fixated on the tabletop, he shifted in his seat. "What, he wanted some toddlers to experiment on?"

"No." She glanced down at David's fingers, curled around hers. "He wanted you."

The kid's head popped up then. His forehead crinkled as his brows knit together. "I don't get it. He hated psychics, and he said he'd never admit we're related, seeing as I'm a mewling mutant."

"He wanted Nkosi to excise your powers, make you a normal person, and then erase your memories of the last two years. It seems like he had plans to adopt you then."

"Seriously? Like I'd be a lost puppy he could rescue?" Sean shook his head as a scowl darkened his face. "Think I could cut out the DNA I got from him? Don't need that crap inside me."

"This may be hard to understand, but I think, in his warped way, he was trying to protect you."

Sean closed his eyes. When he opened them again, the scowl gave way to a look of solemn determination.

"Are you okay?" she asked. A dumb question, but she couldn't think of anything else to say.

"I'll deal." He pushed his chair back and stood. "Need some time to think, that's all."

He headed down the hallway to his bedroom. The door clicked shut.

The silence returned, but only for a moment.

David squeezed her hand. "He'll be fine. After everything he's been through, believe it or not, this is probably the easiest for him to handle."

"You know him better than I do." She knew Sean was a tough kid, though, and he'd have the two of them to guide him through this. Besides, she had another matter to discuss with David. "I remembered something else."

"I thought you recovered all your memories the other night."

She noted the manly satisfaction in his tone, prompted by the knowledge that their lovemaking had restored her Swiss-cheese brain to wholeness. Her body tingled at the recollection of that night, but she forced herself to concentrate. "I mean, I remembered how I forgot. How I developed amnesia."

His chair scraped on the vinyl flooring as he rotated it toward her. With an ease that sent a shiver of desire through her, he lifted her chair to turn it toward him so they faced each other sideways to the table. One glimpse of those fathomless blue eyes, and she developed a new kind of amnesia.

"Well?" he said.

"Huh?" His lips begged for a kiss, a nip, a—

"You were going to tell me how you got amnesia."

"Right. I was." She flattened her palms on her thighs and squared her shoulders. "I did it to myself."

"I don't understand."

"Neither did I, at first." The amnesia had set in on the day her parents were killed. Six months ago, thanks to JT's torments, she'd regained the memory of that day, when Jackson Tennant used his drug-induced psychic abilities to cause a car accident. She had sensed their peril and traveled to them, with RV, but had been helpless to save them.

David patted his leg. "Come over here."

She hopped over there, perching on his lap, and looped her arms around his neck. He hooked his arms around her waist, linking his hands over her hips. She loved this new-and-improved, uninhibited David. He lavished affection on her and grinned with unabashed joy. He could still be stoic, when necessary, but their night in the cabin had freed them both, in their own ways.

"After I saw my parents die," she told him, "I was so devastated and terrified, I lost control of my powers. While I was in the crossroads."

Silent, he watched her without expression.

"My mind got, well, sort of fractured." She dug around for a better way to explain it but came up empty. "The barrier around my memories was built from my fears and guilt. I couldn't save them. I'd lost you too, in a way, because you were imprisoned at the California facility." She squirmed on his lap, which encouraged him to tighten his hold on her. Part of her wanted to break free, run, hide. Mostly, though, she longed to stay right here forever. "I flipped out and caused my own amnesia. I'm not strong like you think, but I'm getting better."

He lifted a hand to her face, his fingers curving over her cheek. "You've always been strong, Grace. What you went through, it would make anyone flip out. You came back from it, stronger than ever, and that's what counts."

"I think you're a little biased."

His hand drifted down to her throat, his fingertips teasing her skin. "I'm thoroughly biased. And from here on out, you'll never have to suffer alone. I'll be with you, always. So if there are any more villains out there, we'll take them out together."

My warrior angel to the rescue.

His brows rose. "Explain this 'warrior angel' thing to me."

"It's silly."

Smirking, he trailed his hand down to the slope of her breast, his skin warm through the thin fabric of her shirt. "I like you silly. Giggling and jiggling."

"Excuse me? Jiggling?"

"When you laugh, your breasts jiggle." He sealed his hand around one mound. "Tell me."

She shrugged. "I started thinking of you as my warrior angel back when you were Mr. Stoic-and-Standoffish. You have the face of an angel, and you're very heroic, so warrior angel seemed appropriate."

"Stoic and standoffish? I guess I deserve that." He brushed his thumb over her nipple. Her breath hitched, and he did it again. "I like the heroic part."

"Me too."

She ground her bottom into his lap, fully aware of how it would affect him. He gritted his teeth and kneaded her breast with ferocious pressure. She smashed her mouth to his.

Footsteps clapped down the hallway.

"If Mom and Dad are gonna screw around, I need to go for a walk. Your happy-sappy horny feelings are wrecking my sulky mood."

They peeled their lips apart to stare at Sean.

He gave them a playfully exasperated shake of his head. "You guys are so weird."

David let go of her breast. "Sorry we're ruining your sulk."

"I wasn't really into it, anyway. I figure it like this. I never really knew my grandfather, and my mom was totally cool, so who cares if I shared some genes with a whackjob. I take after my mother." He hustled toward the door, swung it open, and glanced back. "Besides, I've got a new family."

He strode out the door, head high, a faint smile on his lips.

She stared at the door for a few seconds, but then it hit her. Sean was a tough kid. He was smart and resilient and not just a kid anymore. He was becoming a man.

And with a role model like David, he'd do just fine.

The man whose pants were straining at the crotch tapped a finger on her lips. "He's okay."

"I know."

"Good. Then we can move on to other business." He jumped up, hefting her with him and depositing her on her bare feet. "Let's fly to Vegas tomorrow and get married."

"Yes. Let's."

He threw his arms around her and kissed her with unadulterated passion, proving once and for all that he was no chaste angel.

But to her, he always would be her warrior angel.

EPILOGUE

Two Months Later

THE CORK BURST OUT OF THE CHAMPAGNE BOTTLE, CRACKING INTO the wall and plopping down on the fluffy pillow where David's head had rested a few moments ago. Champagne frothed out of the bottle onto Grace's naked body. She shivered from the sudden hit of cold and giggled from the tickly sensation of bubbles on her skin.

She gave him a sly grin. "You did that on purpose."

The bubbles foaming on her breasts captured his full attention and made his pupils expand into dark pools of desire. Her nipples pebbled from the chilled liquid, an invitation no man, not even a stoic warrior, could resist. At least she hoped so.

Bending his head, he licked the champagne off her skin. His deft tongue raced up the slope of her breast.

Her breaths quickened. "Honestly, David, I thought we'd use the glasses."

"So did I." He glanced up at the flutes on the bedside table. "This is more fun."

Grace lay sprawled on their new bed in their new house, on new sheets woven from silky Egyptian cotton. David had insisted on the highest thread count for their bedding after she'd made the mistake of oohing over the buttery smoothness of the silk sheets in the five-star hotel where they'd spent their wedding night. They couldn't afford silk, but Egyptian cotton did nicely.

Tonight, he subjected her to the sensual pleasure of soft sheets against her backside and hot, sweat-slicked male flesh mashed to her front side. The combination drove her batty with need and transformed her into a sex-crazed idiot.

"Stop that," David said in the low, throaty voice he assumed whenever she was nude, and sometimes when she wasn't. His tongue flicked over one nipple.

"Oh… stop what?"

"Feeling guilty about stripping me naked every chance you get."

Damn. There were times she wished he didn't share her feelings quite so much. "You're the one who stripped me this time, so it's your fault."

He closed his mouth around her hard peak and suckled gently. When he set her nipple free, he flashed her a sexy grin. "We're newlyweds. Everyone assumes we're ravishing each other on a daily basis." He chuckled, dissolving her willpower, if she'd had any left. "Or hourly, as needed."

"But we should be concentrating on Sean and Cari. They both have powers they can't fully control." She struggled to sound convincingly stern, but his talented tongue kept toying with her flesh. A woman had her limits. And this man knew exactly how to push her past them. Still, she had no intention of ending this conversational thread yet. "We also have defunct ALI facilities to check out and abused psychics to rehabilitate."

He exhaled with an exasperated grumble. "The poor orphan psychics can wait, and we've helped Sean and Cari plenty, every day, for two entire months. For the first time in weeks, we're alone in our own house. Tonight is for us." He blew a breath over her breast, eliciting a deep shiver in her. "It's our anniversary."

"Anniversaries are once a year."

"Grace, my eternal soul mate—"

"Cut the crap, David. This two-month celebration is just an excuse to goof off."

"I was thinking more about getting off."

The phone rang.

Grace fumbled to grab her cell off the bedside table. The instant her fingers closed around the phone, David snatched it away.

He frowned at the caller ID. "Wickham. I thought Brits were supposed to have impeccable manners, but he manages to call at the exact wrong moment every time. I think Amador's given him instructions to interrupt us."

"As if he could know when we're in the midst of things." She grabbed for the phone, but he swung his arm behind his back. "David, it could be important."

"Then he'll leave a message and we'll deal with it later." He rubbed his body against hers with delicious friction. "Even world-savers get a night off."

"But it'll just take a sec—"

He hurled the phone across the room. It bounced off the wall with a *thwack* and clattered to the floor. "Amador might be funding our new project, but that doesn't give his lackey the right to pester us ten times a day."

"He's only making sure we've got everything we need."

"At least Amador doesn't call you."

Because he knew David hated him like a cat hated a bath. Sequestered at the private hospital he'd bought, Amador had made no attempts to contact her in the last two months. She was fine with that and with David's insistence that she shouldn't visit Amador. She'd never intended to, anyway. She might sympathize with the trauma that drove him to madness, but she didn't know if she could ever forgive the horrible things he'd done in the name of vengeance.

David patted her thigh. "You're thinking about Amador, aren't you? That ends this instant."

"Yes, sir." Her thoughts circled back to their self-imposed mission of aiding the people who had been held captive by first JT, then Tesler and Nkosi, which led inevitably to more thoughts of Gabriel Amador. Here she was in bed with her new husband, and she kept thinking about a whackjob. "I'm trying not to, but my brain has other ideas."

"I can shut down your brain in a heartbeat."

Her body awakened at his words. Oh yes, he could do that. He'd proved it on numerous occasions.

With a flourish of his hand, he spritzed champagne along the length of her body. She willingly rewarded him with a long, husky moan. He cleaned up the liquid with his lips, his tongue, lapping up every drop with impressive focus and thoroughness. She arched into his ministrations. He nibbled her hip. She plunged a hand into his hair.

The light glittered on her diamond engagement ring and sparked on the gold of her wedding band. She was married. To him. At last.

She ought to tell him. He deserved to know. Well, maybe she could wait until after…

He abandoned his quest to cleanse her body of champagne, slithering up her body to settle down alongside her. "What's wrong?"

"Nothing." She'd slammed that opening shut. Why? She longed to tell him the news, but she worried about his reaction. It was stupid. Then again, they'd never had *that* talk.

"Tell me, Grace. My wife, the love of my life, my most splendiferous goddess."

She laughed. "Splendiferous is not a word."

"Yes, it is. Look it up in the dictionary—later." The contentment on his face faded into concern. "Are you okay? You said your doctor's appointment was nothing, just getting a refill on your allergy pills."

Yeah, she'd fibbed about that so he wouldn't get his hopes up or freak out. "Well, you see, that's not entirely accurate." She clasped her hands over her belly, tapping one finger. "We're having a baby."

His smile beamed into her with the heat and brilliance of a hundred suns. His elation spun through her mind and accelerated both their pulses. His mouth opened, then closed, then opened again as he finally rallied his voice. "Really? We're having—"

He gasped for air, too happy to breathe. She knew this because he fed his joy into her, and she accepted it with all her heart and soul.

The anxiety sluiced out of her. She stroked her fingers down his cheek to dance them over his lips. "Yes. Really. I'm about two months along."

"Two months?" She practically heard the cogs turning in his brain. Then realization sparked in his eyes. "The night in the cabin. When we merged our powers."

"Yep, I think so." A new kind of anxiety iced through her. "Do you think the process of merging our psychic energies will have any effect on our baby?"

"If it does…" He rolled on top of her. "It'll be a good effect. Nothing bad could come out of what happened between us that night."

He was right. She felt the truth of it deep inside, a glimmer of hope and faith she prayed would burgeon into a twinkling star in the form of their child.

David shut his eyes, his lips curving into a contented smile. He nuzzled her belly and painted kisses across her flesh, then raised his head to gaze at her with rapt adoration. "Our baby. This is…" He burst into laughter, startling a tiny cry from her. "This is the best day of my entire life."

"Just wait until our kid's born."

Their child, his and hers, another link bonding them on a new level, somehow more profound than even the psychic connection they shared. She focused on his sapphire eyes, letting herself dive into their gleaming pools, drowning in the passion and love she found there.

He swirled his palm over her skin, down to the sensitive skin at the apex of her thighs. "I hope our daughter is just like you."

"Daughter?" She raised her brows. "I thought I was the only one in this family who had premonitions."

"Let's call this intuition. It has to be a girl because I love you too much for this baby to be anything but another version of you."

"You think you love me enough to affect the DNA of our baby."

"Damn straight I do."

"Okay then, prove it." She wrapped her legs around his waist, pinning his arousal to the dampness between her thighs. "Show me how you did that."

His mouth found hers, and his tongue explored with delicate strokes. She tugged his head down to deepen the kiss.

When their mouths parted, she licked her lips. "You taste like champagne."

"Hmm… good idea."

He snagged the bottle and dumped the last of the champagne onto her chest. It splattered onto the sheets and fizzed on her breasts.

Then he showed her. Everything. And they both knew, with a certainty that resonated in their souls and empowered their psychic faculties, that their daughter would be perfect. Their life would be perfect. They'd have ups and downs, and sometimes they'd drive each other nuts, but when it really mattered, they would stick by each other through whatever lay ahead for them. Nothing would tear them apart again. She knew that.

Call it intuition.

Ready for Sean's story?
Grab book three, *Kinetic*, available now.

Did you love

Intuition?

Visit
AnnaDurand.com

to subscribe to her newsletter

for updates on forthcoming books
&
to receive exclusive content!

ANNA DURAND IS A BESTSELLING, MULTI-AWARD-WINNING AUTHOR OF contemporary and paranormal romance. Her books have earned bestseller status on every major retailer and wonderful reviews from readers around the world. But that's the boring spiel. Here are some really cool things you want to know about Anna!

Born on Lackland Air Force Base in Texas, Anna grew up moving here, there, and everywhere thanks to her dad's job as an instructor pilot. She's lived in Texas (twice), Mississippi, California (twice), Michigan (twice), and Alaska—and now Ohio.

As for her writing, Anna has always made up stories in her head, but she didn't write them down until her teen years. Those first awful books went into the trash can a few years later, though she learned a lot from those stories. Eventually, she would pen her first romance novel, the paranormal romance *Willpower*, and she's never looked back since.

Want even more details about Anna? Sign up for her newsletter to get exclusive content and updates on forthcoming books.

VISIT ANNADURAND.COM TO SIGN UP.

www.ingramcontent.com/pod-product-compliance
Lightning Source LLC
Chambersburg PA
CBHW051300210726
48287CB00002B/590